PENGUIN BOOKS

THE LOVE PARADE

'A compelling snapshot of the language and mindset of a generation . . . and also an affirmation of Branton's own powers as a writer and ironist' *Daily Telegraph*

'Undeniably sexy . . . a literary piranha eschewing the angst of so many first-time novelists for a coruscating attack on the media . . . a show-boating début novel' *Big Issue*

'This début novel . . . has a sharp-edged prescience' *Sunday Times*

'A veritable feast of popular culture . . . Branton has something important to say, and he says it with style and skill' *Literary Review*

'What a media-surfing dude he is. He is connected with a capital C; he is the e-male' *The Times*

ABOUT THE AUTHOR

Matthew Branton wrote *The Love Parade* in London, Manchester and Sheffield between the ages of twenty-five and twenty-seven.

The Love Parade

MATTHEW BRANTON

PENGUIN BOOKS

PENGUIN BOOKS

Published by the Penguin Group
Penguin Books Ltd, 27 Wrights Lane, London W8 5TZ, England
Penguin Putnam Inc., 375 Hudson Street, New York, New York 10014, USA
Penguin Books Australia Ltd, Ringwood, Victoria, Australia
Penguin Books Canada Ltd, 10 Alcorn Avenue, Toronto, Ontario, Canada M4V 3B2
Penguin Books (NZ) Ltd, Private Bag 102902, NSMC Auckland, New Zealand
Penguin Books Ltd, Registered Offices: Harmondsworth, Middlesex, England

First published by Hamish Hamilton 1997
Published in Penguin Books 1998
10 9 8 7 6 5 4 3 2 1

Set in Bembo
Printed in England by Clays Ltd, St Ives plc

No memory of having starred
Atones for later disregard,
Or keeps the end from being hard.

Better to go down dignified
With boughten friendship at your side
Than none at all. Provide, provide!

– Robert Frost, 'Provide, Provide!'

I met your children / What did you tell them?

– The Buggles, 'Video Killed The Radio Star'

I forced my way into the middle and stood near the croupier;
then I began experimenting, staking two or three coins at a
time. Meanwhile, I kept quiet and looked on; it seemed to me
that calculation meant very little, and had by no means the
importance attached to it by some players. They sit with papers
before them scrawled over in pencil, note the strokes, reckon,
deduce the chances, calculate, finally stake and – lose, exactly
as we simple mortals who play without calculations.

– Fyodor Dostoevsky, *The Gambler*
(transl. Constance Garnett)

It was the day in my life when, were I F. Scott Fitzgerald, Zelda would break off the engagement at the weekend. I touched the roll of tired banknotes in my pocket and pressed my forehead to the streaming window. Outside, the pirates appeared to be regrouping for their final pyrotechnic assault. This seemed as good a moment as any. I strode with purpose back to the desk, typed the final period-return-centre-caps-THE END-caps-return, and sat back in the chair. I had planned this – I was in control. He still had to quit the ad agency, go home to his parents, and rewrite the draft that Scribner's had turned down two months previously. Crucifying himself in this room was fifteen years off. I was way ahead of him.

This was clearly a moment. I had expected to push back the chair, twirl the Taittinger from its sweating silver bucket, maybe flick my battered brass zippo to one colossal Havana purchased twelve hours before and kick back for a while – drug some cheerleaders, elope with a truckstop waitress – whatever. But I knew it was never going to happen.

I thought of sleeping, but the damn pirates were sinking the galleon every hour on the hour with no indication of fading zeal. In the absence of anything else to do I pushed back the chair and surveyed the room. It was, after seven days of solitude, an infernal landfill of the kind of junk I have come to require in order to do this stuff: pizza boxes, Ben & Jerry's, spent six-packs of diet Dr Pepper; Chesterfield cartons, stacks of biographies from the library back home, discarded fillets of matchbooks with the name of the hotel embossed on the cover in a scripty font I don't recognize, monstrous flow-charts magic-markered on to the blank backs of A2 promo posters and Scotch-taped to every available wall-space; piles of Italian *Vogue* and French *Marie Claire* with all the perfume strips torn out where I, taking it anyplace I could find it, was trying to conjure the incarnate loveliness of my flagging heroine one last time there about four hours ago.

There was, I blush to admit, a Taittinger bottle in there somewhere. I had gone out the last time I woke up (around ten in the evening three days ago) and picked up a bottle of the choicest champagne that the 7−11 on Sunset and Ocean could afford, along with the usual supplies that I require to get this over.

The *roi des champagnes vintages* had gone west thirty-four hours ago, slugged straight from the bottle with one hand still typing, as I worked through the diner scene for the sixth time in as many hours. I'd run out of tapes and all I could find on the headboard radio of my Cadillac of a bed was an AM cheesy listening station out of god knows where. Vegas remakes of Broadway show tunes were not enough to get me through the night, though I personally owned several CD compilations; but, lacking anyone on whom I could inflict my impeccable sense of irony, I had to content myself with using snatches of Wayne Newton to compose answerphone jingles that only seemed to frighten the caller off. At least, every time I used the touchtone phone in my room to check, transatlantic, my calls this last week there were always a dozen or so that consisted of a single, exasperated exhalation and the clunk of receiver hitting cradle. I bet they were only from my agent − screw him − since I gave him the slip ten days ago in London and was definitely not returning his calls, the jerk. If he had the slightest ounce − no, quarter-ounce − no, one-hit deal in a ten-spot fucking *bindle* of imagination he'd know where I'd escaped to.

Which was here. Incidentally, the Cadillac/bed conjunction back there was no figure. I can't believe what they did to this place. My bed is a Cadillac − tail fins, whitewall tires, the whole deal. You have to open a clunky door to get into bed, unless you use the window like Starsky. The headboard is a dashboard, the speedometer the clock/radio face. The whole place is themed. The old writers' building, for the love of God. I can't begin to describe how I felt when I saw what I'd booked myself into, and where I intended to cloister myself for seven days and seven nights. The horror, as my visions of me at a fine old leather-topped desk, quill in hand, in maybe a frogged velvet smoking jacket and Turkish silk pyjamas, dwindled and died. I mean, I'd really been looking forward to this. The last time I was in LA we were stuck in some lousy Ramada Inn because the promoter was too cheap to book us anywhere else, and I was determined to do it right this time. So I sparked up my PowerBook, slipped on a Frank 'n' Nancy tape and thought it was pretty neat for about ten seconds. Then I got down to work.

Fame costs, and here's where you start paying. Six years before, Shelley Volante had brought me to LA; in sixteen hours I was seeing her again. She would have sooner seen me in hell, but I was pretty sure she wasn't about to welsh on me. It wasn't her style, but then neither was I. I should explain.

Shelley Volante was the author of my destiny, and my problem was that I didn't want her rolling the credits just yet. It had been her idea that I should thrust my pelvis at scaffolding for the best part of four years, as the surly fifth member of boy-band sensation High 5. I'd been just out of school, and it had seemed like a reasonable career option at the time. Now, I figured she owed me. Ostensibly we were meeting to discuss *Jump and Dance: Life in the Dream Factory*; the very last piece of High 5 product ever; some glossy coffee-table thing, that featured some of my own photographs. I had claimed that the copyright was with some ex of mine, who was cutting up rough about it. Now I was going to pretend I had sorted it, figuring it might soften the blow when I presented her with the real business on my agenda – viz. my at-that-point vaguely half-written screenplay – and begged her to read it.

So I'd needed to lock myself away someplace and finish it. Where else but Hollywood? Particularly, since the studios got turned into theme parks, you could stay in what used to be the old writers' offices on the lots. I got the actual, authentic room where Scott Fitzgerald wrote a script-polish on *Gone With The Wind*, over a Remington and a bottle of Scotch; clearly oozing from the wainscot every kind of vibe I needed to assist in bringing this particular confinement to term. I was practically supernova with excitement when I flew in. And what do I get? There is a for-christ's-sake *galleon* outside, which, as I've indicated, is boarded and sunk once an hour – with maximum recourse to firecrackers and yodelling – by Captain Actor's Guild Minimum and his band of Cut-Throats.

I took the first afternoon out to go on the tour, mostly to get away from the swashbuckling. But it sucked. All the rides were hopeless; spin-offs from movies I hadn't heard of, built because the back end was sold before the front. The only good one was from a movie that really bit the big one – can't even remember the title. But the ride was pretty cool. It seemed a shame they had to make the dumb movie, and couldn't have cut straight to the ride. But this is my life; tell me about it.

So I came back here, feeling all the more guilty for having lost half a day. I really ought to have expected it. Perversely, my disappointment might have helped; or maybe, in an unprecedented moment of self-knowledge, I had understood that this was my last chance. Whatever. For the last six days I had avoided the maid and punched the keys, stopping only to drop exhausted into my terrifying bed and pilot that churning vortex of cotton through the night, crossing unspeakable latitudes, riding nameless swells that bore me, like, inexorably toward morning. Which was where I was headed now. I watched the sun go down and watched it rise, and then it was time.

Shelley Volante, my handler, has this page on her hard drive. She's that good. She scares the hell out of me and if she had the time she'd scare you too.

I wish I could say I used to meet people like her all the time when we were famous, but it wouldn't be true. We never met anyone: not celebrities, nor record company suits, nor teen mag hacks, or even the Nobel-laureate novelist sent to interview us at the zenith of our notoriety. We might have blown it. We might not have been sufficiently in character, in realtime. Flickering from a million screens, we were pure light; satellites bounced us around the stratosphere and we were signal, to be encrypted and scrambled and decoded. But in analog – in the flesh – we were substantially nothing. And the more visible they made us the more insubstantial we became.

The circuit retains its integrity by jealously guarding its weak points. The names of the key players were available to anyone who read the trades, but everyone I ever met in the business had a name you could pronounce at least three ways. If you got it wrong, when you were trying to bypass their assistant and have someone give you a direct connection, then it was clear, even to the skivvy answering the phone, that you were some kind of loser; and you'd be forever shifted sideways into a voicemail void.

So soliciting a meeting with Shelley had been hell. She was way beyond me. I was CV material for her, if she hadn't been beyond those too. I was ago. So was High 5, pretty much; though I'd long suspected the whole project was something she would gladly have put to bed years ago, but for the tiresome fact that we had to do four Xmas singles and three summer stadium tours if our revenue curve was to be maximized. You have to be frontlist before you can be backlist. Tell me all about it.

A summer breeze dried my hair as I walked from the dead studio to the lair of the multinational entertainment conglomerate that owned the rights to my past and possibly my future. It was just before six a.m. and the sun was low in the sky, drenching the city with a platinum wash. This was the best slot Shelley had offered, after I'd wheedled and flattered and begged for almost thirty seconds of her time on the phone two weeks ago.

I'd stayed up all night, to avoid my usual morning cotton-headedness, but I was glad I had. There was the pleasant early-morning feeling of a hot day and, as I negotiated the financial district, I walked on behind a man pushing a roller that printed the name of the corporation that owned me on the sidewalk in damp letters every five yards or so. I guessed UriZen were planning another takeover. The sidewalk was hot already, and the name, written in water, evaporated in front of my eyes. I remember wishing, not for the first time, that reality was a little more like life.

Fast-track graduate trainees hurried past me, hungry for the hour before the markets opened, when they could cast about desperately for some panacean evidence that might impose order and form on the half-understood chaos that was the fruit of their hopes and aspirations so far. The boys looked like the living dead, but the girls were all skin tone and cheekbones, as though Audrey and Katherine Hepburn had staged a genetic coup d'état. I walked unremarked among them.

If you ever stayed awake till a summer dawn and watched people going to work, knowing that cool sheets are waiting for you whenever you want, you'll know what I mean. You feel as though you're in another dimension, a different time zone. It's like waking up on the first day of the summer holidays. It's also a pretty facile way of deflecting unnecessary self-analysis, of holding yourself together: go home alone at 2 a.m., and your empty room will give you a hard time about the way your life is going; stay out till seven and it'll greet you like an old friend. A baby trick, but it works. I stopped by at news stands and stuff to prolong it. I felt I deserved this. The day was alive with possibility; the world no longer receded to something I squinted at before dawn through streaming windscreens. This was going to be pretty cool.

On my only other visit to the offices of UriZen, at the incipience of our commercial viability, I'd tried to memorize the faces of everyone I met, in case they could be useful to my future career. It was the same receptionist as four years ago, but he didn't appear to recognize me; which I found momentarily disturbing, as I knew for a fact that a High 5 shot had been amongst the star clientele portraits in the lobby opposite his desk for at least six months two years ago. The fact had figured prominently in the marketing progress reports we'd been sent bimonthly, as evidence of the slick and costly operation translating exposure into sales on our behalf. But there was no flicker of joyful recognition in his face as he punched me in and snapped together my laminated visitor pass. Maybe it had been a bad year for him and he was trying to forget.

I would have felt less weird if I'd been ushered into her usual nightmare office, and Shelley had waved me to a chair without looking up from her crowded desk. But it wasn't like that anymore. The lift doors opened on an artful reconstruction of a SoHo loft dominated by one single desk – constructed from what was, apparently, a single piece of ash four feet wide and twenty yards long. Its blonde patina was interrupted by a modem port every six feet, with pairs of artsy chairs on either side. Shelley sat, her back to huge cast-iron casements, about two-thirds of the way along, with only a laptop, mobile and half-litre Evian bottle marking her territory. She stood up.

'Forgive my not coming round the desk, but it's a bit of schlep,' she said, drawing me by a proffered hand over her PowerBook and kissing me on the lips.

Shelley was English, but way out of my league. Her features bespoke a lineage of post-colonial sanction-dodging and studio-era Hollywood glamour. Money and furs. The beauty of the mother and the evidence of her father mixed with felicitous discord in her face, because women as gene-surfingly gorgeous as her mom were only married, every biography I'd read conspired to suggest, by thick-set tycoons or hawk-faced card-swipers. Shelley's flesh sat as opulently on her bones as a labrador's. She made me almost faint with love. This wasn't going so well.

'Hi, Shelley,' I said. 'Okay. Enough jerking me around already. I'm here. It's whatever the hell time it is. You made all the points you need to. What about my proposal?'

'Which proposal?'

'My book.' This was, I was pretty sure, the industry term. Like any loser, I was addicted to jargon.

She threw back her head and laughed. Three laughs.

'The High 5 book was written five years ago. I wrote it. Before you were even hired. All you were required to do was follow the plot. And now, if you don't mind my saying so, you seem to have lost it.'

'Not that one. My screenplay. The treatment, the typescript I sent you. E-mail, and post when I got no response.'

'Do you think I didn't bozo-filter you years ago? Jesus.'

Right. Because we'd always been wired. Our market consisted of the first human beings not to have existed before DOS, so we accessorized with tech. High 5 were celebrated, amongst other things, for giving virtual interviews. If anyone wanted to know, and nations bated their breath, what we had for breakfast on any given morning, what kind of Lycra undershorts we had on, or which gaudily stippled fruits and midnight chocolate derivatives stocked our personal refrigerators at any particular juncture in history, all they need do was click on the chill-out room link from our home page. And we, so it ran, would supply their deficiency from fizzing laptops as we soundchecked, rode the bus or lounged in departure suites.

Of course we did nothing of the sort. Children deluded enough could interrogate us in real time, but were fed a range of stock answers – based on the unswerving banality of their questions – from a server here at UriZen HQ. It worked quite well, though I was heartened to learn that every now and then some obstreperous little swine would crash the system by asking deliberately abstract questions – 'What's your favorite favor?' – throwing the spellchecker-derivative program for a loop. Me and Max telnetted into the host once from a promoter's office in Oslo and changed the answers – What things do you always carry with you? *Cards, keys and a nameless dread.* How would you like to die? *Very much* – but no one noticed and it all got reprinted in the lifestyle section of a Belgian weekend national. We got in trouble for this.

We were made to carry our laptops everywhere, even on stage, wearing them slung about our hips, right where other generations may have slung a carefully battered Fender. I took the insides out of mine because it gave me bruises when we danced; I got in trouble for this also. But our online accessibility patched us in to vast information-brokerage networks, pioneering new star-fan paradigms in realtime, empowering us to respond to market fluctuations as they occurred – we had the tools if not the talent. The project, from conception to execution, enhanced the product, and was not half good for our USP.

'So you haven't seen it?'

'In fact, I have. And I'm surprised at you.'

'You're surprised I could do it?'

'I'm surprised you'd want to. You have been famous. You have been paid. Writing screenplays is for people who can't get famous or paid any other way.'

'Or for people who're so famous they can't do anything else.'

'Yes. But you aren't. You've had yours; now you're over. No one is interested in you. Don't you know anything?'

I didn't know. She rolled her eyes and huffed her exasperation.

'If bringing this kind of project to term represents an hour on a clock face, then Mickey's left hand is still over his ear, buddy. Until he's scratching his cartoon balls, you are going to be raising finance.'

'I knew that.' I said it a little too quickly. I tried to brazen it out. 'That's why I *came* to you. Jesus.'

'What do you think goes on here? You think we're here to ante up whatever you need?' She looked at me incredulously. I had kind of hoped that this was, in fact, the case. 'You want to get this made, you're going to need to show a hundred people a writer. A real writer. A credible, level-headed individual, preferably with a track record of making sound returns on investments. *You* walk in to a bunch of VCs, they're going to laugh you out the window. And it's a long way down, sweetheart. Forget it. You've had yours. I can scarcely believe I need to point this out to you. You did what you did, and no one will take you seriously doing anything else. You got four years on the circuit. You don't get anymore.'

She had a point, but I was here to persuade her otherwise.

High 5 was conceived in a commissioning meeting on the seventeenth floor somewhere in downtown LA seven years ago. The vast multinational communications conglomerate to whom I belong had paused, momentarily troubled in its lumbering progress by a minor registration on its peripheral senses, like Godzilla taking time out from the razing of skyscrapers to lift his head and snuff the air, as a buzzing cloud of eminently swattable helicopters rounded the cheesy-looking mountain: there was a gap in the market far away to the east. The boom of the Eighties had launched the stars of that insane decade into the stratosphere and it was time to begin again, from the bottom up. The boy-next-door band. You take a bunch of losers and put them where the stars should go.

'You, of all people, ought to know how it goes. Consider yourself. You know the story as well as I do.' She spun her chair around to the windows and stretched her lazy long legs into a shaft of sunlight. 'Five years ago. A market was identified, demand was stimulated; songs were written and tracks laid down. You were hired. You were in the right place at the right time. You were also the right race, the right colour, the right height, and the right age. Our market research required that each of you represent a different demographic, economic and geographical profile. Your character was explained to you. You were to be from Manchester. The box-room poet who ran with the street gangs. Huh.' We both sniggered, even after all this time.

The literate one. Remark me now in the teen-mag poster feature (for which UriZen paid nine thousand pounds), Vaseline lens, louche and languid in my celebrity bath, moisture beading my sinuous neck, uncapped Montblanc and elegantly scrawled vellum illuminated by a single candle in the soap-tray; or sepia-toned, in round rimless specs, discovered glancing distractedly up from a thick paperback Goethe that had been tied to the bumper of the photographer's Jeep and dragged around the block three times; or in a gondola on the Silicon Canal in Manchester, deep in the Village.

'I can still do the accent. "There's this Borges shart starry." Ha ha ha.'

'Huh, yeah. "The Library". It was already written, and all you had to do was progress from act to act.' Her voice became distant, as though in reiterating it she was somehow pitching the idea, but to herself. This was the dope, from one of the best in the business. 'England. Local radio and press. PAs at malls, and cattle-market nightclubs with names in the possessive case. Schoolgirls and petty criminals. You grow from the bottom up. The premium cider promotion and tailored workwear tour. Lipsyncs in lunch hours and dance-offs to deadbeats. First single. Syndicated regional radio drivetime, down the line from theme parks, cable, satellite, sitting in with the children's TV anchor. Second single. The virus-spread of mixes. Get *out* there. Third single – the ballad. A nasty moment when our parent company's stock goes into play and it looks like you'll get dumped after the hostile takeover. It doesn't happen. There is massive corporate restructuring but I broker a new deal, and the project continues. You keep your jobs. The tour. The arenas. The stadia. Radio mikes and choreographed spontaneity.'

On the tourbus listening to a tape of last night's show to check for duff bits. Spontaneously Max and Joe start doing a different harmony, really lovely, and we all join in and it *is* a moment, and the manager stands up livid and hungover and barks will you just shut the fuck up and listen? You are working. You are at work.

'The first CD. Overdrive. Charity. The Xmas No. 1. Act Three. Europe, America, winterland. From the bottom up. More of the same, to healthier-looking children.'

Pimpy-looking guys and whorey-looking blondes in hotel lobbies. The smell of swimming pools at dusk and the smell of swimming pools at dawn. On the podium, collecting the award for which we'd paid forty grand; and maybe it was the constant reiteration that all promotional spend above a ceiling (which we'd apparently reached within half an hour of signing) was deducted from our royalties triggered my one moment of adolescent posturing rebellion. I was supposed to be the one who thanked our manager and producer and record companies and families. And maybe God. Unfortunately I was horribly drunk, because we'd been there five hours already and magnums of Krug was all there was. I surveyed, from the podium, the archipelago of white tablecloths, the gangs of tan corporate slags in tuxes they *owned* – we had to rent ours – and snarled, with an intensity of scorn that surprised me, 'Live forever.' There was a general consensus, even among the band, that I had gone too far, and UriZen used this as evidence of unprofessional conduct when we sued them for royalties, at the end of our careers. When we were finished; when we were twenty-two.

'Act Four. The second CD. The world tour. Major sponsorship. Massive marketing spend. No messin'.'

Sitting on my bed in a Tokyo hotel room full of presents from fans thinking, how do they think I'm going to get all these on the plane back? Es and whizz. A heartbreakingly beautiful Japanese girl lurching round Ollie's room, feeling no pain whatsoever. *Here!* He grabs a wastebasket and shoves it under her nose. *Don't you dare be sick in my bed. If you're going to be sick, do it in this, you hear?* Shelley was talking to herself.

'Second CD. Merchandizing. We dump a hundred in the back end. Third. Artistic reinvention. Politicization – your audience are growing up, so are you. Goatees and shaved heads. Piercings. Benefit gigs. Time to wrap this one up. You take time out. You travel. We sell the shit out of the backlist. Fourth CD but we don't promote it. It sells anyway. The acting careers. The box-office poison. The final slump in sales. And you're washed up with forty in the bank and your face a bad memory of a bad decade.'

'I'm twenty-four and I can't work again. What can I possibly do?'

'You're twenty-four and you've made forty thousand pounds that is yours to keep. I don't care what you do. But I suggest you dump this project. Jesus, can't you see? You have been public property and you will never be accepted as anything else again. *You* can't do anything.'

I wasn't sure I liked this. I'd written the screenplay because I wanted to be more than who I was. I wanted people to know that that twirling, prancing dork wasn't me; that had been someone else's book. This was mine.

'That's as much as I can give you,' she said, waking up her laptop. 'If you want to discuss the High 5 book I've got you brunch with Brody Blur, a marketing guy. He's good. He does the key accounts. And some other stuff. But I don't want this project. It's worth shit and doesn't have the sell-through. It's going nowhere. So I'll see you. And I shouldn't imagine I'll see you again.'

She didn't get up.

She didn't show me out either, which was a bad move on her part. I was halfway to the lifts before this occurred to me, and I cut a sharp left down a dark corridor in case she was sending security up to hoof me out. I strode briskly, and with aimless purpose, through open-plan prairies scattered with Swedish-wood workstations, past moulded traffic-flow-enhancing walls painted the colours of raw beef and pus, yellow fluttering flocks of Post-it notes, sighing diasporas of networked PCs asleep and dreaming behind their screensaver programs.

I was profoundly unhappy, but I'd been up for maybe thirty hours after a largely sleepless week, and felt kind of anaesthetized to it. I sat down at a random workstation and turned the PC on. I lit my fiftieth cigarette of the day while DOS woke up and dusted down its clothes, and, as Windows 95 kicked in, I patched myself in to that nebulous, self-reflexive kind of hopelessness endemic to office environments first thing in the morning.

Smoke wreathed my lips. It was over, and it felt like it had never really begun. Now I had to think, with wearying self-pity, of growing old: of waking with my heart pounding, and washing my hair twice a day; of drinking on my own on a cloudy afternoon in a bungalow somewhere; of turning thirty, which must be kind of like the milk turning when you go away for the weekend, and you have to trawl round the 7–11 late on Sunday night with all the other returnees, thinking about Monday. I rummaged around in the desk drawer looking for a miniature bottle of Canadian Club, anything. I knew, if I had a job in a place like this, I'd definitely keep a few snifters of something around the place, to invert briskly above a diet Pepsi on mornings when there was nothing else for it. But there was just the usual crap – treasury tags, staples, a mini Clinique bonus-time moisturizer, hairbrush, a bunch of wadded-up serviettes with the logo of the corporate caterers on. I took out a clotted old plum lipstick and faxed a smeary kiss on UriZen letterhead to my sister in Manchester.

The clock in the transmit address LED said it was nearly eight. People would start coming in fairly soon. I thought maybe I would see this marketing guy, listen to his stupid crap just because I could force him to give it to me; god knew, this was probably the last chance I'd get to do that kind of nonsense. But I thought I'd better have a lie-down first, just clear my head a little. My bedroom seemed impossibly far away. Going there and coming back would take half the morning. Far better to find the sick bay, where there would be at least some kind of, I don't know, gurney I could compose my scattering self upon. I rifled a few more desks looking for floor-plans or directories but, finding nothing, set out at random, taking care not to retrace my route to Shelley's office.

I seemed to walk forever, only occasionally passing someone hunched at a desk, barely looking up from their coffee and trade. I got into a series of corridors that seemed to lead only to themselves, and had twice passed the same copier when I noticed that someone was using it this time. The machine hummed and flashed, and the girl who stood over it, wearing Jackie Kennedy sunglasses against the slow strobing, seemed oblivious to me as I came to a halt beside her. I leaned forward into her field of vision and asked where the sick bay was. She said, *Twelfth, room 402*, out of the corner of her mouth without looking up. She maybe mistook me for one of her co-workers, I don't know. I thanked her carelessly and made to move off, and only then did she turn and follow my progress, no doubt realizing too late who I was. I didn't care. I didn't wish to think about her life, although I was momentarily intrigued at someone who knew the address of the sick room by heart. I found the place and fell asleep.

Summer rain, and dry pine needles in a dripping churchyard. The girl from the copier walked around the trunk of a cedar tree and said, *Not you. Not now.* And I said, because I couldn't help it, *Does that just mean not yet?*

'Hello? Excuse me?'

I floundered about on the edge of consciousness, then, remembering where I was, recalled myself as abruptly as possible to corporeality. I opened my eyes and focussed, a little dizzily. Someone who smelled faintly of Calvin Klein's Escape was leaning over me.

'Are you sick? Can I get you something?'

I brought her into view and sat up. It was a girl, about the same age as me, and dressed – in a powder-blue tailored suit – far more slickly than I had any right to expect a nurse to.

'Uh, no. Sorry. I shouldn't really – be here. I had a meeting. I felt kind of . . . faint?'

'Are you all right now? I'm sorry, I shouldn't have woken you.'

'Nuh. No. I'm, uh, fine. Much better. Must have drifted off. I feel fine.'

'Then rise, big guy, from that semi-recumbent posture.' She giggled – in rather a fetching way, my bleary senses conspired to register – and held out her hand. I extended mine, expecting to shake, but she took hold of it and tilted gracefully backwards, pivoting me round so that my legs swung over the edge of the trolley.

'Better?' She smiled, and I smiled back. I felt like I knew her from somewhere.

'Much, thank you. Do you work here?'

She laughed, richly. 'No, I had a meeting too. And now I have lunch. But the seam at my shoulder has come apart – see? – and there isn't time to go back to my hotel' – she shortened the first syllable like she was French – 'and change. Where d'you suppose they keep the safety pins?'

She swished around the gurney and commenced a rapid inspection of the various cabinets.

'Damn! How do they plan to patch people up, if they don't keep a decent supply of equipment? Oh. Here are some needles. And here is some gut. But I can't sew.'

'Let me.'

She turned, surprised. 'You can sew?'

I nodded.

'Jesus. You want to watch it. You'll be joining self-help groups and playing softball next.' She took off her jacket and handed it me matter-of-factly, along with a pack of surgical needles and some suture thread. I turned it inside out, threaded one of the curved needles and stitched briskly and closely, so that the repair wouldn't show from the outside. I was aware of her watching intently over my shoulder, of her quiet breathing and the slight shifts of her skin against her sleeveless linen blouse. 'There.' I handed it back to her.

'Smart work.' She slipped on the jacket and pirouetted, her arms outstretched like Mary Tyler Moore. 'You wouldn't know at all. Where did you learn to do that?'

'Oh, my sister taught me. We used to make our own clothes, when we couldn't buy what we wanted.'

'Well, I congratulate your sister. And now you really must let me buy you lunch.'

'I thought you had a lunch to go to.'

'Only with my agent, the loser.'

After my heart. 'D'you think their parents send them away to agent-school, to learn how to screw up?' I was doing all that stupid crap, like seeing whether she leaned toward me when she spoke, if her pupils were dilated, whether she was going to touch me unnecessarily, which is, so I understand, almost as good as giving you a voucher. I couldn't help it, and had recently had to learn to incorporate surreptitious glances at the left hand into the routine as I entered the arena of my mid-twenties. 'Which one's yours?'

'Juuuulian Fenton-Carter,' she drawled, accomplishedly replaying the jerkoff jingle my agent employed when he answered the phone. What the fuck was he doing out here? But I looked at her with new respect. 'I don't know anyone I'd rather have stood up for lunch. And I hope they charge him cancellation. So where?'

And then we were in a cab, sailing along Wilshire on to Santa Monica, out to some deco place. She sashayed in and over to the bar. A guy about my age but classier looking turned round on his stool, and she leaned close into him, whispered something, and kissed him quickly on the cheek. He looked unhappily up, then quickly down at the floor, so that thick parentheses of raven hair slipped forward to his cheekbones, before he tucked them irritably back behind his ears. The girl turned to me and smiled. I felt I ought to introduce myself.

'I'm . . .'

'We know who you are,' the girl said happily.

'We used to get you on cable,' the guy said. 'High 5, right? You really sucked.'

'Oh, right,' I said. 'And what did you ever do?'

That was nasty, and I was shocked at how quickly it had come. But I'd had this exchange so many times and I was tired of it. It got to me especially because just for once I would have liked not to go through this stupid assertion of power – I, the consumer, declare myself dissatisfied with the quality of your ex-merchandise and should like to point out that if I, my fabulous potential quite deliberately as yet unrealized, ever got it together to do anything at all, it couldn't help but be infinitely superior to your stuff. The assumption that that had been the best I could do – that I had even been vaguely in some kind of creative control – made me sad beyond measure. I couldn't have been happier to agree that we did, in fact, blow, and on a scale of Old Testament proportions. And not even in a way we haven't seen before. But just for once I would have liked to have gone into some kind of social contract without the scales weighed unevenly against me from the outset; without this fucking monkey gibbering on my back. It would have been nice to have met these people as just a regular kind of person, without this prepackaged notion that I was some tawdry, spent maleficent who had spread his soul before the world and been found wanting.

I was, however, kind of surprised they knew. We'd been so tightly niched that you had to have fitted the demographic profile almost exactly to have known who we were. We were only available to an endlessly focus-grouped selection of children at a precise socio-economic juncture in dollar-friendly post-industrial high-maintenance nation-states of the late twentieth century. Any idea of crossover would have been laughed out of town. There was no point in trying to expand our market; we were there to make a specific margin and nothing more. Unless these two were researching some kind of FMCG marketing textbook there was no excuse for them to know anything about me. It just wasn't fair.

For a moment there I thought the girl was going to rise to it, and I had a bizarre notion she was about to do the personal-political equivalent of tearing away the hip suit to reveal Okie gingham, delivering a homily-ridden lecture on the real achievements being the unsung ones – the ones to do with taking the strain a little for the ones you love; and I was ready to counter with the suggestion that maybe that was what we'd been doing for poor hick kids, and just because she wasn't the target market didn't give her the right

19

to dump all over it – which, while it wasn't really what I wanted to say, might have afforded me the stunned silence I needed to rise up and stalk off, with a transparent pretence at dignity that would have been wholly appropriate to the moment.

Fortunately my face gave me away – she must have seen how instantly the anger gave way to realistic, wrenching sorrow, because she said, 'Hey, c'mon. That's okay. You were our favourite one. You really looked like you were hating every minute of it.'

I brightened, in spite of myself. 'Jesus, do you know I really did? But that was part of the plan too. The whole idea with these things . . .'

'Is to appeal to every section of your market,' she finished for me. 'To give everyone someone just like themselves to identify with. To project themselves on to. So along with the quarterback and the boy next door, you have the disaffected one. The malcontent. The dark and brooding Malvolio. Which is you, Jake. I, however, am Brett.' She arched an eyebrow and extended her hand. 'And this is my brother. River.' She indicated, with a jerk of her head, the dark figure beside her.

I smiled as I took her slender hand, realizing that, for the first time in a long time, I was talking to someone without having known of and dreaded it for weeks beforehand, and without there being the slightest element of transaction involved.

'Can we get you a drink?' said Brett. She had a lovely lopsided smile that turned her mouth up ever so slightly at one corner. I never thought that eyes could sparkle but hers did; and, when she spoke to you, it was difficult not to feel that, though your life may have had the requisite number of seconds and minutes, they hadn't been cast from the same mould as these. That all the dull grind of your life had been worth it, since it was bringing you here.

She had the most extraordinary face. It wasn't like she just missed being beautiful, or being ugly; nor that she was beauty incarnate, but with one, like, fatal flaw – a scar above an eyebrow, a crooked tooth that served to throw the transcendance of the rest into sharper relief. Rather (and this was not lost on me, my consciousness orchestrated as it was by Hanna-Barbera) she had no business having a face like that outside a cartoon, and yet she was beautiful. Everyone flowers for a couple of years around the turn of their twenties – even Lou Reed – but this was different. I could imagine seeing her in thirty years' time, in a metropolitan setting, and wondering at how beautiful she must have been, all the time I was wasting my life.

'Yes please,' I said, 'I'd like a Cap de Corse.' Which seemed about right.

They both looked at me quizzically, then River waved over a waiter. He ordered my arcane liqueur and a *fine à l'eau* for Brett. And with that, he left.

'Forgive my brother,' said Brett. 'I made him go to the agent-lunch on his own, and now he's mad at me. One of us really ought to have gone, and I wish I could have, but I don't want to. So what brought you to UriZen?'

'The book of High 5 – just some contractual stuff, really.'

'Why did you do it? It seems so unlike you.'

'Oh, you know. It just came along. Of course, my modelling career was more glamorous, and I was making pretty good money at the law firm . . .'

Thankfully she laughed. Law firm, my ass. There was a pleasant, familiar air of skipping school. I really should have been seeing the marketing guy, so I wanted to know what she was bunking off from, to seal our complicity. I made some general remarks about winding up High 5, and asked her.

'They're doing a new biography of our mother. She was –' and here she named a woman, one of the brightest stars of the century that invented them, whose beauty and grace were such that she founded and dislodged dynasties with an arch of her eyebrow. Blow me, I thought.

She had been the first media virus. Her fame came too late for it to be borne by the infirmities of a studio system in its dotage, and so had spread, infecting print media, terrestrial broadcasting, the music business, the art markets, publishing. Her face, just before she died almost twenty years ago, had a better recognition factor than Coca-Cola. Though she never did anything.

She was a real UriZen girl. She never committed to a product. The machine was in overdrive, but never did the thing it was there for. The perversity was too much; it couldn't have been borne by any one person. Her death, in the mid-Seventies, had been the media circus of the century. Her billionaire industrialist husband, derangedly scrabbling at her planted coffin with his bare and bloody hands, while the world looked on in horror, or turned away its face. Dante Gabriel Rossetti exhumed Lizzie Siddal to retrieve the manuscript of an unfinished poem he had buried with her. This was abject, but he'd waited seven years and not done it on live TV. When Brett's mother's broken body came apart in her spouse's desperate embrace, he had allowed half as many people as have ever walked the earth to view the depths of his personal abyss – on primetime too. It had been worse than the Zabruder film: Jackie in Chanel couture scrambling over the trunk to retrieve her husband's cerebellum. Whatever. He'd found it expedient to assuage the horror by systematically bringing to its knees, whenever circumstances permitted, the currency of every country that had broadcast the moment when they could have helped it; that is, not live, but after the event too. Which was most of them.

I hadn't thought she'd had kids. It was widely opined that she had suffered from a condition familiar to most people who've had a spotlight trained on them for any length of time. That high-intensity beam bores a hole straight through you – deep, huh? – and she had sought to fill the vacancy with a consummate disregard for discretion or discrimination. So it was said. Naturally the most powerful man in the world was not centred by the news that his snow-white bride was on her hands and knees for the poolboy, particularly after he (it was still whispered, two decades later) had, as an admonition to greater modesty, put questions to the pleats of her hidden flesh that no one ought really to conceive of asking. This had, unsurprisingly, curtailed her progenitive career, despite arduous and crippling reparative surgery. So it was said.

'It was an affair, and before she was married,' Brett said, looking hard at me. 'We're twins. Our father was a writer, at Fox. We were packed off to her brother in Australia. He owns a camel farm. We grew up there.' She lit a cigarette. 'I only ever saw her once. She came to stay when we were five. We didn't know she was our mother. There was a big party for her, that went on all night, and I remember her screaming at us to go back to bed when we came down. She wept when my uncle told her it was seven in the morning, and we were getting ready for school.'

I thought about my own relatively default-option upbringing, that even so had driven me half-mad with fear and guilt. 'I'm really sorry. It must have been dreadful for you.'

'Don't be. It wasn't so bad. We have a percentage, though a small one. Otherwise, all we have of her is a Persian rug, from her apartment when she was my age. There's a worn patch that, our uncle says, is from men falling to their knees in front of her.'

I couldn't help but smile, and she caught me: we both laughed. After that it was okay.

We drank and we ordered, and we ate and we talked; and were still talking when we'd run out of courses to prolong it. She seemed to know an alarming amount about me, even about my forthcoming marriage to my teen sweetheart, which I was surprised was in the public domain as I hadn't thought anyone would have bothered to report it. Even I had almost forgotten it, and was finding the prospect receding further into the realm of the distant and improbable with every passing minute. I had expressed this, but we were both pretty caned, and she seemed happy to torment me about it over our fourth untouched double espresso *con machiatto*.

'You can't fault yourself for feeling odd about it. It's supposed to be peculiar: there wouldn't be any point to it otherwise. I think it's fascinating. I've often wondered whether the point isn't simply to have you take, you know, this private thing you felt together, and make a spectacle of yourself in front of everyone you've ever known; that way you'll be too embarrassed ever to renege on it. Did you have to be interviewed by a priest?'

'Yeah. It was hideous.'

'Oh God. Was he a hip one?'

'Quite old-school, actually. In a dress and everything. We had to go into his house. It was appalling. He made some dorky joke about the reading of the banns – how they have to do it three times in case someone wasn't paying attention. And Cara started twittering on about how wasn't it odd it has to be three times, because the Muslims or whoever just have to say whatever it is – I divorce you – three times to get out of the other end of the deal. And I'm like, discreetly trying to shut her up and look as though I don't know what divorce is – I don't know if they're allowed to turn people down so easily, but her parents are keen on this particular church because they didn't get a proper wedding themselves – you know, the Seventies and all. And I expect the old goat could refuse to do the business if he thought we were frivolous, or not especially infused with the fear of God. It's curious. You don't know what the variables are with clergymen.'

'It's absurd, isn't it?' The only trace of an accent she had was an occasional drawly elision, a little like Gwen in *Mallrats*. 'You should just be allowed to cough up and have them stage-manage the whole do. Surely they understand that people don't really care. And don't they insist you show up for the banns too? So you have to go stay with her parents three weekends in a row. Nightmare. I can't believe the church hasn't cottoned on yet. All you want is a theme-park thing, with costumes and horses and . . . chorus girls on *elephants*, and cheerleaders – d'you have cheerleaders?'

'I think we have a choir.'

'Well there you go. Trick them out with pom-poms and letter sweaters and you're away. Go team! Yay! And doing little dances. C'mon, you're paying them. You should insist on it. You should get to specify. Don't they have a brochure?'

'I couldn't say. Cara's flat has been like, carpeted with them for almost a year now. God knows why I agreed to go through with all this. I can't even remember who suggested it.'

'Don't you like it?'

I was past caring. 'I don't recall. I can't even remember what irritates me most about her. I was trying to think, earlier. The best I could dredge up was, she was at some ball or party at university while I was on tour, and had her photo taken by accident and put in *Harper's & Queen* – you know? The parade-of-the-aliens section at the back? – and she cut it out and it's still tucked in the corner of her mirror in her old room, at her parents'. The place is a shrine to this squeaky-clean, Burberry and Barbour-ed youth she imagines she had.'

'I once had a Barboured youth. And one in a Burberry too. Yuk yuk.' We both laughed. We were drunk, okay? 'Where are you going? For the holiday thing?'

'Nice. I insisted. She wanted to go to Bali. But I want to go and find the Divers' villa. From *Tender is the Night*.'

'No. When?'

'A month? Yeah. Month on Saturday.'

'Excellent! River and I shall be there, for Cannes. We still get invited by the studio – we must be on some stupid mailing list. Anyway, you must give her the slip, and come have a drink with us. Here, c'mon. Let's sort it out before we've time to change our minds. Five weeks on Saturday. You'll be sick of having sex with her by then. Four o'clock. Les Trois Diables – best bar in Nice. In the old town. Can't miss it. Here, let me inscribe you.'

She produced a lipliner and scrawled it across my forearm. I should stress that this kind of thing doesn't make a habit of happening to me. But that appeared to be that.

The house of your parents arouses untenably high hopes. It can't help it. Things were so relatively uncomplicated when you lived there that it seems natural to expect the relatively pleasant prospect of a short convalescence there – of taking time out from dancing on the edge of the abyss – to solve, and satisfy, and set unchangeably in order. Thus the triumph of hope over experience. Home is really the smell of damp plaster in a cold bathroom on a rainy Sunday night; the persistence of a streetlamp against the darkness of your bedroom; and an unsatisfactory poverty of spirit that suggests that, having come from this, you can't possibly be going anywhere else. But when you're skivvying your way through your twenties this is the kind of thing that has to sustain you, or else you really wouldn't bother.

I got in so late that the hall and kitchen were dark, but I had to concede there were certain consolations, as I sloshed kahlua into a crystal brandy glass. I'd bought them a box of crystal last year as a twenty-fifth anniversary present – fourteen years of marriage, six of separation, then a calmer new arrangement in this calmer, newer house – and it didn't look right. I'd ordered it from the Shopping Channel when we were on tour, and it kind of clashed with the rest of the place. One of the compromises traded by my parents when they elected to retreat once more into the fallout shelter of their marriage was that they both throw out all their kitsch and clutter; now the whole place was clean lines and utility. Consumer durables artfully constituted in colours and textures to suggest an infinite remove from the institutional winked their powersave LEDs from the semidark around me, as I tilted back the chair and drank. The kahlua was a sweet throwback to the deceptions of youth. My sisters and I had swiftly discovered that the correct method of raiding the liquor cabinet was to avoid the mainstream spirits, whose clear glass bottles revealed with artless candour any drastic fluctuations in their levels; and to take enthusiastic swigs only from flasks whose opacity disguised the quantity of liquor within. And so we drank our way around the world: Calvados, kirsch, slivovitz, jambava; raki, sake, Pastis, Pimms; curaçao, Cointreau, *crème de menthe* and kahlua; often mixed together if supplies were especially low. These last we called Disney drinks, for their technicolour sweetness.

I knew every hazard or nuance of the staircase's groaning idiosyncracy from a thousand 2 a.m. arrivals, and made it to the top floor with scarcely a sound. I felt my way along the corridor to the attic stairs, using peripheral vision to see by – a trick I learned from the junk-shop James Bonds I'd inhaled in the dreary-drugged holidays of my childhood. The only room I could count on being empty was my younger sister's, and I hauled my pack up to the narrow room at the top of the house, still balancing the balloon of kahlua in one hand. I eased the door shut, flipped on the bedside light and sat down to smoke.

My mind was full of Brett. I could not get her off my mind. Which was the long and short of it. A thousand songs had been written, recorded and marketed especially in celebration of this condition – we had been guilty of a couple of especially low-rent variations on this particular theme, amongst others – and a slobbering K-tel compilation kicked in my head as I lay back and applied the glass to my mouth, then lolled this way and that, rubbing my fevered skull against my sister's headboard, still plastered with *Charlie's Angels* and *Nancy Drew* stickers. This was ridiculous. Even being in my sister's room made me feel closer, somehow, to Brett. Knowing next to nothing always helps; maybe she had a room like this somewhere. Maybe there had been a thousand myriad summer nights when she'd flung open the door there and fallen on to this bed, then got up and poured herself a stiff one, winked at her reflection in the mirror, and tossed it off in one. And opened the window against sweet subtle darkness to smoke a covert cigarette. Her chiffonier, where anything worth remembering had been prepared for with toner and tweezers and perfume; her desk where she'd inscribed her letters and endless diaries; her ramshackle wardrobe, still bursting with the costumes of her youth. Lying late at night in someone else's room is always like being at Disneyland, on their own personal ride. As I fell asleep the glass slipped from my hand, and cracked across.

I woke early, to the fading lament of woodpigeons; and lay in silence awhile, the better to store this dawn up against the months when I would be away from here. Or rather, the months when my immediate course of action would not be so self-evident. Even so, it felt like I was operating in a vacuum that morning. I got up before it could gather around me and swallow my day.

Downstairs, and the sun licked through the windows. I was juicing a bunch of blowsy grapefruit, making a pulpy jugful of freshly squeezed as a treat for them all, to show I could still be spontaneous in ways that didn't involve getting stuff flown in from Marseilles or the Volga or whatever, which they only seemed to regard as a kind of showing off. Usually this was my least favourite Bank Holiday, seeming only to spin out the false starts of April even further, but it was a late Easter that year, and the sky outside could almost have been a billboard on Sunset for the First Day Of Spring. I was impatient for my sisters. I wanted to fix them individual coffee and *pain au chocolat* as they appeared, and have them question and confide in me about their transitions from home into the realms of like, preferment and capital. I hadn't been half close enough to any of them for the last couple of years, which made me feel like I was only picking up a couple of the available channels, or missing the premium-ice-cream aisle at the superstore. I sat down to wait.

I'd read the paper once for news and once for nonsense by the time anyone appeared. My younger sister wasn't at all surprised to see me, and lifted back a veil of hair to give me a perfunctory kiss, as she sleepwalked to the kettle.

'Hello,' I said it warmly, 'how've you been?'

'Hiya. Bloody awful. How 'bout you?'

'Oh, okay. About the same. You want some juice?'

'Yes. Yes, I think I do. I've been swilling pints of coffee all night. I've got this kind of *urn* in my room. If I so much as smell any more I'm going to spew.'

'Have you been up all night?' I asked resignedly as I poured it out. The last time I had anything worth staying up all night for seemed horribly distant. And any future opportunities were beginning to seem rather remote. Young people make you feel so old.

'Yeah. Christ. You wouldn't believe the amount of coursework we get. I came back two weeks early and I've still not caught up.' She selected a chair at the table, laid out her smoking apparatus and commenced to prepare a cigarette.

'What were you doing? D'you want any help?' I had, rather famously, done my degree by correspondence course while on the road with High 5. I don't know why. I mean, like, *I* can go on a graduate trainee program. As if.

'Women's studies. No, thanks and everything, but I doubt you could follow it. I mean, it's probably changed since you did it.'

'Why, what are you doing? Binarisms? Essentialism? Earth Mother versus Cyberfem? That kind of thing?'

'Naw. We just analyse the press releases from whoever's over from the States with a new book. And try and see who's got the slickest marketing. You know.'

'Oh.'

'Yeah, and identify the fad-cycles and so on. It's okay. I didn't get much done tonight though. The foxes must've kept coming into the garden, and I was trying to work out where they live from watching the time-delays on the security lights. The last one to shut itself off must be closest to their lair, d'you see? But I kept getting distracted.'

'I didn't know we had foxes.'

'Oh, yeah. They've been coming for ages. They all emigrated from the town because they've got like, *wheelie* bins over there now, and they can't get at the trash to forage. Or scavenge or whatever. I felt sorry for them so I've been bringing back leftover fries and chili and stuff from my excellent holiday job – Taco-A-Go-Go – and they must eat it because it's gone every morning; but whenever I see them they look even mangier. So I was trying to wean them on to healthier stuff last week – I got a big bag of marrowbone rolls at the market – but they don't seem to want anything that's good for them. I suppose you can't have someone feed you junk half your life and then suddenly expect you to get with the program. Bless me. A parable for these times.' She laughed sardonically.

'Can I have one of your cigarettes?' I said, a little too quickly. She pushed the package over toward me and I helped myself. 'I got a paper, if you want a look. It's over on the side.'

'No fear! I'm allergic. It's my new luxury illness. I can't have any newsprint or TV or radio or anything. It was taking me over. I couldn't bear it. I used to run out of every available emotion before lunchtime. Before breakfast on weekends.' She squinted at the window. 'I miss the weather report, though. Did you see any?'

'There was one on the plane when we landed last night. You know, when they tell you to set your watch. Sunny spells. Fifteen or sixteen maybe.'

'It doesn't look like it. This bastard cloud hasn't lifted for weeks.

31

It's gathering already. Christ, I'm gasping for a bit of sun. Do you want some coffee?'

'Not really.'

'Neither do I. I think it's cruel to say it's going to be sunny when it isn't. They shouldn't be allowed. It even affects the markets this time of year. Apparently. Everyone's pining away for summer, and whenever there's a decent forecast on the breakfast TV there's really optimistic trading till ten. Then some trader glances out the window and sees the same damn cloud rolling up the river to squat over the city again, same as yesterday – and the market goes down the toilet again. There was a study done. I saw it on the . . . shit, there I go.' She clutched her head theatrically. 'Setting it off. Quick, talk to me. No, actually, don't. I'm going to go sleep a while. Are you around today?'

'Uh-huh.'

'If I get up at twelve will you buy me lunch? Rich boy?'

I smiled. 'Okay.'

'All right. What are you going to do?'

'I don't know. When does everyone get up?' This house was lousy with lazy bastards.

'There's no one else here. Didn't you know? When did you get in?'

'Late. Around two. The lights were off so I went straight to bed.'

'Oh right. No, Julia's off having sex in Shropshire. Fi didn't come home – she's pretending she doesn't need to anymore. And the Ma/Pa config are scoring their last hit of Euro-thrills as we speak. They went to Prague for the weekend. They're flying back tonight. Will you stay that long?'

'I can't. Got to work tomorrow. Well. Meet my lawyer, anyway. Whatever. You know.'

'Actually, I don't. I'm sorry. I didn't mean that. I'm horribly tired. Look, will you do me a favour? And go visit our grandfather, if you're not doing anything else? I'm the only one who ever goes to see him, and he really feels it. Do you know where the place is? Okay?'

'Okay. I'll see you at lunch.'

'Right. 'Night!'

Left alone, I opened the paper and closed it again. My sister would have killed to have had my problems, and I would have killed . . . no. Not really. It was endless, and not worth thinking about. But while I was here, there was a shiny green 205 with all the stuff on out in the driveway, and this was the only chance I got to drive cars.

This last phase of late capitalism has nothing to show more fair than the smell of a new car on a morning flush with the symptoms of summer. It smelled, as I pulled out of the driveway and slipped into second then third, like good times, like impossible solvency, stealing me back to the aroma of new carpets and fresh vinyl paper permeating the house, years ago. It worked on me like lithium carbonate, tripping the pleasure-switches then as now, because the outlay it represented meant temporary respite from the bust-section of my parents' cycle, a metaphorical 1986; a break from post-Opec frustration and hopelessness, heralding a Merchant–Ivory wave of picnics and theatre trips, cottages in Dorset, Provençal gîtes in the bullest years. When equilibrium came it was too late, and I was long gone anyway. My mother had seemed beaten into a kind of half-life for a long time there; I'd spent whole dead hours turning over old photographs and wondering where the lethal young princess had gone. It wasn't enough to admire her selflessness, her thick-and-thin regard – it wasn't any kind of a life. But I failed to imagine what else could have been available, and to extract conclusions to apply to my own life made me almost frantic with a tired kind of nausea. The only emotion I could dredge up without it making me want to spit was a frustration at not being able to see her any other way. This wasn't any good at all.

I got up into fifth on the brief dual carriageway into town. The only other traffic was an interminable queue in the inside lane, waiting to turn into a playing field for a boot sale. I negotiated the new one-way system with mounting alarm and found, halfway through, that the High Street had been paved over. This irritated me because I wanted to drive down it and see what was new, but I had to park and walk instead, which made me feel like some kind of impostor. Most of the shops had whitewashed windows; it was like walking between rows of dead spectacles, with no eyes behind them. I couldn't endure the sensation of imminent denouncement, so I went back to the car and drove out into the country around home. It was maybe between nine and ten and the cloud was piling up now. Even out here it didn't feel right at all. I could remark the green mists of elms, the roadsides alive with flowering grasses, the insouciant meadows and bluebell-decked woods; could almost overlay them with the requisite filter, and imbue the serene certainties they once carried. Almost, but not quite. I was too conscious of the desire and everything it implied. The car didn't have a stereo, which was a big mistake. Driving, usually the one time I can get the interior monologue down to a bearable level, just felt dumb today. I could even hear the machinery moving and, beneath me, the tyres on the road. No good. This trip was a bust. I headed back into town.

The residential home was built on my old school playing fields: it was weird, this new toytown palace of primary-color bricks and twee tube-steel gables, artful little arbours and flowering borders shielded from the road by full-grown ashes whose adolescent configurations I'd memorized through hour after stultifying hour in freezing shacks, that had been razed for the carpark I pulled into. My grandfather was brought here six months ago, after his second stroke. This was my first visit. I operated the entryphone and was buzzed in, warily regarding the pastel uniforms of the carers, who were wheeling stuff and old guys about.

I was back inside the car and spinning the wheels before I even knew what I was doing, and when I had to stop at a red light I couldn't make the car go again. I put my hands in my lap and looked up at myself in the mirror. 'Okay,' I muttered to my reflection. 'Okay.' My eyes were bigger than I remembered them, and it was as much as I could do to put the car in gear and drive away again. For a moment there I thought I was going to go back and find an empty room in that place and get into bed and not get out. But I could drive again, and I headed home on autopilot. As I was coming back through the village I saw my sister walking on the other side of the road and I swerved over to her so sharply that she had to jump out of the way. She opened the door and sat down.

'Shit. That bad? Tell me about it. Last time I went I got the whole spiel and then some. "Let me die." And then I go home and find Mom chewing vita-pills and Dad off out to play squash. Come on. You need a stiff one. How about the Crown?'

Dark oak and spiralling smoke of the saloon bar, and two glasses of something thick and purple in front of us.

'What is it?' I said, picking one up and sniffing at it suspiciously.

'Red wine and orange juice, equal parts,' Phoebs said, taking a slug of hers and smacking her lips appreciatively. 'My trademark drink. I was worried I was getting a bit forgettable at college so I start drinking this, and suddenly everyone knows who I am. The one who drinks the funny drinks. It's about the only thing I can touch anymore. You get vitamin C in the orange, and also – bonus – it disguises how nasty the wine is. Go on. Chin chin.'

I took a sip, then a swallow. 'It's all right. Where did you learn it from?'

'Nowhere. I just tried to think of an unlikely drink. These fragments I shore against my ruins. Pathetic, *n'est-ce pas*? *Quel pays sanguinaire*.' She was inclined, of old, to start coming on like Colette with the cramps when she was bored. I changed the subject.

'So how's the jobhunting?' I was genuinely interested. Real life fascinates me.

'I don't know. I'm beginning to hope I never find out. We get it drilled into us all the time about how there isn't any work left so we've got to be better than anyone else. Work the room. Network network network. I don't think I have the energy. It's been too long a haul as it is. You spend half your life putting up with all their silly ideas about education only to have them like, shrug sheepishly, and admit there was nothing at the end of it all along. I thought you were supposed to get all the adult stuff at the end like some kind of prize. For endurance. And then, when they tell you it's all run out, you want it even more for a while; then you wonder what the fascination was to begin with. There isn't any point in feeling bad. A bunch of people just thought they could do as they pleased, and that it would last forever. And bless me if it hasn't. So what do you do? Start wanting something else?'

'Or not wanting at all?'

'Yeah I guess. What brought you over so suddenly? Cara-crisis?'

Cara was my unfortunate girlfriend. I don't know what I mean by that.

'Actually, I've come back to call it off. I've come back . . . to call it off. It's been over for ages anyway. I mean, I've barely seen her for two years. And I've met someone else. Kind of.' I'm afraid I hadn't broken news of the marriage at home yet. Yeah, I know, what a scumbag. But there'd never been, like, the right moment.

'Jesus. Thank God for that. I can't bear her. I hate running into her in town or wherever. I never know what to say. She's awful.' She took a whoof on her drink. 'I drove by her house the other day and she was out with her father in the garden. Probably air-brushing the lawn green or something. That road is like, Californ-i-a. So who've you met? What's she like?'

I was in no fit state to say. Brett could have led me to fire. I could cheerfully have swung for her. She was trouble, but she was so worth it.

'She knows how to build a house of cards. She can sing the *Top Cat* theme. She's trouble and I don't care. She's called Brett.'

My sister received this information with one eyebrow aloft.

'And everything she touches/Turns to fake fur and glitterballs/Martini glasses/Royal flushes . . . ?'

'Yeah.'

'Shit. Must be hellish.'

'Not half. D'you want another?'

She nodded her assent, and I trailed off to the bar with our sticky glasses. While the crispy-haired youth was incredulously mixing the drinks, I slipped round the side and called Cara on the payphone. She sounded dimly effusive to hear I was back, but I think she knew. I think they always know, when you ring them up out of the blue and say you need to talk. It would be a whole lot easier if the dumpee could acknowledge that call for the shorthand you both know it is. But we can't help wanting to hear the words spoken, at either end of an affair. Co-stars of a thousand cinematic kisses, we must have our final scene. And so we did.

After school I got a job in a theatre, as an usher. It was a hell of a place: too hot or too cold, a snakepit of insufficient legroom, chafing collars, choked-back coughs and unmanageable frocks. My duties, as far as I understood them, involved pencilling a kind of insolent leer across my features as I lounged, in rayon waistcoat and junior dickybow, with my back to a gilded pillar, and indicted patrons through this particular circus of hell. My favourite was working the dress circle, where sweating tossers in nasty tuxes escorted tired-looking MBAs to fractured modernist operas. They'd never been before and didn't understand the interval drinks orders, so had to sit through the interminable half-times in excruciating silence, terrified of having to essay opinion, and so feigning absorption in the programme's drooling career histories: Penny took leading roles in *A View from the Bridge* and *Death and the Maiden* in rep at Telford; her TV credits include *Casualty* and *The Bill*.

Here I met Cara. She was twenty-one and drifting. She'd done some dumb degree that her redundant ex-middle manager father considered to exhibit the same kind of business acumen that had helped him make such a success of his own life. Like, she'd been really into Jacobean tragedy, so he made her to do Leisure & Heritage Management so she could run the ice-cream concessions at the Lyceum. She'd consequently done nothing at university except get dewy-eyed over TSS and VAT on tampons at some old meeting or other, and to permit herself to be drunkenly assaulted once a semester by blue-eyed young men whom she met in nightclubs. She espoused a vague kind of feminism that involved owning *Wild Swans*, a Betty Blue poster and the soundtrack to *Thelma and Louise*. She had a rather frightening collection of Athena naked-male-model-cradling-naked-baby posters in clipframes. She wore lipstick as red as a stop light. She was the first girl I slept with, okay?

The moment I'd said it she irritatingly fumbled forth a pack of Silk Cut Ultra from the Gap jeans that didn't fit her right and lit one. She didn't look at me. She chuffed out thick columns of smoke for a few histrionic moments. Is there someone else? she said. Her voice failed to catch between syllables as I had a feeling she hoped it would.

I still don't know what you say to this. I tabulated the options. Did I want to make it easier for her? Or for me. Did I want to hurt her now so she'd hate me within a week and get it over sooner? I could have done without her puppy-dogging around for weeks on end. Not that I was planning to stick around, but you know. Or did I want to live forever in some shrine of her synapses for the saintly way with which I like, discharged our mutual obligation?

'Of course not –' opting naturally for the path of least resistance '– I don't want anyone else.'

Visions of her deflating future service-industry boyfriends (preferably still wearing their dayglo Ribs-R-Us visors) with shiny-eyed narratives of my magnanimity danced through my head like sugarplums. I hope she mentions my abs – also how much money I've got.

'Then why? It's been so long. We were okay.'

'C'mon, Cara. Of course we weren't. We've barely seen each other for months. In two years we've probably spent about a week together. Real time.'

'But with you away on business all the time. And you never took me with you. Max took Kate, and Oliver took along Lucy.'

'I wasn't allowed. Strategy. I was the unapproachable one. I couldn't be seen to be available, not to anyone. And that was all over a year ago.'

'But you've been recording . . .'

'I'm sorry. I haven't. There's no studio in Belize. I've been goofing off. In America.'

I'd see her in hell before I told her I was writing a screenplay. I didn't need any further complications. It would have sounded dorky anyway

'Oh.' Teartracks on her face. I guess her world was falling inwards. This had irritated me too. She did have a world, that she had created; with her as my, jesus, anchor or something, getting on with her life with all the consolations of a boyfriend but without any of the trouble. Like seeing him ever, for example.

'Don't you love me?'

'Cara, give me a reason to.'

This wasn't fair. Not fair of her as well. She'd always left everything up to me. Starting it, perpetuating it, now finishing it. I wish she'd slept with someone else. Then I could have behaved how I wanted for a while, without feeling guilty, until it came to this.

She was doing big orphan-eyes at me. I nearly gave in. But the thought of never having to worry again about what a mess I was making of her life was too much. I became brisk and manly.

'I'm sorry, Cara, but this is no good. For you or for me. I don't want to risk hurting you by saying things I don't mean, so I think we had better stop this now. I shall put it all in a letter when we're both calmer.'

And so I split. I left before my parents got back and got the train, tube, train to Waterloo, where I bought a single to Ho Chi Minh City, mostly to watch the guy's eyes get round. I changed my mind over a mocha in the Gare du Nord, and spent ten days parading myself in a stupor past the monuments of Europe. In Vienna I bought a handful of euro teen mags, mostly to yuk over the latest bunch of losers. This was how I found out Charlie was dead. I almost missed it, tucked away on page nine of *Mädchen*, between Courtney Love's latest arrest and Agent Scully's latest baby. My German is lousy, but there was a picture of him, and a bunch of negative-looking Teutonic words in the caption. I rang the girl who used to do our press in London. She seemed torn between embarrassment and boredom at having to fill me in. Charlie had driven into a tree ten days ago. No one was saying he'd done it deliberately, but he was full of gin and 2C-B, and there weren't any skid marks on the road. I rang off not knowing how to feel. The funeral wasn't for three weeks, till after the inquest, and I got the idea we were expected to go. I knew it would be scripted. I knew there would be press. I imagined the key accounts were being restocked already. I could see us all, in black suits and sunglasses, looking like Blonde, Pink, Orange and

Brown. I wasn't going to do it. This was real life. His family would be there. Absolutely no way whatsoever.

So away: away from the tainted wedding-cakes of Paris; away from Prague, ornate and mad under the lowering sun; away from the smart credit cards and cartoon cars of the west. I rode a motorcycle to Moscow and hung out a while, but it made me sad. Trams and dusty trees – AirMax and tight jeans. I picked up a carmine-lipped fortysomething Fascist countess among the furs and Homburgs at Smolenskaya station; between whose immaculate alabaster thighs I rocked with the rhythms of the train along the spice trail to Samarkand, Tashkent, Urmqui and Shanghai, where she disembarked for Hong Kong. She traded in pornography and plutonium, and only took trains and cabs. She objected to flying: now that airlines forbade the consumption, if not the sale, of cigarettes she missed that moment, after you'd flown through the eye of a storm, when the No Smoking light winked out again, and you knew you were flying through some department of Heaven that forgave the recent sins of air travellers and vouchsafed them free passage. She found this denial of the evidence of divinity unforgiveable. I continued south, simply to use up my ticket, passing through points of confluence whose names were familiar from the buzzing static of napalm-bearing helicopter radios in mid-to-late eighties VietNam movies, to Ho Chi Minh city. I threw away my Gap clothes, bought a linen suit and a flight to Bangkok–Cairo–Stamboul–Nice. My month was nearly up. My obligations were discharged. It felt like home had never existed.

The sea was too blue to look at, and the stones on the quay would not cool, night or day, for months. Summer had arrived a week before me, and now Nice hung in the heat beneath the blue glare of a Mediterranean noon.

The honeymoon apartment in La-Croix-de-Marbre had been shut up for a few days before I arrived, and the melting chocolates and dead roses on the pillows made the hot, airless rooms seem even more oppressive. I'd slung them out, left it to air, and cabbed up to the hotel on the east cliffs that I'd seen from the sky as the plane made its long slow sweep from the Maures, over the sea, to the estranged airport of Nice.

I was drinking pastis out on the terrace in my linen suit (and a Holmes T-shirt and sky-blue Vans, the jacket tied round my waist by the arms), gazing dreamily though the smoke of too many Gitanes Blondes at the city below me. Summer seemed to be taking its best shot at being sweet and meaningless, and the Promenade des Anglais shone with iridescent traffic. This was beginning to feel a bit special.

Most people's careers don't live up to the private image they have of themselves. My career hadn't lived up to my public image. This had made reality checks even harder, and I had kind of lost the knack for them. I wasn't sorry about knocking Cara on the head because that would have been silly. How far would we have got on forty grand? It's not like either of us could do much, and she'd wanted to have children besides. She'd get maternity leave from her school – she had done teacher training, finally – but she'd have to go back, and I had decided that I couldn't face househusbanding her baby because it would unquestionably have her feet. But I was beginning to feel less than entirely sure that coming here on the off-chance was such a hot idea, even though the apartment was already booked and paid for (I'd made myself do it three months ago, as though the transactions would force me into shaking off the nameless dread and mental cringing that accompanied every reminder of our destiny together, honeys till the end of time). But I still felt weird. It occurred to me that I had been reading too many novels with stylized representations of the Chrysler building on the cover, but I suspected that things weren't going to happen unless I made them. My previous life-experiences appeared to contradict this, as I had fallen into the High 5 thing without the slightest effort or inclination of any flavour, but I felt that had been a negative development rather than anything else. It had simply deflected me from having any kind of a regular shot at things, closing off options, Shelley seemed to be telling me, rather than opening them.

Moreover, I'd spent about a quarter of the pay-off from High 5 in the last two months, and it was beginning to look as though a bottle of jellies might soon come to seem an attractive career option. I mean like, right, I can go and work in telemarketing. Neither did nametags, hairnets and blue band-aids seem likely to figure in my working wardrobe. I could maybe blag a celeb column on a teen mag, or a broadsheet anxious to wear its irony on its sleeve, but I'd be in precisely the same position a year or two down the line. UriZen, so far as I could decipher Shelley, wouldn't give me finance 'n' distribution because the circuit was tired of my face – what they wanted was a new one, a *tabula rasa* with all the cheekbones and personal weirdness that the circuit demanded. I thought I could maybe help them there. I was going to give it some kind of shot anyway. I was running out of chances, and I wanted to have something other than High 5 on my résumé before undertakers commenced giving me the glad-eye.

★

The bar was where Brett had said it was, and she was right, I couldn't have missed it. Being in Los Angeles had been difficult because I grew up in this dozy provincial town, and if you saw anyone wearing black you practically leapt upon them – in LA, where every other loser tricked themselves out in shades of sable (maybe as relief from the cute toxic palette of that cartoon city), I'd been hard at it to stay in my seat. So when I walked through the old part of Nice, and caught a snatch of Portishead wafted along by the afternoon breeze, I just followed my nose till I found it.

It was pretty cool. It was inside some sort of crypt, but above ground, with domed ceilings of brick supported by arboreal columns. It felt like being in groves. The seats were all from railway carriages, with pearly bakelite seat numbers in Gill Sans, and string luggage racks overhead.

Brett was there, and looking even more fetching than I remembered her. She had her back to the door, and I skulked around a while because I wanted to remember this moment of being, so it seemed, on the knife-edge between one life and the next. Her hair had been bleached a little by the sun, and was held back by some white fly-eye Jackie O. sunglasses, pushed back over her forehead as she smoked. There was no River. She was tan. She wore a pink Fred Perry tennis dress and matching Dunlop pink flash. She looked adorable. For the space of a whole cigarette I wanted to spare her whatever kinds of weird sadness I would clearly lead her into. Sweetness, do yourself a favour – treat yourself – and go away from here. I waited, but she didn't, so it seemed I was engaged to mischief. Besides, you have to really fancy someone before you can consider messing up their life on the scale I had in mind.

An hour later (can you ever wholly recollect the time you spend in bars? Could you stand it if you could?) we were on our fourth bottles of Belgian cherry beer, and she hadn't stopped talking.

Unfortunately about Cara. I might have preferred the evening to be a little later before we got on to the old *affaires de coeur*, but there you go.

'Were you ever in love with her?'

'Yes, I think so.' It would have been caddish to say no, and besides I wanted her to know I was cool about expressing my emotions. Not like, share-your-feelings-with-the-group, but you know.

'And can you still see why?'

'Actually, no.' I didn't want to push it.

'That's good. If you can still see how you once loved somebody then you're not over them. Do you blame her?'

'For what?'

'For wasting some years of your life. For wasting your sweetness on desert air. She did, didn't she?' I blushed and nodded. It was, I'm afraid, true. I'd been too embarrassed to sleep with people after the show or whatever. 'You shouldn't feel bad. She comes from a world of Reeboks and clip-frames, MX5s and scrunchies. How could she possibly help you? She wouldn't know what she needs if it kissed her on the nose and asked her to Charleston. What did you do after you gave her the Captain Frosty?'

'I spent some time at my parents'.'

'You have parents? What's it like?'

'Oh, you know.' Of course, she didn't. 'We sit around and talk about sex the whole time.' Thankfully this got a laugh.

'Were you ever happy with her?'

'Nothing ages like happiness,' I said, with relief to have something to say at all.

'And nothing propinks like propinquity.' We clinked glasses and saw off the rest of our drinks. I got more.

'So what now? Will you be loved again?'

'I don't know. You get so you feel, I don't know, that maybe shorthand is all we can give each other – just random symbols instead of whole phalanxes of joy and fear and longing. Just stupid anecdotes and throwaway banter instead of infinite passion. You can't even just give the other one a stack of diaries to read and say – there, get on with it. They need context, the flung-on-the-bed desperation of a thousand grey November Sundays. Or February midnights. When you're coming down.' I was laying it on thicker than a CNN anchor's foundation. Brett seemed, however, to be up for it.

'Because you've had affairs – whatever – that you felt very deeply, and now you can't help seeing every potential one becoming just like them,' she said, and took a lingering whoosh on her Kool. 'So you need to have a series of dissolute, sickening, heartbreakingly meaningless ones before you can appreciate it again.'

Blimey. Recalling this now is like couching in front of the TV on a November evening, and thinking about how you slept naked under a single sheet three months ago.

'I can't help feeling that my friends talk about me when I'm not there,' I said, pushing it, 'and look grave, and wag their heads and say, I hope he finds whatever it is that'll make him happy. They love me but they can't understand why I throw things away the way I do.'

'You're not much of a boyfriend,' she sang along to a snatch of something on the breeze. We'd left the bar hours ago and wandered around the quarter, feeling the extent of evening as the clocks chimed around us. I wanted to sweep her up in me, feel those brown arms around my neck. We were both quite drunk, and looking out over the sea now.

'But what is there for people like us to do? Model? Marry? Work for some trustafarian's crappy style mag? Then knock out some drug-impaired novella?' She could do the most extraordinary things with her eyebrows. 'Or do you do something else; that *you* can do because no one else dared consider it. Do we plan a murder, or start a magazine? What colour are my eyes?'

'Green,' I answered, reflexively.

'And do I walk, and talk, and tango?' She turned to me, her eyes shining, and suddenly her voice was hot and smoky against my neck. The milky sea. The angel hair filigree descending into her nape. Whatever.

'I have to go. River and I have stuff to do. Meet us here at noon tomorrow.'

It took around ten minutes before I noticed I was alone. I went back to the bar and got stupid, stinking drunk. I tried to go on to a club but there didn't seem to be any. I drunkenly essayed a walk along the shore but all the beaches were private and possessed of loosely-tethered pit bulls. I thought of picking up one of the rich old broads, lousy with rocks and a poodle in tow, who'd thronged the Promenade des Anglais in the flattering pink light of dusk, but there weren't any in evidence now. I didn't want to go back to the flat alone since I had this horrible feeling Cara was going to be there, hysteria replaced by a calculated zeal to exact four years of roads not taken from my tented flesh with a kitchen knife. She wasn't, but this didn't mean I slept any better. At a quarter past four, when all the world was perfect blue, I stole up to the roof of the apartments to smoke some cigarettes. I wasn't feeling too great about myself, if you want to know the truth. I'd meant that stuff earlier about people I loved feeling sad when they thought about me, and I was inclined to agree with them. There was something in me that was like biting on tinfoil. I'd even taken fame with the bad grace of Richard Carpenter, adding surly atonal keyboard trills to crowd-pleasing standards at Caesar's Palace the year I was born. I thought, perched on a ledge above the city and looking like hell, of the Bell-Jar babe, out on the roof of her hotel, floating her silks and taffetas away on the wind as a way of finishing something. My stupid cottons – my Oxfords and poplins and jerseys – would just flop to the floor. This was an unsatisfactory end to the day. Was this the right thing to be doing? Maybe I just needed a nice vicar's daughter in a Morris Minor. The hell with it. I didn't know then and I don't know now.

'There is really nothing quite so much worth doing as simply messing about in planes.'

I was perfectly willing to concede this, but when Brett hopped off her Vespa, climbed on to the back of River's and said, 'C'mon, buddy. We're going to get tight on the wine of the country, and then we're going for a swell plane ride,' I understood the day was not going to go quite as I'd planned. I folded the copy of the *Züricher Zeitung* that I had bought for the romance of it, tucked twenty francs under my coffee bowl and mounted the scooter. I'd ridden one before, for a photo-shoot, so I had no trouble keeping up; though River went very slowly at first for my benefit and Brett kept turning round to give me reassuring waves. We puttered along the bay towards Antibes. It felt nice riding along under the girl-drink theme-bar palms, and we went quite fast and made a good breeze.

I wasn't sure what was going on, but they were both giggling irrepressibly when we stopped in the square of a little village on the Antibes road. Brett explained everything over lunch, with enthusiastic interjections from River, whose spirits were so high he seemed positively chummy for a change. We sat outside in the shade; there was a warm wind and you could tell it came from the sea. They had been to the casino the night before, it transpired, and had taken a suite at the Carlton this morning on the proceeds from baccarat and *chemin de fer*.

'Simple exchange of values,' remarked River, waving his glass around airily while Brett chortled uncontrollably. 'You give them a couple of thousand francs, they give you such piles of cinq-mille plaques you can't stack them up in front of you.'

'We bought stuffed dogs –' Brett was giggling so hard she could barely get the words out ' – stuffed *dogs*! From the *concession*! At the front!' And she was racked with such paroxysms that River, sniggering away himself, had to pound her on the back to stop her choking.

'But stuffed dogs, River,' and she looked at him imploringly. They both doubled over then and I sat back and lit a cigarette, and laughed a little myself, feeling uncomfortably like an indulgent uncle. I didn't want to be their uncle. I wanted to be their lover, their accomplice, their deranged teacher. When they had recovered themselves a little, Brett wiped her eyes and informed me that the road to hell was paved with unbought stuffed dogs. This set them both off again.

This was getting tiresome. It's never much fun to be outside a joke that someone you fancy is sharing with someone else. But after a while Brett got up, threw her arms round my neck, gave me a big smack on the cheek and said I had to come with them again that night.

'But I don't know how to play,' I admitted miserably.

'Oh, the hell with that,' said River. 'We'll teach you. We'll have time, won't we?'

'Sure we will,' said Brett. 'Have you got a tux? No matter, we can rent you one from our hotel. God I love the Carlton. Oh.' She pushed away her bowl of cous-cous and held up her glass for a toast. 'Come on, let's drink. To the things that almost got us, but couldn't quite. To phoning in sick on sunny mornings. To escape from the north, and tomato *soup*, and stupid boring guilt. To Eden and forgetfulness. The warm South!'

And we threw back beakers full of it.

Which I began to regret when it became apparent that they were serious about the aeroplane. River, moreover, was going to pilot. And when I saw the plane they had in mind, my desire turned back like the pilgrim's at sundown.

'Isn't it darling?' squealed Brett, grabbing my hand and dragging me across the apron toward it, while River argued in French with a grease-smeared bald man in blue overalls.

Darling it possibly was. Airworthy, and capable of being flown by the half-cut bastard son of the most celebrated woman of the century, and his clearly barking, though avowedly louche, lovely and possibly into me, sister, was another matter entirely.

It was a biplane, of a marque and vintage that suggested it may have been parked on the lawn at one of Gatsby's parties – a succession of tragically lit flappers cakewalking along the wings. I began to suspect that I had come on holiday by mistake.

'Jesus,' I said, as we rounded the fuselage, 'Brett, no. We can't possibly.'

'Yes we can.' She caught up one pretty ankle in her hand and hopped a few steps.

'It's insane.'

'Staring at WordPerfect all day is insane. We lived in a tent last week, because we didn't have enough money for a room. That was insane. Lying looking at Orion through the mesh windows, swigging ten-franc vin ordinaire. Putting my mother's necklace in hock for our stake last night seemed insane.'

'Are you from hell?'

'No,' she said in a low voice, glancing over at River, still in heated conference with the mechanic. She let a light hand fall on the back of my neck. 'But I know the way to heaven.' And drew me to her so that I didn't know she was doing it. 'Or would you rather not be saved?'

'Brett, that is the worst line ever.' I kissed her forehead. 'Come on.'

She smiled with her eyes, and we scrambled onto a wing and up into the fuselage, me first. She climbed in after, sat across my knees with an arm round my shoulder and waved excitedly to River as he strode, beaming broadly, across the grass toward us.

'Disco!' he called over. 'Fuel for an hour and a half.' He climbed into the cockpit in front of us and commenced interfering with the controls. 'Hah! Electrics. We don't have to spin the prop.' He whistled 'Something Stupid' as he adjusted various dials.

I swallowed. Brett was tying her hair up in a white chiffon scarf. All her weight was in my lap and her out-thrown chest was practically in my face. I swallowed again, dryly, and croaked, 'You seem to know a lot about the Riviera,' to take my mind off it.

'I know a lot about everything,' she said, fixing me with an impish smile that didn't help matters. 'We grew up on a camel farm, didn't I tell you? Three days' drive from the nearest town. That's how we learned to fly. But until there was satellite all there was to do was read.'

'Didn't you have friends? From school?'

'Our school was a four-hour flight away. We had to stay there all week. It was the hell of a place. *Caning* was still allowed. Yes, of girls. I was only beaten once, and that was for telling the truth. It certainly cured me.'

River gunned the engine, and the propeller spun into noisy life. 'After a while we stopped going. Our uncle's library was way superior. He had a first edition of *La belle dame sans merci*, and a Mask of Anarchy pamphlet. But he was kind of into Rimbaud – troubadors and shit – and there was a lot of Provençal history. And some excellent stuff about the Côte d'Azure. I loved the title, so I read it all. See that eagle on the wing?' She shouted as we began to bump over the grass to the tarmac. 'It's from the coat of arms. See how there's a painted-over patch by the back of its head?' I nodded vigorously and tightened my arms around her. We were taking off. 'The Italians must have done that in the war. The eagle's head points to the left or right depending on whether Nice is owned by France or Italy. Someone must have painted it back after the war! Yesssss!'

The ground was suddenly staggeringly far below us, and we

were climbing hard. The engine screamed. It was nothing like being in a regular plane – the whole thing shook as though it were in the grip of some monstrous palsy. I wailed as we swerved sickeningly upward again.

'Look!' shrilled Brett, leaning over the side with an expression of ineffable glee. 'There's the Murphys' house! On Garoupe beach.' She sat back down and bellowed into my ear, 'D'you know when they first came here it was total hicksville? They couldn't use the telephone between twelve and two because that's when the operator was having his lunch. Or after seven at night, because he'd gone home.' She shook with laughter.

'Were they the first people to bring writers here?' I hollered.

'God no. Chekhov stayed at the Pensione Russe in Nice for the winter of 1903. He loved it. He said that even the dogs exhaled sophistication. Yeats was buried at Roquebrune; they missed some bones when he was exhumed and taken back to Ireland. There're still bits of him down there, though nobody knows which ones. Also Joyce, got the idea for *Finnegan's Wake* at Nice.' She ticked them off on her fingers. 'And Cocteau wrote *Orphée* at the Hotel Welcome in Villefranche.

'But the Murphys were the best. It was a wonderful time. Fish were jumping and the dollar was high. Though it wasn't just about money: you need to go away to freshen up the scene at home. The Jazz Age wouldn't have been the same without the long perspectives of summer. Like Ibiza and the Summer of Love. Isn't *Tender is the Night* dedicated to them?'

I nodded. We'd levelled out and were sweeping over the Cap d'Antibes. River turned half-around and took his hands off the joystick to wave at us. The little plane lurched sickeningly, clearly to his delight. Brett pulled out a compact and started applying lipstick, to demonstrate how unconcerned she was. He shrugged, winked at me and turned back to the controls. Brett pressed her lips together to distribute the cosmetic evenly, then dropped the mirror back in her bag and leaned comfortably back, with her head resting in the crook of my shoulder and her hair flying in my face. It felt good to be flying about a bit after lunch. I had to hand it to them. This was a pretty cool thing to do.

'Don't you love hotels?' said Brett, as we waited for the PC she'd ordered from room service to be brought up.

Yes, I did. My miserable, lonely debauch in the city of angels aside. Staying in hotels in High 5 had been like forever having to go pick people up at the airport, but never going anywhere yourself. But one of the few compensations as you plummet towards thirty is the thought of weekending with the strange sunlit someone who'll maybe stick around long enough to re-establish the link between sex and love forever. Heating cranked up to 11, bathroom awash, drapes billowing out of the windows, room service and champagne and thick white sheets ironed so flat and tucked so tight you could bounce a coin on them. If you fancied. I tried it with Cara once, somewhere in Cumbria. She wouldn't let me play any tapes at a reasonable volume in the car on the way up, and she'd only brought jeans and jumpers and her usual heavy-duty M&S pants, all bulky cotton and twanging elastic. I'd been looking forward to a weekend of Lanson and languor, major room service abuse, and generally being disturbing behind the Do Not Disturb sign. All she did was take endless swampy baths, as though she'd never had one before, as though all getting away from her parents' house meant to her was a chance to spend as long as she wanted in the bathroom. Zero imagination. Admittedly, the gang of sales reps in the oak-panelled bar did cast envious glances when I managed to drag her down there for, for the love of god, two halves of dry cider; and I did derive a certain satisfaction from the thought of them later in their rooms,

Burton's trousers puddled around their ankles in the blue glare of the hotel's fifth channel. But that was about as good as it got.

'You should have seen the state of this place when we left it this morning. We'd trashed everything. It looked as though a bomb had hit it.'

I could imagine. But now the suite was immaculate, starched and aired, even new chocolates on the pillows. I'd been a little surprised when I came in and saw there was only one bedroom, and not even twin beds, and thought that River must have a room somewhere else until I noticed a pair of Dockers in the press. Brett saw me checking them out, and said something airily about there only being one room free when they had breezed up in the early hours and that there was another the next day, but I thought it was kind of sweet. Certainly, if I'd had a sister I was as close to as Brett seemed to be to River, I couldn't think of anything nicer than having them around to wake up with once in a while. I was almost jealous of that sweet sibling matter-of-factness that was generated between them by the simple facts of living – of never having to face up to too many nights on your own – the satisfaction of being able to be there for someone without really having to try. Of course, I was not naïve enough to imagine there mustn't be some kind of negative balance to the account, but there seemed an enviable reciprocity none the less.

The sleek Italian PC arrived and was installed, jacked into the phone port with the switchboard on bypass. Brett booted up Windows 95, signed on to the hotel's MSN account and got a connection to a server with a Cannes std code almost immediately. She tapped in the URL of Caesar's Palace (triple-dub dot vegas dot com – I mean, how cool?), and we both lit cigarettes as Netscape commenced to download the over-elaborate, un-amber-enabled graphics on the front page. River came out of the en-suite dressing room wearing an unbuttoned white dress shirt and white Calvins: he peered half-interestedly over Brett's shoulder for a moment, then got himself a red-checkered bottle of Kronenbourg from the minifridge and sauntered out to the balcony.

'Right,' said Brett, 'here we go. *Faites les jeux*. Roulette –' and she clicked on the appropriate icon '– the game that built Vegas.' A wheel appeared on the monitor, rendered in high-res verisimilitude, that rapidly changed to low-res QuickTime when she clicked to spin it.

'Roulette is *beautiful*,' she said, as the wheel blurred on the screen, mimicking the optical illusion you get in movies where the wheels of cars seem to lurch and spin slowly back when you know they're going forward and fast. The ball dropped into a slot – red, 33. 'Roulette is the point of casinos. They couldn't exist otherwise. Without roulette every casino would be just a back room in a bar. It pays for everything – the plush, the gilt, the sophistication of the staff, the surgeon in the cellar to patch up people who've shot themselves.' She laughed. 'Really. One at Monte Carlo used to have a fully equipped operating theatre in the basement. Roulette pays for it all because it has the most gratifyingly consistent house edge. And it gets people in and playing. Any imbecile can figure out how to do it, and the house does everything it can to keep you at the tables – complimentary drinks and cigarettes, regular stage-managed apogees of suspense. If you're really playing high they'll give you a suite at the hotel. Anything to make you feel like this is the big time – anything to keep the losing majority happy and playing, while the house edge ticks away like a meter. Rather like life, wouldn't you say?'

She gave me a sidelong smile as the virtual ball dropped into virtual zero with a satisfyingly real clatter.

'There is no room for skill, and no possibility of inclining the odds away from the house. People expect a run on red to even up with black sooner or later but it doesn't have to happen. We're conditioned to believe in fairness, and things evening out eventually, but when you get older you find that they don't. If you play roulette when you're young you can find this out early, and save yourself a mid-life crisis.' She lit a Lucky. 'Every spin of the wheel is an isolated event in time and space, with no relation to the previous one. Red or black are both equally probable with every game, even if red came up the last hundred times. The last billion times. Which is why roulette permits the existence of casinos. Of organized gambling at all. Things don't exist unless they have a margin. Natural selection.' She smiled to herself. I frowned, leaned in closer and put my chin in my hand.

'Roulette is just thirty-six numbers and a zero. But say you throw two dice a hundred times. Eight will come up more times than nine because there are five ways to make an eight and only four for a nine. Do you know why so many people say seven is their lucky number? It's the easiest one to throw – six ways with two dice. Next are eight and six: five ways each. There's only one way to throw a double, which is what cuts the chance of even numbers down. And of course things get worse as you get higher. There's only one way to throw a twelve.

'So. The wheel has no memory. There's a green slot – zero – that pays the house, so each number has a 1 in 37 chance of coming up, but the house pays as though it were 1 in 36. Hardly anyone notices even *that*.' She shook her head despairingly.

'So why do people keep playing?'

'Because it's easy. Because it's a no-brainer kind of buzz. Because it feels like you're really living. Which is why most people go to casinos to begin with. To escape time. There aren't any windows, so you won't see the sun coming up and giving the game away. And there are no clocks. It *is* Arden, or the nearest we're going to get to it. Stasis. Do you smoke?' She inclined her head towards River who had skinned up on a deckchair in the sun, his French

cuffs unfastened and floppy over his languid wrists, his face impassive behind a slick pair of Cutler & Gross.

'I used to a lot, actually. In the band. The manager used to dole
it out on tour like it was pocket money. Great wads of hash. To
keep us docile I suppose. Make us go straight to sleep after shows.'

'How'd it make you feel, after you'd been doing it a while?'

'Disconnected, I suppose. In neutral. Idling.'

'Exactly. That's how you feel when you've been playing roulette
too long. You don't notice how much you've lost, and you think
you remember patterns in the wheel when there haven't been
any. But people come back, because they want that feeling, of
everything else being on hold. We, however, are here to take the
dreamers to the cleaners. So we play baccarat.'

We ate at our separate hotels, and met in the bar at the Ruhl at
ten. River and I were transformed in our tuxes, but Brett was
dressed to break hearts – a short bias-cut black dress, beaded with
long strings of jet below an empire-line, black patent Mary Janes.
She ordered Tanqueray gin martinis, dry as you like with three
olives, and passed round unfiltered Sullivan Powells from a slim
silver case. We had all combed our hair back with Sweet Georgia
Brown on Brett's insistence – to keep it out of our eyes, which
we must be able to consult at all times – and the low light shone
from us, making us look like the lethal young blades we felt, as
we shot our French cuffs and leaned forward over the low table
as Brett began to talk.

She'd explained baccarat earlier. Some rich old sanction-buster
buys the bank from the house for a fixed fee and plays as banker,
with eight players making the game. S/he controls six packs of
cards shuffled into a silver shoe, dealt by a croupier and watched
over by a *chef de partie*. The banker sets the stake for each game,
beginning the evening at ten thousand francs, and the first player
to the left has an option to either accept the bet or pass it on. If

the *banco* is exceptionally high and there are no takers, the stake can be put up by several or all the players, and even some spectators, acting as a syndicate and regulated by the chef de partie. The house takes a fraction of each game – the *cagnotte* – that's usually paid in advance by the banker, to keep his or her working capital at a round figure.

'It's not so different from twenty-one,' she'd said, back in their room, tucking an errant inverted bass clef of hair behind her ear as she clicked on the screen to deal. 'The bank and the player get two cards face down. The object is to get as close to nine as you can. Pictures and tens count nothing, aces are one. You only take the last figure of your score – eight and six are four, not fourteen. The best hand is a "natural" – eight or nine from two cards. The bank can only beat it with a better natural.' She turned over the player's cards on the monitor: nine and seven – six. 'The odds say you ought to stand on six or seven. It's impossible to count cards because there are six packs, so you really don't know what's coming.' She clicked on the bank's – jack and five. 'Five is the critical point. It's dead evens whether drawing or hanging tight is better. This is where the bank has its edge – if you draw, the bank knows you're holding five or less, and your new card comes to you face up. With the bank holding five against what it knows is six or better, it has to draw, and hope for something between an ace and a four. Right now there are a hundred and ninety-two cards that it doesn't want and ninety-six it does.' She clicked – a three. 'And there you go. *Huit à la banque*. Bank wins. Draws are replayed, by the way. Again.' Click. 'Player holds two. *Une carte*. Four. Bank knows player has something between four and nine. Bank plays – ace and five. Player may be holding four or five. Sticks on five and player wins. Now play as the bank against the computer. It's holding. We've got three and know it must have five or more. We draw . . . a six. Yes! But the bank's got a natural eight. We lose. Now you do it.' After fifteen minutes I was bored.

'But when there's a minimum two and a half grand on the table, and you've chosen to take the bet, after sitting and watching the bank take the other players for an hour, then things are very different. And when you're ten grand up and can triple your capital with two cards, you will be someone you wouldn't recognize if you saw yourself across the room.'

'You'll be delighted to know,' said Brett, at the casino, after we'd drunk to losers and lit our second cigarettes, 'that the bank on table four has been bought by a UriZen stockholder. Lucy Norton. I had the chef de partie fax lists to the hotel. Used to write for American *Vanity Fair*. Inherited money and married it. Owns a bunch of fashion PRs. She paid just under thirty thousand francs for the bank, and she's probably got twenty times that to play with. So if we bring her to her knees, we will have made enough to buy a helicopter. Or pay Shelley Volante for two years, in one night. So no fucking mercy, okay? She's hard as nails, but we don't care what she's done in the real world because this isn't. We won a hundred and forty thousand francs last night from six games. We're staking a hundred tonight. If you put in fifty that'll give us twenty in sterling – can you?' I nodded, as though eight grand was nothing, thanking God for the pressure of my deposit account cheque book against my breast. I mean, I hadn't thought it would be something I could put on Visa, but nevertheless. But the martini was crisp and powerful, and the Turkish cigarettes tasted of tobacco, not the smoke. Now, I would pay twice as much money again just to be there once more; at the beginning, which was worth everything that came after. But Brett was speaking.

'We play fourth. We'll get to watch her a while, but we take the first game we can and *suivi* if we lose. The other players are kind of loaded, so don't be dazzled. There's a Ferrari and a Guinness. We're the youngest, but only by about four years. The average age is probably early forties. But it doesn't matter. They can either make her richer or poorer along the way – we don't care. We're here to double our capital twice over, then we leave and never come back. Agreed?'

She and River looked at me hard; but I lowered my eyes and leaned forward, with the nonchalance turned up to eleven, extinguished my cigarette, made eye-contact and nodded curtly.

'Okay. Let's go watch roulette. We start at eleven.'

The buzz inside the *salle de privée* was deafening. It was like cocaine. You could do it again and again and it would have exactly the same emotional effect on you. The air hung heavy with perfume and smoke, elation and despair, and it was impossible not to feel the rush as we changed cheques for chips at the caisse. No one was as they were outside. All around us eyes shone, colour rose, and pulses beat visibly in tan necks. It was damned sexy, if you really want to know. Many, many people in this room, one could feel, would need the lightest touch to get them hot, and maybe a few would require the smallest push to send them spinning into the abyss. For a moment I didn't care about the money. Then all at once I did. Everyone here looked so sleek, so thoroughbred. Their bone structures signalled that fish fingers had never salted their infant lips, nor that they'd ever walked to school with someone named Kevin. I was a tourist here: I had yet to understand that this is how successful people live their lives. I turned to Brett, who was staring raptly at the ivory ball as it made its descent, and had her intervene with myself.

'Aren't the biggest games along the coast?'

'Monte Carlo is no different really. We can play for more or less the same stakes anywhere. The reputation's just a Rainier thing. There's always been like this mad competition with Nice. It was worst during the last *fin de siècle*. The Monaco syndicates were so scared of bad press that if loser punters topped themselves they'd parcel up the bodies and send them out of the principality in the post. The Nice cartel found out, so they started to raid mortuaries for cadavers that'd died naturally, shoot them through the temple with a revolver, smuggle them into Monaco at night and leave them lying around near the casino. Then call the newspaper. Look, do you see that guy scribbling away over there?'

A slack-jawed fading gigolo-type was writing down numbers, staking, losing, then crossing them out and writing more.

'He's using a system. Probably the reverse Labouchère. It's a staking system. You've heard of the Martingale? This is a more refined version. You write out four ascending numbers representing units of your stake, add your stake to the lower end when you win, and cross off the first and last in the list when you lose. Then the new numbers left at either end should add up to your next stake. It acknowledges the house edge – it expects you to lose – but permits an outside chance of winning.' She blew out smoke. 'But all it really does is regulate your losses. Systems only really favour the biggest pot – which is the house – and they keep you at the table while the house edge works. This is really such a mug's punt.'

'Aren't his rings obscene?' I said. 'God, I hate jewellery on men . . .'

But Brett wasn't listening. She had on that expression that women wear at 2 a.m. on a dancefloor, when some guy is shouting in their ear whom they don't want to go home with, but don't want to shoot down entirely. We'd been crushed right up against the table, opposite a woman who was playing alone and winning. Brett watched her avidly. She was maybe in her mid-forties, and wearing it well: she seemed not to care about the unwritten rule that all women approaching the change should cut their hair off and get into serious tailoring. But neither did she look like Tina Turner. Her hair was smartly but not severely cut, and she wore a scarlet skinny satin shirt with long collars and black cigarette pants. As we watched she staked four yellow mille-franc plaques on even. She had rings on the third finger of both hands. She was smoking Kim. The wheel went round and thirteen came up – she lost. She staked again on red and drew heavily on her cigarette when it came in. She left the stake and winnings on red and it came up again. Then she put half on one to eighteen, and half on the fifth block of six.

'She's playing one bet against the other,' Brett murmured. 'The *sixain* pays five to one, but she's got a two to one chance on her *manque*. She's not entirely covered, but those are okay chances.'

The world turned and the wheel span – 32. Piles of chips were placed before her. She put half on manque, changed her mind and shoved it to passe, then split the rest between two sixains either side of ten. Sixteen came up, and she raked it in again. Then she put the whole pile on black. She seemed to be about to rescind, but the cry of *rien ne va plus!* made her translate the movement into shooting a cuff, then cupping her chin in her hand. The tension was unbearable. I couldn't bear it, anyway, and Brett was gripping her jet-bead evening bag so tightly the tendons on her arms stood out.

'Quatre. Le noir gagne, pair et manque.'

The woman smiled, closed her eyes a moment, then opened them and breathed out. She looked beautiful – beatified. She watched with amusement as the croupier converted her winnings and stake into large denomination chips, and deposited them in a neat pile before her.

'Christ,' said Brett, 'that's a hundred and forty thousand francs.' The woman let the wheel spin once without staking then, seeming to make up her mind, slipped the seven slim plaques into her square evening bag. She got up and left the salle, ignoring the caisse. A few envious eyes followed her, but quickly returned to the table, looking for the next action.

'Stay here,' hissed Brett, and walked quickly out of the salle. I looked around. River was talking to some rich girls over by the trente et quarante. I wandered over to the portals and peered round, just in time to see Brett disappearing into the bar. As I walked past the heavy glass doors I saw her go up to where the woman was sitting at the bar. I continued on past into the commode, sat down in a stall and pulled out my tabs. What the hell was going on? When I came out and walked past the doors again, they both had drinks and were laughing at something the woman said. Brett offered her a cigarette and she took it. I loitered around, with one hand in my jacket pocket like an Eton boy out on a lark, making it look as though I were waiting for someone. The vestiaire eyed me suspiciously, but I stared insolently back for a moment then looked at my watch and took out my cigarettes. I smoked one slowly, and was about to light another when the woman came out, swinging her bag breezily, and disappeared into the night. I pushed the heavy door and went into the bar. Brett saw me coming, grinned broadly and sauntered around the fountain to a palm tree.

Astonishingly, she spun around, did a little bump and grind against it, then tossed her hair and regarded me over her shoulder.

'Yunforgeddable,' she sang to the canned music, 'thasss whad you arrrre.'

'Brett,' I said, 'shouldn't we be starting? What's going on?'

'I was just looking for a mother figure.' She snickered, and slipped her arm through mine. 'Come on. Where's River? Let's go to work. Let's go *play*.'

Back inside, we found River still with the same bunch of rich girls. It was ten to eleven. Brett interrupted him, rather abruptly I thought, and sent him off, scowling, to an all-night chemist to buy Pro-Plus.

'Tout de suite!' she called after him, and turned to me. 'Come on, you. Let's go out and take the air. By the time we're finished here we'll be so jaded with cigarettes and nerves we'll have forgotten it exists.'

I followed her out on to a balcony. Below us was a garden, secret and enchanted in the moonlight. Its leaves and petals were already curling shut in the warm dampness of the air, surrendering the last sweet scents of a thousand pollens to it, and floating them up to us. Suddenly I felt very tired, and dangerously content. I wanted to go back to their suite, drink a nice lazy glass of oaky cab-merlot and go home to fresh sheets, and the hope of sleeping faster to see them again. It seemed that I didn't want to do this casino thing, and the realization that I was feeling something real kind of surprised me. I'd become so inured to everything. Couldn't we just have a nice holiday? We had the money. Although perhaps there was the feeling that there was nothing left to us but holiday. We had to work to earn it. And besides, I guess I had to go through their hoops if I wanted them to go through mine. I exhaled heavily without meaning to and Brett, who had been silently smoking a cigarette, her arms crossed below her empire line, turned around with an impishly amused look.

'Do you like my *parfum*? It's called Swelegant.'

I couldn't help but laugh. 'You smell like a summer afternoon in heaven.'

'You say the sweetest things.'

'Look, Brett, we don't have to go through with this. You don't have to if you don't want. Really. I won't mind at all. We can just, you know, get some cocktails, go dancing. We can do this another night.'

'No.' She remained looking over the garden.

'You're sure you want to do this?'

'Search me,' she said brightly. 'My desires are artificially stimulated by marketing departments. Which I think is rather sweet of them.' She blew out smoke and turned to me, twisting one leg back and forth on the heel of her Mary Jane. 'So I can't be sure what I want anymore. I was rather hoping you'd show me.'

She turned back. I looked out over the trees to the horizon for a moment, my mind racing. I couldn't help it. I faked a kind of overbalancing thing in her direction and let my arm fall around her waist, as though to steady myself, then let it stay there.

I snuck a glance at her out of the corner of my eye. She was looking the other way. Her diamanté earrings stretched her lobes ever so slightly, and her hair was lighter at the roots than it was at the ends. Then she turned her face to me but her body the other way, so that she spun out of my manly embrace, then pirouetted slowly to do big kohl-eyes at me.

'You and I need to talk. But not now. The game will be starting. We must go in.'

'But, Brett.'

'Not now, Jake. Soon though. Come through.'

We found our place and Brett sat down. There was no sign of River. I sat just to one side and behind her on another of the fake Louis Quatorze chairs. She set out her cigarettes and lighter on the green baize, and a huissier appeared from nowhere with a heavy glass ashtray that he placed at her elbow. She lit up, blew a swift shaft of smoke obliquely upwards, then turned round and winked at me with both eyes, without smiling. She held my eyes for a moment, then turned back, put her elbows up on the table and smoked her cigarette.

The whole table was smoking – it was like a smokers' conference. But no one was drinking, and I swiftly ditched my Pernod and black so as not to appear an amateur. I thought for a moment that the absence of booze must be down to the need to concentrate, but this probably wasn't the case: it wasn't like poker, where whether you were bluffing or had the nuts, you had to be made-of-stone sober not to blow the gaff; or blackjack, where you need to count.

But I think the real reason no one was drinking was because they didn't have to. They weren't bred to a culture where speed-swilling was part of the national character, thanks to a bunch of Great War regulations designed to get the proles into the munitions factories by nine and which were never repealed. This is at the back of everything I can't bear about England – binary nation, equally probably open or shut. You grow up knowing you've got to chuck it down your neck because you're out on your ear in a couple of hours: no time for subtlety, just kick and fizz; no time to talk about anything that doesn't get an instant, easy response – nothing that needs context, or digression. It's leaked into everything about us, and is going to take forever to unlearn. I looked around the table again. They all looked so *relaxed*. I guessed that, to them, money wasn't a way of storing time. I used to feel bad in High 5 about taking cabs and limos everywhere. I couldn't help but remember how poor I'd been when I worked at the theatre, and when it was all over I got buses and stuff for a while. Then it occurred to me that all the time I was fannying about outside Mammouth with six bulging carriers I was wasting writing time, and if I wrote four hours a day for six months to finish the damn screenplay and sold it for Writers' Guild Minimum, then every one of those hours was worth ten dollars. And the cab home was three quid tops. Not to mention getting soaked and stressed and letting myself watch junk TV for two hours as compensation. It occurred to me how unnatural it is, this thing we do. This sell-your-time-to-buy-the-time-that-someone-else-has-sold. My four hours selling ad space over the phone for some crappy business-to-business trade mag is worth one of your hours when you fix my shower, or a quarter of an hour when you grant me a credit line, or four thousand of your hours and your sanity besides, when I buy a ticket to the movie you threw away your twenties and broke the hearts of everyone you loved to get made.

Enough already. The real reason no one was drinking was that they'd pretty much all chased the dragon an hour before. This was during the glut, when the relative purity of heroin meant that shooting up was no longer a necessity, so junk became, once more, a hip luxury. The woman who had bought the bank had arrived, nodded to the table and sat down. The croupier mixed six packs of cards in a flat-shuffle. When he was done, he offered them to her to cut, then fitted them into the shoe while she sat back and watched. She was pushing forty, quite attractive but in a sad kind of way. You know, Chanel but not couture, Wonderbra and heels, incipient upper lip shrinkage and hair so big it seemed like it was some kind of a mission with her. She turned to the chef de partie and smiled perfunctorily, big tombstone teeth beneath wide Rouge Sublime matte lips, then said something curtly that no one caught, though the table had gone quiet.

'Messieurs, mesdames, les jeux sont faits. Un banco de vingt-mille francs.'

The banker looked up at the table expectantly. The couple at number one – obviously married, obviously American, obviously tourists – flickered a glance at each other and deferred to the next player.

Number two was dark, maybe thirty and weekending from the Bourse, total Armani, with a black Caesar cut like David Schwimmer. When he smiled, which he did often, turning to his ditzy blonde companion, he showed a discoloured front tooth, like a Marlboro tucked into a pack of Gitanes. He smiled now and tapped the table in front of his fat pile of ten-mille plaques with a spatulate finger.

The banker remained impassive. She gave the shoe a slap to settle the cards, then leaned forward and pressed the pink tongue to dispense two for herself and two for Caesar. The croupier slid his long wooden spatula under the player's cards and deposited them a couple of inches from his tan hands. He gave it a histrionic second or two then, without leaning forward in his chair, tilted their edges twenty degrees from the horizontal so their value was just perceptible, then let them fall.

'*Non.*'

The banker faced up her own cards, a jack and a five. She had to assume that the player was holding a minimum five, so unless she was feeling really lucky she had to draw again. She slapped the shoe and slipped out a three.

'*Sept à la banque,*' intoned the croupier. '*Et le cinq,*' he added, as he turned over Caesar's loser ace/four. River showed up with a bunch of Volvics, and discreetly handed out Pro-Plus, which he'd thoughtfully pre-popped from their bubble pack. We all swallowed. He looked quizzically at me, and I indicated that we hadn't played yet.

'*Un banco de quinze-mille francs.*'

'*Suivi,*' said Caesar at once, exercising his right to chase his lost bet before it was offered to any of the players. The game was dealt.

He looked so sulky anyway that it would have been impossible for him to give it away, but I knew his cards blew even as he set them back down on the table. His sort was not looking so special neither.

'*Carte.*'

The croupier flipped over the three of hearts. The banker licked her top lip. The three meant that, had he been holding his best possible five (though it was evens he would have stood on it again as he looked the sort to bluff disconsolately), he might now be holding eight. But she needn't have worried. She had a natural eight to his six.

Caesar did his best not to look irritated or ruffled, but didn't *suivi* his bet this time. The third player – the Ferrari – accepted the next coup, and took the banker for twenty thousand with his Queen-three-nine against her worthless ten-king pair. The table seemed to heave a collective sigh of relief at the spell being broken, and the Americans in pole position even looked for a moment as though they were going to take the next bet, of thirty thousand francs. But the banker's bullishness with the increase of the stake (generally things moved in cinq-mille increments once the game hit twenty) perhaps inclined them in favour of electing to prolong their cheap evening. The game fell to Brett.

There was a moment of unbearable tension as River and I stared at the back of her neck. Then she turned round, looked coolly at each of us, and turned back. She shook her head. River and I looked at each other aghast. She didn't turn again, and the bet moved to the next player. Five and six were both men in their fifties who seemed to know each other. Five resembled a waiter in his tuxedo, and six looked like a bad comedian from the Seventies, like he'd be happier in white slip-on shoes and maybe a golfing sweater/Lacoste polo-neck ensemble. The reek of Paco Rabanne had been wafting over from them all evening. I figured that five was doing a spot of corporate entertaining, or maybe they were partners. They did a big show of being two good old boys deferring good-naturedly to each other, with much showing of palms and shrugging of brows, but ended up passing the game anyway.

'Banco,' said seven, who was no better really. He was about the same age, but clearly thought he was pretty tasty. He was wearing a double-breasted wool tux by Versace, a wing-collar jacquard waistcoat by Kilgour, French and Stanbury, a cotton poplin high-collar dress shirt by Ralph Lauren, and a checked cummerbund/bow-tie combo from christ knows where. Tie Rack? These people, when they screw up, go supernova. It was excellent to watch his Terence Stamp suave good looks crumble when he got a nine as his third card, leaving him four tops unless he had baccarat to begin with. The banker turned up five and stood, wisely, as all the croupier discovered under the pink backs of hot stuff's cards was a six and a five. Brett turned to us, delighted. Her decision to pass up the bet had been vindicated, and the three of us felt like winners, though we hadn't even played yet. Like people who get married straight after graduation.

Seven didn't *suivi*, and a bank of forty thousand francs was passed round the table. River and I were willing it to come to Brett. We couldn't wait any longer. It was like reaching that moment on your third date with someone, when you know that if you don't end up dancing on your back tonight then you never will. So I understand, anyway.

Eight, nine and ten were apparently barely settled in for the evening, and with the bank thirty-five thousand up after four games, had every reason to expect rich pickings later. They all declined, leaving the Americans on the blocks looking distinctly unnerved when they passed up again. They knew the whole table suspected the game was already out of their league, and adopted especially stern and calculating expressions to imply that this wasn't the case. Caesar elected to join them in this, and the table turned to Ferrari. But he chuckled, and turned and whispered something I didn't catch to Brett. She laughed quietly, gave him a fond look and turned back to the table. *'Banco,'* she said. River and I looked at each other, and he passed me a cigarette. I produced my silver Zippo and lit us both, without either of us taking our eyes off Brett.

More than a quarter of our stake was on the table. Her cards came to her, and she barely looked at them before requesting another. Of course she couldn't lift them high enough for us to see. A seven slid face up across the green baize. The banker faced hers – eight and three, giving her a count of one. She had to draw another. Brett sat with her back very straight, her hands folded on the table in front of her cards. The rings on the banker's fingers – they were like doorknobs – clicked against each other as she slipped another card from the shoe, regarded its inscrutable back for a moment, and turned over another seven. This was bad.

'Huit à la banque.' Brett remained perfectly nonchalant as he slid the spatula under her cards. *'Et le sept.'* She remained as still as a summer dawn, and *suivi*'d the next banco of forty-five thousand.

When she asked for another card and got a nine, River and I lit our third cigarette in as many minutes in perfect synchronicity. Running my hands nervously through my hair, I found out also that I had a spot beneath one of my sideburns, which is the same as having one under an eyebrow. The banker had a pair of twos and had to draw a card; Brett had nine at best, though it could be anything else at all. Quite unnecessarily, the woman drew a five. Brett, it turned out, was holding a nine and a four.

She *suivi*'d immediately, on a banco of fifty thousand francs. The Americans drew in their breath audibly, and even the nice old guy at four was looking at her with concern, as if he would take back if he could the Lysol-brimming chalice he'd passed her. The woman with the bank gazed across the table for a moment then half-shrugged, as if to say, you want it, kid, you got it. Her bejewelled and carmine-taloned hands rattled like giant insects as she pressed pink cards from the shoe and slid them on to the table. Brett examined hers with extra insouciance, then turned to us and smiled. She didn't ask for another card. I gathered the smile meant she had better than a five, maybe even a natural. The banker turned hers over: nine and six; five. Brett ran five fingers through the hair above her nape. Maybe it wasn't a sign. I hoped to God.

The woman looked curiously at Brett. Was she bluffing, with her histrionics? And if so, to what power? She had no option but to take a card – the chances were that Brett had better than five anyway. She flipped over the ace of diamonds. Brett inclined her head good-naturedly and allowed the croupier to turn over her own cards.

I couldn't bear to look, but I could tell from the croupier's voice as he called six for the bank on a flat rise, like the final-score announcer on *Grandstand*, that she had stood on a five, though there was no indication in her demeanour. But of course she had, and we had lost everything.

River had turned the colour of a personal computer. I was

pretty sure I had too. Brett, apparently imperturbable, breezily opened her evening bag and drew a thick white envelope from inside. She turned to River and handed it to him.

'Stay in the game for me, will you, darling?' She beckoned the chef de partie and explained that, though she had a slight headache and would like to take some air, her husband would continue to play in her absence. River nodded in a surprisingly businesslike fashion, and matter-of-factly inserted the envelope into his breast pocket.

There was a general murmur of sympathy from around the table as Brett rose. The heat, the excitement – but of course. The chef de partie clasped his hands before his chest and put the facilities of the establishment at her disposal. Brett graciously demurred and motioned for me to take her arm. But some aspirin, a *fine à l'eau*?

'Vous êtes trop gentil, monsieur,' said Brett. 'But I'm sure I shall be perfectly well presently.'

River set his face to a businesslike scowl and began marshalling the small denomination chips that Brett had left on the table. The huissier hurried to unfasten the velvet rope for us, and the spectators fell back solicitously to let us through.

'Keep walking,' Brett hissed through a fixed smile. When we hit the vestibule, I turned and liberated myself from her vice-like grip.

'Where are we going? Can't we all leave?'

'We haven't finished yet.'

'What do you mean? We're all cleaned out. What was in that envelope?'

'Bunch of comp slips. It's to buy time until we get back.'

'Brett, come on. Why don't we just go? We've still got a couple of thousand sterling in chips. We can still have a cool week or two.'

'The hell we can. Come with me.'

And she had the vestiaire grab us a cab.

'Are we going to get more?'

We got in, and sat at opposite ends of the bench seat. She wound down her window and stared placidly out.

'Yes, we are.'

'You didn't say you had any more.'

'That is correct. I didn't.'

'Then where are we going?'

The cab sizzled down the long black reach of the Avenue Jean Médecin, the plane trees going sha-sha-sha through the open window. She turned to me.

'Look, don't tell me what you want to say. Tell me what I need to hear, okay?'

She turned back to the window, and narrowed her eyes against the breeze. I sat back in my corner. This was going great. You know? Fuck my luck. I expect the driver thought we were having a standard domestic, but there wasn't going to be any tearfully imploring each other to allow sole deposit of the blame. It was all my fault, dwarling. No, dwarling, it was mine. Say it was mine. No you say it.

This was it. They had lost most of their capital, and I assumed we were going to pick up whatever paltry remnants they had left. It made no difference. They had lost badly in there, and I had been a party to it. And you don't want to hang around with people you've been a loser with. Not until you're a little older than we were anyway.

But we weren't headed to their hotel. The cab climbed the coast road above the cliffs, and pulled up outside the hotel where I had lunched yesterday. It seemed like weeks ago. Brett paid the driver and got out.

'Well come on then.' She regarded me coolly a moment, then turned on her heel.

I followed her, and shut the door behind me with a dull chunk. The vintage black DS pulled away on snuffling treads, and disappeared behind the lemon and eucalyptus trees by the gate. Then she pulled me up short, and led me away from the hotel in the direction we had come. I was beyond questioning. We walked back down the cliff road for ten minutes or so, until we came to a huge deco apartment complex we'd passed on the way up. Brett led me up the drive.

'What are we doing?' I felt it wasn't unreasonable to ask.

'We're just dropping in on a friend.' She climbed the steps and buzzed an entryphone.

'Who?'

'Never mind. Leave the talking to me.'

A woman's voice answered. Brett spoke rapidly in French, too fast for me to follow: there was a light laugh from the other end, another buzz, and the door clicked open.

'Come on,' said Brett. She grabbed my hand and pulled me in. In the dark atrium, I stopped and pulled her up short.

'Will you tell me what's going on.'

'If you needed to know, yes. But you don't.' She tugged at the door of a cage elevator and shoved me inside. 'All you have to do is be charming. Do you feel as though you can do that?'

'Oh, right,' I said. 'It's alarming how charming I feel.'

She smiled, and kissed me quickly on the cheek. Old Brett. You could always count on her knowing the same junk as you. So that was that.

We were buzzed into an apartment so spacious you could see the curvature of the earth across the stripped wood floor. There were four floor-to-ceiling casements looking out over the sea, sparkly with moonlight below the emerald cliffs. The only furniture was a low glass table between a pair of white leather couches. A studio-quality reel-to-reel tape deck stood between two doors at the other end of the room, playing 'L'amour est un oiseau rebelle' with, I still think, Maria Callas singing soprano. Leant against the opposite wall was a billboard size canvas bearing a silk-screened reproduction of a *fin-de-siècle* print of the *Débarquement*: a restaurant built on twin rocky outcrops by the point at the end of the last century; a gazebo with kitchens implanted into one and an ocean-going clipper grafted seamlessly onto the other, where the diners would sit, waves breaking below them, for all the world as though they were launched out into the Baie des Anges.

One of the doors opened, and the woman who had won at roulette earlier walked in, carrying an open bottle of Cristal by the neck in one hand, and three crystal flutes in the other. She smiled as she ticked past us to the table, sat down, and poured out some drinks. She looked up at us and laughed.

'Are you going to stand there all night? Come over.' Her voice was low, but without a trace of an accent to her English.

We did as she said, and sat on the couch opposite her. The music segued into 'Drowning in a Sea of Love' by Joe Simon. She offered us a drink, and gave me her hand to shake.

'I'm Désirée.' She pronounced it the French way. I suppose she had no option.

'I'm, uh, Jacques,' I decided. 'Didn't they name a streetcar after you?'

The woman gave Brett a perplexed look; she, in turn, glared at me. What? This was my idea of being charming. Even though she laughed, after Brett explained, I decided I had better shut it.

We drank the drinks and there was smalltalk. After Désirée poured some more she did a curious thing. She gave us both a weird look, then took off her wedding ring, and slipped it over a slim white candle so that it fell down to the heavy wooden candlestick. I understood immediately. She wasn't married for the time it took for the candle to burn down to the ring. Which was a neat idea, but, christ almighty. I took a *big* old slug on my Cristal.

Brett remained cool.

'So where did you start to gamble?'

'In Osaka, actually.'

'Not pachinko.'

'Yes.' Désirée smiled. 'Do you play?'

'I did, when I was in Kyoto.'

'What's pachinko?' I interjected, then wished I hadn't.

'It's the most excellent game,' said Brett. 'It's a cross between pinball and a fruit machine. But faster, and with dozens of balls at once. The word means, slingshot?' And she looked at Désirée for confirmation.

'Yes. It comes from the conflation of two other words – *pachi-pachi* and *gachanko* – which describe the sound of the balls. They're both onomatopoeic.'

'It got popular after the war. Pinball came over with the GIs and really caught on, but space costs in Japan. So they turned the tables upright and invented pachinko. It's huge. It makes four times as much money as the automobile industry.'

'When were you in Kyoto?' asked Désirée.

'Oh, a couple of years ago,' said Brett. 'Travelling. You know.' She hadn't told me this. 'How about you?'

'In the Eighties. My husband is a diplomat.'

'Where is he now? If you don't mind my asking?'

I was glad she had. I was beginning to feel that some sweaty old suit was watching all this on closed-circuit TV.

'Not at all. In Nassau, with his mistress.'

I didn't like the direction this was taking, and no mistake. Désirée got up, and leaned her back against the wall.

'My husband has affairs. I –' and she gestured with her champagne flute around the room '– do this.'

'Tell us,' said Brett, leaning back into the sofa and stretching her legs out in front of her.

Désirée hesitated a moment, then brightened. 'Sure.' She came back and sat opposite us, slung one leg elegantly over the other, and began to talk.

'We were married young. Twenty-one. I don't think Édouard saw much beyond a stag night, a party and a honeymoon. And that was twenty-five years ago, or near enough. So we had a decade of muddling along, as one does, while his career took off. Brussels, Strasbourg. Then ten years of being so terribly civilized. Hoping it'll go away, hoping it will stop happening. Here –' She walked off into a bathroom, and came out proffering a razor blade. She handed it to Brett who, to my amazement, pulled a plastic envelope of cocaine from her evening bag, and commenced chopping lines on the low glass table. She looked up.

'He had affairs?'

'Not exactly. More – oh, there's no word in English. I suppose a language only names what it knows. *Flings* is nowhere near. I don't think he could stand a real affair: not because of me, but because of her. If anything became more than a series of one-night stands, she would begin to bore him. If there were demands, if there were scenes. If there was sadness.'

Brett had cut three lines. 'Why do you think so?'

'I wish I could tell you something more than I'm sure you already feel you know. But I can't. I can't even say that we should never have married, or that I shouldn't have stayed with him. It has worked, as much as anything does. We have a beautiful home, successful children. We have always done as we ought. We've made something good in this world, even if things haven't turned out the way I thought they would. Or the way he did, for that matter.'

Brett's eyes twinkled. 'Do you think that men, when they say they'll always love you, expect you always to remain lovable?'

Désirée threw back her head and laughed. 'At least to them anyway. But of course, one cannot always be what he loves. I can't always be the reassurance that he needs, that he's still attractive; that he can have any woman he wants, but has chosen to have me. That I am always going to be available to appreciate him for what he is, not what he can provide. Neither can I forever be discovering new selves within him, thrilling new *hims* beneath the habitual and the everyday; inside the two of us, who live and function and do what we do for most of the year, with the minimum of unnecessary disruption. Romantic love doesn't have to be the point, you know. Nor does physical love, even family love.'

'So you have an arrangement? That lets you try out other selves?'

'You could say that. Every six months or so we allow ourselves a proportion of our surplus income, and take three weeks away to spend it, however we please.'

I was tired of being quiet. 'But don't arrangements just benefit one party and not the other? One does all the living while the other does the letting?'

'Forgive me,' she said, 'you are a young man, and you should relish what you have. But life is not something you can put in a box and label. One can be happy with the way one is, and not need to be anyone else. But, with the passing of years, one cannot help but wonder about the roads not taken. Could I not have been anyone? How might that have felt? So I take holidays, and become other people. Which, I'm sure, is all Édouard does.'

Brett inserted a thousand-franc note into one nostril and did a line.

'So who are you tonight?' She handed the note to Désirée, and both their smiles widened in complicitous concomitance. She leaned forward, holding her sweep of hair back with her free hand, and hoovered up a line herself. She passed the banknote to me.

'Why don't you prepare some more and I'll show you.'

She rose, and swayed off elegantly through the door she had come in at, shutting it behind her.

I held the banknote between my fingers, and thought better of it.

'Brett, I don't want to do this. Christ, what's that?'

She had pulled a bindle of white powder out of her bag and emptied it on the far side of the table, in front of where the woman had sat.

'Smack,' she said. 'Practically pharmaceutical grade, and easily strong enough for our purposes.' She pushed it into a line with the blade, then cut another line of coke between it and the untouched one.

'Where the fuck did you get heroin from? And what – christ – "purposes"?'

'In the ladies'. And just enough to put her under for a while.'

'While we do what?' Then I finally clicked. Désirée hadn't deposited her chips when she left the casino.

'You're not serious.'

Brett regarded me evenly.

'It's this or law school.'

'What?'

'Haven't you heard of the mid-twenties crisis? I'm having mine early.'

'Oh dear god.' I buried my face in my hands.

'I already have a place on the twelve-month conversion course,' she went on, gleefully. 'I start in September. Then Bar school. Or maybe I could do teacher training. Come on. Save me from myself.'

'But that's not so bad . . .' I could see us in a little flat somewhere, making solicitous cups of tea as she hit the books, combed her wig, whatever.

She stared at me, incredulous. 'Are you kidding? Jesus.'

The door opened and the woman came in. I'd thought I was beyond being shocked now, but I seemed to have infinite reserves to draw on. She was wearing a clingy chiffon Dolce & Gabbana number and not much else. She'd slicked back her hair like Brett's, and put on heavy chandelier-type earrings. She wafted over on a cloud of Sun Moon Stars and sat down. Brett stood up.

'I shan't be a moment.' She indicated her evening bag, and winked. I looked at her, aghast. But she was gone, into the bathroom and I was alone with old Désirée, quite beyond rational thought. But I'd seen Mia Wallis, you know? I knew that if you inhaled uncut heroin it didn't just knock you out. While I felt that her vocabulary and tone deserved some form of retribution, this was too much. I had to do something.

Désirée smiled at me. 'What's the matter? Don't you like me?'

'Uh, no, yes, of course.'

She laughed. I flushed deep red, bent down and did the line of coke in front of me, out of sheer embarrassment. It hit fast and hard, and fireworks went off in my frontal lobes.

'Why don't you come round here, and we'll both do some together.'

I got up uncertainly, walked round the table and sat on the arm of her sofa. She giggled, and patted the leather next to her coquettishly. I slid down. What if she made me go first? I thrust the note at her.

'Okay,' she said, 'but then you must take your medicine.' She leaned forward, put the bill in her nose and bent over to do the line.

What could I do? I picked up the candlestick and brought it down as hard as I dared on to the base of her skull. The ring shot along the candle and clattered across the floor. She groaned and sat up for a moment, then her eyes rolled back beneath her lids, and she collapsed sideways on the sofa. I checked she hadn't swallowed her tongue, then tilted her head back to give her an airway. I had to think fast.

Brett had taken the real coke into the bathroom. Bugger. I turned the table around as carefully as I could, so that a spent line was in front of Désirée's sleeping body, and tried to think how Uma Thurman had looked at the moment when the music stopped. Désirée didn't look half ill enough.

I picked up the razor blade, hitched up my trouser and rolled down a black silk sock. I took one practice shot, then gripped the blade between my thumb and forefinger on the flat sides, and let my hand fall with the weight of my arm on to my ankle. An impressive amount of blood welled up, and I smeared some with my finger beneath Désirée's nose. I sat back and checked out the effect, then added a dusting of coke for good measure. Then I rolled back my sock before any blood fell somewhere it shouldn't. I checked her breathing again, got up and pressed my forehead to one of the windows. Then I remembered the ring, and skidded across the floor to retrieve it. I heard the lock slide back on the bathroom door, and kicked the ring away under one of the sofas, shoving my hands into my pockets and turning to face her.

Brett came out of the bathroom, and looked at me, then over my shoulder to the sofa. I saw her eyes shift focus. When she saw Désirée, and what we appeared to have done to her, the colour drained from her face like it does from a cheap ice lolly after you've sucked it. She turned back to me.

'Okay. You're in. Her bag with the chips is on a chair by the bath. Go and get them. Try not to touch anything.'

I went in, picked up her bag and put it down again. I couldn't do this. But I realized what I could do, and despite the coke, felt quite lucid for a moment. This way, all Désirée would think when she woke up was that we were a pair of weirdos, and wouldn't have much reason to go to the police. I looked around me. There was a vanity case on a rattan chair over by the basin, and I snuck over, opened it as quietly as I could, and extracted some slim eyeshadow cases that were about the same size and thickness as vingt-mille plaques. I slid them into my breast pocket and hurried out, scared Brett might be checking out Désirée and discovering she wasn't OD'd. But she was still standing where I'd left her, her face ashen, so that her make-up stood out in sharp relief.

'Have you got them?'

I tapped on the breast of my jacket, and the eyeshadows clicked against each other with a satisfyingly plasticky sound.

'Okay. Get the glasses we used, and wash them out in the kitchen. No. I'll do it. You flush the cigarette butts. Wrap them up in tissue first, or they'll just float.' She half-smiled. 'Boarding school.'

I did as she said and we met back in the main room.

'Okay?' I nodded. 'Then we're out of here. Come on, back door.'

She led me by the hand through the kitchen and down a fire escape. We walked back along the road to the old town and hailed a cab there. She directed the driver back to the casino, then sank back into her seat and exhaled. She asked for a cigarette and I gave her one, but she didn't say anything else, which was just as well because I needed to think. The coke got in the way though, so I decided to postpone it. I couldn't help starting to feel absurdly happy. We hadn't actually done anything wrong – except maybe minor assault and eyeshadow-larceny – but I thought Désirée would be so relieved to find nothing else missing when she came round that she would just let it go. Besides, it might be kind of embarrassing for her to explain it all to some hick gendarme.

When we arrived, and I got out and opened her door for her, Brett looked up at me so tiredly I almost forgave her then and there. But I decided to take charge. I packed her off to the ladies' to compose herself, and went to the caisse, where I cashed a cheque for a hundred and forty thousand francs, and ditched the cosmetics in a potted palm. I went out and waited for Brett, and when she came out, handed her the seven vingt-mille plaques.

'Let's go and play,' I said. She nodded, seeming to understand. I followed her into the salle.

The game was still going, but River was nowhere to be seen. We found him at the bar, three sheets to the wind. Brett was indignant.

'What the fuck are you doing?' she hissed at him, while I ordered us a couple of stiff ones.

'You didn't come back for hours and hours. So I assumed . . .'

'You assumed what?'

'I don't know. You tell me.'

'Don't-you-be-so-absurd. Christ. Oh, never mind. But we can't go back to the game now. Come on. We might as well go.'

I didn't want the night to end like this.

'Brett, if we leave now then it's all for nothing. We can't stay here, can we?'

She looked at me for a while, and seemed to make up her mind.

'You're right. Come on,' and she turned, leaving her anis de loso untouched. 'You too,' she called over her shoulder to River.

We trailed after her, but she stopped in front of an empty roulette table. The lone croupier, who had looked half-asleep, snapped into animation. Brett turned to us.

'How much have you got? Come on, empty out your pockets.'

River fumbled around and produced the remainder of the chips from earlier. Brett took out the seven vingt-mille plaques and placed them on the baize with River's chips. I handed her everything in my wallet – a couple of thousand. The note we had used to do the coke rolled straight up into a cylinder the moment she placed it on the table. The croupier noticed, but remained impassive. She was probably used to it at this hour of the morning.

The cash bet looked incredibly, wildly reckless next to the neat pile of chips.

'Roulette, Brett?' I said, without expression. 'What about what you said? The house edge?'

River turned away and groaned. Brett looked at me flatly and said, slow and low, 'It only works against you if you want to hang around and let it. Play fast and leave, and it's nothing. Doesn't have a chance.'

She turned back to the table and considered the baize for a

moment. I guess she knew then, as she must know now, that sometimes you have to play the worst game – the one you know is the dumb one. And you have to put it all on one spin.

'Red and black,' she said. 'Dionysius. Sex or sleep; blood or death.'

She shoved the whole pile on to red and nodded to the croupier. I understood. This was her way of consulting the oracle; of checking with the gods if it was okay.

It was, and we won. She made no flicker of recognition, just left the bet where it was and inclined her head to the croupier again. We won again. There were more than half a million francs on the table. She flickered her eyes closed, then opened them wide and instructed the croupier to send the pile straight to the caisse. But then she seemed to change her mind, and told the girl to put a thousand francs anywhere she liked and spin again. The croupier shrugged, dropped a chip into the *cagnotte*, and spun the wheel. It seemed to take forever. Then the ball dropped into green zero, and Brett fainted dead away.

She came round terribly embarrassed, but I told her women fainted all the time in cartoons. While River was getting her out of there I had the money translated digitally into my holding account by the debiting and deposit facility at the caisse.

I found them collapsed on sofas in the lobby. We collected ourselves and tottered out into the dawn. The air was sweet and sharp to our jaded lungs, the sky shot through with cruise-brochure white and blue. We ran over the prom to the rail and leaned over, just to stand and breathe and look for a moment. Waves broke gently on the beach below. I was way, way too tired to think anymore. All I knew was we needed to get out of here.

Brett turned away from the rail, sunglasses hiding her eyes, wind whipping her hair back.

'What now?' she said. She may have been as tired as I was but she wasn't showing it. 'What do you want to do?' She sounded so calm, like she was about to suggest going to a Häagen-Dazs or something.

'We ought to make ourselves scarce,' I said. 'Jesus, someone might be looking for us already. Here's the first place they're going to come.'

'Okay,' she said, 'so we leave. You want to split the money?'

'Let's just go,' I said. 'For God's sake, let's get out of here. We can talk about it later.'

'Go where?' said River. 'Why do we have to go anywhere?'

'Tell you about it later,' Brett said curtly. She turned to me. 'You want to stay with us?' she said, but I barely heard. I didn't see an option. To stand there and calmly write out a cheque and then go home and never see them again seemed suddenly far more improbable than anything we could do otherwise. So I nodded. 'Then let's go home,' she said. 'Let's go back to Cali.' We left immediately.

Twenty-six hours later I was looking down the barrel of a Beretta at some kid in a tweed jacket and oval glasses. Oval glasses! I mean, get real. For sure they make you look creative and sensitive and intelligent. They make you look like Sylvester Stallone in a straight-to-video romantic comedy. They make you look like every other dork with no imagination. You may as well magic-marker TEACHER TRAINING IS A REALISTIC AND POTENTIALLY SATISFYING LIFE OPTION FOR ME across your forehead. Back-wards, so when you haul your sorry ass into the commode at some ungodly hour each morning you can read it in the mirror and remember how you sat on your imagination.

'Is that thing real?' said the kid, transfixed by the weapon, eyes as round as his lenses.

'It ain't licorice,' snarled Brett, totally in character behind me.

Though I did know how he felt. You've seen them so many times in cop shows or whatever that you can't quite believe it when there's one there in front of you, looking you in the eye with its single, dilated pupil and asking you, how lucky d'you feel? I was totally in character, the pumped-up rookie steadying his piece with both hands while his disdainful new partner, the old-timer who's only fired his weapon once in thirty years of active service, rolls his eyes to the heavens and pictures, momentarily, the clapboard retirement place upstate, the cool verandah, the troutstream, the folksy friends and neighbours, all waiting to rewrite his epilogue after this one last case.

Except this had been Brett's idea. But I knew how the kid felt. I'd said the same thing, two hours earlier in Brett's apartment.

'Where'd you *get* that gun?'

'Weapon or piece, never "gun".' She slid back that slidey thing on top and let it snap back in place.

'Where'd you get it?'

'I know everything and I can do anything. You're just going to have to start trusting me on this.'

She drew a bead on a poster of Scott Baio, and jerked the barrel up theatrically as the hammer ker-chunked on an empty chamber, supplying the SFX deficiency with a credibly realistic silenced-automatic sound from the side of her mouth, the kind that generally precedes gouts of blood issuing from the corner of Joe Pesci's lips.

'Bang on the button.' She blew smoke from the barrel, put her head on one side and studied the poster. 'Poor Scotty. You get *Joanie Loves Chachie* in England?'

Although catching cool American programming when I was a kid, before satellite, was like being in Hungary in the Fifties, only picking up Radio Free Europe if the wind was blowing in the right direction, there had been a short run, back to back with *Metal Mickey*, sometime in the early Eighties. I nodded.

'Major synergy,' said River, coming in from the kitchen. 'There were so many *Happy Days* spin-offs, no one in the producer's family went to college for like, two whole generations.'

'He had more of his kids working for him than Aaron Spelling,' said Brett. 'Let's go.'

So we left, but I'd wanted to stay. It was a major information-density apartment, and I needed more time to check out the artefacts. While River was running his head under the tap and Brett was rummaging in her closet for the Beretta, I had tried to make a systematic sweep of as much of the cool stuff as I could.

The place was awash with stills and lobby cards, of Gary Cooper, Jimmy Stewart, Katherine Hepburn and Claudette Colbert; stacks of screenplays, bound in black vinyl; teetering piles of biographies on every available surface – Selznick, Laemmle, Capra, Howard Hawks, yeah, but a hundred others whose names meant nothing to me: Max Busch, Bruce Cabot, Beverly Byrne, Bud Schulberg. Hundreds of them, whose broken horizontal spines ran through all the typographical triumphs of the mid-to-late twentieth century. I picked one off the nearest pile, at random – a 1975 life of Charles Boyer, last reprinted 1982, last checked out of Van Nuys public library nine months ago. I tried another, and another, and another again – all from libraries, all monstrously overdue. Brett came back in while I was engaged in this research, and I had to feign interest in an A2 blown-up Xerox of some weird, geeky-looking guy, that seemed incongruous among all the slick publicity shots on the walls. I didn't feel ashamed of asking who it was because there was no way this guy had ever been on a soundstage.

'Who's that?'

'Harold von Brunhart,' she said, brusquely. 'Inventor of Sea Monkeys, X-Ray Spectacles, and the Graduate Trainee Program. Check this out.'

Which was when she unhid the gun.

This had started on the plane. When she talked animatedly, as she proceeded to through three time zones, there was so much infinitely fetching stuff going on all over her face that it was difficult to keep up with; though you didn't want to miss any, and knew you'd kick yourself later for not being able to replay every nuance. I was hopeless, but she was once-in-a-lifetime, and I had fallen in love like you do with your first Disney heroine, your first time in the dark there. Maybe before you die, in the depths of downtown in a city far away, you will stumble upon your personal perfect nightclub. They will play 'Just My Imagination' and 'Get It While You Can', and make you ache at your table; the bartender will know how to make your drink, and won't run out of Mount Gay before you do; the sloe-eyed strangers in the booths around will behave like they've known you forever; and the dancefloor will be dimpled with Brett's heelmarks. From long ago, buddy.

When she'd finally talked herself out and slipped away, I stayed awake, gazing upon her, now I could do so with impunity. Her pulse fluttered at her temple. She was absolutely right. Everything I'd ever wanted was starting to happen.

As we stood behind floor-to-ceiling glass in the DIS, Inc. corporate flagship building the city rolled out before us under a California moon, the one you never quite believe in movies. From the aqua nitelites of lit pools, west of Beverley and Glen; to the headlights raking the sky in the hills above Encino; to the downtown office towers, lit sporadically now, like hospitals at midnight, the city was laid out like a Monopoly board, zoned as closely to income as the seating plan on a 747. Later that summer some industry suit would tell me that the movies first came here because LA was the Union's biggest open-shop, non-union city, and each new street was built for a specific grade of studio employee. It didn't change. You didn't move out of your tax bracket and you didn't move house, because there was either nowhere else you could afford or nowhere else you'd be seen dead in. This was, of course, when there was some kind of relationship between money and the value of one's labour. It stuck, anyway; LA is a perfectly zoned city. You can still go to practically any part, and have a pretty good idea what kind of lives unravel themselves behind the walls around you. So we'd known exactly where to go to find our victim.

It was a coffee shop, in the basement of an arthouse; the genre or sub-genre of third place I'd spend half my life in if I had time, the kind of place that functions as one of the core sets in situation comedies featuring displaced young urban winsome types. You know the kind of thing: abstracts on the walls, Dietrich on the decks, twenty kinds of latte and French cigarettes. You expect incidental music by W. G. Snuffy Walden to kick in any second.

This place was pretty empty and the kid was sitting alone at a table, ostentatiously frowning over the kind of paperback, to the selection of which on the way out of his apartment he'd probably given a disproportionate amount of time, the loser. He practically fainted with relief when Brett followed up eye contact with the kind of comment on his book selection that invited intrigued-but-not-irrevocably-committed response on his part.

We are sweet. We need to think, as we sit in these places, that someday someone somehow is going to decode all the details into whose composition we have put so much triumph-of-hope-over-experience care: the number of buttons on my jacket, the width of the bar on my Mary Janes, the white filter on my cigarette, the absence of the strapline, Now A Major Motion Picture, from the cover of the hip novel I'm narrowing my eyes at. Of course, they don't. Or even if they do, the conclusion they draw is that some-one who puts this amount of thought into details has way too much free time on their hands, and is therefore lacking focus, and probably a life; so they hit on the fatneck in the boat shoes-chinos-Polo combo, or the dork in the DM shoes and collarless shirt, depending on their taste for passive-aggressive or aggressive-aggressive. You don't realize this until later in your breathing career. I suspect that the Gap owes its entire existence to the moment when each successive generation finally gives up on hoping someone else is ever going to decipher our complex semiotic résumés. The day finally dawns when you're like, the hell with it. And you start to dress like everybody else, and it's only then that anyone looks at you twice.

Of course, sticking up loser twentysomethings in Pasadena parking lots was not precisely how I expected us to begin reinventing ourselves, but we were testing a theory expounded thirty thousand feet in the air. Down here on the ground, it was the kind of night when you don't hear the motors of cars as they pass on the road; just tires and slipstream, a swish and a sigh. We didn't have to worry about cruising patrol cars or CCTV; this was the wrong place. This kind of thing wasn't done here, which was precisely why we were doing it.

'Oh, fuuuuck,' moaned the kid. 'Leave me alone. Lemme alone, you *cunts*.'

'Jesus,' said Brett behind me, genuinely shocked. 'You kiss your mother with that mouth?' The kid's jaw dropped. 'Hand over your wallet, or we pop a cap on your ass.'

I'd long been looking forward to rolling the pristine sheet of twenty-pound bond I was saving for my autobiography into the old, retro-type typewriter and picking out, in caps, the chapter heading 'Gunplay', but this, sadly, was not going to make it. The thing in my hand was a replica, though the kid wasn't in any position to cast aspersions on its integrity.

'I don't have any money,' he said, miserably, extracting a slim faux-crocodile number from his hip pocket.

'Really,' said Brett, sarcastically.

River shot her an irritated glance as he tossed her the wallet. 'Why not?'

'I'm an intern,' confessed the kid, hanging his head.

'Where?'

The kid named a media conglomerate.

'*Dis*co,' said Brett, pulling out his smart-card security pass.

An hour later we were sitting in the oatmeal glow of a networked Pentium in an otherwise dark office, and Brett was changing the desktop colour palette to something less offensive.

'Pas*tel*!' she said, outraged. 'Jesus. I mean, whatever happened to psychological profiling? Don't they have loser-detector tests at recruitment stage anymore? I worry about these places, swear to God.' She wagged her head darkly and clicked on Wingtips, with a pale blue Marquee screensaver – there wasn't time to do a custom one.

This was all news to me, because I only ever had a PowerBook. I still like Macs over PCs, but I was in total hog heaven anyway. I wished we could come here every day. All the neat stuff! Laser-Writers and Styluses and Sportsters and colour Canons – far out. Aside from anything else, one of the main reasons I went to Shelley first with my screenplay was I didn't want to have to deal with some production company who wouldn't have lots of spare office space. I hated the thought of being some shitbird writer, holed up in some ratty apartment in his bathrobe, only coming out for lunch with a bunch of other loser writers, or his agent once in six months. I wanted ergonomic deskroom, surrounded by discreetly humming technology, and soon.

'Right,' said Brett, clicking up File Manager and pushing in a floppy. 'Where's that kid? Get him, willya?'

I found him down the hall, playing Quake with River on the PC of a corner office.

'It's so unfair,' he said, walking back with me. 'Only the VPs have games on their computers. They put a sentry program on everyone else's to make it go beep if you even boot up Solitaire.'

'Who're the VPs?'

'The ones who have their own money vested. Actually they're not. It's like, title escalation? Anyone on payroll is a Vice-President of something or other. But these people are like, el Generalissimo doo-*chay* Master of the Universe President of marketing, north-western seaboard.' I saw his point. Job titles have got like warheads were in the Eighties. It's the only way some kinds of people can keep score anymore.

The kid had changed his tune – in fact he was sweet as pie. Brett had told him, in the cab on the way over, that we were a decadent multimedia performance-art terrorist group, dedicated to making the corporations of the postindustrial west die a bloated, rock-and-roll Elvis-type death – if only metaphorically on the commode full of cheeseburgers and speed. I don't think he bought it, but she needn't have worried. The kid hated his employers. He'd been on work experience almost a year, without experiencing any work commensurate with his MA in media communications, or any pay commensurate with sixty-hour weeks. They kept him at it with the Fear.

'You're ever anything less than eager and sunny, they sling you out and get another intern. There's a waiting list of like, fifteen hundred? They hoof me out, I'm back at the bottom of someone else's list. I may be a loser now, but at least I'm a loser with a hope in hell of getting on health insurance someday, you know?'

Brett had him point out the directories she wanted, then she drag-copied them to the A-drive. The kid shuffled his feet.

'That's okay,' she said to him, singsong, like a kids' TV anchor. 'Go play.' He scampered back down the corridor.

'What's that one?' I indicated the files paging through the dialog box.

'Story archive.' She wriggled back into the lumbar-support chair and lit a Kool.

'What's story archive?' I tried to sound like the only reason I didn't know was because I didn't care.

'Where the loser ideas live.' She took a long draw on her Kool, and regarded me through the smoke. 'You ever notice how movies or books or whatever come in bunches? Like you get one Vietnam movie and then there's a whole shitload? Or a song that suggests that if only you'd express yourself, you'd feel a whole lot better?'

And I'm like, tell me about it.

'This business works on fear. No one likes to go out on a limb in the frontlist. You have to be so damn sure that what you're doing isn't going to piss your market off. But if something comes out of left field – a sleeper – everyone falls over themselves trying to copy it. You see it all the time. A book or a movie or whatever about, jesus, an idealistic lawyer in a corrupt judiciary hits the top ten and stays there. Suddenly everyone's falling over themselves to sign up idealistic lawyer stories; but if you're smart, you kept notes on everything you turned down in case something suddenly acquires some currency. Someone pitched you an outline with a lawyer in it two years ago, so you look in your pitch archive. You call them up. If you can't find them then screw them. You make the lawyer movie anyway, hire some other hack, whatever – just get it in the theatres for Thanksgiving. Which is what this is. Stories waiting to happen.'

I didn't get it. 'Why do you want them?'

'Most of these were turned down, not because there was anything so wrong with the pitches themselves, but because the authors weren't marketable. Or wrong for the project. Geeky, ugly, old, fat, common, whatever. But hand them out to the youthful and the gorgeous and you're in business.'

'Who youthful and gorgeous?'

'I've got a stack of application letters for some internship at the apartment,' she said. 'Boosted it from UriZen. Two thousand or so.'

'You stole it?' I was trying not to laugh. You really had to hand it to her.

'What? It was just lying around. I thought, I'll have that.' She sniggered.

'Still don't get it.'

'At least half of them don't really want to be interns, they just want to get a foot in the door. They think they're getting nowhere not because their stuff isn't any good, but because they don't know anyone in the business. They're totally wrong on every count, but some people haven't had the privileges we have – always remember this. So we do them a favour, and we do ourselves a favour too.

We find out who can do what, give them decent story ideas to work on, which is all they don't have right now, help them develop, then we sell the product. All of the variables fall into place. And we control a unique young creative agency. The biggest in this town, and therefore the world. Close your mouth.'

'But . . .'

'But what? This business is ass backward. You're on your own when you most need not to be. You're shit-poor when you most need not to be. Almost everyone would do their best work at the start of their career if they didn't have any distractions. The responsibility for developing talent has been abdicated. Jesus, we went to UCLA, and no one gives a fuck. There's this stupid myth that it's somehow good for you to waste away through your twenties getting nowhere. Waiting fucking tables or standing over a copier. I think the products of this industry would be a lot better if people got to make them before they got something kicked out of them by penury and overwork, and thinking you're mad because your life is slipping away and you're getting nowhere. So we redress the balance. And of course we acquire money and influence in the meantime. Then we get to do what we want with our movie and not what someone tells us to do.'

'But . . .'

'This is us and them, Jake. Okay?' She ground her cigarette against the stem of a potted fern. 'C'mon. I shouldn't have to tell this to you, of all people. They think letting people like us in here to skivvy around for them isn't a problem. They think we're the same as they were when they were our age. They don't think in a million years we'd have the imagination to screw them right back. They think we're such a bunch of desperate losers that we're going to eat whatever crow they give us, and be grateful for it. You know all that stupid slacker crap? That's how they want to think we are, so they don't feel bad about exploiting the hell out of us. What are we trying to prove here?'

We were trying to prove what she'd said on the plane; and, I couldn't help it, I'd had to agree.

'This is so weird. This is so cool.' She'd waved her champagne cocktail around the club-class bar, empty except for us three. 'We shouldn't be here. Should we?'

I shrugged. Search me.

'Everything we've done, we shouldn't have done. The card game, the money – everything. It was all *way* out of our league. But check this out. We're doing what everything tells us we shouldn't, and we're getting away with it.'

This I couldn't contest. This wasn't our milieu at all. It didn't even feel like we were in this decade anymore. It was like we'd entered some kind of Andy Warhol timewarp parallel dimension, somewhere between Studio 54 and San Tropez: where women called Kiki and Suki, wearing sunglasses of billboard proportions, were squired at five hundred miles an hour to hyperkinetic disco-theques by the luxuriantly moustachio'd sons of shipping magnates, cough syrup heiresses, pantyhose tycoons and yoghurt barons, profit-skimmers and bottom-liners and sanction-busters of every *modus operandi*; being impossibly successful and glamorous, and doing it everywhere at once and much faster than anyone else, ever.

'So what do you want?' she said. 'Most people get out of bed every morning and know that's the best they're going to feel all day. We, however, have escaped. You want this to be some kind of holiday from reality? Or d'you want to never go back? Your choice. You want to live how the world says you have to be, or you want to make it up yourself?'

River cut in. He was the most pumped I'd seen him, smoking up a rocket on his Lucky.

'It's like when we were in film school . . .'

'You were in *film school*?'

'UCLA,' said Brett, coolly. 'Our mother may have lacked a

number of things, but she did have a damn good accountant. I think she slept with him and broke his heart, and maybe he never dropped his torch for her. It doesn't matter. He made sure we got money – it's not a lot, though maybe it's enough to give us the kind of problems that some people would kill to have. Whatever. It was enough to send us both to film school.'

Me, interior: *yes yes yes yes yes yes yes.*

'We didn't fit in at all,' said River, and they both snickered. 'We like Capra, Howard Hawks. Everyone else in our class thought movies started with *The Godfather*. Movies was a dirty word. *Cinema*, please. Morons in collarless shirts whining about the Integrity of the Western. Creeps.'

Brett took it up.

'It was when *Clerks* was just out. The industry was beside itself. This was something else. Someone makes a movie for nothing, but they still have to come to you for distribution. So you market it the same as normal – as if it cost you the same as something with twenty exploding helicopters and a bunch of prima donnas – and you get the same return. Better, because this is something new.'

River. 'Our class caught it like a virus. Everyone else just immediately junked all the projects they'd been working on – the stuff that got them on the course to begin with – and jumped on the ol' wagon. But we wouldn't do it.'

'Why not?' I thought *Clerks* was pretty cool. We had a private screening in New York, mostly to pick up tips for our next image-rethink. Brett exhaled, exasperated.

'Don't you know anything? All those movies weren't meant to be movies. They were meant to be calling cards, for chrissake. What you max out your credit cards for, to show that you have some ability; like a résumé, plus. But you remember all that stupid Generation X stuff? The industry was going insane trying to figure out how to sell it back to us. Then they got it; make like the calling cards are real movies. Market something that was made for twenty grand just the same as if it cost five million. So now that's the only kind of movie you're allowed to make if you're young. Quirky, jumpy and cheap, buddy. Who's going to fund a big project by a kid our age when they know they can market someone's college home movies and make the same margin? We say we won't do it. We kept right on with what we started. Everyone thought we were mad. *We* thought we were mad. But you've got to do it. You've got to draw the line and say, enough already. They say we have to make this kind of movie; we say, in a pig's arse. We were never like anyone else to begin with and we're damned if we're going to start pretending now.'

I was hoping when we were older, this would be one of the times she'd be thinking of when she'd turn around one day and say, apropos of nothing, we never talk anymore. Not like we used to. I checked it out.

'The defining characteristics of your existence don't mean shit anymore. I have a dumb job – so what? I can't hold down a relationship because – ?' Her eyebrow supplied the question mark. 'Because there's no real future to project things into. Because the present feels like an insignificant preface to the rest of your life. Terminally unsatisfying, because it's supposed to be. It's time, Jake. We've got this far refusing to behave like we're supposed to. I want to try something when we land. Are you up for it?'

Yes I was. Back in front of the VDU, she said, 'What did you learn from the casino?'

I shrugged. 'The more you play, the more the house edge can work against you?'

'Yeees,' she drawled, a stunning-but-straitlaced schoolmistress humouring a particularly young-dumb-and-full-of-come adolescent. Kelly McGillis in *Top Gun*. 'And?'

What? You separate yourself from your shirt, you turn over

some loopy old lady-who-lunches? I shook my head, hoping to look perplexed rather than just thick.

'Come on,' she said, 'I told you this already. The cards have no memory. You can throw tails two hundred times in a row, and it's still just as likely to come up next time. Things aren't going to even out eventually; life isn't fair. If you think it is, then you're going to start thinking there must be something wrong with you.'

I could, it has to be said, second that emotion. I'd begun to suspect I had unsuccessful genes. Everyone I went to school with seemed to be making a better job of living, and loving, and providing. Something inside them seemed to draw them to law school or teacher training like it was a magnet. Prams, promotion, package holidays; they were hauling themselves into the next century. But I had *unsuccessful* genes − I was programmed to screw up. It has occurred to me that loser DNA just mimics the characteristics of superficial success. Maybe it could make it through another few generations of working for the government, marrying, buying Victorian terraces and stripping the floors. But then all that will be over, and they won't be able to cope. They'll just die away. Really triumphant genes run a program to make you think you're a loser, so you never stop being hungry. You never stop pushing yourself, even when you think there's nowhere left to go. This was where they'd pushed me.

The percentile-complete bar in the copy dialog box pushed to the end, and the drive fell silent. I didn't really understand it right then, but this was our kind of ultimate heist. Adidas bags full o' cash, Head holdalls of cocaine, whatever − they were for the birds. They were just money. We wanted *lives*. Stealing information, developing it, and fixing it to the face the market demanded would bring Brett the seed money she wanted for the feature they'd been trying to get past the cigarette concession in the Sainsbury's of production for the last four years already, since before they even went to film school. But more; it would make her three-dimensional to everyone who'd responded to her few desperately won pitches so far with dictated-but-not-read rejections. 'Sent by fax modem' under the 'I wish you every success in your future career' to excuse – or maybe emphasize – the lack of signature.

But there was another way. She didn't need to do this. *I* could be Shelley. I had product, and it was, despite what Shelley had said, exactly what was wanted. I knew it was good enough, or at least different enough, for someone to want to put into development. It featured disaffected teenagers, for christ's sake, which is one market you know isn't going to dematerialize. And Shelley would have fallen on it like a vulture, if it had come from anyone else. Sod her. I lacked her legions of contacts – so what? I had all the other things she didn't have, like desperation. I was just as capable as her of taking this project out of turnaround with a new face.

Or two, I rather thought. The time had come. I told Brett about my screenplay, misty-eyed with gratitude for every miserable, wasted minute of the life that had brought me here.

There was a horrible moment when I finished. I'd thought about this so much, going round and round with it till it drove me almost mad, but I still didn't know whether they would do it. Of course, and it would be rather a bore to have to bring this up, there was the matter of complicity in murder, at least as far as Brett knew. This suggested to me that she'd be at least reluctant to risk my taking this to someone else and losing her hold on me. As for River, I had no idea how much she'd told him and didn't care. He'd go along with whatever she did; that was the point of him. It wouldn't have been any fun being her if she didn't have a foil when things were good or a support group when they weren't. I envied him that, of course, and hadn't entirely put the idea of supplanting him out of my mind, however clinically I seemed to be surveying the situation. But if there was to be any kind of future for me and her then it was up to me to make it happen. And I wanted her to be with me because she wanted to, because she saw me with new eyes; not the patsy in a joke everyone already knew, but as what the world was waiting for. Then, of course, I'd tell her everything.

Because I didn't know anything about them, and I'm hopeless at that sort of thing – can't help but be, when I can't even do it myself. I puzzle, I frown, over the events of last year, last week, this morning, pushing my hair back till it hurts and giving myself lines, trying to figure out where it all went wrong. I beat myself up over this. I whale on me, I let go on me. I've been doing this as long as I can remember and I don't seem to be able to shake it. My backstory means nothing. Wipe the backups and burn the negatives, babe. There is nothing I could show you, if I really took you back. There isn't much of a tour, at my own private Disneyland. The rides all suck, and the concessions went bust. Welcome to Jakeville, home of the hopeless. Alt.binaries.pictures.freshman.psych. Let's go.

Fade in, to the bedroom where I didn't read Dostoevsky at three and Dante in the original at five, where I didn't sprout a fetching smatter of freckles across my nose, that didn't complement my gappy smile, which wasn't cooed over by the dizzying succession of successful Groucho-type friends who didn't drop by, and who didn't whisk me away, put me in front of a camera and inveigle me to say, Mummy – why are your hands so soft? Track out the window – come fly with me – into the garden, and the apple blossom I didn't sit under, precociously inventing sagas of goblins and fairies, that I didn't sew into little booklets that didn't charm everyone who saw them; or the wonderful extended family I never ran to, who would have laughed or had me sectioned had I ever been myself. Dissolve to the school, where I didn't use laughter as a defence against bullying, where I never played Puck and brought the house down, where the editor of the mimeographed magazine stayed distinctly undazzled by my Dorothy

Parker-lite doggerel. Dissolve to montage of dizzy summer nights, when there weren't cider and haylofts, or flush-faced girls who didn't grab my hand and pull me, playfully protesting, from the strobes and four-to-the-floor beats, and never said, breathless, *you*. Fade out. I swear, my adolescence could have been planned by the army. Nothing happened, and then more nothing, and then cars on fire, and some burnt-out cars; and the rest you know about.

But Brett – Brett had backstory in spades, and it all worked perfectly. It was a wrap. Looking at people's appearance and clothes and setting, and drawing assumptions about their character is something you get from TV or the movies. Every shot is filled with significant detail: one single 35mm frame would swallow 40 meg; you couldn't fit ten on to a clean hard drive; but there isn't anything there that needn't be. This is why people always have such enormous apartments in movies – to make the accumulation of significant detail appear less forced. Her and River's apartment was tiny, but it was the same kind of thing.

There were pictures of her mother all over the place. They fascinated me. She looked, herself, fascinated herself by the camera. Caught, but smiling, transfixed by the flash like she split the spectrum and the shards pinned her to the set; or turning away, entering a limo, leaving a restaurant, but never completing the action she was caught in.

There was one I liked especially. Just before her marriage she'd lived in the famous Pad o'Gals apartment in Bel Air – with *that* actress, daughter of a Forties child star, *that* writer, daughter of a Fifties Nobel laureate, that prototype supermodel, that Biba girl, that Factory girl. Whether any of them actually lived there was always kind of doubtful, but it was a cool idea, and was always a facile story – Cosmo ran a big feature in its first-ever issue – when real ones were thin on the ground. It was a UriZen thing, back when UriZen was still a baby just born of a bunch of competing factions. It kept the heat on them all, on a slow simmer even when none had had a specific product to sell. This was where you could be, the captions said. In the Pad o'Gals, with the eyes of the world upon you. Everything used the same idea after.

Brett's mom's marriage was the media event of the decade, against a backdrop of OPEC, the Cold War and a vicious Vietnam hangover. It was milked for all it was worth; America needed it bad. The spin started almost a year before, was feverish when this picture had been taken. It showed her symbolically moving out of the Pad o'Gals, an event to which half the world's media had naturally been invited.

She was coming down the steps, looking like Katharine Ross in *The Graduate*, halter top, cut-off jeans, penny loafers, carrying a cardboard carton of paperbacks. On the front of the carton was printed SPECIAL CORNISH HEN FROZEN CHICKEN KEEP AWAY FROM HEAT and this was supposed to be some kind of major big deal. I suppose it was. The idea was kind of, look: she's an ordinary girl, she moves out of her apartment with boxes from the grocery store, but she's the most famous woman in the world right now and she's on her way to marry the richest and most powerful man. This could be you. I touched the glass with my fingers once when Brett was out of the room. *I met your children/What did you tell them?* But she never told them anything, and she left them nothing but photographs, whole warehouses of press cuttings, footnotes in media studies textbooks. And nothing else.

She was a star whose ascendancy hit on the mother of format crises – network vs cable, movies vs TV, video vs everything – so she never actually *did* anything. And she was more famous than anyone else, ever. For a short while. She was the person-equivalent of the Rubik's cube, the hula hoop, cuffing your jeans, sundried tomatoes, wearing your baseball cap backwards, or having a social conscience. This was evidence of the extent of UriZen, though no one knew it yet. They could sustain the Heat, while fending off the Fade, without committing her to any real product, ever.

She was *the* 20th Century star. Pure image, pure hype, pure spin, pure light. Nothing. Keep away from heat.

I found it almost frightening, that picture. The confluence of ordinary object and extraordinary situation killed me. Like the cop's ear thing in *Dogs*. Which doesn't have anything to do with a razor or an ear. That happens out of the frame. The horrible thing is the song – that ordinary piece of Seventies' playlist. It's the wrong music, and it doesn't stop. It goes right on after the ear's been sliced away and tossed aside. There's no crescendo, no screaming atonal violin chords. But the worst thing is the psycho knows the song as well as the cop does. He sings along; he dances to it. The guy who breaks into your house in the middle of the night, breaks your ribs with a baseball bat, ties you up, makes you watch while he rapes your partner; he watched the same shows as you did six hours ago. He maybe even ate the same microwave dinner. That photograph of Brett's mother carried something nameless inside it. It made me think of Marilyn Monroe – there was a time when she was just a dime-a-dozen bottle blonde, riding the streetcar to work, running out of blouses, waiting on line during the late night at the market, thinking about the things you do, and wondering if you aren't mad to hope that it's ever going to change. I could have stared for days, and if I'd been less concerned with semiotics I might have noticed something else: that the pictures were all razored from magazines, and not terribly old ones either. But I wasn't, and I didn't.

When Irving Thalberg was my age, he fired a director for using a shot that recurred in every movie he made. There was always a girl sitting by a window in an empty room, then a bunch of sloppy old labradors would flood in the door and engulf her, and she'd laugh and the moment of tension would be past. I suppose the director had once, his grubby freckled nose pressed up against the railings of some whip-cracking old litigator's estate, seen a girl doing the doleful, silhouetted against a window, and maybe somewhere else a rich girl with a bunch of dogs, and it had stuck in his mind as kind of shorthand for glamour. I've no idea what mine was, if I ever had one; probably something to do with a shot from some dumb video when I was twelve, a convertible Morris Minor with the top down, disappearing round a country lane in bright sunlight, clean hair streaming back in the wind on mornings when I wasn't up yet. I don't know where I saw this first, but Brett and River flipped all the same kind of switches for me, and I saw them only as rarely as I could bear to; I didn't want this feeling to end.

Because we didn't share an apartment, even when we decided to go for it with my screenplay. Though I'd kind of expected to move in, it was pretty obvious there wasn't room – they were practically living on top of each other as it was – so I stayed in a hotel for a couple of weeks until I found a couple rooms in a building out toward Santa Monica, though just the wrong side of the freeway. It was much better that way. Though everyone our age is supposed to be like, living in group houses and shit, this is just a budgeting constraint on behalf of the producers of *The Real World*. We'd all live apart if we could afford it. You know? Who wants to have other people comment on your obsessive fifteen-hour viewathons of time-porn TV shows (where you ogle people with free time like other generations ogled flesh); the way you like to gibber incoherently at news anchors after too many bowls of cereal; and your habit of sitting in the glow of the fridge light for a couple hours when you get back from the market, and have to go back and buy everything again the next day. Sharing things is like, jesus, *thirtysomething* : dinner parties, *Granta*, jogging – all kinds of weird sickness; shared vacations, resentments, tensions rivalries; unfulfilled dreams of Creativity, unsatisfactory parenting, inability to express feelings – *ick*. I hated that show, not least because everyone in it scared the hell out of me. I thought Shelley was going to walk on any moment. The one time I tuned in, some woman in a swanky kitchen was whining about her needs. Then some beardy-weirdy in a rich-guy office was shooting executive hoops and whining about his needs. And I'm like, what about my needs? I need to watch TV a couple hours. Can'tcha blow up a helicopter or something?

But it was best I have my own apartment if I was going to write. This was what we decided. I was cool about my screenplay getting the money to make theirs. They had this major story – I mean *Kane, Zhivago, Gatsby*, though I never read it – and their project for the next few years was to get enough money together to make it themselves. This was what they were doing at the casino, though that was kind of pissing in the ocean. They'd given up on trying to go the usual route. They knew it sucked. River did an excellent skit of the director who'd get hired by the money guys – there was no way anyone was going to let two kids with no track record direct and produce it themselves.

'You know –' drawling in a terribly bored, terribly moneyed voice ' – there's been a lot of talk about how the, uh, happy ending . . . caused a rift with the writer. But let me put the record straight. *(Frees underwear from between cleft of buttocks.)* I did it not for commercial reasons but because I fell in love with these characters *(demonic glare into camera)* and I wanted to see them survive. I'm kind of a romantic at heart *(bares teeth)* and I wanted to know the sun was coming up on a world where they were still alive. *(Picks ear and examines residue on finger with childlike wonder, for four beats. Appears to remember where he is.)* I shot both endings and spliced them together, and still my heart reached out for the happy ending.'

It could happen – I mean, *Less Than Zero* for christ's sake – and, as Brett pointed out, once the possibility was even on the dry-erase board, everything else would *de facto* carry the taint. So we'd do mine first; it would give them track record, money for leverage. What we already had would sustain us and pay the rent, till we started to see the four points of unadjusted gross from dollar one that we were planning to insist on for mine.

But we were stymied. I couldn't pitch to Venture Capitalists because I'd be laughed out of the room. Which was why I was cool about ditching the usual round of pitches. I never wanted it to begin, so I took it to Shelley. I wanted a change from High 5; I had four years of doing the same routine day in day out for a bunch of over-sugared brats, and pitching to VCs would have been more of the same, though maybe with less to help me look myself in the face every morning. Wind me up and watch me go. The faded marionette, lap-dancing a gang of disinterested bozos. Blowing dentists for a few bucks. Beam me up.

They had the same problems as me. I'd thought it wouldn't be a problem for them to pitch instead of me, but Brett said people knew about their mom − it was like this open secret − and there had been too much money pissed up a wall by nepotist fuckwits just lately. A couple of years ago, fine, but not now. We went round and round with it for a few days, and then she was hammering down the door of my apartment one night around three. She burst into the living room and flipped all the lights on. I'd fallen asleep in front of *The Twilight Zone*. It was the episode with Burgess Meredith as a specky bank teller whose irritating boss and nagging wife are always dumping on him for reading books. He starts hiding in the bank vault in his lunch hour with his eyeglasses and his book, and one day while he's down there the bomb drops. I fell asleep right at the start, but I'd seen it about a billion times cubed.

'I was watching it too. I got it. It's perfect.' Brett was babbling, she was so excited. I was still kind of woozy. 'Novelize it! Do it as a book.'

I was aghast; I had just woken up. 'A *book*?'

She bubbled with laughter.

'Oh, come on, Jake. It's not that bad. We'll still make it into a movie after. You should see your face.'

I had no desire to see my face. I was still kind of unpeeling it from the couch, and I was pretty sure there was a runner of dried spit from the corner of my mouth. I rubbed at it, I hoped surreptitiously.

'You said, uh, do it as a book?' I couldn't believe I was hearing this. I mean, what was this shit? The bank clerk was inside the vault.

'Uh-huh. I met this guy, when we were pitching for agents last year. He had the spot before us, but they made us wait half an hour, so we got talking. I forgot all about him, then I saw him in *Variety* a couple months ago. He's doing novelizations of screenplays. Clay Bartleby. He just finished *The Double*. I bet he'd do it for ten if I hit on him. And if we didn't want it too interior.'

'Hello?' I was making an effort to be as reasonable as possible. 'What the fuck are you talking about?'

'This is the easiest way to get yours made. I don't know how I didn't think of it before.' She sat down on the couch, and put her Che's on the coffee table. 'Flip me some pleasure switches.'

I took the four paces into the kitchen, and rifled the cupboard. There was an emergency package of Oreos behind the linguine jar – I kept the regular supply in the fridge, but I didn't have time to go to the grocery store today. I wondered whether I ought to put them on a plate or what. I elected to be, you know, casual, like it was no big deal her stopping by, and tossed them over the open-plan-because-there-isn't-room-for-a-wall counter. She caught them, bit off a corner of the package and spat it on the floor, not taking her eyes off the TV.

'Uh,' I said, eloquent and urbane, 'you were, like, saying?' I picked up the remote and hit mute.

'Oh, yeah,' she said, chewing vigorously, spraying crumbs. 'I was thinking about DIS and everything. What's the one thing the industry runs on?'

'Fumes?'

'C'mon. Scarcity of product, buddy. One corporation acquires *rights* to a property. And they sell the rights to other content-providers, or put it into development themselves. The unique value of the product – its scarcity – is always in the center of the equation.'

'Yeah. So.' I didn't see where this was getting us. 'We have my screenplay and yours. We need to get someone to buy one so we can make the other.'

'But that's precisely it! Don't you see? We've both got screenplays. So has practically everyone else our generation. The market conditions are not favourable to us. We are looking at a glut.'

'And? Um, can I have one of those?' The cookies were going pretty fast.

'Sure.' She held out the package, then took one herself and gestured with it. 'So. A spec script by a young kid is not a rare commodity. Neither is a showcase reel or a demo tape or a pitch disk. What's the common factor?' She popped the cookie, whole, into her mouth. I was having a hard time dealing with the fact that she was in my apartment at three a.m. and I was practically naked. I shook my head.

'The *tech*. They're all trying to break into high-tech entertainment sectors. Which is why we love them. But there's one practically zero-tech sector, where there's no competition at all.'

'No.' I didn't want to hear this.

'Yes! Books! *Disco*, Jake. The only people who write books now are the ones who've blown out everything else. They're all like thirty, minimum. It's wide open.'

I thought on this a moment. She did have a point. I tried to remember the last time I'd seen a back-flap mugshot on anything that hadn't totally bitten the big one, that hadn't been cut off at the top of the forehead if it was a guy or vaseline-lensed to disguise the upper-lip shrinkage if it was a woman. I couldn't.

'It wouldn't make enough money. What's the maximum number of units you could hope for?'

'Domestic and England? Hundred thousand. Hundred and fifty maybe.'

'Don't you see what I mean?' I said exasperatedly. 'This is a negligible market. A million is a negligible audience for a screenwriter.'

'Sure it is. But then you can make the movie,' she said, pausing a beat and shifting down. 'If a hundred thousand people buy the book, domestic and England, that's a hundred thousand people who'll go see the movie. And take their dates.'

'People who read books don't have dates,' I said. I mean, I read books.

'Oh, c'mon. They must all get together sometime. They pick each other up in bookstores. Say half of them do. A hundred and fifty thousand, guaranteed. That's a million gross first weekend. You have a guaranteed market to show your investors. They'll give you five times that. Then you've made a five-million-dollar movie. Who cares if it bombs? You've handled a five-million-dollar project. Next time they give you ten to play with.'

She was right of course. It was kind of a downer, but it solved everything. The clerk was in the vault reading, oblivious to ground zero outside.

'It'll be fun too. We'll be hip. People will be so shocked we chose to do it as a book, they'll fawn over us. I mean look at us. The fact that we chose books as our format will be a story in itself.'

I knew it. Her face should have been launching a thousand movies, magazines, CDs, personal freshness products, Gap franchises. Not books.

'One thing though. I don't think we should do it here. We need to maximize impact. We need focus. America is too big. Oh, that's okay.'

We'd both gone for the last Oreo at once.

'No, you take it,' I said.

'Split it?' I nodded, nonchalant as hell; but I'm thinking, like, yes! Shared food. She handed me my half.

'The way to be cool here is to be cool in England first. Like America only got into dance music after Chicago house went to London and came back acid. So we do the same.' She took a slug on her diet Dr Pepper. 'Jesus, think about it. The pound is so weak, it's like the franc in the Twenties. Everyone cool is going to be in London, just like Paris was then.'

This really swung me. I mean I wanted to go back to England like I wanted to be, I don't know, godfather to Brett's children. But I love the idea of a scene. Dorothy Parker and the Algonquin; Tricky and Portishead and Massive Attack. Cool. Creativity is as much a matter of context as ability. I've always thought that, like, success should come from your sensibility rather than as a result of a bunch of slick career moves. When you find some other people who share your tastes and obsessions and a whole new 'tude is born. And everyone else discovers that they felt the same way as you all along.

'And they'll come to us, because we did it first. This is like noticing Ben & Jerry's stock price ten years ago. Or making out with Madonna when she was in high school. We must be the only people in the world having this conversation right now. I know it seems incredible that anyone like us could be out there, but they are. Imagine owning the very first fax machine – it's sitting quietly now; you can't even send to anyone. But you wait. If you build a new motorway, even in the middle of nowhere, the traffic to choke it will arrive out of thin air. We're going to start a scene, and we'll be the first.'

But I saw the same old problem.

'What about publicity? People will know who I am. If they see my picture. Journalists'll just do little snide pieces – y'know, guess what.'

'We do it. Me and River.'

'Both of you?'

'Uh-huh. Think of the angle.'

'You'd do it?' This was a bit much, but I was kind of thinking about homing in for the big scene now. I didn't know. Sometimes I wake up looking – not okay, but different. With my hair all flat and all. Gamine, little-boyish, but hey sugar, you want to make me a man? Jesus. I really don't believe myself sometimes.

'Sure. It's going to take a while, but it'll give us a new angle out here too. To be writers already. Writers who've gotten paid anyway. What're you doing?'

I was trying to imply, with my body language, that I was the proprietor of infinitely-adaptable-to-unstable-economic-conditions genetic material, and pretty cheap and slutty besides. But it occurred to me that this wasn't the way. I didn't want to be cheap; I wanted to be a multisaver. So I changed it into reaching for my cigarettes. I was getting the feeling she was going to leave if I couldn't keep her talking. It was awful late. I wondered how long it would take to climb out of the bathroom window, swarm along to the fire escape and the street below in order to disable the distributor cap on her Japanese motor. She'd never get a cab now. I played for time.

'How long's this going to take?'

'Say three months for the guy to write it. Month to pitch and sell. Four months to build it up and get it out there. Three months for it to give us some figures.'

'This is putting things on hold. That's a hell of a delay.'

'But it's not like we won't be doing anything else. Man, I don't know what they do all day, book writers. We can use it to network, polish, whatever. We'll have piles of time to do all of the stuff that, face it, we're going to have to do anyway.'

'Won't it mean getting a different kind of agent?'

'There's only one kind.'

Which was ours. Certainly in my case, and I imagined in hers too, 'agent' was a total misnomer, since it implied some kind of action on one's behalf. He only approached me after I was hired and my contract was tighter than an MBA's ass already. I think he only pretended to be hot for me, and for about five minutes, so he could kiss up to Shelley by letting her walk all over me. You want to barbecue my client's *cojones*? Sure! Go ahead. Beverage with that? Otherwise, he never did anything except vacation and complain. And serve writs on me, the bastard.

'Anyway, what's the point? We can do it ourselves. Now that the studios are gone you have to take responsibility for every part of your career yourself. And besides, that business is way simpler. You know? Where's the deal? Piece of piss. I'll call the writer guy in the morning. G'night!'

Peck on the cheek and door. I listened to her gun River's Honda Civic in the street below and pull away. It was quiet. I hit mute again and got the sound back. It'll be cool, I said to the TV, as Burgess Meredith came out of the vault and surveyed the destruction. Amongst the ruins, the one building still standing was the library. His eyes lit up, and he ran toward it; then tripped. His glasses fell off and smashed; he groped blindly in the rubble. This was too cheesy; I flipped it off.

So four months later, here we were. Of course, I couldn't have let some other guy in on my baby. No way. Besides, I was kind of glad to get another shot at it. I've always thought your first thing should come out of you like it's shot from a gun, or you end up being pegged in second league; hustle premature product or not enough of it and you turn into Lush. It's not your fault, because some record company wants to see margins made now, even if they're a tenth of what you could do, given time and belief. But, like Brett said, now the studios are gone no one's looking at the big picture.

She'd been bitching once, not long after we got here, about how they'd done all the usual rounds in the last year of film school.

'Your first project has to come from nowhere, and that's good; but because you don't have a track record, no one's going to take any notice unless it's some kind of manifesto.' She had a cigarette in the corner of her mouth and was speaking out the other side, her face screwed up against the smoke. 'No one cares if it's a good story, a good picture. What's new about that? Never mind that that's the most they expect from someone who's been around a while. Once, years ago, at a studio, they'd say, yeah, this kid's got something, give her a couple. And you'd rewrite scenes on a dozen movies, and say six went into production, and two did okay. Then you might get a chance to work on something good.

'But now they expect you to come up with the best work of your career without any help at all. If you don't blow everyone away the first chance you get then that's it, they don't care about you and you're over. There's no patience, no reciprocation. All they care about is that its new – that it tells them about some world they don't know about, or, rather, some world they haven't cleaned up in yet. So you have to make what you have into some form of despatch from some kind of front line. A proposal for new modes of existence. Like, oh yeah, we know. We've done everything. We've plumbed every depth. Who're we kidding?'

Actually, I'd had to restrain myself from pointing out, we had kind of broken the bank at Monte Carlo, gone on a minor killing spree and were proposing to pull off the media equivalent of fixing the World's Series. Not to mention having been so famous by the time we were twenty that we couldn't live any regular kind of life using our real identities. But she'd had a point somewhere.

'It's all so backward. Like you only get a shot at the money at the end of your career – when you're too old to know how to dress, let alone live. Not at the start, when you need it, when you could really use it to come up with something cool.' But my story wasn't there yet.

It was weird coming back to it. In the rash of features that appeared on quantum mechanics a few years ago, when it was sexy for about five minutes, there was something about the results of an experiment depending upon whether or not it was observed. I felt the same way about my characters. I'd taken my eye off them for a while, and they'd probably been off playing softball, tossing salads, hugging sprogs and participating in personal-growth programs meanwhile. Now I had to recall them to the closed world I'd defined for them, for reasons that didn't seem so important anymore, and they dragged their feet coming back in a way that suggested the first day of school after a too-short half-term. When I finally had them assembled the problems began.

It didn't help the damn thing that I'd written in it in the midst of High 5. I wasn't at my best then. I was just so fucking poor, and every day we were getting in worse and worse debt to UriZen. It scared the hell out of me. I hated everything, and it kind of came out in the book. It wasn't going to make for any usual kind of feelgood teen-movie sensation.

There wasn't much to it. I couldn't help feeling that all the best themes got turned into theme parks years ago. It was about being seventeen forever. When you have friends you'd die for, but they all die on you instead; in cars that are too small and too fast. Their mothers' cars, cars they've stolen, doesn't matter. Golfs, 205s, MR2s, MX5s. Being in charge of too much power before you know what it can do to you. Because you think that somehow you're different, and you're going to live forever.

It was set in middle anywhere; you know it. The kind of place people *come* from, because there's no earthly reason to stay: post-everything smalltown orbited by superstores, ex-industrial estates, dead railtracks, a bypass that doesn't have much to avoid anymore.

The time was now; a dragging, drawn-out hiatus between two centuries. Like someone hit the pause button around 1989 and we've been on hold ever since. The *fin de siècle* already happened, and we didn't notice; Old Testament plagues and hurricanes, falling towers on Wall Street and Broadgate. The Thirties paid for the Twenties, the Seventies for the Sixties, the Nineties for the Eighties. And how. So if you got yourself born in the wrong decade then sorry, kid, party's over. Now we need you to sweep up the glass, corral the beer cans, empty the ashtrays, scrub at the vomit. And put your damn back into it, won't you? Is this going to go on forever? Nothing happening except perpetual wars of pre-medieval savagery and incomprehensibility. And the feeling that if anything else significant went down, we're so blanded out with news of nondescripts and nonentities we'd be unlikely to notice.

Yet this urge to record it. I don't know what I was thinking of. It wasn't that I had such a good time, just now, when I was young. I suppose I just miss it, and that's not the same thing at all. I saw hugely misguided significance in the fabric of the lives my friends and I lived, before school broke up; before some became teachers, some went to Australia, and the rest went to prison.

It was especially weird to be feeling kind of happy with here and now, because violent dissatisfaction with wherever the hell I am had appeared, up till now, to be the point of me. I've always hated here and having to be here. It was ironic too, because the whole dynamic of the story was about hating here, and trying to get away, only to find there was nowhere else to go. Just around here. It was called *The Car-Crash Age*. I like it when the title and the story are the same thing. I was going to shoot practically the whole thing inside automobiles. Minimum exterior. It started out with a bunch of kids who hung out together, having occasionally cool times in a small way. Then they learned to drive, and things changed forever. Having the means to get from the bar to the party to the club to stoner central out by the lake meant they never stayed anyplace for more than ten minutes. Now the good time was always happening somewhere else, and if you could only keep moving then maybe you'd catch up with it. Couldn't you? Catching up with it would mean that now your life was starting. Far better that you couldn't; that the better time, the better relationship, the better self, remain always somewhere up ahead. Whatever. The old gang fell apart, and there was never going to be a new one. A few people got killed in car wrecks, but mostly to add metaphorical weight.

It had seemed okay at the time, because I was expecting my casting choices to supply the deficiency of my lazy and suspect talents. If real people doing my lines didn't sound real persons then, and only then, would I reconstitute it. And cut the lines of whichever actors I'd taken irrational dislikes to. So what I did now, after a couple of weeks of flaying myself alive over a hot PowerBook, was cast it in my head, and watch every movie I could lay my hands on featuring my choices, then translate their on-screen mannerisms and attitude into prose. I used Creative-Writer too. It's this totally cool program that helps you write stories like you're in a platform game. More like a MUD than AticAtac or Sonic. But there's a cartoon character and everything.

I suppose that I ought to have been considering what was happening, but it didn't feel like decision time. I was trying to liberate myself from this cycle of feeling like every action, however insignificant, was going to have some irrevocable effect on the freeway to loserville. But I never felt like, I don't know, whoever it was who had to come up with the first PC/TV interface. Tough call, because TVs were always matt black and computers were always oatmeal. But, jesus, way to screw up. Matt black, but oatmeal keys on the keyboard. Gorgeous. It could have been any colour at all – grape, lemon 'n' lime, cherry-flavoured antacid – y'know? It wasn't like cars, where you can always tell who's really anal about the resale price because they go for the dark blues and greens and greys.

But I never doubted that what I had in mind wasn't good for us. We were trammelled by fame; it hadn't worked for us as it ought; so it wasn't unreasonable for us to expect another dose of it to act like a vaccine, or an antidote to the surfeit of bad stuff we'd swallowed already. It was what I'd been working towards, since I started sketching out a story, not really knowing why I was doing it; then since the earliest absurdity of High 5 I had clung to it, even as I jigged and twirled and pranced, my face in a rictus-smile so long every day that after the flashbulbs it took 20mg of diazepam to prise muscle from cheekbone. I had only the vaguest idea of how I was going to do it but, by the time I'd worked through enough stuff to stop writing about myself and start something saleable, I'd been alive for over twenty years, with my eyes not entirely shut for most of them. And so an outside chance began to develop that maybe someday I could get back on health insurance and afford to die slowly.

I had four years of touring to work on it, and did so with varying levels of enthusiasm and application that roughly corresponded with wildly fluctuating predictions of our future economic high jinks. Ironically enough, when the worst case applied and we were finally paid off, my resolution derived instead from a sense of my own wasted youth; and, perhaps, my own wasted fame. If the two weren't analagous, then I'm afraid that they appeared near enough to see the cliffs of one from the shore of the other on a clear day.

However, I guess I always knew it was never going to be a great movie. It was the sort of thing you ought to see with your inbetweener, never your steady. With Cara rather than Brett. You shouldn't go to see a good movie with someone you're just treading water with. You need it to be as forgettable as they are. You don't want it to be too good, because then you'll want to see it again someday, but you won't be able to because you know it'll remind you of them, and how badly you behaved.

Brett was never going to be anyone's B-feature. She was someone you'd go to see only straight-into-the-all-time-top-twenty-or-forget-it movies with. You wouldn't want to squander your time with her on everyday stuff. She looked like an ad for humans. So did River. I could see what she meant about critics fawning over them, once the book was out. I used to go over to their apartment that summer, maybe a couple of times a week, and the door would be open if they were in; some honeyed afternoon around five, finding them facing each other in the window seat, as the sky turned pink behind them; talking quietly but animatedly, each with their backs to the frame and their sharkskin pants tapering out before them, ankles crossed over one another's, each tapping a Wannabe idly against the other's calf.

I'd stand where I was and gaze on them a while – wrapped up in their twin-world, a place that extended only so far as the other would allow; lazy humour tweaking the corners of their eyes and mouths, murmuring back and forth and forth and back words that slipped out the angle of the window with the smoke from their Luckies, and were carried away on the breeze.

When I went back to the door and made a show of coming in again they'd smile, and raise their knees a moment so I could sit between them with their ankles in my lap. They asked me where I'd been and what I'd done and what I'd seen. They had a stack of Coca-Cola crates against one wall, and one of them would go over and get you one; and they'd watch you drink it, like you were appreciating this rare Coke. It felt like home. It felt like a gang. They were perfect and, by extension, so was I.

Too perfect to stay under wraps forever, and we'd known it all along. All I ever wanted was the brashness that comes with a gang, and now I had one. We didn't have to mess around with this kind of crap. We didn't have to stay behind the scenes. It was time for us to walk in brightness down the middle of Old Compton Street, St Mark's Place, the Strip, as if to say, go on – have another look. We could be an idea everyone wanted to steal.

This was, I felt, perfect timing for everything. I wouldn't have wanted to have met Brett much earlier. She was out of the wearing-too-many-rings phase, but not yet in the one-ring-pointedly-on-the-long-finger-left-hand one. Also, any earlier and I was still such a mess. But I felt a lot better now, and she was pretty together about most things. I guess she had to be.

They'd been born in an earthquake, at Cedars-Sinai, she told me. Everything since then had been a process of reinvention, forced upon them. Reinventing themselves as their uncle's kids. Reinventing themselves to get out of Australia. They didn't have any accent at all. They drummed it out of themselves when they were fifteen with a stack of old elocution 78s from the Forties, with guys from downtown Sydney trying to be Noël Coward. River used to sound like Tony Curtis in *Some Like It Hot*, Brett said. But they had to get rid of it. No one would take a couple of Australians seriously. Brett used to get quite heated on the subject.

'Can you imagine if Tarantino was from WA? People would just laugh if you shot *Dogs* in downtown Perth. Or stick you straight in the arthouse. Arbitrary, unwritten rules, but just you try and break them. You'd be amazed how many Australians are doing the same as us in the northern hemisphere. Fading in, taking over. Coming north and never going back is pretty much your only option if you're young and creative and don't want to spend your life shooting flatbed truck ads in Brisbane or Durban or Adelaide. And we were lucky – we had dual citizenship (we have Mom's accountant to thank for that too. He's just like this total fairy godmother).' She giggled. '*Totally*. See how long we were in LA! I'm just a Valley girl underneath all this. So by the time we got to UCLA, we may as well have come from nowhere.'

And Los Angeles was the place to go if you wanted to start over.

I hated all that crap about, you know, just as night is when things come true, LA is supposed to be where things go sour. The hell with that. This was the city of *Moonlighting* as well as *Sunset Boulevard*, *The Rockford Files* as well as *The Player*. It was a place to get into character. I loved it. I'd frequently find myself, late afternoons in my apartment, sitting by the Venetian blind in slats of orange sunlight the colour of a Clinique woman's cheeks, like in *LA Law* when there was a tough decision going down.

One day I was doing it, smoking cigarettes in the heat and pretending my ass was on the line when, right on cue, the phone rang. The only person who ever called me, the only person who had my number, the only reason I had the line sparked up again was Brett. I snatched the phone up and started talking right away.

'Hey, I had an idea for your author biog. What if you guys were from someplace else? Somewhere, you know, more literary. More elemental. You said yourself no one takes you seriously if you're from Australia. And you know, you don't want anyone sniffing around too closely . . . hello? Brett?'

'Jake?'

Beat.

'Who is this?'

'Jake, my name is Nancy Stuyvesant.'

'You have the wrong number.' I hung up. It rang again, immediately. I went away, into the living room, put my Walkman on. When Janis Joplin was done notifying me that I should get it while I could, I clicked it off. The apartment was quiet, except for the sirens and the whimpering and weird slapping sounds from downstairs. I swear, that building was lousy with perverts. I got on with some work, but it rang again about a half-hour later. First thing next morning I went out and bought a machine, installed it, and went to Santa Monica for the day.

Playing back the tape the next evening, I was trying to look for things that weren't there. Strange intonations, unnecessary pauses, that kind of thing. The sort of thing I was making my characters do fourteen hours a day – on top of everything else – but reality is never like you write it. There was nothing – just that name again, and a number to call. I checked the exchange against my list – Paramount 956, Disney 560, TriStar 280 and so on – but it wasn't there. It was a loser number. And the name – Nancy Stuyvesant. It meant nothing to me. It sounded like a Gerry Anderson pilot that would never have gotten made. A woman puppet in a non-peripheral role – yeah, right. But I couldn't leave it alone. I'd said too much, just for a change. After maybe a week of executive insomnia and premium-rate nausea I called her number, and got her first thing. I almost hung up right then. I mean, she didn't even have an assistant.

She made no reference to our first exchange. She said she was the ghost brought in by Shelley to finish the High 5 book when the original writer went into detox and refused to come out. She seemed cool and I prattled away a bit, slipping back into character like it was an old and familiar lover, where you know what goes where without breaking stride.

'That's all I need, Jake. You've been, uh, great. One last thing – why weren't you at Charlie's funeral?'

I'd hung the hell up there. She didn't call back this time.

I didn't want to talk about it then and I don't want to talk about it now. I still feel bad, though for a different reason.

I didn't go to the funeral because everything was too fucked up. This is what I told myself. It wouldn't have been fair. It would have been inflicting the joke all over again. Your son's life was a joke. We weren't the first bunch of patsies, but it had never been done with so little grace, or so cheaply. Mostly so cheaply. I counted it all up once, and allowing for all the pizza we ate and everything, and counting all the hours we were on the job in one way or another, we would have made a better hourly rate at

Taco-A-Go-Go. As teacher trainees. Answering the phones at UriZen. That's why I didn't go. It wasn't even like they could say Charlie had taken the fast lane, and burned out too soon. It was all just too cruel.

I didn't want to see the others, either. There isn't anything worse than having to go get drunk with people you used to be a loser with. It makes you feel like, even if you have finally clawed your way out of here, you don't deserve it. You have to cut those kind of ties. You need to immerse yourself in what you're doing even if it means losing sight of the kind of person you thought you wanted to be. If it means hanging out with empty people who can help your career – flatline suits, dorky celebs – rather than people you share something with, you have to do it, even if it means alienating your past. If you ever want to get away from here, because just being *here* becomes a self-fulfilling prophecy after awhile. This is why I didn't go.

I'm being too hard on myself, but if I could slip back down the long perspective I wouldn't know what to do, even now. Or maybe I could, but it's beside the point. I was in a hell of a situation – we all were. Out at the end of an event there. It wasn't like there was a Witness Protection Program or anything. It wasn't like there was a brochure. I'll take this new identity, and this new gameplan. You had to wing it, you had to make it up as you went along, and I hate that, I really do. I could say that I didn't know what I was doing. I could say that I could have done much worse; it could have got much more out of hand than it did. I could say that I might have wound up where I am without doing any of it. But what's the use? It wouldn't change a thing. The only thing I can change now is me, and I think this was beginning even then. I can understand, if nothing else; I can see motive, means and opportunity. I can still see where I was coming from, though the reception's not what it used to be – the picture's ghosting, and the vertical hold flips, and sometimes I can't get the station at all.

You get so you thank sweet heaven for that, some days. Perhaps this is not the best kind of self-knowledge, but it's all I have. One day soon I'll locate the volume switch that controls the inner monologue, and then maybe my life can start or finish, depending on whether the glass is half-full or half-empty. But for now – since honesty is generally more shocking than deceit – we say screw the glass, I ordered coffee. Triple-wet-skinny, buddy.

I tried to push all of it out of my mind and get on with the summer, still kidding myself that it was, in fact, going to end, and that there was a deadline on the cool times. Quite apart from my book-authoring, there was way too much to do to have the time or the inclination to think much.

The principal character amongst the cast that conspired to waylay these days of my life, lurking behind low walls with tyre-irons, was what brought us here, a cool morning in late August, with traces of dew still on the tall Monterey pines that line Beverley and Glen. Today was a courtesy call, a treat. It was the payoff we were getting, for a whole summer's work.

It had been Brett's idea, and this was even before I talked her into letting me reformat the screenplay. We'd procured ourselves jobs, of a sort, as interns too. It meant nothing to me, though it was a big deal to Brett, and to be fair, to almost anyone our age in this town. We'd had to apply, and interview or audition or whatever, for some old love of an agent along with about a thousand other kids. Quite literally a thousand, and it hadn't even been advertised. Brett had spent a whole week in the library beforehand, and had drilled River and I until we were bored silly. To work for nothing too. I should explain.

Some epochal old Director was putting together his collected writings; or rather, some margin-scraper at a publishing sub-division of DIS, Inc. was paying him for the right to publish them. I don't think there was any special urge to black-and-white on the Director's part – it was some ancient contractual fall-out that he couldn't wriggle out of, so he'd had to agree. Since all that an initial search had dredged up had been a sheaf of obituaries, written by the Director over the last ten years – when time began to catch up on his friends and associates and get relative to experience again, after the Sixties, Seventies and Eighties and all – this involved some poor schmuck spending two days a week in his crawl space marshalling whatever could be trawled up. It was alleged that the Director had written a number of essays and reviews when he was just a critic – this was back when the studios still had it in them, though gasping their last, to prevent critics inflicting themselves on the camera. The only extant copies of these were allegedly in the guy's loft. So, however, was almost every reference that had appeared in print in the last four decades to not just this guy's films, or any movies in particular, but to all films, in general. It was claimed that this landfill of yellowed newsprint needed to be indexed and cross-referenced and who knows what else.

Brett had pitched for us to do it and won. She claimed that the cachet of having been this Director's PAs would repay us like cubed; though I was slightly sceptical about this since she fabricated the most outrageous résumés for us all to get the gig, and I didn't see why we couldn't just do this again. But she said it would also give us some kind of insight into the publishing industry. Like that was going to be useful.

A few of her friends – there was a whole gang of them, which surprised me – were publishing interns, though they weren't much help. They worked at the kind of places where the first thing they make you do on your first morning is build your own flatpack desk from IKEA. This was not a personality test. When they gave you the can you had to put it back in the box again. These places were run by the kind of people who'd be a nuisance anywhere, but have special opportunities in publishing. Some Dead hanger-on who knocked out tributes to Jerry Garcia by other old liggers;

some jittery old fruit who got canned when his family firm was swallowed by conglomerates in the Eighties. Like reformed smokers, they were people who professed not to believe in the bottom line, but found that the only way to fund their lifestyles was to exploit the shit out of everybody else. River's friend Loulou was a publishing junkie.

'I'm like, bite me,' she said to me once. I was desperate for information on my non-teacher peers, so pumped any I could capture. 'I mean, Tipp-Ex and Scotch tape are all very well, but working in publishing makes it so much more satisfying to steal from your employer. Books have a 10 per cent resale factor or 20 per cent exchange. So you can swap your stack of mind, body and spirit trash for hip Japanese literature. You just tell them they're promo copies. This also means that cute bookstore guys who look like Eric Stoltz think you're some kind of hotshot agent.'

I liked Loulou – you had to, someone who'd reconstituted herself from trailer park mail-order-limited-edition-ceramic-kitten-for-real hell to hip LA cigarette girl vampishness. If she'd played the hand America dealt her she'd be the kind of truckstop waitress who calls you 'hon' and gets bothered by tattooed guys with bad teeth named Slim. Which would actually have been pretty cool. But now she was a publishing slave who called you Sailor and got bothered by jowly guys in slip-on shoes who wanted to take her to Martha's Vineyard. But she was a representative sample of most of Brett and River's friends. I only ever saw any of them by accident, if I dropped by the apartment when they had company over. But after a while it got so I'd let it slide and go back home if I saw the windows of their apartment all flung wide to emit the smoke of a dozen Lucky Lights. They became kind of depressing to me.

I understand that most people, in corporate cathedrals of glass and light, have to do the economic equivalent of feeling up children in the bogs. But the alternatives were beginning to seem not so terrific either, judging from the evidence here. I mean, I knew UriZen, but I had been kind of hoping that smaller places might be different. To discover that this was not the case made me begin to doubt that trusting to attitude over acumen was such a hot idea. Because it was these kids' attitude, their enthusiasm for whatever it was they were doing, that seemed to lay them open to the worst kinds of exploitation, by people who really ought to know better. Brett's friends didn't even answer the phones, or type invoices; they got bozos with no ambition to do that, and paid them enough to live on too. It was the ones with the passion, the ones who couldn't help themselves but *loved* books or art or music, who were inveigled into doing all the things they wouldn't have dared ask the pudding-brains on salary. But they weren't even honest about it; there was always a 'Can you bear to . . . ?' about it. Like it's us and them, and we're in this together. Like the Party and the proles in *1984*. Bosses and interns vs secretaries and receptionists. Which it was, in a twisted kind of way.

It reminded me of High 5 a little. When we weren't on the road or being rehearsed, we had to go into the office and do the filing, stuff envelopes, Xerox the press or whatever. I know, as well as anyone my age, that hell will smell like a hot copier and the synthetic creamer in vending machine coffee. Although I was pretty sure Ben from Curiosity never had to do this, it wasn't such a big deal. I mean, we had a sell-by date and everyone knew it, and Shelley said it would be useful for getting jobs afterwards. You know, media office experience, to put on your CV. I'd hoped she was kidding at the time. Still, the friends of Brett and River should have been the industry's future, but the people with the power weren't going anywhere yet, and didn't seem to want to look beyond that.

I was doing something on the Director's PC one day that summer. He had a load of old stuff that had been done in MS Works, but he'd just upgraded to Word; like, welcome to the twentieth century. But though it let you convert files from competitors' programs – WordPerfect, ClarisWorks – there didn't seem to be any facility to import Works files. I called Microsoft to find out how you did it, and they said the only way was to buy a new, supplemental convertor from them. This struck me, because it was so totally English. Like, if you're a new, first-time customer defecting from another supplier then hey, welcome aboard, and here's everything you need. But if you've been a loyal customer all along, and you've faithfully bought all of our products one after the other, then happy fucking birthday, asshole. This appears to be the universal, at the late twentieth century. The turncoat gets a big old soul kiss, the faithful get dumped on.

Their friends made me feel like this. It caught the sadness exactly. It made me sick. If you didn't care, you were okay; if you had any passion about you then someone was going to use it to exploit the shit out of you, until you hated what you loved. Loulou used to love books – now she thought they were a joke. You shouldn't parade your love; you have to keep it to yourself, or someone's going to make you sorry. They took the fun out of everything, and it didn't end there. They ruined everyone's love. If you loved movies, they ruined your love. They had no business being in the business. They had no imagination and no ability, but they wanted to stay; so they dressed up trash and sold it like it was the same as the things that made you love in the beginning. Until you were just tired, and you gave up.

So I wouldn't have gone over to their apartment much even if these hadn't been inbetween days, when the only thing to do was keep my head down and work. I did and I didn't understand why Brett and River wanted to see these people. Like my friends in England – the ones I never saw anymore – they weren't like we were. They were getting it kicked out of them, until they became civilians, who would shun us the moment they took the Fifth – teacher training, law school, whatever – preferring the company of other dual-salary floorboard-sanders. They had a kind of avidity about them: the kind in people's eyes, in clubs at 4 a.m.; when the drag queen in the ladies, who held court all night, checks her reflection one last time and knows it's time to go home. What it came down to was that Shelley and all her friends only did business with each other. Brett's friends would be exactly the same in ten years, given the chance. You could tell; it had started already. I asked Loulou once if she wanted to go to the movies and she said, right away, who else is going? I hate that. They were just playing at being drowners like us. Like those restaurant chains that only hire actors as waiters. The whole world was turning into High 5, and I did not need to know this.

I guess that solved the actor problem though. There are four types of people in LA: corporate sleazebag emotional thugs; genuine gangsters, who understand concepts like honour, integrity, character, and the long-term view; actors; and Mexicans. The last two were as ubiquitous as each other, but it was the Mexicans who ran the city; who trucked in the food, who carted the garbage, who hosed down the streets, who swabbed away the mess. Without illegal immigrants LA would catch an unsavoury disease and die.

We were illegal immigrants too, and our visas were nearly up. But working for the Director had given us another kind of visa meanwhile. We had an in. The Director was still on the mailing list for all kinds of studio parties, but he never went. Because Brett got to open his mail, she'd accept for him and get us on the guestlist too. This made me uneasy, because that damn journalist could be anywhere; she knew what I looked like, and she could have been anyone. I hadn't told Brett because I didn't want it complicating anything. I tried to override my panic, be cool, see the parties as just another necessary drag, as well as another reason to be glad I was tired of her friends. If I hadn't been I should have found it impossible not to cotton on to the people my age at these things, pathetically trying to relive some kind of dorky early-twenties thing I missed out on. This would have been such a mistake. You can get freeloading drunk with a bunch of whining losers any time of your life, but these parties were like air miles; work the room at enough of them and you get a free ticket out of your twenties.

It was at these things that I began to learn the value of research. Southern California is, like, the Trades Belt; the same idea as the Bible Belt, but everyone reads *Variety*. We were at a party somewhere in Burbank one time, and Brett dragged me over to some old UriZen money guy.

'You're English?' I had to admit it, though it pained me. LA was full of eager young faded aristocrats over from London – they were everywhere – all with Hugh Grant hair, all called things like Jasper or Fergus, all urgently needing to be kicked to death. Doltish rich kids with no imagination, following the conduit of money here from London or New York, then finding that they couldn't do it. In London or Manhattan you can hustle eighteen hours a day and get away with having nothing else to recommend you. Here you couldn't – the climate would kill you. Unless you were born here, you had to have something good about you, some species of talent or originality – something that would make people come to you, rather than you hustling them till they gave you half a deal to get rid of you. Bluff energy, a facility with racquet sports and a plausible manner were not enough. This was a secret shared by the hip cognoscenti. But there was a constant turnover of jerks from London, trying to do what they could get away with back there, full of empty hustle; trying to be players with nothing to play with. Running on fumes. It made you even more ashamed of being English than you ought to be.

'You know Johnny Marlboro?' he said.

I didn't, but I read the trades. It had been the talk of all the parties all week. I'd seen a feature on it back home, months ago, and remembered how improbable it seemed when I was reading about it. It had occurred to me that if we didn't get newspapers in the morning when our faculties are kind of dulled, we'd soon give them up.

This Marlboro guy ran a production company that made low-budget British films. It was called Tautology, and *Canary Wharf* was their third feature. Set in the tail-end of the Eighties, it was about a delayering, deadwood-stripping management consultant who puts hundreds of people out of work every day and, at night, tortures and kills homeless people, slipping what's left of them into the foundations of the docklands development scheme. Pretty deep, huh? But it had achieved notoriety for its graphic realism, done with cuts of meat, editing-suite trickery and genuine homeless people as actors; but after the single edition of outrage when some editor finally noticed it (*Ban This Sick Stunt!*), interest faded. It did okay in the art-houses.

But – I don't know, six months ago? – there was an IRA bomb, and part of the Docklands Light Railway had to be rebuilt. They had to dig up what was left of the original foundations, and they found human remains, dismembered and mutilated, and dating from the same period as the film. The tabloids picked up the story again and the police hauled him in. It was absurd, but he couldn't prove anything: the actors he used were homeless, weren't on residuals and couldn't be traced; he had produced, directed, and edited himself; and his cameraman and everyone else who worked on it were away, on some odyssey of a self-financed documentary shoot in Goa, and couldn't be contacted.

Something like that, anyway. The ruckus generated finally drove the owner of a lock-up leased by the real killer to put two and two together and turn him in, and the guy got acquitted last week.

'That was so fucked-up,' said the guy from UriZen. This seemed to be the complex and considered conclusion, on the circuit. What no one was talking about was that he'd been set up by the industry itself.

The cuts-of-meat thing had just been something for the press. Tautology had never expected anyone to take any notice outside the usual circuit. The graphic shots were a showcase for the program that created them: those weren't real eyes getting razored, real hands being microwaved; it was all done on a Mac. Everything you see in movies now has been manipulated. If there's a crowd scene, I don't know, a sports stadium doing a Mexican wave or whatever, that's a sample section duplicated ten thousand times. Or that classic process photography shot, interior of a moving car, city at night playing unreally in the back window. That's finished now. That's why it was played up so sweetly in the cab thing with Butch and Esmerelda – it was the last time anyone was going to use the old process.

Johnny Marlboro had been working with a bunch of programmers who were developing some new software for FX – the people who did the morphing in *CyberCop* and *Time Commando*. FX had needed a flesh simulator for *Prehistoric!* and *Good Money*, and these coders were making one. They had a whole series of flesh construction and deterioration sequences they were using as a showreel; once they sold the software, no one needed them. Johnny Marlboro, thought, cool, he could use this stuff; after all, all this excellent software was being used for otherwise was sight gags involving Dippy the Dinosaur. They did a deal, and he shot *Canary Wharf* in three weeks. It had needed to be that kind of story – torture, dismemberment – because all they had was limb shots, skin shots. Faces were a real problem for the coders. And hair.

Anyway, the studios who bought the FX programs had gotten wind of it, and slapped an injunction on him making any connection between his film and theirs. So when *Wharf* got all that stupid attention, he'd just said, offhand and kind of flip, that he'd used cuts of meat, and spliced it together with footage of real people in the editing suite. He hadn't really cared what anyone thought, since the movie was just a technical exercise anyway. But then – well. Things got a little prosaic in the interrogation suite. The police didn't understand it hadn't been real flesh, and Johnny Marlboro couldn't get anyone to go on record that it had been software that had generated it, because it had turned out to be the same software that was used in next summer's blockbusters. It had suddenly become, like, a billion-dollar project. One guy's little movie was all over the front pages, broadsheets too, and when things get that big, no one wants the slightest whiff of scandal. He could very well have gone down for ever, but the real psycho had confessed last week.

It was really kind of twisted, the way everyone was having some kind of outrage-fest when they'd been pretty comfortable with letting him swing for it two weeks ago. But now Brett and the money-guy were having some kind of impenetrable conversation – Brett had really flattered the pants off him earlier – about the cultural dynamics of video rental (*'The freeze-frame and rewind buttons on your VCR remote prefigured the invention of the mouse. Image selection and manipulation is the technological triumph of the late twentieth century.'*). When I tuned back in the UriZen guy was on to the rest of the future.

'Betamax. Nobody had any idea everyone could be so wrong. It was the better format. Still the industry standard, but Sony screwed up. They assumed the superior product was going to walk off the racks . . .'

'But the pornography licenses had all been nailed by VHS,' I interrupted.

He stepped back and spread his hands, impressed. Brett beamed at me. But this was something I knew about.

I'd begun to feel a little ashamed of how little I knew about movies. Up till now I'd kind of disdained all that. Creepy-looking guys in their thirties, with faded quiffs, pointy sideburns and an irritating line in waistcoats, who hang round arthouse coffee concessions talking loudly to pale pudgy women with downtown artsy coifs about Ford, Walsh, Lean–Powell–Truffaut. Fanboy film guys 101. People who write the name of the director as well as the movie on the spines of their alphabetized videotapes. Creeps. Film Buffs. Like English graduates who keep a shelf of smooth-spined Penguin Classics on parade in their apartments for the next forty years. Like, yeah – I bet you read them all the time. It was enough to put you off. Besides, listening to these people whining on about Fellini, Bertolucci, John Collier, Timothy White or whoever was like playing a CD of old TV themes and wondering if they'd mean anything more to you if you knew the shows. *Petticoat Junction* and *I Dream of Jeannie*. You could probably get them on cable or something but like – yeah, *I* have the time.

I was tired of all that horse's ass about the greats. Some loser old phoney whining on in the Weekends about the Western, about *noir*, about rewriting the syntax of film grammar. I hate that. It's like, you start liking movies just because you think they're pretty cool, and because maybe they take you out of yourself for a hundred minutes and leave you feeling like, I don't know, you're more like the kind of person you thought you were going to wind up as. But it's never enough just to like something anymore. You have to start justifying yourself, ransacking a vocabulary that meant nothing to you when you were just some kid with square eyes, isolating and dissecting whatever it was that made you like anything to begin with. Then you aren't so keen on the movie anymore, but what you do like is your reasons for liking it. This blows. I'd be happy to illustrate this with an example from my love life, but there aren't any. However, I'm prepared to speculate that guys hate to talk about their relationships because we know how much fun it is to take something apart – Walkmen, Shimanos – but we know also how quickly your interest fades when the bonnet is up and the guts are all over the floor. You don't know why your heart flips/You only know it does; it won't stay that way and when it doesn't, you need to leave it alone, and let it force the issue on its own.

You learn not to parade your love. If you do, you just sound dorky. I loved movies because . . . oh, the hell with it; because of the kind of videos you used to rent when someone's parents were on holiday. The kind you watch with shafts of low sun filtering through gaps in the curtains, over a rubble of squashed pizza boxes and beer cans, through a haze of Camel Lights. Movies featuring the photography of Tak Fujimoto, the total star presence of Bronson Pinchot and Anthony Michael Hall. With Andrew McCarthy and James Spader as the creeps who get the girl. Movies that were supposed to be eye-candy, catch a market, then fade away. I won't let them. Film Buffs may jeer all they want, but screw them; this is, after all, what *Bringing Up Baby* or *The Philadelphia Story* were made for. I'm an encyclopaedia of the kind of tapes you feel sorry for in the video store, tucked away even further back than the ones that feature helicoptors exploding in mid-air, or Michael Douglas's flabby white ass oscillating wildly. Of course, this is from when there were video stores galore, not just Blockbuster. *Pretty in Pink, Fast Times at Ridgemount High* – timewarps to the simpler, more innocent decade of the 1980s. *Ferris Bueller's Day Off, The Breakfast Club*; movies with kids stuck in some lousy situation and saying, time out here. What would we do, if we could do whatever we want? Because when you know what that is, there seems to be less in your way.

I'd love to know what it would be like to be totally sequestered from every cultural artefact after a certain period. Say you took a kid from birth and only exposed it to records and movies and TV shows up until the year I was born. If it wrote screenplays, would it write *Grease*? If you taught it to play guitar, would it come up with 'Hotel California'? I need to find out. I had an idea that the people who did all the things I thought were cool when I was a kid had already sat through all the old stuff themselves, so I could absorb it through them, by osmosis. But I'd begun to feel an unpleasant suspicion that this was not enough. I was also terrified of having Brett think I was, in fact, some semblance of my character in High 5. I set about rectifying the situation.

I read a few biographies, but knowing that Frank Capra was once a door-to-door salesman was about as useful as knowing that Humphrey Bogart never in fact says, play it again, Sam. They made me realize that I hate biographies, and everything they stand for. It's not enough that some guy made some cool movies. The star/fan paradigm has shifted from love and admiration to a kind of calculating jealousy. No one's interested in just watching the movies, and liking them, and going home happy. They want to know how Tarantino or whoever it was arrived at that precise stage in their life, as if by mimicking every convolution, they might find themselves someday whispering tips on being supercool to Tim Roth too. They don't want to trust to their own abilities in case they're not enough, and everyone knows how fast the turnaround is. It's difficult not to. I used to think it was funny, how no one wanted to be an old-style star anymore – the kind who had the one thing you couldn't force upon yourself. But now I knew; this industry is like someone handing out flyers in the underground, meant for tourists but during the rush hour, until the floor is thick with them. Books were no use to me; I needed information. I needed to be able to say, why don't we do a cutaway from the tracking shot then dissolve to a pan intercut with a three-way reaction like whoever did in whatever. There was nothing for it. It was time to involve myself with the fanboy pantheon.

I found a video store called ViKTRS Video on Hermosa Beach. The title was short for 'Video Killed The Radio Star', which was what drew me to it in the first place. It was a cool place; it was like the anti-Blockbuster, so it stocked almost everything I needed. I took out a different tape every day, to watch when I'd otherwise be poodling about, drinking my coffee and having a look at what was in the printer from last night. It was usually deserted, so pretty soon the staff commenced to take the piss with my film-fag choices, putting Sonny Chiba tapes in my box of *North By Northwest* or *Holiday* or whatever. Like, yuk yuk, fellas. But I trounced them one day when I overheard two of the clerks arguing about a peripheral character in *Nightmare on Elm Street 4*. I pointed out that the actress in question had also been a camp counsellor and one of the token hot-chicks-in-bikinis in *Halloween 3* and *5* respectively, as well as a headless prom queen in *The Return of the Living Dead*. Their interest, or possibly chagrin, aroused at getting faced down by someone as anal as them, they pressed me, and I reeled off the names of every bit-part player John Carpenter ever used. What can I say? I had too much free time when I was growing up. But when they found out I was the John Hughes-meister, they thought I was dope. They thought I was superfly. It was cool with them, in the way it's cooler to say you like the Carpenters over the Velvets. Not just because The Velvet Underground is like, muso fanboy 101, but it's like, in order to acquire bad taste, you must have knocked yourself out already, assembling a flawless sensibility. Which was what I was working on.

It turned out they were kind of the same as me, after all. They'd started the store with the money they would otherwise have used for film school, figuring that hanging out watching movies all day and arguing about them was a more productive way to spend their time. Emil said, film school is where you learn about the industry rather than where you learn about movies – who's allowed to piss off who, how much, and at what stage of development. I could buy that. They turned into my friends – kind of – that summer. I wished I'd had more time, now that my existence seemed to be less divorced from my life. But having far too much to do is pretty much the same as having far too little. This wasn't something I was ready to know yet. And then it was time to go.

Emil and Robert notified me once that the director of *Five Easy Pieces* got the money to make it from his role in the deployment of The Monkees. They didn't know why this broke me up, because they didn't know who I was. I was just some kid who kind of obsessed on the back catalogue of Winona. I don't think they'd ever watched TV in real time; as far as they were concerned, there was too much else you could choose from, and control the rate and frequency of information flow besides. They also told me about the video format wars, and this was how I impressed the money guy at the party. I felt my stock with Brett rising, even as I said it.

But as the money guy initiated a monologue about DVD vs CD+ she commenced to look distinctly thundery. You had to know her pretty well to see it, because she was still smiling away at the guy, who was maintaining exhausting eye contact with her. I nudged River's arm, and we turned away like we were having a conversation of our own.

'What's with Brett?'

'Search me. Maybe she thinks he's hitting on her. These old guys still think people don't know that sleeping your way into the business means you're never really going to get anywhere.'

I could understand her pique, even if it was probably misplaced here. But everyone hit on her, and all the time. Even the Director took a shine to her, the old goat. It brought me up kind of sharp. It had become difficult for me to see her as the world saw her – as a genuine, girl-type girl, and one you probably knew once, back when she'd been the infant proprietor of woolly red tights and a lazy eye. Sweet and ugly. Maybe a couple of years later, when she beat you up and ripped your shirt and made you cry, because she liked you. Then you lost track of her trajectory for a while, and suddenly she was the kind of young woman who found it expedient to be squired around by guys in singlets in dinky urban jeeps, rather than hang out with skinny losers with a nice line in smarts but an unhealthy familiarity with the back catalogues of Patsy Cline and Johnny Ray. But she was back. Just when you thought you were safe, and it was difficult to deal with. I'd kind of put a lid on it, not long after we started working for the Director. Something happened. The kind of thing you don't want to think about too much.

It had been a terrifyingly long day – I'd been writing all the previous afternoon and night, we'd arrived at the scary Munster-type mansion on Sunset Boulevard at eight, and it was now around seven. The Director had gone out for pizza, and Brett and River and me were out on the back lawn, smoking cigarettes. I really shouldn't have been, since the air had kind of sucked that week; though I'd always been better in America, because they've had catalytic converters since the early Seventies, so they've even had time to filter down to poor persons' vehicles. We were just kind of shooting the breeze, when the llama of the Director's third wife – who lived in Prague now, with the daughter from his first marriage – sauntered over the lawn to us. It nuzzled River's shoulder, then walked away a few paces, stopped and regarded us over its shoulder.

'Look,' said Brett happily. 'He wants us to follow him.'

It was like *Lassie*. We trailed after it, down over the lawn, into the jungle of eucalyptus and cypress between the house and the pool. It didn't seem to have any mission for us – no smugglers pretending the old house on the cliff was haunted so they could unload their swag there, no old skinflint to unmask as the real Terror of the Abandoned Mine – so we walked over to the pool and reclined on the grass, propping ourselves up on our elbows. Brett lay back, put her head on the meat of my thigh, which was no big deal, I reminded myself, and closed her eyes. It was so quiet we could hear the crisp, tearing sound of the llama cropping grass the other side of the trees.

I felt light; light as a whisper on the breeze. Every cell in my

139

body seemed to tingle. I had felt the first, not unpleasant, symptoms of oxygen deficiency enough times to know them for what they were; send feelers out to the tendrils of my lungs, feel their incipient tightness, and gulp down some Ventolin before it really kicked in. But this time I thought I was just trancing out on the afternoon; so when my throat filled with Kleenex and my chest with cotton wool, I went rigid with shock. *I'm back*, shrieked the asthma from my ribcage, shrill with joyful malice. *And whaddaya know? I'm tired of you, fat boy. How d'you think I feel, riding around in a dork like you? Think the time's come, buddy. Can't jerk around with you forever.* I scrabbled at my jacket pocket, other hand going straight to my collar and tearing it open. I pulled out my inhaler and slammed the canister down into the mouthpiece; it gave half a *phut*, and died. I held it up to eye level, hands shaking as I twisted the canister round, then jammed it back between my lips and tried again – nothing. By now Brett and River were sitting up, eyes wide with dismay, mouthing things at me from another dimension. I struggled upright, choking, drowning in air that had acquired the consistency of warm Häagen-Dazs, and held out the Ventolin for them to see. It dropped through my fingers and fell into the pool.

Then my head was in Brett's lap, sweat pouring through my shirt and darkening my jacket. I heard River shouting instructions, but his voice sounded like it came from the bottom of a well. Brett sat down with her knees drawn up and her head tucked between them, and River pulled me over, draped me over the curve of her back with my legs either side and my arms hooked over her shoulders. Then he ran away up through the trees, back toward the house.

I don't recall how long we stayed like that. I remember admiring my pulling technique, which appeared to have developed to include suavely wheezing and perspiring over the girl I'd set my heart on. Presently, the imminence of my demise receded like the tide at Camber Sands. Of course they'd done all the right things;

my thorax was raised, the pressure was off, the bound-up muscles in my chest had a chance to reacquaint themselves with their function. Presently she helped me down, and lay me in her lap again, her hair falling around her face as she stroked mine back off my forehead. She was murmuring all the while, but I was kind of tuned out, and it was a while before I realized she was actually talking, not just mouthing reassurance.

'. . . something I've never told anyone before. I've carried this round for so long.' My eyes fluttered open. She was gazing out over the pool, the fingers of one hand still twined in my hair. 'Not even River knows all of it. Okay?'

I must have made some gesture of assent, or maybe I didn't need to – she went on anyway.

'I know you must think I'm some kind of monster for coolly suggesting offing that woman after the casino. It wasn't on my mind when I took you there. It wasn't on my mind at all. I was just thinking about, I don't know, maybe making friends with her, getting her to make up a syndicate with us. I mean, she did ask me to come over earlier. And then . . . oh, things were crazy anyway. All night. All day before. Things fell into place. It didn't seem so real. And you see, there was a precedent. It isn't the first time I've – oh, I don't know.' She traced a finger around my eyes. 'Been there when someone died.'

I blinked up at her. I didn't want to hear this.

'Our uncle used to freak out for a few weeks once or twice a year. It didn't matter when we were away at school, but if he felt it coming on during the holidays, he used to send us away. It was kind of exciting; being woken at four to find the housekeeper packing our luggage and the plane fuelled to fly at dawn. We got sent to stay with his first wife's children from her second marriage. They were two boys and a girl, but I hated her – ponies and ribbons. I used to stick with River and the boys. Every now and then they'd get full of testosterone and forbid me to come with them.' She laughed, briefly. 'I even had to fight them a couple of times to make them let me come camping, or fishing, or whatever they were doing. Then one time they went skiffing out on the lake. We'd done it lots of times the summer before, but this was spring recess, and the weather wasn't so predictable. They didn't want me to come, and there was a dreadful row. Even River turned on me.'

She took a breath and went on.

'They were going out to the middle of the lake to look at, y'know, some copies of *Playboy* or something. Where no one could catch them doing it. I'd heard them talking about it, and I definitely wasn't invited. I hung around anyway and followed them, then confronted them again out by the jetty. I said I knew what they were going to do, and if they didn't let me come I'd tell on them. I really wanted to go. Partly because I hated being left out of their gang when it suited them, just because I was a girl. But mostly because I was curious too.

'You are at that age. You understand that there are parts of the world that are being deliberately kept from you. Like terminal illness, or madness. Sex is just some kind of particularly colourful rumor when you're eight, unless you're especially unfortunate, I suppose. This would be confirmation of it. Along with real, documentary evidence. Like the instruction diagrams from a pack of condoms someone brings in to school one day. D'you remember? Anyway. Eventually they let me come, partly out of fear that I would rat on them, but I think partly to gauge my reaction to whatever they were planning to do. For once I was going to be allowed to come along as a girl, not as an honorary boy. I wasn't actually sure if I liked this. Anyway. We rowed out to the middle in the skiff, and Steve produced some cigarettes – to get the transgression under way I suppose. We all made a terrible job of smoking them, but with as much aplomb as we could muster. Then they hemmed and hawed around, trying to get the conversation round to it. I was impatient. I suppose most children see their mothers coming out of the shower or whatever. But I hadn't the faintest idea of what a woman looked like under her clothes. The only women I ever came into contact with were teachers, and one pilot we used to have. I'd kind of assumed that their, you know, figures were just part of their clothes – like bustles, but in the fronts of their dresses too? But I'd heard them talking about pictures of naked women, and I wanted to see. So I was like, trying to get them to cut to the chase, but they were just getting sillier and sillier. Like boys do. So eventually I just lunged for the knapsack. Steve went for it too, and overbalanced, and then the boat tipped over.

'I was furious. River and Andy swam for shore and I started after them, but when I turned round to look for Steve he was back, by the skiff, holding his knapsack out of the water in one hand and trying to swim with the other. We'd all been wearing quite heavy clothes – it was only spring – and he wasn't staying up so well. I went back to help him, but when I got there he was going down.

'People panic when they're drowning. When I grabbed hold of him he started to fight me. I think he thought I was trying to get at the knapsack, because he held it in the air behind him and pushed at me with his other arm. He started to go down again in like, seconds, but this time he was pulling me with him. I don't really know what happened next. For all kinds of reasons, I overreacted. I grabbed at his head and pushed him under, maybe so I could get free and back to the surface, maybe to calm him down. Anyway, he didn't come back up. I looked round for him, but there was no sign at all. I tried to call out to the others, but they were still splashing towards the side, and I was having a hard time keeping my head up myself. I swam out after them. I remember persuading myself, once I'd got enough momentum going to be able to breathe properly, that Steve had just been playing a trick on me, and that if I turned round I'd see him. But when it got shallow enough to stand, the lake behind me was still as a millpond. The other two were lying on the beach, too exhausted to turn over. Neither were very good swimmers. I sobbed out some of what had happened – I already knew I'd done something terrible, and so diminished my part in it – and we just kind of stood around and cried and wailed at each other for a while. We were terrified of someone finding what we'd been up to, most of all. I think Andy and Steve had stolen the magazines from their father's closet, and Andy was almost apoplectic with horror at the volume of admissions he'd have to make if the whole thing came out. So by the time we went for help we were all totally hysterical, and it was too late. Way too late.

'They had to dredge the lake for Steve's body. It took a whole day. I remember us sitting in the movie we'd been packed off to – *Smokey and the Bandit* – ashen-faced with fear they'd find the knapsack. Steve had been quite forgotten, for the moment. But if they did trawl it up with the corpse, they never said anything about it. We were sent back to our uncle, who was still pretty loopy; we had to go and stay with the housekeeper. The horror of what had happened only really set in then. I never told anyone what really went on. Not even River. And so you see, I was a murderess by the time I was eight. And no one knew.'

I had listened quietly, furiously computing the new vectors of bluff and counter-bluff this implied. I was breathing okay now, if a little wheezily. Clearly it behove me to say something.

'Poor thing,' I croaked. 'Been awful.' Wrong tack. I went to touch her face, but she batted my hand away and held it firmly.

'I don't want sympathy. I just want you to understand. I'd done it before. Even if it was kind of an accident. But no one knew. Only me. I've carried it around with me ever since. Can you imagine? I've always known how easy, how really inconsequential it can be, to make some life just . . . end.'

She fell silent, and looked away. Nice, which I'd practically forgotten about, slithered unwholesomely back into the frame. Clearly I could never tell her the truth; this would imply that I'd let her carry that volume of guilt, on top of existing trauma, and let the old wounds run fresh, almost for my own amusement. Jesus. The woman she thought we'd killed and robbed probably just imagined she'd passed out from the purity of the coke, counted herself lucky not to have OD'd, and, after a couple of days with a headache, felt nothing more than embarrassment over the whole incident. We'd probably even done her a favour; it might have shamed her into giving up on that stupid fooling around. But I could forget it. There was no way I could tell her the money we'd played with had come from High 5. Maybe one day – and *please* let it be soon – when our futures were assured, and bound together inextricably, I could tell her we never killed anyone. When I could afford to. But of course I had to let it remain the dark backdrop for now, for whatever reason I chose to present to myself.

She was quiet for a while, and I lay in her lap, trying not to think about the current feeling that I had, which was kind of like being some guy up on a minor coke bust who'd told the desk sergeant he was a writer, simply out of whatever drunken bravado remained from the debauch that had brought him here. Just so he wouldn't have to say he was unemployed.

'Do you feel bad?' She was looking at me, warily.

I didn't know what to say.

'A little, I guess.'

'Then don't. We are here now. Come here.' Which wasn't necessary, because I was here already.

Well, you try and rewind the tape. One moment someone isn't lithe and alive in your arms, the next they are. You don't know how they got there. Star of a thousand kisses, and you don't remember one.

Somewhere, ten years ago, I'd made the decision that, because the jocks and prom-queens were doing it all over the place, copping off was somehow pushy and beneath me. It had never got me anywhere. All it seemed to have involved was treating myself like a locked car, with a big showy stoplock across the steering wheel but the stereo still there for anyone to take. I could give it up now, if I wanted.

We sprang apart after a while, and kind of mentally circled each other, gasping like wrestlers. It was the moment to start something forever, or let it go and not be sorry. Now the time was here I wanted to push it away back into the future. The urge to extend deadlines was nothing new, but there was something else here too. I was scared. When you're young you love and you hate, and you really love, or you really hate. But I was twenty-five in a few months and things were very different now. What you feel when you're fifteen and what you feel when you're twenty-five is like the difference in your respective smoking styles. At fifteen you don't inhale properly, and the smoke is thick and rich and random, rising in the air; but when you're twenty-five you suck it right back, and though you can blow rings with it, and let it slip over your lip and up your nose, and do all kinds of neat tricks with it, it's thinner and less surprising to you. You begin to suspect that you have got to the end of smoking. It occurs to you one day, and in a way that you can't instantly dismiss, that it's time to give up.

Besides, the Brett situation was too complicated. It would mean problems with River, who was, even though he didn't let it show too much, a bit weird about his sister; though given their background, I was thankful he wasn't worse. He'd need time to get used to the idea, if Brett and I were to start anything. There was too much on the line for that to happen now.

Also, amongst the many delusions I was labouring under, I had the idea, in the way that you do after you've just dumped someone like a really scaly piece of trash, that I knew all about how not to screw it up next time. It seemed like, you know, you meet someone in your or their early twenties and you know they're right for you; but you also suspect you're both going to go to hell and back over the next few years. So either you try to wait a little while, and risk them going round the block a few times with even bigger morons than you, and ending up totally beyond repair. Or you hang on to them now, and risk finding out that love is like the news: there isn't enough to fill a whole bulletin every day, so ministers cheerfully admitting to being arms dealers on the sly get the same column space as some actress's commonplace. The monstrously inconsequential receives the same headline time as things that ought to scare you to death, just to fill the half-hour slot. Soon you can't tell the difference anymore, and you discover you don't care.

But it felt like there was a third option now, this late in the game. I was almost done with the book at this point. It was okay. Everything was going to be okay. We weren't going to have to do any of the stupid grinding circuit, pitching to every chancer that felt like wasting our time, while desperation and despair drove deserts between us. We weren't behaving like every other loser in this town, and there was no reason to start doing it now. I felt a hot flush of pride at having got myself in a position to swing it. Some kind of creative working relationship for the next few years would keep us close as lovers to the exclusion of everyone else, yet keep the burning of the boats at arm's length, till we were finally ready to reel one another in.

We were quiet for a long while, and eventually River and the Director came back with a new inhaler. They'd had to drive ten miles to get it; I didn't really need it now, but took a few theatrical gasps on it anyway. It would've looked pretty silly otherwise. We went back to the house, and after I'd assured everyone I was all right about a million times, we lounged about in the garden a while, talking about nothing.

★

Brett used to laugh at me for the way I digress when I talk. She said if you could see the words coming out of my mouth, they'd be in cyan. I can't help it; I get distracted. Anyway, why stick to the point when nothing else does? I can't take trying to live my life like it was a story, replete with motivation, upholstered with significance, and heading for a neat conclusion. I can't help feeling that when I'm finally wrapped, it will not be a wrap. Though maybe I'm alone in this.

So anyway, back at the party, the money guy was still talking. I was surprised he was wasting so much time on us, but Brett had done her now-familiar trick of researching everything there was to know about him beforehand, then playing it back to him as flattery disguised as inquisitiveness. It generally worked, because no one in the business ever knows about anything except the events of the very recent past, and usually only those that had a direct bearing on them personally.

'You know the first instinct was to try and buy out the VCR manufacturers? Suppress production? And when that fell through they tried to limit the functions of home VCR, so it couldn't compete? No one saw that it could expand penetration far beyond the theatres without significantly altering the original form. When everything else failed, retail cassettes were pegged at hundreds of dollars, actively to discourage purchase.'

He was assuming he knew more than we did, simply because he'd been in the business thirty years and we hadn't. He couldn't have been more wrong. The people outside understand better because they're far enough away from the randomness to see patterns emerging. He was totally wrong about VCR, even now. The killer app of the product was that it allowed consumers to disrupt the linearity of time. This was a big, big deal. I can't remember what the world was like before home VCR, but I imagine it must have been like banking was before ATMs or debit cards. Imagine, having to take time out to queue up inside buildings that were only open when no one was around, and pick up huge rolls of cash to last you till you had to do the same damn thing again. It must have been the same with TV and movies before VCR. You had to see what you wanted when someone else decided you could. This was why VCR was so excellent – you finally got some control. You could do what you wanted without missing out. I was not surprised it had worried these people.

'Now cassette and cable are where you look first for pre-sales,' he was saying. 'Not to the theatres. A good percentage of the time we can cut them out of the margin altogether.'

'But you're talking about multimedia,' said Brett, sounding for all the world as though she didn't know everything there was to know about it already.

'No one is going to make the same mistakes again. Control the formats! Fuck the writers, and fuck the stars. Control the formats, and they'll have nowhere else to go.'

'Formats!' spat River, aside to me. He was drunker than he ought to have been. 'Someone ought to reformat *him*.'

About a half-hour later, the money guy fell over and began to make strange noises. He was carried out on a stretcher, and *Variety* wrote it up as stress fatigue. Later River claimed that he'd slipped him some trips, but we were both caned at the time and I didn't know if I believed him. It was a week after I'd finished the book, and Brett had just finished a polish. We'd been talking, naturally, about the lengths you had to go to in this business. They'd tried practically everything before they met me.

'We did a spec treatment for a sitcom once. We spent weeks on it. A young woman comes from an ethnic minority family that still keeps its old religion. She upsets her community when she marries a corporate-type guy with no religion except stripy shirts and golf; he expects that she'll give up the traditional practices of her people to be his career woman counterpart. She kind of agrees, but her family go supernova – this guy is, like, secularity cubed, and they're the last members of an ancient faith. So there's the premise. The husband tries to network his way to success, but the wife's family mess things up, and she has to use her spiritual savvy to sort it. We'd done two whole episodes before we realized we'd written *Bewitched*.' River puffed out smoke and rolled his eyes.

'The critical thing right now is scarcity of ideas,' said Brett. 'You know? This whole generation got rich recycling the stuff they liked when they were young – *Star Wars*, *Indiana Jones*, *Batman*, *Star Trek*, everything, even our stuff: *Tank Girl* – *Dredd*, for heaven's sake – and loused them up. What's left for us?'

'It's the same in music,' I said. It was the night after we went to see the Director that last time, our last night in LA. We were all pretty drunk, and trying to justify to ourselves that we were doing the right thing. There was an end-of-term, end-of-vacation kind of sadness, but I was secretly up about getting out of here. It had been a pretty good summer but now I wanted the next phase to begin; it was going to be cool, and I'd been too long away.

I guess it was different for Brett and River. They were about to do the thing their mother never did, and commit, in the eyes of the world, to a discrete item of intellectual property, a piece of business.

'You know? Was this an exercise in regret for the loss of a presumed simplicity that didn't know its future?' River was pretty good at the film school stuff. 'A seeking to revive national common imperatives by drawing on narratives from the final era of ideological coherence and common belief? Or were they just too fucking lazy to think up their own ideas?' He lit his Lucky and winked at me. 'Find out, after this message.'

'The point being,' said Brett acidly, shooting him a look, 'that it doesn't matter if you control the format. The format is just hardware. The really valuable thing is the software that convinces the market they can't live without it. With home VCR it was pornography; with PCs it was the spreadsheet. Interesting, no? That it takes things that blow to make cool stuff freely available? The guy who invented spreadsheets didn't make a cent out of it, but they're what put a PC in every company. Once that was established, and accountants felt okay about PCs, wordprocessing and database put one on every desk. It's just the same in this industry. Everybody wants to be Apple and IBM at the same time. They want to be fly, like Apple were, and come up with the killer innovations that are going to turn the industry around. But they also know that in ten years they won't have the energy to sustain that kind of drive, and they don't want to find themselves usurped; so they try, at the same time, to be big – so big that no individual ever has to take responsibility for a decision. But of course Apple and IBM both cut their own throats by refusing to license. We are, young men, entering the entertainment industry at a critical time. Like that old sonofabitch said . . .'

'I wish I'd given him more,' said River, languidly. 'I'm not sure it should have had any effect. The CIA used to administer sixty times that to squaddies, but it didn't do sixty times more damage.'

'I still can't believe that.' I didn't think it was so damn funny.

'It was as much as he had on him, leave him alone,' said Brett. 'And besides, that lousy old twister negotiated our mother's contracts. He was the one who stopped her ever doing anything except the circuit.'

This was like, the same reason why it's a really bad idea to go out clubbing with med students. You're recounting some hilarious drug anecdote and everyone laughs, except one bastard who says, with quiet sincerity, I saw a fourteen-year-old girl die of that yesterday. This is the same ex-good old boy who just told a story featuring beer, a boarding house bedspread, and dual incontinence. *Salud*, buddy.

'You see what we're up against? No one has our interests at heart. They're all at profoundly unstable junctures in their careers, however entrenched they might appear to us. This is going to make things even harder than they usually are. It's important we're clear on this, otherwise we might start thinking there's something deficient about us. Okay?'

This was not the giddy last night I'd envisaged. We were all feeling kind of weird, but I could understand that this was just the shoreward swell of undercurrents that had been gathering all summer.

It had been easy to avoid noticing. This is one true cliché of LA. The only way to hold yourself together in the inhuman light of broad day is with work and the pursuit of money. Otherwise you'd be vaporized, like the single brief whisp of white cloud you might see some day as you went out for a paper, dissipating in front of your eyes into the uniform deep blue. If you didn't assign your existence as much purpose as you felt you could bear, you'd feel forever like someone who's on their third drink at lunch when they know they shouldn't be; and though the declaration of unilateral holiday feels just dandy now, you know the evening will make you pay. You know when you've earned something and when you haven't; this is why you never do everything you promise yourself, when you're working, that you will, if you get a break between contracts. When you do finally get a month or two off, you walk into town, and however nice a morning it is, all you see are retired guys and dead-eye guys. You don't want to be either yet. For months now I hadn't had time to notice anything except the immediate obstructions to getting to tomorrow, but it had seemed totally natural to be that busy – kind of instinctual. Likc the way cell-building stuff in your body travels down to your hand, and works out that it's just so far from the tip of your finger and so far from your wrist; so it'll construct itself as a knuckle-cell. It was always the same, whenever I went to Los Angeles. It happens to everybody. You take on a priority function in the hive when you enter 213 or 818. You don't want to think about how it might feel to be there with nothing real to do. This was what stung most about Loulou and the rest. With the desert and the mountains between you and the rest of the planet, you know you're going to whale on you forever if you didn't use this while you could.

It was only now, when it was over, that I noticed things I'd been feeling all summer, things I'd been too busy to pick up on at the time. There had been, under the rush, some kind of – I don't know. I don't know whether it was just Brett or what, but if something small went right for me, if something good happened – like I was, whatever, at Gelson's and I asked for some oranges and the guy picked out six for me, including the only one that was wrapped in tissue paper – then even as I unwrapped it and spread it out on the counter at home, tracing my fingers happily over the exotic print; if anything nice happened, I'd always give an involuntary inward shudder of dismay, because I knew that even tiny things going my way could cumulatively queer the big one, and that was the only one that mattered. It was like, I was happy if I went out without my wallet and had to have the cab driver circle all the way back to be paid. This was good, that a bad thing happened, and I wanted lots more. I didn't want young women making eye-contact with me across grocery aisles and notifying me that ordinary, relatively happy existence was going on everywhere. It broke my heart that people could be nice in an everyday sort of way. Talking about it makes you sound like a dork besides. So, I had that trepanning kind of empty-apartment regret and unfocussed dread that seems to be automatically brought on by the smell of raised dust and carpet cleaner, as I shut the door of my flat for the last time and drove my meagre stuff over to Brett's for storage. I didn't feel like I'd been dumped on enough to deserve what ought to start happening now.

It complicated things that we were going to London. It was all very well for Brett and River, but I came from there – well, England, anyway – and in the ablative case was where I was keen for it to stay. Moreover, I was known there. The cheerful anonymity of Southern Cali, where waiters had a higher profile than me, suited me just dandy. I was counting on Brett being on the money about the weakness of the currency making London like, you know, Hemingway's Paris. I wanted very badly to believe it, and like, Paris, yeah, okay. But London? Right. Paris wasn't full of dorks to begin with.

I know if you're a certain kind of kid growing up in the provinces, then London is supposed to be your insurance. Like the way I'm saving everything Lou Reed did post-Velvets for when I turn thirty. In the same way that someone tries to avoid hearing the football scores so they can watch the game later, I go to the bathroom in a club if anything that sounds even vaguely like Lou Reed comes on. I'm reserving it for my dotage; for after I turn thirty. I'm pretty sure there won't be any other cool music around then, and I think of it as insurance.

So London's supposed to make up for twenty-odd years of having your consumer impulses frustrated by the lousy rural facilities. I'd barely even been there. When I was caught up in what I'd never allowed myself to dream might be possible, all I saw of it was Wardour Street, White City and Wembley Arena. I supposed that one day I'd have to earn my disdain.

Fortunately even if I'd wanted to see any of it now, I couldn't have lured Brett and River out of the apartment we rented with promises of Scott Baio lapdancing the Queen in Piccadilly. Beyond business, they were so not interested. Brett said she'd once had a high school economics textbook called *The Decline of the British Economy 1945+*, and I wasn't in any position to argue. I had to ditch the heavy-lidded West wonderland cool that I was planning to alternate with a dumb Hackett-and-Peter-Jones kind of Englishness I'd thought I might need to affect while squiring them round Chatsworth, Stratford, Salisbury, declaiming on Pugin, Vanbrugh, William Morris. Without it, I felt kind of at a loss. I felt I ought to make some kind of an effort, but what would you show someone who's never been to England, to mark their card with what it means to be at the edge of a continent, at the end of a century? You could, I don't know, maybe drive them up the M1 in a Ford Mondeo wearing polyester suits; eat oat bran cereal at Newport Pagnell; make them trawl the aisles of Meadowhall in matching his 'n' hers Gore-Tex and Timberlands; take them windsurfing on Grasmere? I was profoundly thankful they didn't care. They wouldn't have paid any attention anyway. We sure do love your English faux-Edwardian personal freshness product franchise. The only aspect of England they were remotely interested in was TV, but not even the programmes. They were fascinated by the commercials, which they said they'd read a lot about, and quickly became adept at spotting imports that hadn't been tweaked for the home market: Ferrero Rocher's astounding ambassador; the monstrous cheesiness of the Pringles and L'Oreal-bopping teens; and the Fruitopia Strawberry Passion Awareness and Citrus Consciousness campaigns, which kind of doubled it back, having maybe seemed a little weird in America but worked okay here. They liked the billboards outside churches best – You're not too bad to come in, you're not too good to stay out. River said that was almost as good as the classic Roach motel – 'Roaches check in, but they don't check out'. But I had the hell of a time explaining any that I thought was good. The Boddington's 'Cream of Manchester' series was running a showcase retrospective:

RIVER: What's a Cornecko?
ME: Cornetto.
BRETT: What's a Cornetto?
ME: It's a kind of, uh, individual semi-premium ice-cream product.
RIVER AND BRETT [*in unison, and quite genuinely distraught*]: But you said this was a commercial for a *beer*!

The hell with here. We had work to do.

It was the day in my life when, were I Patty Hearst, I would be making my first appearance on surveillance cameras. It was the end of summer. An actress had slept through June in a glass case in a gallery; politics had come, once more, to mean about as much as the Pepsi Challenge; the living had outstripped the dead. Statues of gods had woken up and drank, living aliens had been dissected on primetime TV, Milan *carabinieri* had found themselves picking lead out of the last of the Guccis. And somewhere, out there, had been millions like us; sitting up straight on the back of the bus, dressing like the victims of Seventies' serial killers, walking the dog through endless mass-produced streets, flipping with resigned longing through the magazine rack at the superstore. It had felt like the cruellest punishment in the world to have to work so madly through a summer, but knowing this only distilled our resolve. It felt like the interminable waiting was over.

So I sat on America, and got ready for England. I tried to forget I'd just come from a nation where going to the casino is just like going to the supermarket, only even more darkly exciting. I tried to forget I was back in a country that was stuck in some kind of throwback to the worst of America, the Disney-drought of the Seventies: half the citizens chilling in consummate self-regard, anaesthetized on trash; half dangerous rednecks who could turn at any moment. So on with it. Various matters were expedient.

Going over to the Director's that last time was fatal, not least because it was finishing the process of turning an employer into a friend. This has been abused too much already. I had all kinds of alarm bells when Brett first suggested it, but she brooked no argument.

He'd started the summer by having nothing to do with us – he'd been pretty resentful about the whole thing, having not noticed, two decades ago, a clause concerning rights to his writings patched into a finance package for one of his movies – but Brett went out of her way to charm the pants off him, and make it clear that we were at the vanguard of a new generation, who had done their research and felt very keenly the debt they owed him. I was pretty disdainful about this, not least because it meant Brett got to goof off with the Director the whole time, leaving me alone with her brother, who was about as keen to be foraging about in a dusty crawl-space all day, trawling through sheafs of cliquey puff-pieces, as I was. Moreover, I detested his movies. They started off okay around the end of the Fifties, when he'd been one of the last directors to be contracted to a studio, but swiftly degenerated in the Sixties and Seventies into the sort of horrible allegedly-iconoclastic critical circle jerks – featuring attacks on privileged schooling, satires on middle-class bureaucracy, and the Grim Epiphanies of the Working Man – that inspired the foundation of film schools, and permitted the perpetration of arts programming. It was disconcerting for him to become more than two-dimensional.

Brett went ahead and did it anyway. She'd told him all about her being at UCLA by then, and had worked on him to such an extent that he readily agreed to an exclusive interview for the film school journal, which Brett planned to conduct just before we left. I had been pretty dismissive of the idea at first, but ultimately it came to seem a logical extension of my movie-history project. Even if I didn't like his movies, he had, after all, worked with practically everybody.

So this is where we went, just before we left. It was the saddest day I've ever seen. It wasn't just that we were leaving; it was him.

It had never really occurred to me that the two main indexes I filed him under – old guy, industry darling – might be sources of profound unhappiness to him. But it was excruciating, listening to him. It must be a terrible thing to be old and feel that you have been wrong. I mean, I only had twenty-four years to deal with;

he had three times that. It must be repetitively, surprisingly painful to see women – women who used to be in your gang, when you were young and swell and clever – described by journalists as 'feisty', when everyone knows that this is just shorthand for old, bitter and mad. I wondered how I'd feel if it was Brett, rouge besmeared across drooping lips, rings clanking on her wasted fingers, holed up in one of those creepy Munster-type houses on Sunset, being called 'feisty'. It would have hurt more than I can say.

This was what had really brought me down when we got to London. We were about to do everything that was a source, albeit indirectly, of sadness to an old man, who had only got a senile llama to remind him of the last person who loved him. It had never occurred to me that he might not have loved his movies; that he made them because no one was going to pay for him to make his own; and that once he'd made enough to do what he wanted, the impulses that would have made them good had upped and gone – undelivered with the papers some morning. It hadn't occurred to me that he might have once been as desperate as I thought I was now.

There wasn't much time to moon over it. We were here to do a job. Brett had certainly done her research, though when I can't imagine. Whenever I inquired how she knew some ungodly nuance or bizarre foible of the industry we were about to scam, she said she'd had to bone up on it to deal with UriZen over their mother's biography, while I was authoring the book back in LA there. It was unlikely River had been much help. I supposed she'd done all the work while he goofed off. Such a stoner, honestly.

Even her short-term plan was not concerned with the book itself, but what its existence as a kind of résumé on the open market would do for us. ('It's like Windows 95,' she'd said. 'Remember the launch? How much money they threw at it? It was make-or-break for Microsoft that it sold. There wasn't anything especially new about it, except that it was a platform to run future products, without which they couldn't work. Once the computer equivalent of VHS vs Betamax had been done to death, they had to come up with something new. Don't be so linear. There are three of us. We aren't going to live off books alone.')

Left to my own devices, my efforts at submission would have been some kind of nightmare Betty Blue thing, but Brett went straight for the money-shot. She rented two rooms and a kitchen above a shop on Westbourne Grove, bought desks and chairs at IKEA, and leased a PowerMac and a Pentium, a colour laser, a scanner and a couple of phones. She set me up as an agent, with her and River my sole clients. This bothered me, because agents were becoming more interesting than the people they represented, and if anyone started sniffing around, it would complicate matters in a way I didn't want. Brett said it was more evidence of the business being more interesting than the product, but that was the only way I was going to be able to come along to meetings and stuff, and I wouldn't have missed that for the world. I did, however, go so far as to bleach my hair and start growing a goatee, because I assumed the publishing people would recognize me from High 5 – they were, after all, industry – but Brett and her brother found this almost unbearably risible.

'Do me a favour,' she said, when I'd confessed the reasons for my new degeneracy of aspect, and she'd finished chortling. 'These people wouldn't recognize Ben from Curiosity. Jesus. Go and shave. You look like a farmhand.'

We needed to present it as a *fait accompli*, a total package. While we were waiting for the stuff to come through I whisked them both back to my parents' house when I knew they'd be away to take their picture. I used my retard-proof Olympus in my sister's attic room for a *trompe-l'oeil* version of Henry Wallis's *Chatterton* that I saw in the Tate one time; River, powdered wan to look consumptive, draped along the bed beneath the dormer window; Brett lying underneath at the other end, face-on to the camera, chin propped in her fists. It was excellent, though we had to wait all afternoon to get the light right. My sister was around – it was just before the start of term – and acted very weird around Brett, though I'd kind of expected it; the two women you love most in your life always end up, if not exactly hating each other's guts, then existing in some uneasy symbiosis for your sake. I kept contact to a minimum and got them out of there before it could deteriorate any further. Brett was supremely unconcerned, I might add.

We needed to begin again. Just as my past was invented for me in High 5, I needed to invent one for Brett and her brother. It was difficult to improve on reality, which was a shame, but there was no way I could have used it, even with their acquiescence. Better that they came from nowhere, with faces like angels and tongues of holy fire. Australia certainly wouldn't wash. I thought instead remote rural Ireland – think flame-haired girls in emerald velvet, pretty mouths and green eyes, tall pale guys with sable locks and frock coats, thunder brewing on their brows; Bushmill's and oysters, morning mists on the Liffey. That kind of thing. The rest would have to come from them.

So I'd sketched that out. I'm aware of in how unflattering a light it casts me, and I really had to force myself to think like that. But success on your own terms, artistic or otherwise, requires extraordinary effort, and thinking my way into the head of a UriZen exec is not my idea of fun. Whatever. We scanned a crop of the photo on to a bunch of outsize address labels, stuck them on Jiffy bags, and mailed them off with the typescript to the six places with the most money, omitting the local UriZen subsidiary for obvious reasons. Brett had read up on which editors were buying what and for how much in a year's worth of the trade press at Kensington library the day we arrived, and did an unfathomable spreadsheet thing that incorporated their interim results, stock price, differential margins and employee/turnover ratios. I really did try to understand, but I'm hopeless with that sort of thing. She knew exactly who to send it to, so I trusted her. I didn't have much option.

There was a week when nothing happened. We went into the office and hung out, scripting the media interviews they would ultimately have to do. There was no point in pretending it wouldn't happen, so we might as well be prepared for it, if we were going to use them to our best advantage. I was chosen to orchestrate media-practice because I'd told them lies about the depth of involvement I'd had in High 5's campaigns, which, incidentally, generally involved keeping my mouth shut and sticking to the autocue.

Finally, however, the phone started ringing. And how. Brett took the calls, as my assistant, and drove them mad for a few days with my incessant meetings, flights to Geneva, workouts with my personal trainer, uninterruptible focus group sessions and so on; and when she'd finished toying with them, and leaked the photo and their interest to the trade press, she set up an auction for the very next day, only permitting me airtime on the speakerphone with a short, strict script in front of me, and her finger poised over the mute. We stayed up all night drinking then teleconferenced it, still utterly caned; Brett in the living room, me and River on the extension in the kitchen. Brett shook us awake just after lunchtime; we had a deal. The money wasn't great, but like, this was books. It wasn't the issue.

A bike arrived with a draft contract the next day, along with a letter inviting us to lunch with our shiny new editor at a venue of our choosing. This was to be followed by a meeting with our new key contacts at Ellmann, Westlake; some English publisher that had been swallowed up almost by mistake years ago by DIS, itself then a mere food multinational, in a parcel of choice growth-industry entities. Brett loved them more every minute.

'They're perfect,' she explained, over our own celebration at the Ivy, where we'd forced the barkeep to make us a pitcher of Mai Tais and put on my Hawaiian medley tape after the other lunchers had quit flattering each other and scuttled back to their desks. 'The key Nineties' marketing strategy is to spread your product over as many formats as possible – like Wannabes in pastel suede, pink patent leather, mock-croc and snakeskin. And Swatches.'

'Or Michael Jackson doing the same dance in every video,' put in River. Don Ho was singing 'Tiny Bubbles'.

'Ellmann – or rather DIS, Inc. – own, like, everything. Everything UriZen doesn't, anyway,' said Brett, and itemized the media architecture we could infect with ourselves. A whole bunch of cable and satellite networks, one and a half studios, big fat stakes in slick magazine houses, a rash of radio stations from the Midwest to the middle East, two of the major online server hook-ups, and big chunks of the best broadsheets on both sides of the Atlantic. We could also, if we fancied, exploit their interests in cartoon-character endorsed pre-sweetened breakfast gunk, crystal-clear personal grooming products and sanction-busting, dissident-mushing, ultra-carnage anti-personnel devices. Brett had spent all morning drawing a spider-chart that outgrew, almost immediately, the dry-erase board purchased especially – 'I just can't write any smaller,' she'd wailed, kicking it over.

'They have to understand that we're an infinitely diversible cross-platform property,' Brett continued. 'If they think we're just going to churn out books they can forget it. We want to spread through their corporate architecture like a virus. We're going to infiltrate every circuit we possibly can without crashing the system. Until we're ready for it, of course.'

'Snow crash,' said River. 'Total meltdown.'

'Then we make some fucking movies,' said Brett. We toasted the annihilation of the circuit as we knew it.

★

We chose the place on Kensington Church Street where Dexter Fletcher got stood up in *The Rachel Papers*, and informed our new editor, Didi Roman, by e-mail the day before ('She'll probably have to get one of her slaves to show her how to use it,' snorted Brett). On the day appointed we went shopping for outfits early in the morning, as lunch was set for 12.30. Vindictively early, I felt, but I supposed they wanted to scuttle off to lunch as soon after they hauled their sorry asses into the office as possible. River and I wore old black Sulka suits over white Ben Shermans with vintage black cotton ties, all from Dolly Diamond. We looked like a couple of mid-Sixties Mormons who'd just been sold some reefer as an asthma cure. Brett chose a black knee-length second-hand leather crombie ('It's not creating demand for fresh pigs if it's old') over a merino turtleneck, stretch-satin hipsters and cuban-heeled boots, all black. She looked like Elizabeth Montgomery on her way to an S/M party. We spent too long at the flat taking Polaroids of each other grinning and waving the contract, and were late to the restaurant, but the other two hadn't arrived. We ordered martinis, dry as you like, and waited politely.

Eventually two grinning women bore down on us out of nowhere. They were analogues of each other; Prada and Paul Smith, and pushing forty like it was a car stuck in snow.

'Brett? River? I'm Didi Roman, of Ellmann.' She spoke like the Queen, only posher. 'And this is Demi Peignot, our Publisher.' I swear, you could hear the uppercase.

We shook hands, sat down and ordered ('The usual,' they hollered across the room at the *maître d'*, who was actually busy with someone else). The Publisher was a surprise. I was quite chuffed, but Brett hated them instantly – when they both went outside to get better reception on their mobiles, which went off in unison almost the moment they sat down, she made grokking, gagging noises and informed me that these were the sort of women whose sole mission in life was to get their spawn in the party pages of *Tatler*. She considered this disconsolately for a while, then gobbed in their Caesar salads as an afterthought.

When they came back in Brett gave them a big shit-eating grin and told them the anchovy dressing was to *die* for. They troughed away, and I had to grab some corn bread, pretend to choke on it, and go to the men's room, tears streaming down my face, until I'd laughed myself out.

When I returned, Demi was unashamedly coming on to River. Brett was staring incredulously at her water, as though it had just directly addressed her.

'Didi tells me there's a certain androgyny to the *style*,' Demi brayed, through a mouthful of croutons and Cos, emphasizing the word 'style' like it was a remarkably complex new critical concept currently namechecked by all the coolest correspondents. Almost everyone else in the dining room was bowed over their food, pointedly trying to pretend they didn't wish her dead. 'A leashing of . . . testicularity?' She swallowed, hugely, and stretched her lips coquettishly at River. 'So few men succeed in getting in touch with their feminine side. I always say that if a man wants to get in touch with his feminine side, he should cut his salary in half.' Didi tittered sycophantically. Brett flushed pink and set her jaw.

'Actually, as I think our proposal pointed out in fairly unmistakable terms, we both wrote it. We work together.'

'My dear,' oozed Demi. 'No one's suggesting you don't. We're going to make it a cornerstone of our Internet Promotion.'

Brett's jaw dropped. Demi looked at her like she thought Brett was surprised she could be so spry. 'Oh, yes,' she twittered happily, 'we're expecting great things from Internet Sales.'

Brett could contain herself no longer.

'Our contract,' she said, 'articulates that you are going to match our fee with your marketing spend. Don't think you're going to palm us off with "Internet Promotions".' She was practically hissing. 'And anyway, do you understand nothing? Who do you think the market for this book is?'

'My *dear*,' said Demi, rolling her eyes at Didi in an oh–these–young-firebrands kind of way. 'Are you trying to tell me my business?'

'Actually, yes I am,' said Brett. Demi gaped. 'Where d'you buy your paper?'

Demi looked at Didi. Didi looked vacant.

'What paper?' she said.

'Do you make *books*? Do you use *paper*?'

'Oh,' said Demi.

'From suppliers?' offered Didi.

'Suppliers who charge you the market rate for the quantities Ellmann uses,' said Brett. 'Does Ellmann belong to DIS?'

Didi nodded.

'Does DIS publish eight newspapers in Europe?'

They looked at each other.

'Does it?'

'Yes,' mumbled Didi.

'How much paper would you say that uses? A hundred times what you do? A thousand?' She tilted back her chair. 'If you'd ever thought to check, you would find that it comes from the same supplier. They must be pissing themselves when they invoice you. I suggest you negotiate your supply as part of DIS's overall requirement. This will cut your primary overhead in half. Then perhaps you can afford to pay us what we're worth.' She took a forkful of her salad and chewed it calmly. Demi and Didi were silent, then suddenly started talking loudly about their holidays. When we didn't join in, they went quiet again. Finally Demi pushed away her plate as if to say, fuck this for a lark.

'Didi!' she barked. Didi looked up, sweetly surprised, as though some unimaginable treat was about to be offered. 'I have a two o'clock!' ('With your colonic irrigationist,' Brett *sotto voce*'d me, as Demi rose and rummaged in her bag). She turned to us. 'I'll leave you in the hands of my senior editor. Didi Roman!' As though Didi had only just arrived, and hadn't been introduced. Then she sailed out, knocking over a vase of lilies with her Prada shopper as she disappeared out the door. The *maître d'* cast his eyebrows long-sufferingly to the ceiling, clearly used to this sort of thing, and despatched two waitresses to clean up in her wake. The entire room seemed to sigh with relief. Brett glowered at Didi, who seemed oblivious.

'She thought I was his fucking girlfriend, didn't she?' she growled.

Didi suddenly appeared to remember that we hadn't signed the contract yet. She switched off the simpering lackey and turned on the brusque businesswoman.

'I apologize. Demi Peignot is a remarkable woman, but you must understand that she has very little to do with the everyday, ah, operation. Her interface is primarily at corporate level. However, she expressed an especial interest in meeting you, and I think you should be aware that this is quite exceptional. If she appeared to have misinterpreted some of the details of the project then that was my shortcoming for not outlining the, uh, nuances of your circumstances with greater clarity. Now, I don't want you to worry. Everyone at Ellmann is absolutely aware that your collaboration is quite a unique selling proposition. And that this was reflected in what was, if I may be frank, an unprecedented price for a first novel. We expect great things from this book. And we're sure we're not going to be disappointed. Now. Shall we order?'

Brett appeared slightly mollified, and bespoke an onion tart as if everything was forgotten. I knew she was faking it though, and was probably already contemplating making Italian cut-works in Demi's guts. Which would be a lot of cut-works, it has to be said.

River and I both ordered tomato soup with nasturtiums in it. Didi continued, unabashed. You had to hand it to her.

'It's so exciting to come across new talent of this order. And so young!' she gushed.

Actually, minor confession. We'd put in the proposal that Brett and River were nineteen, not twenty-two. 'We use Clinique,' Brett had insisted. 'Prozac for your face!' I'd protested – I mean, did they need to lie? They were twenty-two. But Brett had insisted. UriZen were knocking out novels 'by' twelve-year-olds at this time.

'We see your primary market as less Generation X, than Generation What Next?' She paused for laughter, but carried on regardless when there wasn't any. 'It's a huge market for us, and one that we're confident your book will maximize. These people are multi-skilled, working in the high-pressure world of downsized, delayered organizations. They work far too hard, but working late forms a comfort zone for them. When they leave the workplace they're at their time of maximum exposure, when the emotional hole in their lives opens before them. They don't have time to go out, as many of them have to be at their desks by seven, so they head for late-night supermarkets and convenience stores, to rent videotapes, select own-label wines and buy foods targeted at people too lonely or tired to cook for themselves.' She gestured with a forkful of Trout with Pernod and Black. 'Our focus grouping calls them the Little Luxuries Generation. Afflicted with the Small Indulgence Syndrome. They're either unable or unwilling to make traditional financial commitments, buying, say, a home or a car, preferring instead to constantly reward themselves' (we all shot each other a glance; we'd decided earlier that the number of drinks we would allow ourselves at lunch was going to be directly proportional to the number of split infinitives Didi used. I mean like we gave a crap, but it was the kind of thing Demi and Didi would have professed to care about; like the way they said literals instead of typos, or right ragged instead of flush left. I suppose this was the best evidence they could muster that they were, in fact, in the business. River beckoned over a waiter and began giving detailed instructions for a round of Bloody Marys) 'with little things, like comfort food. Pre-prepared meals that combine the exoticism of a night out – chicken tikka masala, say – with a dessert that anticipates their feeling of emptiness as the lonely evening wears on – sticky toffee pudding, like Nanny used to make. At weekends they treat themselves to CDs and cappucinos. We know how you kids love your coffee!'

We regarded her with polite interest, and chugged our BMs in unison.

'They find meeting people difficult. Office culture is such a minefield of political correctness' – she rolled her eyes – we regarded her, chins in hands, like she was a museum exhibit – 'that they find it more prudent not to flirt. So. Tying all these things together. We're going to aggressively market you' – River waved his glass at the bartender, who nodded, long-sufferingly, and set to once more with the vodka and celery-grater – 'as a Little Luxury. And because you're both very visual, and there are one of each of you, they can project their, ah *frustrations* on to you. Isn't it marvellous?'

'Marvellous,' said River.

'We're thrilled,' added Brett.

'Wonderful,' said Didi. 'I'm so pleased.' She really looked it, too. 'Shall we go?'

Outside, she explained that one of Ellmann's most distinguished novelists – some monstrous git who'd been perpetrating his own brand of well-wrought urn stuffed to the gills with gross sentimentality, philosophy 101 namedropping, dewy-eyed humanism and acutely embarrassing sex-scenes for the past quarter-century – had fallen off his perch that very morning. She waited for us to offer surprise, condolences, hysterical grief at the loss of our undoubtedly revered forebear. But it was like hearing Morrissey was dead. The only possible reaction was surprise that anyone could tell.

Anyway, she had to go and order flowers, and would meet us back at the office. So we got the tube, because I still found it almost unbearably exciting.

Hanging from the straps, Brett complained about our not having mobiles, so we got off at Tottenham Court Road and got one each, then played with them all the way to the DIS building. When we were done Brett clued us up on corporate etiquette.

'If we meet any people our age, don't treat them like shit – they have bosses to do that for them. It's bad enough for them, watching their own lives going down the pan, without us turning up and reminding them of what they could have done if they'd taken the time. Remember that they may yet. And even if they seem haughty; consider how they feel, putting up with the same stupid crap every day, knowing that the people who push them around all day have got another three decades to go and aren't planning to go anywhere. People stay in this business, not because they need the money, but because they wouldn't have a life if they left.' She programmed the number of the flat into her phone's memory and called our machine to see if there were any messages. 'But don't suck up to the assistants either. Don't assume they're going to be doing the real work, so you have to make a big show of condescension. If you kiss up to them, they'll see straight through you, and leave whatever they can get away with undone to serve you right for your presumption. Also, don't clip your visitor's pass on to your lapel. Only salesmen do that. Put it in your pocket.'

We got back before them. We were shown up to Didi's office and told to wait. We went in and sat down. It was uncomfortably silent. Brett got up and stood looking down out of the window at the street below. She kept checking her watch.

'Jesus, look at that town,' she said. 'You can almost see the crap floating above it. The radio said this morning the air was going to suck today. You got your inhaler?'

I patted my jacket pocket confidently.

'Oh, fuuuuck,' I moaned.

'What?' She turned round.

'I put it in there,' I said. 'I definitely put it in there. I haven't used it, have I? D'you see me use it?'

'Maybe there's a hole,' said Brett. 'Check the lining.'

'I didn't drop it on the floor, did I?'

We looked, but it wasn't there.

'How do you feel?' said Brett, looking at me concernedly.

I did feel a little tight, now she mentioned it.

'I'd better go and get another,' I said.

'Will you be all right? D'you want River to come with you?'

'No, I'll be fine. Damn. I'm sorry. Apologize to her if she comes back before me, will you?'

'You got it,' she said.

'Jesus. Later,' and I went back out to look for a chemist.

I had to walk about half a mile before I found one, and when I got back, Didi had shown, Demi also. She obviously had too much free time on her hands. I checked them out a moment through the glass before I went back in. Brett said something I couldn't hear, and they all burst out laughing. I was astonished. They almost looked kind of chummy in there. I waited for it to die down before I knocked, and went in.

'Joe,' said Brett, turning and smiling at me. I almost turned and looked behind me. *Damn* near. Jesus, what a day.

They all looked at me expectantly. I twisted my face at them.

'You certainly have an efficient assistant,' said Didi.

I grinned some more. My face was starting to hurt.

'As well as a couple of remarkable discoveries,' she added. They had clearly run out of things to say, but Brett had primed me on this, and I launched into it.

They would clearly find it odd that they'd never heard of Joe Gillis, agent, before, since almost everyone who was anyone in that industry had practically shared the same bathtub when they were kids. So I told them that I'd started out promoting parties when I was seventeen, then started a dance label and a record shop, and Brett and River had emerged as nascent faces-about-town who had come to my attention as a result of my interests.

'I saw them everywhere, and was struck by their obvious star quality.' I was doing a rich-kid accent and everything. 'I initially approached them with a view to a recording deal, but when they told me they were just finishing a novel, the chance of moving into new markets was too good to pass up. I planned to self-publish it and sell it through the club scene. When I read it, I realized that it deserved a wider audience. And so, my submission to you.'

It was pretty watertight. There was no way they could disprove it. They knew nothing of that milieu. Why should they?

'We're very glad you did,' said Demi. '*Seventeen Forever* is going to be huge.'

'Seventeen For*ever*?' I said.

'We've agreed a title change,' said Brett, briskly, making unnecessarily cruel, I felt, eye contact.

'We felt the *working* title a little, uh, stark? A little – humph! – negative,' said Didi.

I looked back to Brett, who looked nonchalantly to Demi.

'It's a tough business,' said Demi. 'Why put obstacles in the way?'

'Why indeed?' said Brett, smiling up at me significantly. What the fuck was that supposed to mean? I stared back a moment, then let it go. What was the use? Demi gave me a big smile, and exchanged a too-obvious look with Didi. She may just as well have drawn a finger below her chins.

'By a happy coincidence we have several of our key sales people onsite today,' said Didi. 'River and Brett have agreed to meet them, so if you have no objection . . . ?'

I spread my hands in the air.

'Well, it was terribly nice to meet you,' said Didi.

Oh, right. I got shown the door, and trailed back to the lifts. So that was that. I punched the buttons and stared gloomily out the window. It looked through a well in the centre of the building, with a courtyard at the bottom. Across the way, I saw Brett and River and Didi and Demi enter a boardroom full of guys in suits. They all shook hands and stuff. Suddenly I could have cried. The lift pinged. It was like we were on the tube, in different but adjoining carriages, and I was looking at them through the connecting door. Perhaps we were going to the same place, perhaps one of us would have to get off sooner, but, as I watched them through the glass, they moved in different rhythms from me. I stood for a while trying to gauge the progress of the meeting like you can gauge the progress of an incoming fax – quick for gaps, slow for blocks of text – but it wasn't telling me anything I didn't know. I got in the lift and went back to the flat.

They didn't come back. I'd been in the kind of mood where I would have said no even if they had told me they were going on somewhere afterward. But I missed them. This should have felt, once again, like the first day of the rest of my life. We had the deal; things could start now. But it felt like going home after you graduate and sitting in a room for a month, hundreds of miles from your friends; then, someday, getting the slip in the mail that represents twenty years of school; and taking it back to your room, sitting on your bed, holding it in your hand, thinking, and . . . ? I went into River's room, then through the connecting door into Brett's. I sat down on her bed and flipped through a few magazines, then lay down and stared at the ceiling. I wandered back out and through the living room to my room. I lay down on my bed, and pulled the duvet over my head.

I woke up four hours later to Brett and River's voices in the living room. I couldn't hear what they were saying – it was like when someone's got a stereo on really loud in the room above, and you can't hear what it is, the most you can make out is the bass signature, booming through the floor – but it sounded like the sort of thing I shouldn't walk in on. I put my head underneath the pillows and went back to sleep. In the morning, when I got up, they were gone.

The sun had chased away the clouds, and flooded the room as if to reproach me for my torpor. Ever since we'd arrived it had been the kind of freaky Indian summer that's more like May than October, and it felt good to kid myself it was spring. Muslin drapes billowed in a breeze that spoke of fresh-cut flowers: delphiniums, sweet peas, bunches of lilac, carnations; bright awnings in Bond Street, and happy horses in the Park. Floundering around in sheets that smelled of me, I discovered to my disgust that it was a little after twelve.

My room was the smallest in the flat. I couldn't stand to slouch about in it a moment more. I took a hot, brisk shower, scrubbing at myself furiously; then dressed, in a washed-out white cotton Oxford, old Levis and new Vans, descended the stairs and made thick Turkish coffee, the way Brett showed me, on the stove in the kitchen. I didn't really like it – too grainy – but it made me feel closer to her to drink it.

I felt better. It was difficult not to, in the sweet air of the kitchen, coffee vapours blending with the late-blooming vines outside the open window, the sun falling warm on the back of my neck as I sat on the counter with my back to it. I went out to Tesco Disco Metro for bagels and Philadelphia, and when I came back there was a message on the machine from Brett.

It took me a while to find the damn thing – it was an old machine, and no one had read the coffee-ringed manual about how to erase the tape – but when I located it and played it back she said they'd had to go to some DIS party that night, and had been so traumatized they'd gone away for a few days, ostensibly to scout locations. They needed some space. I figured they were probably having some kind of crisis of confidence, which it would be churlish to carp at. Their mother, again, and the monumental attachment of their faces to an actual product-type product. You never know, when someone does something that you'd do yourself without a second thought, what monstrous significances it might have for them that they try to keep a lid on. I tried to make my satisfaction at being so selflessly understanding my consolation for being alone, the same way I can eat a carton of Ben & Jerry's for lunch and congratulate myself on the calcium. After the furious summer, this should have been a time to change down, like coming, aching, off the motorway after four hours at a monotone eighty, and rediscovering how it felt to change gear, to brake, to have visual information again. I should have gone somewhere. There were cars, but where to drive them? Whichever way I went I'd run out of road tomorrow. I wished we were back in America. A couple of nights back in July and August I drove out through the desert, toward Vegas; the roads are so straight and the night is so black; time runs back on itself, and all that exists in the world is the brief self-replicating cone of light from your headlamps. You can't do that here.

So I stayed at the flat and tried to play with some ideas. I hadn't had time to work alone for ages, and so drifted into the opportunity to take my body-clock for a world cruise, with thirty-hour days and twenty-hour nights, touring my way through the time zones. Days blurred into each other, and before I knew it they'd been gone a week.

The weather had taken an episodical turn for the worse, so it was no good going out. One afternoon I was trying to interfere with a short story I'd been lousing up about a Pasadena fraud cop tailing an embezzlement suspect at Burbank (the cop uses his badge to get into story archives, and read all the scripts that never went into production so he can put together the ultimate pitch). But I couldn't really concentrate. The perpetual drool of rain from the gutter to the street below, as I lay on my bed, reminded me not too pleasantly of the sound of our tour manager urinating from the top of a fire escape at the back of a club in Milan, while Max and I cowered on the steel steps a flight below, trying to shield the glowing coal of the pipe we'd been sharing against the dark, while the piss spattered down on to our Schott security jackets. It wasn't a happy time.

After four or five hours of sitting moon-faced in front of my PowerBook not doing anything much, there was the dull plink of incoming e-mail. This brought me to with a start, and when I opened my box the tagline read Brett Brett Brett.

>Jake.
>The hell with this. Cornwall blows. But Cornish pasties are def (Eighties' revival *mot du jour*). They're like eating a bunch of *sick*. We're both horrifyingly rosy-cheeked. Our arms are brown, we're sleeping without even drinking. We saddle up at the end of the week. And then it will be time to shoot some guns, cowboy.
>That party really sucked. You're better out of that side of all this, trust me. You and River are the kind of writers that the system feeds on, and it'll suck you dry and toss your husk aside if you'll let it. But I'm here to take all that strain for you. I'm getting quite good at it, and this one, believe me, was the worst it's going to be. It really was from hell. The industry people were the worst. As products of the English class system and educational monstrosities it was like they existed purely to supply an answer to the question, Why is even American culture so much less etiolated than yours? A room full of people

all with a touch of the James Spader about the chops, all
waving champagne flutes and talking nasty about
people who're successful enough not to have to have
been there. River got high on the roof with Minion
Cyrillic, and I stole Demi Peignot's wallet right under her
nose (yes, I was precisely *that* bored). Cheap cheap
cheap, incidentally – *fake* Vuitton, no gold cards, a
couple of tens. I was waiting for her to announce that
she'd lost it, so I could ask her if it was really worth
having back. Also four cab receipts for less than two
pounds (*can* she walk?) and – get this – a Costco card!
I suppose she must buy her Giorgio in bulk (why doesn't
somebody *tell* her?).
>Anyway, I met our publicist – the girl who's going to be
doing all the press for this book. She's about twenty-six,
but still quite okay-looking if the light's right, I suppose.
Her name is Juliana Bold, and she worked on the Shott
and the Ztiff campaigns, so she must know something. I
thought I was going to have to start her from scratch –
you know, *ecoutez et repetez*: arse . . . elbow. Shit . . .
shinola. Okay? But I think she's going to be quite useful.
There is a swell new *young* (i.e. no faded Eighties'
Groucho wankers) magazine starting, and she knows the
editor and a couple of other key people. The art
director's parents are really loaded and own this like,
theme park of a house by the sea they're going to use
for editorial retreats – kind of planning meetings/
houseparties. I asked old Jools why and she said, if the
editorial team didn't have short vacations dedicated to
simple pleasures, they'd never get any sleep at all. They
sound pretty cool to me. I've always been interested in
people who arrange their lives so they can live in the city
and the country at the same time. Anyway, it's the

weekend after next at this place (JPEG of map follows.).
You go along the freeway and then sort of turn left.
We'll meet you there if you'll take Juliana. Pick her up
Saturday lunchtime at Kartouche, wherever the hell that
is. I imagine it's in London. I rented you a 1962 Porsche
Karmann. We need to do this properly. If you look in the
drawer of my desk, the address of the garage is in the
cigarette case with my initials on it. Get yourself a
Ramones tape and just drive that honey through the
night. There's nothing like it, swear to god.
>Brett.

Far out. I went to bed happy, and spent the rest of the week
getting excited about the party, and seeing her again.

In the newspaper once there was a competition where the prize
was to design your own house and have it built for you. I suspect
this is apocryphal, mostly because it sounds like it ought to be, but
once the winner was notified and asked to submit a rough idea,
he sent in a drawing of a cave. This rather exasperated the under-
writers of the competition, a building conglomerate promoting a
new kind of individual-spec executive home. There was no point
in anyone winning if they couldn't use it for publicity: so they
furnished him with a chauffeur to Swindon, hauled him in, and
talked him through the program they'd commissioned, which
permitted customization of a standard half-timbered double-garage
unit within certain parameters. Generally this extended only so far
as choosing one kind of mullioned window over another, or
clicking dwarf conifers into place with a mouse; but for the
showcase house, which was going to be used in the press generated
by the competition, an especially large lot had been put aside; so
you could, if you felt particularly subversive, put the garage on
the other side to normal, if you thought you could handle it. The

winner listened patiently while everything was explained to him, nodded politely in all the right places, then drew another cave, the same as before. I think they had him sectioned.

I love that story. Most games aren't open to everyone, and the winners are preselected; since they are descendants of the people who seized control to begin with, the successive winners tend simply to be duller versions, albeit taller and with better bone structure. But in a game that's open to everyone, you can't legislate for who the winners are going to be, by definition. So you ought to be able to get a few yuks in.

Saturday came, and it was back to Indian summer. I spent the morning buying socks because I'd run out, then came back and packed, and followed Brett's directions to the garage in a cab. I signed for it and picked up the keys, trying to ignore the monstrous numbers on the invoice, slung my bag in the back and took it off the forecourt. It was, as Brett had suggested, a honey. I hightailed it through a gap in the grid down a miraculously clear Fulham Road, the sexy boom of the twin exhausts bouncing back from the shopfronts. I slipped a quick rat-run to the King's Road – I'd studied this – and I swear, pulling racing changes round the squares was like sliding on ice. I could see why Brett had rented it. It ran so smooth that, if the salesman told you it ran on Guinness and champagne, you'd believe him.

I picked up Juliana as appointed. She wasn't quite as old as Brett had said – it turned out she was twenty-five – but she seemed arrested, somehow. I watched her as we talked about nothing on the crawl up to the Westway, and she seemed, I don't know, stuck around twenty. She was still acting as though she were young enough to be using unsuccessful facial expressions – this is me being sardonic, here I am resignedly amused by all the silly, silly things beyond my control – but my attention was distracted by a series of situationist things sprayed on to the moulded concrete underpass, on to road signs. I didn't know anyone did vandalism anymore. CHRISTIAN? Then WHO IS CHRISTIAN? I took it for some proselytizing take on existentialism, from the original misparticipants in the late twentieth century. CHRISTIAN? I'd tried to give up smoking once, but gave *that* up when it occurred to me there was little else to distinguish my existence from Christians'. *Why* didn't they smoke? I should have imagined they didn't have the same imperative to string things out as the rest of us, given that they were never going to have to hand in their dinner pail. I'd certainly give my smoking instincts free rein, had I sufficient room left on my card to buy the optional extended warranty they had – the one they found it unthinkable not to buy. My trouble is, I don't want to live forever; I can't bear the thought of my own unmediated company stretching out to the middle of the next century: but I have an irritating suspicion that, the moment I'm picking up speed on the long slide, there'll be someone, too late, that I wouldn't mind putting the brakes on for. And of course by then the cables will be frayed and the fluid leaked away.

Christian grew a qualifier. WHO IS CHRISTIAN GOLDMAN? requested a sign prohibiting U-turns. Of course; it was the end of the summer holidays. St Martin's or wherever had finished four months ago for a third of its card-swipers, and they were out on their own. When I was in LA one time there was a billboard at Sunset and Marmont, underneath the Marlboro Man: BabyDol – coming soon. With the 'o' as a lipsticked heart. It was only there for a week, so I guess she paid for it herself. The idea was that content-providers, Jeep-ing past it on the way back to Holmby Hills every day for a couple of weeks, would find the fifty-foot airbrush of the blushing starlet surface in their consciousness next time they were pitched an especially ditzy vehicle. CHRISTIAN was trying a lower-budget version, and though the Westway isn't the worst route from Islington to Wood Lane, I couldn't help feeling that this is as noticed as you're going to get, buddy.

It turned out Juliana knew most of the people who were going to be at the house.

'Oh you know, there was a kind of gang of us up at Cambridge,' she said, one arm over the back of her seat so she was half-turned toward me. 'And then there were houseparties and things, and we'd all go out to Ibiza for summers, and we all kept in touch when we came down. Though it was difficult to keep so close, what with tiresome things like work.' She wrinkled her nose and giggled. 'But we're all basically doing things that complement each other.'

I thought that she was a woman close to the end of her rope. She was the only person she knew who worked for one of the old kinds of corporation, and getting back together with her friends was the only way out she could see. You could tell by the way she talked about them.

'Basically, it's just moving their scene down from London for a few days, but without any of the non-key people as distractions.'

'And are you happy in your work, soldier?' I tried to be light about it, but I didn't want any neurotic scary-mary screwing up the PR. I didn't see why we couldn't have had someone older. I supposed it was because we were young.

'Oh, it's not so bad. Lots of parties, but you do sometimes wonder what it is that you're doing. My mother once said, instead of paying so many people to promote the books, why don't they just keep your salaries and let the books take their chance –' she pulled up her shoulders and giggled ' – and I remember for one horrible moment seeing what she meant. I had flu one morning, and I was kind of coughing and moaning round the kitchen, and my flatmate said, Call in sick. And I said, I can't; if I don't get to a phone and start talking things up it . . . won't make much difference?' She burlesqued aghast self-knowledge. 'It's not like the magazines and chat shows and weekend sections would cease to exist. It was horrible. But then I realized that they'd only be featuring other people's clients.'

'It must be weird, though,' I said. 'Having always to be so pumped up about everyone you represent. How many, say, in a year?'

'A hundred, maybe.'

'Isn't it difficult, to tell them apart? To make whoever you're selling them tell them apart?'

'You do kind of hear yourself sometimes, and you're, like, this guy is Raymond Carver meets Garcia Marquez but with Faulkner undertones and Updike's scope, and you think, what am I saying? I wonder what it must have been like to be doing, I don't know, Defoe's press, or Sterne's marketing. You know? When there wasn't anything else. "Well, it's not *very* much like the Bible."'

I laughed and changed up.

'But what I do is mostly about making things happen – bringing people together. Which is what this thing is going to be about. What's the point of having all these talented people floating around if they aren't brought together? It's basically a PR thing for the *Post*. Why not? They already have all the printing and distribution in place, and all these people kind of half-attached.'

'What people?'

'Well, you see, the *Post* is way ahead of the rest; it sees itself as a brand. You don't just take the *Post* – you subscribe to the whole *Post* lifestyle.'

'That would be a cool concept for a magazine. Post-lifestyle.'

She considered this for a moment.

'What would be the point?'

'Oh. Yeah.'

'Anyway. So the *Post* isn't just a newspaper, it's a whole cultural stable. Across the board. They have stakes in rep cinemas, arts suppliers, cable, publishing.' She ticked off the points on her fingers. 'You know? And their big thing now is online-service provision. But instead of just having straight Internet access, you go into this pre-prepared online environment that's already tailored to your interests. Like the difference between going on a package holiday to a resort, and just getting a plane somewhere. It was supposed to happen ages ago, but when we thought the Net was cool, suddenly everyone thought it was cool, so we had to think it was a loser idea for a while. But it's still there! And it's so cheap! And we can feed the content into the paper when they're short of staff. So it's finally being launched next week. C'mon, you must have seen the campaign. The giant safety net, with the business guy falling through it. My friend Robbie wrote the copy: "Net? Nyet"; and, "If you didn't flip over e-mail, wait till you see the *Post*." You must have seen them.'

I hadn't.

'Jesus, where've you been?'

I didn't like to tell her I hadn't watched TV, turned on the radio, sparked up Netscape or gone to the newsstand in months now. But it's the only thing when I'm trying to work. I remember the first time I essayed a media-free weekend, and couldn't believe how much more time there was. I don't know if I could recommend it, though. It depends what you're doing with your life right now. If you want or need to make your time disappear, we sure have things that can help you with that. Have a nice life, now.

'Well, whatever,' she went on. 'They've sort of picked up all these people the last couple of years to work on whatever project within the brand. They're all young, they're all vaguely talented, but none of them are really, you know, pushing the envelope doing what they were hired for. Why not bring them all together and start something new?'

Uhhh, Houston? We have a problem. The whole point of being young was that you were underpaid, undervalued and exploited.

This was how you learned to be adult about things, and move hell and high water to protect your own interests as soon as you were conniving enough to have any. I couldn't believe I was hearing this, especially from her.

Because she was definitely on the shitty end. When I picked her up, though her clothes were immaculate and she was hauling some big-league garm-carrier, she was sitting behind a lime-and-soda that the ice had had time to melt in, and there were dark vitamin-deficiency bruises beneath her eyes. It was all kind of obvious. She could probably rely on her parents for deposits, damage limitation, whatever; but she had the sort of job where you were doing pretty much the same thing as your ten-years-older boss, and you had to look and live like they did on a third of the pay. So what was left, after she'd paid for a pit with a postcode, had to go on Clinique and Clarins, Hobbs and Hilfiger, Agnès B and Aristoc. She probably didn't lose much on going out because I imagined even her evenings weren't her own and she'd have to spend them schmoozing. And there was probably a tremendous amount of fearful making-do, but something had to give, and I don't think she got enough to eat. When you take people to lunch you're too busy flattering them to eat anything, and you have to be careful about being a bit obvious with the deli spread in the evening. I knew this from High 5; we never got enough to eat – it always seemed to be left out of the itinerary, like someone had just forgotten, so we all smoked like fuck to compensate. And of course no one took her on to supper afterward, because she wasn't important enough. How do you explain that to the 'rents, at the same time you're telling them you were at a party last week and had half the Cabinet making inefficient passes at you? Which was odd, because I didn't see any evidence to indicate that she wasn't exactly the same kind of person as her handlers. You have to assume that they pay the juniors so little because they enjoy it; the juniors are, after all, far better educated, since they've had to stay in the educational system for as long as possible, simply by virtue of there being nowhere else to go. Poor cow.

It made me melancholy of a sudden, because she reminded me of Brett and River's friends in LA; and my own friends, the ones I never see anymore. It made me sick and sad, and I wanted to be here to say, enough; some day, in some small way, years from now, if that's what it took. The Groucho generation say, oh yeah; you want to work in this industry, you have to accept that it's not going to pay you like it paid us. No one buys books anymore, no one wants to see a good movie anymore, yada yada yada. So even though it hasn't put a crimp in our style, and Martha's Vineyard or Provence aren't going to get lonesome for us for a while yet, we don't have the money to let you live like we did. Sleazy old jerks. If people stopped buying, it was because they were tired of the crap that that generation foisted on them out of laziness, out of thinking that sitting on your imagination was what it meant to be a grown-up. It depressed the hell out of me. Like my friends, who used to be so vivid; but got it beaten out of them in a couple of years, then took the Fifth. Teacher training, because it was the one last thing you got a mandatory grant for. This was not a free lunch. Junior teachers get half what senior teachers do. You get a glut of juniors, you dump the seniors – your overheads are cut in half. My parents used to be teachers, so did most of my friends, and the kids that permitted their forced retirement took ultra short-term contracts themselves. They were retired, in turn, at twenty-five rather than fifty, replaced by twenty-two year-olds. And there were thousands waiting their turn behind them. This was what kept me in High 5, even when it became clear the way it was going. Enough already. She went on.

'The magazine – it's going to be called *There*, by the way, as in *Out* There – is excellent kudos for the *Post*. It's a real shot in the arm to the competition, for the *Post* to be associated with something new, something hip – they can point to it and say, look. We've got all these bright young things, they're doing something totally new and they're doing it for us.'

She was starting to depress the hell out of me, but we were moving onto the eight-lane, so I cranked up a specially-prepared tape of fifth-gear selections, and let 'Night Train', 'Roadrunner', and 'Come Up And See Me' drown her out. An hour and a half later, we were pulling up outside the house, and I felt all kinds of better.

It was perched on a cliff, somewhere between Bournemouth and Poole. We overshot the approach to the house on our first shot at the coast road, and drove through the strangest streets by the sea there. It was like Venice Beach meets Malibu; stucco deco next to cantilevered cedar and glass, all under Monterey Pines and thirty-foot palm trees. I'd had no idea it was like this, but money seemed to have moved here in a big way in the Twenties and Sixties. I exclaimed at it to Juliana, and she said that a bunch of merchant banks had big offices here – 'Chase, Manhattan built, like, an *air*port'. The place we were going to was much older money though. Juliana had been there before, and told me about it while we searched for the drive. It had been built as a bet by some fading eighteen-nineties' exquisite in 1921; when we finally pulled up in front of it I saw what the bet had been. It was like someone had sampled a section of a Tudor mansion in Photoshop then clicked randomly all over the screen, reduplicating it over and over. It was extraordinary, like something Cecil B. De Mille saw in a dream after a bad oyster. I loved it.

'There's a Real tennis court out back, but nobody knows how to play,' she said. 'C'mon, the door's open.'

No one was around – Juliana thought they were probably at the beach, two hundred feet below – but there was a PowerMac on an occasional table by the staircase, with a floor plan done in Illustrator. But someone had put some kind of a hack on it – you clicked on your name and a little red line crept along the stairs and hallways to your room. Juliana showed me to mine. At the top of the stairs she pointed out an offhand pile of straw hats that had last been worn, she said, by the Bloomsbury group on a weekend visit in 1929. When I was alone in my room, I found the drawers of my armoire lined with newspapers bearing headlines of the Spanish Civil War. There was a queer little door under a window that opened into a tiny crawl space, and I ran my finger through dust that had lain unstirred since the Jazz Age. There was a half-bottle of slowly warming champagne on the bedside table, but I felt floaty enough already. I lay down on the tapestry-covered bed, and entertained daydreams art-directed by Cecil Beaton a while. I was interrupted by a smart rap on the door.

'Who is it?' I called, peeling my face off the pillow.

'Robert Poste's child,' said Brett's voice, irritably. 'Let me in.'

I hurried to the door, pushing my hair back with my hands.

'Hey, cool room,' she said, brushing past me.

'Hello,' I said brightly. 'How've you been? No hug?'

'Since that damn party, I've become suspicious of the practice,' she said, picking up the champagne. 'Can I have some of this? I already saw mine off.' She tore off the foil and snorted. 'Only half-bottles. What kind of hell-hole is this?' I giggled, and she shot me a dry one as she poured it out. 'They're sponsors, actually.'

'The drinks company?'

'Mmm-hmm. They're paying for the fashion pages. Every section of the magazine's been sold to some FMCG marketing department or other, so don't worry about swallowing all the booze. There are cases and cases, buddy. Everything down to, like, the potato chips. The *dip*. Charlie told me earlier.'

'Charlie?'

'He's the editor. We've been to the beach.'

'So what's the plan?' I asked, accepting the glass.

'Talk, hang out, be cool. I'll be talking up *Seventeen*, so you needn't worry about all that.'

'When's it start?'

'Cocktails at seven. There's going to be a kind of pretend editorial meeting soon after. Brainstorming, sort of.'

'Why "pretend"?'

'Oh there's a hack down from the *Post*, who's going to write it up for the lifestyle section. It seemed the best way to do it – a kind of set-piece, for their benefit.'

Which was typical. I mean, aren't we ever going to get tired of this? Whenever something cool gets started, there always has to be some damn hack getting all superior about it on the features page. Why couldn't they keep their snouts out for once? Or, at least, hang back and give it a chance before they started turning it into something it wasn't. But I suppose the *Post* was bankrolling the whole thing, and that gave them dibs. I made a mental note to find out which one this hack was, which shouldn't be difficult as he'd be at least ten years older than everyone else, and give him the swerve.

'What are you going to wear?'

'This.' She was wearing a white skinny New York *Herald Tribune* T-shirt, gunmetal PVC trousers and para boots. 'Sort of millennial *À Bout de Souffle*. What're you?'

'I don't know. I thought maybe I'd, you know, throw something together from the extensive and, uh, infinitely interchangeable range of male clothing options.' I was trying too hard and she knew it.

'Whatever. Look, I've got to bone up on what all these people do. Jools sent me some stuff. I'll see you downstairs, okay?'

'Okay.' I didn't want her to go, and kind of made two abortive attempts at getting out of her way. Then I just stood there. 'I missed you,' I said, looking at the ground. She sighed, probably with irritation, came over and put her arms around me.

'Come on,' she murmured into my collarbone. 'Come on, old Jake.' I tried to keep my arms by my sides, but they seemed to creep up around her back of their own accord. I let my cheek descend, till it rested on the spent gold of her hair and I could feel her voice humming through her skull, and buzzing in my back teeth. 'There's no problem here. This is what we need to do. We can't keep you hidden away for ever. Okay?' She nudged my head up, regarded me a moment, then put her mouth to my collarbone and let it rest there. I could feel her eyelashes brushing my neck as she blinked, and we stayed like that a moment.

All at once it seemed that now I was here, I just wanted to get away, and fast. These people scared me. My one overriding sense of what it meant to be young had something to do with the suspicion that maybe there were deadlines, but youth was the currency you paid to get them extended. High 5 had helped, because we never met anyone our age. There was a nice fat cushion of slick industry people who felt the push of a different decade behind them, so it seemed less unreal that we – me, Max, Ollie, Thom, Charlie – were stuck in some kind of generational stasis. But now, it was like being the infant genius at your small-town school, and suddenly you're sent away to a bigger one in the next town. So you look around at the other new kids on your first day, and there's hundreds of them, all aching to prove they're smarter, more driven, and more focussed than you ever suspected might be necessary. It felt like a brochure had been handed out at school ten years ago, detailing the moves to make and the turns to take if you wanted to go somewhere. Anywhere. But I suspect I bunked off that day.

'Come on, Jake,' Brett insisted. 'Let's go, buddy.' It was time to get with the program. I let go, and we talked briefly about selling-points and shit like that. Then she went back to her room.

I finished dressing and tried to do some motivational stuff in the mirror, the old surreal stuff we'd been instructed to do backstage as the house lights were going down. *You're a fuckin' Beretta*. It hadn't worked then and wouldn't now. The same face I'd learned to flip my eyes away from on magazine racks regarded me disinterestedly from the glass, looking older and more drawn than I remembered it. I went back to the dressing table and put in some eyedrops, and a smear of Vaseline on the lids, the way we were shown to before morning PAs when we were still coming down from the night before. This seemed to improve things slightly, so, to make sure, I downed about a third of the bottle of Southern Comfort that I'd brought along as insurance, just in case we had to hole up in my room sometime over the weekend. I watched my reflection toss off a final histrionic capful, and finally I felt ready to rock 'n' roll. I was late.

I'd worried about having to do some kind of hideous Eliza-Doolittle-at-the-Embassy-ball kind of descent down a staircase, into a room full of chatter which stopped in mid-sentence to let everyone once me over; but nobody seemed to notice when I finally made it down. It took a while to locate Brett – the room wasn't that huge and it was heaving in there – but I found her somewhere under the cloud of Silk Cut Ultra, on the other side of a mêlée of waggling cigarettes and expansive gestures. She was talking fast and low to people I didn't know, and only interrupted her flow to give me a quick peck on the cheek, a cursory introduction and a shot glass of something purple from a tray on a table behind her. I couldn't really follow what she was saying – everyone was talking too fast in a room full of voices, and my hearing is, I guess, slightly shot from a thousand nights in front of a million screaming children with a backing track thumping out of billion-watt Marshall stacks behind me – so I hung back a little, tried to smile in the right places and finished my drink.

'Hey,' said a girl at my elbow.

'Oh, uh, hi,' I said. I was so nervous my stammer seemed to

have come back. Which was like, fuck my luck, because I knew this was it. Being here was a form of validation, and I wasn't going to get a chance to hang out with these kind of people again. Something was really happening here, and the best thing was, it wasn't some dumb industry thing. These people were my age and there was no need for any of that kind of crap; but, at the same time, there was the feeling that, being here, you were a player, or at the very least, among the players. 'I'm, uh, Jake,' I said, and held out my hand. I was off the blocks with a bullet, it seemed.

I needn't have worried, because she was only a computer geek. She'd been working on the *Post*'s online thing, and was doing the OOP for the web page of *There*. She wasn't going to be involved for long. Her name was Polly Chesterfield; I thought she was just kind of short, but when she asked me what the song was on the stereo ('Rio') I asked her how old she was. It turned out she was sixteen. She didn't know who High 5 were either – too hip – though she'd been, I suppose, prime market for us. In fact no one seemed to know. No one looked at me, twice, though whether this was genuine ignorance, or loser ex-celeb overload, or simply not caring, I don't know. I glanced over at Brett once or twice but seeing her here, surrounded by all these people, was like hearing a French person pronounce the name of Tin Tin. I sat on it fast, and tried to get Polly to point out who people were, but I'd scarcely had a chance to sidetrack her when there was a casual exodus from the room, like the movement of wedding guests into a marquee; I tail-ended and came out in the kitchen.

This was a huge room with red stone flags on the floor, chunky aged-softwood fittings, utensils and strings of bay leaves and dried peppers hanging from the ceiling. It was the same kind of Richard & Judy kitchen as the ones at parties you crash when you're fourteen. Everyone sat on whatever space there was, along the counters, on the floor. I walked quickly to the far end of the room, to avoid being the last person left standing; and half-sat on a window ledge by the back door, propped up like on one of the 45-degree half-bench coffee-and-Danish-almost-to-go things at Pret A Manger. The last person into the room was a girl I hadn't noticed before, who crossed the room to the only free space left, which was on the floor with her back to the door below me. She looked like Alice: sullen, dark-eyed Alice, from the original illustrations to *The Looking Glass*; but this, rummaging in her record bag, was Alice who'd somehow contrived to step off the page and grow up. I thought she must be looking for cigarettes in there, and it was only when she pulled out a Walkman, and set it on the floor before her and hit the red button, that I realized this was the hack. I'd thought they'd have sent someone much older. I suppose they thought she was their *enfant terrible* or something. A hip young gunslinger. I tried to pay her no further notice.

The buzz of conversation began to diminish and Charlie, the editor, sat up on top of the range. He consulted some crappy Tag-Heuer he got for his birthday, cleared his throat and welcomed everyone, including, with a sardonically deferential remark, Nancy Stuyvesant. I felt my face break out with instant eczema. The *hack*. There was nothing I could do. She was between me and the door. But this wasn't the worst thing.

Charlie opened his mouth and began to delineate the contents of the first issue, and you can fill in the blanks here. Whatever fatuous crap is going down right now, insert it here and save me the bother. It wasn't even like it was anything new. It was stuff even I already knew about, and, like, I had the information equivalent of anorexia. I was aghast.

He spooled on. Listening to him was quite disproportionately boring, like waiting for a video to eject when you've got the blank tape in your hand and the show you wanted to record is started already; or watching the grey of an operation-complete percentile status bar in Photoshop nudge forward, like encroaching desert, when you want an okay-res picture from a 2-meg 3.5. I still wanted to hear if there was in fact anything they were going to do that, even if it sucked, would do so in a way that we haven't seen before; so I half-tuned out, until he should commence to cut to the chase. I sighed through my nose and flipped my gaze to the floor in preparation for the first-drinks-wearing-off-now session of the what-am-I-doing-here-what-am-I-doing-with-my-life unwelcome self-analysis that had been welling up for a while. Probably a few minutes passed before I realized I'd let my gaze fall on Nancy Stuyvesant's shorthand pad. I focussed, and saw she'd made two columns or lists, but hadn't written a heading for either.

Orthodontics	Rest home
Contract	Non-disclosure form
Mall	Multiplex
Sociology	Media Studies
Uniform	Costume
Employee	Cast member
InterCapping	Negative Leading
Freeze-frame	Click 'n' Drag
Storage	Frequency
CD	WideScreen
Middle-class guilt	Denial
Strike	Fear
Command line	Dialog Box
Text	Icons

'Fashion,' said Charlie. 'We're booked for Tommy Hilfiger, Ralph, Daniel Poole. The usual suspects. Old school cut to the new breed . . . hey, and we need locations. People, remember; if you're out, and it's all back to someone's, don't get too far off your chump not to remember the address of the place, if it looks like somewhere we can use.'

Nancy was writing, IF FASHION IS THE ONE INDUSTRY THAT

PROFESSES TO WORSHIP YOUTH, WHY IS IT BANKROLLED BY OLD WOMEN? Like someone on a train who knows you're looking at them, she glanced up, saw me, and winked. She wrote, HI JAKE. DON'T YOU WISH HE'D CUT TO THE CHASE?

Be cool. I nodded, and mouthed, 'Not half.'

THERE IS NO CHASE, she wrote. Then she drew a noughts-and-crosses grid, put an X in the top left, and passed the pad and the pen up to me.

I took it, and stared a moment in confusion; then scrawled an O in the middle and passed it back. She won that game, and the next two. I'd forgotten how to keep from giving away a double-branch option.

The thing broke up eventually, after a staged photo-opportunity of the core editorial team faking it up around the kitchen table, upon which the various sponsors' beers, corn-syrup sodas, premium ice-creams and comfort food items were cunningly product-placed. The sound system kicked in, and people worked the room. I wandered around. Juliana was buttonholing the editor about a tie-in book, Nancy was proffering her Walkman for quotes, and Brett was over in a corner with a skinny guy in a ratty suede jacket. I joined them, and Brett introduced me without cutting off his flow.

'You know, the whole post-adolescent disillusionment thing is over. How can't it be, when there're no illusions left? After twenty years of seeing the conjuror show how the trick is done as he goes along? Just to get himself a new angle. So you see, as a consequence, the crisis of disillusionment that should descend like the devil in the middle of your third decade just isn't going to happen. Just imagine. No alarming awakening into the capital world, no trau-matic interpellation into the symbolic order, no realization that the end of your teens was some kind of holiday from reality before life really got a chance to kick in.'

Brett was nodding like a dashboard dog. I mean, I understood that we were going to need to put up with this kind of thing, but jesus, so early? She could at least have warned me, so I could have woofed down a couple of fat ones first.

'It's not our fault,' he said. 'Home VCR manifested itself around the same time we kissed goodbye to innocence and, as the first generation to troll the video stores, we were on the target end of one slick marketing operation whose panicky executives were keen we should get passionate about the sophomoric rites-of-passage movies that got optioned in the Seventies and were only now slouching towards straight-on-to-rental premiere. In the absence of anything else, and because the whole ineffable joy of video rental is to feel that you've made the correct consumer choices for a change, these method-heavy epics of gauche anguish – okay, kids, we have once more to party before we realize how meaningless it all is, and buckle down the graduate fast-track accelerated pro-motion programme – got indelibly engraved upon our collective consciousness. So the epiphany of giving up and giving in holds little attraction. Seen in a thousand times. So the timbre and tempo of life, along with the degree of self-knowledge and ability to be equivocal about one's general life-plan, remains the same at twenty-four as it was at fourteen.'

I couldn't take it anymore, and wandered round aghast, trying to find anyone who wasn't delivering some kind of a pitch. Brett came over after a while and steered me around, while I tried to keep a hold on the idea that these were the people I needed to be around, however I felt about it. If I couldn't, then the Fade was just around the corner. That only seemed to make it worse.

Brett had said that going into that meeting at DIS and having their names and smiles blur before her was like the meet-the-cast sequence of a daytime American sitcom; one that's too lousy even to be on cable, yet somehow contrives to be the same episode whenever you're home and sick. It was like that now, and whenever

Brett moved me around to a bunch of new people I let their names and faces flash before me, kidding myself with the assumption that, if this was to be the halcyon role of their career then I needn't trouble to remember them; and if it wasn't, then maybe I'd see them again later. But I couldn't help feeling that I'd seen them all and done them all already. This in contrast to Brett, who was flitting about from group to group, extending her perfumed hand to people I would have expected her to cut dead. I'd rather hoped that when she'd talked about dissolving the distinction between work and play she'd meant something other than this.

But it occurred to me that I was behaving pretty much the same as I had at parties a decade ago. I knew I couldn't be the kid in black sitting by the speakers for the rest of my life, while everyone else is dancing and laughing and finally living. 'This is a Low' was shaking the windows, and the vocal line, like a plane stacked up on a tight schedule, picked that moment to start its final descent to the tarmac of E major, before it taxied round the solo and took off again. I murmured a rising harmony to the last line, but with feeling. Six months ago I would have sneered at myself for picking up cues for my life from pop songs, but it feels like sometimes you have to take it where you can. Finding ways to stay a loser was, after all, all I was doing, and it was time to snap out of it.

So I tried, but it wasn't any use. Brett seemed to have a knack of interrupting the flow and insinuating herself into people's lives that I didn't. People talk to each other about their common ground; if you don't have any, you construct some. Parties are always full of guys who wish they'd taken the time to read that book, see that film, go to that gallery, so they could answer questions with something more than monosyllabic half-opinions culled from the second sections. This wasn't a regular party, but the same rules applied. Brett had done her research and I hadn't. It was too late now, and I just stood, one hand in my pocket and a drink in the other, while they talked at other people.

I kind of drifted into a corridor after a while, which is always the worst place to be at parties. I got stuck with one of the scarily beautiful girlfriends who barely asked me my name before she launched into a terrifyingly intimate and apparently interminable account of her late adolescence. This involved recounting a series of unrelated and earth-shatteringly trivial events, that she'd somehow cut-and-pasted in her mind into a cogently heartrending account of cruelty and injustice, using pop-psychology magazine article bullet-points as keyboard shortcuts. She was whining on about some stupid boarding school, where they had to have the dormitory plumbing replaced once a year because of all the stomach acid going down the U-bend after supper every night; and I was nodding and frowning in the right places, but really I'm like, yeah, I'm so impressed you were all such major-league fuck-ups. Suddenly she lost interest, practically in mid-sentence, and threw her arms round another girl whom she clearly hadn't seen since a plane crash ten years ago when they'd both had to eat all the other passengers. I drifted away in case she'd forgotten I was there and was going to keep her back to me all night; trying to look, as I patiently shouldered my way back along the corridor, as though I had an idea where I was going.

Presently, I found myself outside the back door, and in that median stage of drunkenness where you're never quite sure how you got anywhere. I wandered along a path between the pines. I just didn't know anymore. Why was this whole thing so bad? When it ought to be so good? There wasn't any excuse. These people had the power of one of the biggest content-providers in the world behind them, and could do what they liked, and yet they were coming up with something that was just the same as everything else. Except slightly worse, because it had been done by every gang of St Martin's graduates for the last ten years. They had the privilege; surely there was a responsibility tacked on to that? I wasn't naïve enough to assume that was what someone in their situation would actually feel. But they ought at least to want to do something good, if only because it would get them another job. But I supposed these people didn't even have to worry about that. The *Post* was bankrolling it. It made me almost angry, until it occurred to me Shelley had probably had this conversation with herself a thousand times before. It isn't people who are bad but the way things are. And if you ever want to change things you have to go along with them first. I could have gone on all night, but a shadow on the path coalesced before my eyes into River, standing with his hands in his pockets and his back to a tree, staring into space. The topless neck of a flat bottle of Southern Comfort was tilted to an oblique angle in his jacket pocket, spreading a large oval dark patch through the fabric. He seemed oblivious.

'Hey,' I said.

'Hay is for horses,' he snorted. He was drunk as a bastard.

'Your, ah, cocktail is spilling,' I pointed out. He fumbled around with his jacket and pulled out the bottle, owlishly inspecting what was left of the contents.

'Ah, shoot,' he said, and drank off the last half-inch, tossed the bottle into the undergrowth, and sank down to the ground, his back to the tree.

'This is so fucked up,' he said, almost to himself.

I sat down next to him. I couldn't have agreed more. I was pissed at Brett. I couldn't bear to see her kissing up to these people, when she didn't really need to. I felt betrayed, almost. I'd had to rely on myself so long, because I felt excluded by everyone else, and I'd kind of got used to being a gang of one. Then I'd let her in, and I expected her to be as reliable for me as I always was for myself. So when she wasn't, I behaved like a dumped yob.

'You don't know,' he said.

'The fuck I don't. This blows. What are we doing here?'

'We're here because Brett said we had to come. And we do what she says. You do what she says.'

'Like you don't.'

'You don't know.'

'I don't know what?'

'You think everything's so neat.'

Say what? I'd already said I thought it blew. I looked blank.

'It's a mess. You don't know.' He pulled out a pack of Luckies, lit one, exhaled heavily. 'You can't just waltz in. Y'unnerstand?'

He was nervous about the book.

'Sure we can. If it wasn't a mess we couldn't. People would look a little deeper. But the way it is, everything's just surface. That's all anyone wants – stick a face on the product and fill the slots. Everybody's happy and we get to do what we want at the end. It'll be a breeze. Don't worry about it.'

'Jesus.' He whooshed out air. 'It's not . . . I don't know why I should be telling you this. She won't leave me alone. I can't leave her alone. We're not like . . . ah, think about it, can't you?'

I was thinking about how people say like. It isn't just an ironic frame. I think it's like, to add extra syllables to a trochee or whatever it is, to make it more iambic. Which is pretty fucked up, when you think about it, since iambics were invented to make blank verse sound more like speech. Like, we have to make our talk sound more like talk by using a talk-simulator. We have problems.

'This is getting out of hand. You can't . . . we're not like, happy little siblings.' He shot me a look. 'Not like, you think we are. Oh fuck this.' He got up and stomped away. I watched him sway round a tree and disappear. I thought he was trying to tell me he was worried about doing the press on the book. At least this is what I told myself he was trying to tell me because I was also having one of those total-clarity flashback moments you have when you're drunk, where our conversation was played back and I watched it like I imagined some day I was going to watch dailies. There was also selected footage, thrown in as a kind of optional extra, of various uncomfortable moments through the summer, and in Nice before, that I had thought nothing of at the time, but were suddenly freighted with significance. I sat on it fast. It wouldn't be sat on. I got to my feet and rubbed my forehead against the bark of the tree. This couldn't be happening. This was not possible. I'd never had anyone tell me to back off before, but I suspected that that was what he had sounded like. I started down the path after him, but a figure stepped out from behind a tree.

It was Nancy Stuyvesant, trailing a huge tulip glass of something crimson from the end of one arm and a bottle from the other. I moaned, and slithered my back down the nearest tree. She sat down beside me and poured out some more.

'Who was that you were talking to?'

Did she hear?

'No one. I don't know. Whoever.'

'I see,' she said.

'Were you listening?'

'Should I have been? No, actually. Hack's honour. I was sitting by the back door with someone. She went back in, I thought I'd see where this path goes. Why? What were you talking about?'

'Nothing. He didn't know who I was, thought he could score off me.' This was probably a mistake. I'd take any kind of money she already knew who River was, but I wasn't really interested in how the game went anymore. I just wanted it over. I looked miserably into the middle distance. I kind of wanted a stiff one pretty bad, but I was damned if I was going to fight my way back through the house to get it. She saw me looking at her glass.

'You want some of this?' she said. These are the sweetest words available to humanity. I didn't have a glass so she gave me the bottle.

'Take it all,' she said. 'I just sent Polly in to get some more.' She had a low, husky voice, like a man talking on the phone to his mistress during his wife's funeral. I waited for her to say something. I didn't know what the hell to say.

'I saw you talking to her earlier.'

I nodded.

'She's a cool kid. She asked to look at my pager, and when she saw I'd set it to vibrate rather than beep, she said I was turning into an android.' She giggled and took a swallow. 'If you feel it rather than hear it, it is kind of like having an implant. She said it's the hungry-cat principle. It's easy to ignore the one who yowls for chunks every time you walk in, but the really smart ones wait, then climb on your lap and get their claws in. And hey, one of those aeroba-girls – that's what she calls them, the aeroba-girls' – she was referring to one of the many irritatingly attractive young women who were there as professional girlfriends – 'one came over and started trying to be cool, saying her political conscience wouldn't allow her to uncritically embrace the new technology because it would end up taking over people's livelihoods. And Polly looked her up and down – the perfect skin, the subtle lipstick, the pro-vitamin hair – and said, "Well, that's something *you* don't need to worry about, sweetie." Hey, Polly!' Who had just appeared at the back door, her arms full. 'Hey, girl.'

Polly saw us and headed over. I stole the moment to look again at Nancy, who caught me, and winked back over the rim of her glass.

'Give me strength,' said Polly, dumping two bottles of cab shiraz and a stack of Dixie cups on the grass at our feet, and cross-legging down behind them. It felt silly to be towering above her so we sat down on the ground, our backs to the log-pile. 'You know what Charlie just thought of having me do for the home page? They want a twenty-four-hour live video feed of the level of the office coffee pot.'

'How, uh, cute,' said Nancy, turning one corner of her mouth up.

'Yeah,' said Polly. She pushed back her fringe and gave me a cup to pour my wine into. 'Like, desperate adolescents can sit in their bedrooms and watch the level go up and down, maybe faster before the copy date, and feel, you know. This is out there.'

'And what's so wrong with that?' Nancy was trying not to laugh. I didn't think it was so damn funny. Polly blew up on her fringe in irritation.

'I hate this damn thing. I wish I'd never started it. Like, this site is really necessary. This whole thing. It isn't real. It's only real for twenty people, and half-real for twenty more hangers-on. It sucks. Roll on bedtime. Hey, you want to play a game?'

She pulled out a pack of Handy-Andies and instructed Nancy to drink up, because she needed her glass. While Nancy chugged the last inch, Polly separated one ply of a tissue from the other, then took the glass, licked around the rim and spread the tissue taut over the top. Then she dug out a small-denomination coin from the pocket of her Dockers and placed it in the middle.

'You all get a cigarette,' she said, looking at me, so I flashed the ash, 'and you take turns to burn the smallest hole you can. You lose if the coin drops after your burn.'

We hunkered down on our elbows round the glass. Nancy went first, just brushing the Kleenex with the coal of her Kent, and a scorch mark flowered into a hole; then spread alarmingly, its edges glowing. When it dwindled and died Polly went, then me. We played quietly for a while, but games get boring for people waiting their turn if nobody talks. I could so not ask Nancy what the hell she thought she was doing hunting me down like a dog, so I asked Polly if the magazine was going on CD-ROM.

She giggled, and winked at Nancy.

'What?' I complained, worried I'd committed some unforgivable tech *faux pas*.

'Oh, s'nothing,' said Polly. 'It's just we were talking about that earlier. The way people accent the ROM, like it's a kind of a new feature of a CD. It stands for Read-Only Memory, which is just spelling out that it's the same as the old kind. It's a limitation, but people accentuate as though it was a feature. The same way having your job title changed to "consultant" sounds pretty cool, but it just means no security, no sick pay and no medical/dental.'

'It's to gloss over the fact that if you want to use CDs on your computer you have to more or less duplicate the thing you bought ten years ago for your stereo,' said Nancy. 'My go.'

By now, the money was at the nucleus of a spiderweb of charred strands, radiating outwards.

'This is where it gets like Ker-Plunk,' said Polly. 'You have to locate the weak points and avoid them.'

'Like the opposite of marketing,' said Nancy.

'Shit!' said Polly. 'That reminds me. What time is it?'

I checked my Babylon. 'Just after ten.'

'I said I'd have lunch with Zeke,' she said, getting up. 'Later,' and she scampered off.

'Zeke? Lunch?' I said.

'Her boyfriend. He's spending the summer coding in Palo Alto.'

'Oh, sweet,' I said. 'They hook up online, right?'

'Uh, no,' said Nancy, patiently. 'I believe they use the phone. Wouldn't you?'

I guessed so. 'Is he her age too?'

'No, he's eighteen. Boys take longer to mature than girls. Jesus, look at her go.' She leaned back on her arms. 'And look at us. We're here because we have to be. She's here to do them a favour. She doesn't care less about it. She's sixteen, and she's already got over this kind of thing. She thinks it's funny to be here, but she doesn't want to come again. God I wish I'd been like that when I was her age. I would've fawned all over these jerks.'

Polly flitted past the kitchen windows and disappeared. It occurred to me that I should have made an effort to talk to her earlier; or just been less rude, when she'd been making an effort that she really didn't have to. But this was me all over, ditching the cool people to suck up to a bunch of jerks. I wasn't going to do it any longer. For once I didn't feel the fear that I generally take for sincerity in myself.

I went to carry on the game, but Nancy said, Leave it, I like it like it is. She poured herself a drink in a Dixie cup, and made me one too. Then she sat back and looked at me. She really did look like Alice, but the antitype of the animated, generic-Disney-face one; she was that first, scary child-savant, older than the rocks amidst which she sat, looking like she could tell a few good ones about the grave and the charnel-house.

'What are you doing here?' she said. 'It's okay, I haven't told anyone else.' It was unlikely they'd know otherwise. When we were around, if you didn't have cable, and it tended only to be parents who used it as a child-minder who did, you could have blinked and missed us. England was not a major market. Fancy.

'You'd laugh if I told you.'

'So make me laugh. I could use a few.'

She saw I didn't want to and let it go. I didn't want to talk. Instead, I told her about some merchandizing ideas I'd had for the magazine when I was still excited about it.

'A screensaver that's a perfect replication of a filled-in spread-sheet, or merge file, or sales letter. So when it kicks in, it makes it look like it's not a screensaver at all, and you only just left your desk. A watch, that instead of numbers, has little signs telling you to go get a coffee, or check out the job ads.'

'I got one,' she said. 'One of those weather house-barometer things, but hooked up to your bedside phone. Instead of a little man coming out when it's sunny, it dials your work number and plays a tape of you saying you have food poisoning.'

'Or a credit card that buys you freedom from the feeling you're wasting your life.'

'The black AmEx!' she said. I looked blank. 'You don't know about the black AmEx?'

I didn't.

'It's way exclusive. Far above gold, platinum, iridium or whatever. I've always wondered what it could possibly be that was so expensive you needed the ultimate chargecard to buy it with. I mean, what, the right to exhume Jackie Kennedy and make her into furniture? But maybe you've got it. Maybe that's it.'

I thought about it. 'Maybe it is. Are you?'

'Wasting my life? I don't know. I think that whether you are or not, it should feel as though you were. Otherwise you stop pushing yourself and start drifting. I think there are a few cardholders here tonight, or they wouldn't be doing something so lazy.'

I looked down at the lit windows of the kitchen. In a room full of people, Brett was sitting opposite the editor at the kitchen table. He was talking intently across the table at her, and in his earnestness I saw his hand fall upon and cover her own. I didn't know how she could let him do it. It was hard to find this admirable, though I felt like total dogpiss for thinking that.

'You're quiet,' Nancy said. 'D'you want to go in?'

I thought about the moment at the end of a wedding, long after the bride and groom have departed, when the last dance has been danced, and it's time to go back to your room. The lights come up, too bright, and all the people, who looked so well in the dark, blink at each other, and at the smears on the glasses in their hands.

'Not really,' I said, after a while. I had the notion all of a sudden that night is when things come true. 'Do you?'

'God, no,' she said. 'I meant not to stay, but . . .' she waved her wine at me and stuck out her purple tongue.

'Do you get time off for being here? On your weekend and all?' I asked.

She snorted.

'I'm freelance. I didn't have to do this, I offered. The features editor on the *Post* tried to have her staffers – the ones who couldn't pull rank to get out of it – draw straws over who had to cover this. They'd been groaning and faking excuses about it for weeks.

She mentioned it on the phone when she was buying something else from me, and I said I would.'

'Why didn't anyone want to?' Though I could see it might be difficult to get a new angle on this.

'For the same reason that I'm just so . . . not interested. Like, the world needs another style magazine. It's just an internal corporate puff thing for the *Post*.'

'But, surely . . .'

'Aren't these people any good? They may be, but not doing this. All their editorial will be is two thousand words about the kind of life you have if you work for a style mag in London. Hanging out with fatuous celebrities in chic locations. Having delusions implanted and then disseminated by the most sophisticated information transmission superstructure that this particular economic hierarchy is capable of.'

I'd tried to keep it down all day but now I let it go. This wasn't me. I didn't need these people. I felt like we used to when we were at the end of a cycle, lip-syncing the fifth single from the LP for the last time, after four months of doing it all day and nothing else; there might be a new CD out next month, and the whole dumb game would replicate itself play for play, but at least we wouldn't have to do that particular routine ever again. I felt like I was waking up, after a long time asleep. I thought I used to believe in this stuff. Now it felt like I'd waited my whole life to see it for what it was.

'This,' she said, lying back on the grass and gazing at the stars, 'is the kind of magazine bought by people who don't have lives, or think they don't; and want some kind of scale to measure things against. What they'll get from *There* is something that's dressed up to look as though it's just beyond their reach, and it always will be. An endless parade of stuff they won't buy, places they'll never go, people they'd rather die than have to talk to in real life.'

'You're not going to write this, are you?' I didn't dare hope.

'Actually I am.' She blew smoke-rings at the sky. 'It would work better for the *Post* than a straight piece of puff anyway. And it's not going to do them any harm. They'll fold after a few months anyway.'

'Even with the backing they've got?'

'Because of. You don't understand at all, do you? But then you never did. Come here.' She reached up and let her hand fall on the back of my neck. 'All the way.' She drew me down until my cheek was resting against hers. Then she whispered, 'This is to get rid of them.'

I jerked back up.

'No.'

'Disco. All of these people are surplus at the *Post*. They were networked into jobs there – part-time, work experience – because of who they are. They slimed their way onto salary, but the *Post* can't afford them anymore. Given the corporate culture and the public face, making them redundant is unthinkable. Folding a financially untenable and notoriously shallow magazine isn't, however.'

I sat up and stared back over the lawn at the house.

'They're all going to get the can?'

'Uh-huh.' She lit another cigarette, and screwed up her face against the smoke. 'Serves them right. They've had all this on a plate.'

'That's a bit spiteful.'

'No it isn't. Getting to do this sort of thing for a living ought to be something you earned. You don't know how hard people work, and for how long, to get the chance to write about things they might want to. I started on the *Wolverhampton Express*, when I was sixteen. Then a series of other regionals.'

'Jesus.'

'Tell me about it. You had to write big news and little news, and when there was no news you went out and bit a dog. I had six years of grinding it out, then three of the same on a national. Now I get to choose what I do.'

'So you chose to come here,' I said, and ducked to avoid the punch. She still got a good one on the side of my head, though.

'I came here, Mr High 5, to remind myself why I want to stay freelance. If I worked for somewhere like the *Post*, they could make me do this whenever they felt like it. Besides, I'm giving up journalism. I'm through with it.'

'Why?'

'Because newspapers are the IKEA of information. You go in there with the best of intentions – to get a lamp – or with no intentions at all, but it doesn't matter. You come out weighed down with stuff you don't want and won't use, regardless.'

'So, what are you going to do? Ghost more books about me?'

She stared amusedly back at me. I should have found this irritating.

'Why did you write that one? Why are you interested in us?' Why are you *following* me, you bastard?

'I covered one of your lunchtime high-school PAs. Four years ago. For the *Leicester Mercury*. One of the last things I did there.' She blew a smoke ring at me, and I let it hang in the air. 'I never understood why you quit like that.'

'We didn't quit. We were shut down.'

'Yeah. So what?'

'What?'

'You heard. So what if they shut you down? You still had, like, a huge fan-base. You could have carried on.'

I couldn't believe this.

'How could we possibly have carried on? They owned us.'

'No, they didn't. They put you together, and they owned the product and the name, but they didn't own you. You could have gone somewhere else.'

'What on earth for?'

'You still had hundreds of thousands of fans. All they got when you quit was more of the same. You could have carried on what you started and done something better. Something that didn't just tell them their lives were going to work out fine if they emptied their minds and got on the dance floor. At the very worst, you could have gone to a smaller company that was trying to put out something good, and helped them fund it by bringing them whatever margins you could generate.'

It hadn't even occurred to me we could have stayed in the music business. Jesus.

'So what *are* you doing here?' she said. 'If you've come to network, you're not making a very good job of it.'

'I'm working on a screenplay. Of a novel,' I said. 'I came with the author. She just sold it to Ellmann, Westlake.'

'No,' she said. 'What for?'

I named the sum. It was only much later that it occurred to me this mightn't have been the question she was asking. What a moron.

It was also only later that I understood the colossal stupidity of what I'd done. I was supposed to be behind the scenes. No one – least of all a broadsheet journalist, who already knew more about me than I cared for anyone to – ought to know I was involved in the book at all. But I was sore at Brett, though I didn't know what for, and feeling pretty fucked up about it, and my mouth ran away with me.

'Did anyone see the lottery numbers, d'you know?' Nancy asked after a while. I suppose I'd gone quiet. I was beginning to feel embarrassed about what I'd said, so poured scorn on it. I said I didn't care about the lottery, that it was a tax on stupidity, that kind of thing.

'Oh, please,' she said. 'It doesn't become you.'

'No I'm serious.' I reeled off Brett's teaching on the subject. 'If the chance of getting three numbers is $55-1$, why does it only pay like it's nines? What's the point of playing when there's so little reward?'

'You don't get out much, do you?' She regarded me with interest a while, then lay her head back to look at the stars. 'Maybe you'll end up in the real world someday. Possibly sooner than you think. And you'll understand you have to get it anywhere you can. You'll play the lottery.'

I thought about the house edge a moment. Suddenly it didn't seem such an astute analysis of the way things were.

'I'm sorry. I didn't mean to sound superior. I don't know what I'm doing anymore,' I said, to the grass. For a moment, in that way you can be when you're drunk, I was serious.

'I can believe it,' she said. 'But that's okay. You have things to do. You have this screenplay to work on. So roll with it. Maybe you'll surprise yourself.'

I shook my head. 'The only time I'm ever going to surprise myself again is when I think I've got no mistakes left to make.'

She seemed to consider me a moment. 'That's a start,' she said, and looked at her watch. It was after one. 'I'm going to bed.'

'Nancy, please don't.'

'I want to be out of here before anyone else is up. What's your e-mail?'

'Don't go.'

'Do you want to talk again or don't you?'

So I scribbled it on a matchbook, and gave it to her.

'Later,' she said. And I'm like, yeah. Right.

When I was done rubbing my forehead against the grass that still bore her indentation, I reviewed the situation, as far as I was prepared to. It was a freak autumn night, warm and heavy. It was still pretty early. I had twelve cigarettes and three-quarters of a bottle of wine. God knew how far the nearest 7–11 was. But I needed to push this through to morning somehow. I dug around in the pockets of my jacket – I hadn't worn it for a while – but failed to turn up the stale, clingfilm-twisted sixteenth I was hoping for. I drank the wine and smoked four of the cigarettes. Then I smoked the rest, and staggered into the house. It seemed everyone had gone on a munchies run to the two-four, except a circle of die-hard hot-knifers around the Aga. I swear, the smog of coke-sweat and dope haze in there was like LA rush hour in August. I declined an offer from the stoners, and was about to submarine a bottle of wine with about three fingers left when I remembered the Southern Comfort in my room. I went back up there and drank, I don't know, half of it, and lay fully dressed on the bed with one wingtip on the floor to stop the ceiling from spinning. I was sort of semi-conscious for a while, tuning in and out, then I got undressed and got into bed. I sure chose the wrong moment to go to try to fall asleep. All of the rest of them started to come up and go to bed, and I swear, it was like a pharmaceutical version of the Waltons. Got any valium, Jim-Bob? There's some Seconal in John-Boy's room. I'd take two if I were you, Mary-Beth. G'night, Jim-Bob. Here's your Rizlas, John-Boy. G'night, Jimmy-Sue.

Six hours later the sun stole into the room like a cat burglar, and licked at my face as I shifted my head this way and that to get away from it. When I finally booted up vision I found myself pinned by a shaft of light, lying where I had fallen, one foot still on the floor. I groaned, and sat up, my head pounding. I found a bathroom and drank a quart of water from the tap, then cold-showered and dressed in my not-so-sharp-anymore suit because I didn't feel like wearing the clothes I drove down in. I'd honestly expected to be up all night having the kind of conversations I'd waited my life to have, so I'd only brought the suit and a change of underwear. I'd imagined us all sitting round half-empty bottles of bourbon, in our shirtsleeves as the morning shadows shortened, like in *The Hustler*. I'm such a dork.

The kitchen was empty, and I got some juice and sat down at the table, my head on my arms. Presently, two of the aeroba-girls came in from the garden, saw me, and laughed at my wretched state. I weakly wished myself elsewhere.

'God, you were going for it last night,' one said, and covered her hand with her mouth.

'Was I?' This was news to me.

'These floors creak rather, you know.'

'Excuse me?'

'I'm in the room over the corridor,' she said, conspiratorially. 'I passed by yours around five.'

I wasn't in any state to deal with this. I didn't even have the energy to fancy them in my half-assed kind of way today. Their faces, that had seemed the epitome of lazy glamour last night, were about as fascinating as a shareware screensaver when you really checked them out. I made some fatuous remark to change the subject, then asked where everyone else was?

'Oh, here we allow for the hangover like the Spanish for the siesta.'

'Have you seen Brett?' I described her.

They both giggled.

'We *thought* she disappeared rather suddenly last night.'

I gave up on them, and went back to the computer, looked up Brett's room, found it and knocked. The door swung open under my hand, revealing a pristine room, the bed neatly turned down and curtains blowing in the breeze. I remembered River's was next to mine and went along, but though the disarray of the bed (typical River) suggested some unimaginable saturnalia, his things weren't there either. They must have got tired of waiting for me to wake up. I wearily gathered my things together and tried again to open the window, so the room might at least be aired, but it wouldn't shift. The hell with it. I took a last look round then walked down to the car as swiftly as my head would allow. I hated this place now; built on a wish with money that stank; I was glad to be out of it. I drove away from the house, parked in a village called Canford Cliffs; bought a bottle of Vittel from a newsagent's and walked down to the beach to drink it. I meant to stay just long for my head to clear, but the sand was warm, and I put on my Oakleys and lay back, looking like a deranged undertaker on a bender in my dishevelled dark suit. When I woke it was after six and I had a sunburn, from the collar up. I drove back to town trying not to turn my head or yawn.

About the twelfth or thirteenth thing I miss most about being young is not having hangovers like I used to. There was a time when a hangover was almost something to be savoured, like the lazy throb of a hickey beneath the collar of your school shirt; an excuse to relive the events that brought it about, in a sweet, sensually convalescent kind of way. You don't get a hangover like that after eighteen or so. Now you get all the pain and nausea, but with attendant BTEC shrilling paranoia, a PgDip ability to see fear in a handful of dust, and a PhD kind of trepanning self-knowledge that might be useful, welcomed even, any other time except when you're otherwise occupied trying to keep your insides on the inside, while hoping to God you didn't do last night what you can't help suspecting you did, even if it was nothing. Especially if it was nothing. But the absolute worst thing, and this is what I was getting now, is when you think you have a reasonable working outline of what transpired, and you think yeah, okay, that's not so bad. I can deal with that, and you manoeuvre yourself around to accommodate it. But then other pieces come back, that don't fit so well into the beginning, middle and end you've constructed. You're drinking your coffee in the morning and an icecube plops into your mouth.

At odd moments, driving back on the motorway, it started to happen. Odd things came back, that struck discordant notes with the sequence of events I'd manufactured for myself. I suspected that I'd only remembered things so far that fitted the general picture I'd wanted to keep – the smell of the trees as it became dark, the taste of smoke drawn over a palate stained with the wine we'd drunk, the way the light from the kitchen window shone on the grass. Nancy's open-necked shirt, the pulse above her collar-bone.

Now there was the rest, disembodied and in unrelated chunks. Like *déjà vu*, but more unsettling. She'd talked a lot more about her work than I thought. She'd said something terrible that I didn't understand, about recording the actual not being the same as telling the truth. Something about the price of newsprint being raised twenty times, till people stopped buying newspapers. What was that about? She was a journalist, for heaven's sake. I just hoped Brett hadn't noticed me with her too much.

As for Brett. This wasn't anything I could think about now. Clearly things were weirder than I'd had any idea. I wondered whether River was talking about something isolated or cumulative. Or whether he was just trying to get me to back off, whatever his reasons. It wasn't anything I could do much about except be there; and maybe get her away from him if things really came to a head. It had been stupid of me to think they ought to pretend to be co-authors; it had just seemed like that was a better selling point. Stupid. He was the weak link, and this could ruin everything. If it was her on her own, I'd be free to go off with her whenever. I'm sure she would have. We could have just stuck him in rehab till it was over. As it was this situation needed more than I suspected I had.

But it was time to grow up about this. I couldn't go through my life dropping everything the moment it started getting weird. People are. If I'd bothered trying to find the weirdness with Cara, and let her do the same with me, that might have worked out. I did love her once, for about ten minutes. We could be in a flat somewhere. I could be, I don't know, doing an MA now. It could have worked out, but I dropped it as soon as she went stodgy on me. I could have found out why and helped her out of it. I'd let it slide then, but I wasn't going to do it now, with Brett and her brother. There was weirdness between them. I shouldn't just walk away from it. Besides, I couldn't. There was nowhere else to go.

It was time I grew up. I felt like I'd been out to watch some shitty new movie, and come back to find I'd missed *The Philadelphia Story* on TV. Something real was happening, not with some stranger at a party, but in my life before I went there – the life I was going back to. I supposed I'd spent so long waiting for it to happen that it was difficult to believe it was now. Finally I did; all that with Brett earlier had been stupid bravado. It was her plan that was going to save me now, not anything I did without her.

But still more disconcerting was how much I'd told Nancy. Jesus, I was never going to drink again around strangers. Even the fact that I was going to be working on the screenplay of the book, given that she knew who I was, was too much. I needed to be distanced from it as far as possible. My God, if anything got out, it would ruin everything. I'd been so wrong about all of it, and it had been staring me in the face from the start. My little room, at the studio; everything I wanted had been there. Behind the scenes, doing the real work – that was what I loved. It could only get worse after that. Being out front was for the birds. I really ought to have learned this already, but I knew it now.

Going back to the flat suddenly seemed like a big deal. I had that feeling, like when you've just finished with someone and half-wish you hadn't; so you call them to see if they're feeling the same, and they say they're just on the way out with friends. You wonder at what you've set in motion.

But Brett was all smiles when I got back.

'Hey, Jake!' She gave me a hug and kissed me on the cheek as soon as I stepped through the door. 'Wasn't it excellent? Come through, let me get you a drink.'

'Just a Pepsi or something,' I called after her, and followed into the living room. River came in from Brett's bedroom and flung himself down on the sofa, while Brett rummaged about on a drinks trolley that had come to resemble, in miniature, the cityscape from the opening credits of *Dallas*.

'Pepsi,' groaned River. He looked how I felt. 'Pepsi float. Can't take another hair of the dog. Please?'

'Jesus, you pair of lightweights,' said Brett, disappearing into the kitchen. River regarded me blearily from his couch. I wondered how much he remembered. I sat down in an armchair. Brett came back in with a couple of Pepsi floats, and ice in a glass for herself. She gave River his, and he padded back into the bedroom, shutting the door behind him.

'Want a dash of this?' She spun the top off a bottle of Cockspur. I declined politely. 'Suit yourself.' She shrugged, and made herself one. She sat down at one end of the sofa, swung her legs up and sank back.

'Chin chin,' she said, and toasted me with her glass. I waved mine back weakly.

'Well, what did you think?' she asked, but didn't wait for an answer. 'Smart work with that journalist by the way. What was her name? She was the only one I thought might be difficult. We saw you outside with her, and Juliana thought she ought to go out and help you, but you seemed to be keeping her pretty sweet on your own. Did you get her on board? About the book?'

Jesus. 'Oh yeah. Pretty much.'

'Excellent. Well, this is all going swimmingly.' Swimmingly? Christ. 'Things are going to move really fast now. We need to be talked about, written about, part of the buzz – we've got to be hand in glove with everyone who's doing anything now.'

She knew it was worthless and she didn't care. If it had been anyone but Brett I would have reacted with adolescent knee-jerk horror. But I could see her reasoning. It was much harder to make that kind of decision than to see something for what it was, and refuse to get involved. I really did ought to grow up about that. I also saw the point of making me travel there with Juliana. I was just supposed to have been like an extra press agent, talking things up.

'Cool,' said Brett happily. 'Well, I think that's as much as we need to do for the present. They've agreed to run extracts from *Seventeen* in the first issue of *There*. It ties right in with publication – maybe the next issue too. And do a big interview as well, and some lifestyle stuff. Hideous, I know, but we need to maximize this in the right places if it's going to work. In fact, I think I've persuaded Charlie to run a regular fiction section. Have you got any short stories, anything like that?'

I looked uneasy. 'Well, yeah, but . . .'

'Oh, you don't have to pretend they're by us.' She laughed out loud. 'Jesus, we're going to get enough exposure already. You can get them to run them under a pseudonym or something. A whole bunch of pseudonyms. You'll still be the one who gets paid.'

Even though *There* blew in every other respect, this sounded okay. I supposed they didn't really need a face to promote it if it was just filling a slot.

'Well,' I said. 'Yeah. There are a couple of things they could use . . .'

'They don't even have to be proper stories. Even fragments will do, if they're about the right sort of thing. You know, junkies, squats, whatever. Charlie said anything that's like, a swift walk on the wild side for Gap kids, is what they want. Just give me what you have when it's ready and I'll sell it on.' She paused, but I couldn't think of anything to say, so she went on. 'You were right. We're the youngest writers that have been around for ages. That's all that it takes to get people really excited, and they'll pay for whatever we see fit to sell them, for the time being. Charlie's excellent; he's going to be a real help. Juliana too.' She stretched her legs out onto the coffee table, and wriggled her shoulders into the couch contentedly. 'This is all working out quite satisfactorily.

Now we just need to tidy things up. We leave in the morning.'

So we were back to LA. Walking through the swish of the doors at LAX, the flesh was seared on our bones by the heat. It was, so I learned later, the second day into the inhuman fortnight when the Santa Ana winds blow; when the air seems somehow to become a new isotope of itself, like air[9]. I didn't know anything about it at the time, and in retrospect I suspect the others didn't either, because it was idiocy to go back to that. Even inflicting London on ourselves for another ten days would have been preferable. The ostensible reason for our return was that we needed to complete our research for the Director's book; in actuality it was pretty much all done, and just had to be FileMaker Pro'd, which we could have done anywhere. It would have been much better to do it elsewhere, but it seemed like we needed to keep moving around, without really knowing why.

The heat was unbearable and incomparable. If anything, it just kept getting even worse. Every day your back stuck more to the car seat, and your chest got tighter and your throat rawer from traffic fumes, and smoking too many cigarettes in the heat. Our additional torture was to be in an enclosed space together. There was no point finding a bigger place because we were out of there in a month, and it just was so not worth the stress of looking for another place after the short-run lease expired on mine. The idea was that we were going to *Friends* it, with me as Rachel, but I had a problem here. After four years in High 5 I had developed a deeply felt need for a well-defined personal space, and sleeping on the couch for a month in anyone's apartment would have been bad enough – I don't need for people to be able to walk past me as I writhe and gibber whenever they please. Also the whole weirdness that going to stay with people somehow implies. Like, this is going to develop our relationship. We're going to get to know each other, to see who we really are when we're around each other twenty-four hours a day. Groo. I hate that. You use up a big chunk of your RAM just dealing with people if you have to live around them; if you want to run something cool, like Photoshop, it needs all the RAM you can give it, so you need to shut down all the other applications first. This can take days of solitude. Also I need at least an hour to assemble my emotional and psychological armour every morning, before I plan to let anyone attempt even the most cursory interface. But Brett had been quite firm. I wanted to go to a hotel, but she said we couldn't afford it. I suspect she just wanted to bring things to a head.

This was the time and the place for it to happen. I don't think any of us slept for ten days. Taking a cold shower and standing dripping in front of a fan worked for about ten seconds. Queues for the bathroom at four a.m. Days blurred into each other. About the most original thought I had the whole time was that the summers had got too weirdly hot like the tomatoes had got too weirdly red. I poured some out of the can into a pan of onions one night, and was shocked at how vivid they were. The sunset outside the window was the same colour. It occurred to me that both have had their DNA fucked with. Which was pretty deep. But that was the kind of thought whose originality startles you after ten days of click n' drag, dropping headers and chunks of text from Word into FileMaker. We took shifts at it, six hours each, two shifts a day. It prevented us interfacing anyway. When whoever was off shift we'd go to Gelson's or the Galleria just to be in air conditioning, or go for a swim, or drive to the hyper-rich ghetto the other side of the freeway, where the winds didn't seem to blow. Time passed. We were three days from finishing. I was semi-conscious on the couch and River was PowerBooking in the walk-through kitchen. None of us had said a word to each other beyond the strictly functional for at least sixty hours. Brett came in from the hall.

'How long has there been a message on the machine?'

I struggled up. River looked sullenly in over the counter.

'There's a message on the machine. Someone must have been working when it came in. Someone must have heard it.'

We both looked blank. It was a weird occurrence, because practically all their friends had left, visas and green cards expired. A few were doing voluntary EFL in Africa, Indonesia – the Fifth but with better scenery – the rest had just gone home. Loulou was still around but there had been some kind of falling out that no one was talking about.

'What does it say?' said River.

Brett walked back into the hall and came in again with the machine in her hand. She hit play.

It was from the Director, just asking how we were, saying he was sorry he missed us if he had, and saying goodbye. There was some weirdness going down, because he said, This is Sasha. Sasha was his nickname, but it was only used by the media, along with all the other people who didn't know him. Some columnist had made it up and started using it three decades ago, to imply some sort of personal intimacy, when actually the Director had hated her guts. Whatever, it stuck. He even joked with us about it once or twice, how know-nothing studio assholes would call across the room at the Four Seasons, Hey, Sasha! to impress the people they were dining with. He had begun to call out for pizza as a consequence.

We went over. It was too hot to think about doing anything that involved staying inside any longer. Besides, the Director had air conditioning.

There was no answer from the entryphone. We scanned the code from the maid's infrared key months ago, so we let ourselves in. There were no cars in the driveway and all the second-storey windows were open, which was insanity in this heat. Brett killed the engine and there was a weird moment in the car. I was in the back, and saw them exchange this weird look. Then we got out and went in.

Somewhere on the edge of every town there is a lake or a hill or a ballpark or whatever that's universally designated stoner central. Where you go when everything else has closed but you're not ready for your life to resume just yet. You wind up there at dawn some sweet summer morning, but there's a car there that shouldn't be – a Scorpio, a Mondeo – with a guy inside. It never occurred to you that regular people came here, except during the day. You try to ignore it and carry on as usual, but when you shut off your engine you can hear the executive motor idling. Then you notice the vacuum hose trailing out of the window. The guy's closed eyelids are turning blue but his chest is still moving. What do you do?

Tumbleweeds roll through my memory here. We found him upstairs, in bed. There was a bottle of Ty Nant water in one hand and an empty flask of Veronal in the other. River and Brett seemed to take it totally in their stride. I was freaking. I checked his pulse, my hands shaking almost too bad to do it, then snatched up the phone.

'What are you doing?' River looked at me sharply.

'Calling 911. Jesus, what d'you think?'

'Put it down.'

I didn't believe this. I gaped at him. 'Excuse me?'

'You heard.' He turned back to the bed.

'Brett.' She looked up. I appealed to her. She looked at River, then back at me, shook her head slightly, and turned back to the Director.

'Oh, right –' I began pacing about '– we're just going to like, sit and watch him die. Cool. Am I the only one who is aware of the existence of security cameras?' I was frantic. 'There will be an inquest. You understand? They'll look at the tapes. They show us arriving. It'll be obvious we were here before the time of death. We'll be accessories. They could even say we did it. We need to call a paramedic, and we need to do it now. For fuck's sake! What's the matter with you? Brett?'

She looked again at River, who held her glance with a fixed glare. She got up from the bed, and walked to the window.

'Be quiet,' said River flatly. 'This doesn't concern you.'

'The hell it does.' I was practically hysterical. 'Do you know how much money's tied up in this guy's estate? People are going to be suing each other out the wazoo. This is not going to be some thing that's no big deal. There'll be insurance investigators from hell to breakfast and I-am-not-going-to-jail, okay?'

River stood up, walked round the bed, and interposed himself between me and the door.

'Sit down,' he said.

'Jesus, what's the big fucking deal here? We call a doctor, we're out of here. And don't you gorilla on me, River.'

We glared at each other. I couldn't believe this was happening. Brett was still on the bed. We held eye contact for a moment, then she looked away. I hated this most. Watching her accede to River was like seeing the strong sassy girl you fell in love with wilt before her parents. It was unbearable.

'Did you *know* about this?' My voice was weak. I hated it. She didn't look up. I turned away in disgust, and went to push past River. He gave a brief, involuntary noise of exasperation. Then he slugged me.

The Director took hours to die. I sat in the bathroom dabbing at the horizontal split on the bridge of my nose, burning the Kleenex in the bathtub when they were too bloody to absorb any more. My eyes puffed up like I'd had rhinoplasty. I looked like some camera-sneaked-into-Pia-Zadora's-clinic shot from the *Enquirer circa* 1980. I felt totally traumatized. Like Christopher Walken says, it fucks you up.

Brett had come in for a while, and shut the door behind her.

'I'm sorry,' she said, looking at me uncertainly.

'Are you sleeping with him?' The time for subtlety was way

past. She looked keenly at me, then dropped her glance. She went over to the mirror and started doing her eyes.

'Wrong tense. Once. At Nice. The night before you arrived. It just happened, okay? You know how the casino makes you feel. And I don't want to talk about it. Here.' She handed me a tissue she'd used to blot for me to burn also. 'Besides, don't we have more pressing things to consider?'

And that had been that. We went out to the Food Mart about an hour after his death rattle started, twenty minutes after his body had evacuated itself. We got a six of sodas and maybe some dip and came back, me wearing sunglasses to shield the damage from the security cameras. We needed to kill another hour or so. Brett and River checked out the house for a while, all the rooms we'd never been in before. Then they made me make the call.

We were interviewed separately. We told them we just came in to work, that we didn't usually see him, that he didn't like to be disturbed, that there was resentment on his side about the project to begin with. I said my face was from fainting when I found him. They checked everything out with UriZen. It checked out. So we were out of there.

Four days later we were back in London. River did a nicely understated apology that had more sincerity than something effusive, and I could see that this wasn't the kind of thing that anyone could put their finger on and say, there, this is right and this is wrong. I think they both knew he was going to kill himself all along, that it was all arranged. It made a kind of sense; they, who spent much more time with him that summer than I did. I wished, if this was true, that they'd told me before, but at least this way the only damage was my nose – I might have really gone overboard if it hadn't been happening right in front of me, and therefore more difficult to stop.

Though the Director wasn't the issue at all. She had slept with

River. She said it was over. He had claimed back in England that it wasn't. This blew, but the worst thing was that, as if things weren't complicated enough, we had, once again, all the associated stress of killing with none of the actuality. We were on to our second victim but still hadn't actually zedded anyone. At least, if we'd just popped a cap on someone's ass, mown them down and reversed over them, things would be slightly more cut and dried. As it was there was an awful feeling of inconclusiveness.

An uneasy stasis was painstakingly generated over the next couple of weeks, but we were so not talking about it. We drank a lot. We never got up before noon, and earlier and earlier into the p.m. Brett would disappear into the kitchen, and come out shaking up a cocktail that, poured out, looked and tasted suspiciously like liquidized Deep Heat. She said she'd read somewhere that for every new thing that came into the world something old disappeared, and she was trying to sabotage the effect by keeping post-Prohibition cocktail recipes alive. She'd hold her latest Technicolor concoction up to the light and regard it appreciatively, and when she said, see off a couple of these and see if you can find the door, you didn't doubt it for a moment.

I suspect now that the booze had nothing to do with the Director or even with the other two. The ease with which I embraced it seems to suggest it was more a reaction to the last few years than anything else. It wasn't like, it eased my passage back from the frantic tunnel-vision of creation. Right. It was more that I needed to be anaesthetized. I hadn't really got used to doing nothing yet. I'd worked like a madman, like an imbecile, for five years, driven like a crazy person by managers, producers, choreographers, directors; and when there was no one left to push me, I pushed myself till I thought I'd go mad with the strain. The hoops got higher and the biscuits ever smaller, till they both practically receded from view.

But I'd been issued with this invitation before, had a hell of a time turning it down then, and couldn't let this get out of hand now when I was so close to the tape. It would have been easy, so long ago now, to have simply followed the prescribed vectors of precocity, as far as I understood them, and sunk my winnings into a swamp of self-destruction: allowed my success to become my identity, let drink – mostly rum drinks – become a part of me, as much as the way I liked to sleep late, to linger over the newspaper, to buy American cigarettes and the New York *Herald Tribune* in convenience stores late at night. I could have become the sort of ex-celebrity who stole ashtrays from the Orient Express, got hoofed out of Nell's, turned up drunk or wired or both on late-night short-run minimal-reach chat shows, until finally I couldn't get the silk rope raised at the Atlantic anymore and woke, with a horrible start one night, to find myself swaying in line outside Stringfellows. Then maybe I'd leave town, become interested in conspiracy theories, join anti-abortion groups, a cult; get kicked out when the money ran dry, fall apart, move back, renegotiate the foot-hills of the circuit. Call my agent, fax my agent, break down in front of his intern, stand shivering outside Mezzo waiting for him to emerge. Network, flatter and beg; be a source, be a guy, be available. Make up the panel for commercial radio quiz shows, take bit-parts in TV movies, wait for what went around to come around, until finally I could appear in the B-list pages of *People* magazine to tell the world how great it was to be straight. And round we went again.

The best case scenario was that we all successfully forget the last few weeks, and pick up somewhere we left off way back. This could have been total free time, like being seventeen, when your parents go on holiday. You get the house, the car, the consumer durables; you get to choose what and when you eat, drink, live. Everyone comes to crash for the duration, and your boring old house turns into Party Central. But even if this were possible, the jaded, nauseous drive to the recycler with a dozen black bags of cans and bottles, the frantic search through the *Yellow Pages* for a glazier who works Sundays, the wall-eyed mornings spent blearily hosing flowers of vomit off the patio, had all lost their edge. There was nothing to make them worth doing anymore.

It began to seem like it was a regime with Brett and River, in those few weeks, an anti-health farm we'd booked into for the duration. They meant to stick to the program if it killed them.

One Friday morning it was especially bad. I woke at five and staggered into the kitchen for cigarettes from our duty-free arsenal in the kitchen. It had been a week of shimmering pressure confluences, the air quality indices scoring off the charts; my asthma had been straining like a balloon ready for flight, testing the slack in the tethers of my medication all week, and I'd barely been able to bring myself to smoke at all; now it was colder, the sky was darker, the city exhaled again. I drew it gratefully over my palate, counting off the six seconds until the tightness behind the bridge of my nose as the nicotine kicked in, bringing with it the usual panic. Hemingway was running the bulls at Pamplona on the nine thousandth, one hundred and thirty-first day of his life – I was failing to blow coherent smoke rings in a breakfast nook in Battersea. Oh, the hell with it. Grace Kelly was twenty-two when she made *High Noon*, the same age as Winona Ryder was for *Reality Bites*; Lauren Becall was nineteen in *To Have and Have Not*, the same age as Juliette Lewis in *What's Eating Gilbert Grape?* Besides, I was twenty-five today. It seemed rather draconian punishment for having been twenty-four for twelve months. I rose and walked out to the roof garden, sat near the edge with my knees drawn up to my chest, and looked out over the roofs to the river and Chelsea beyond.

A dull pencil had been taken to the bright sky of yesterday overnight, and now the future squatted over the city, humped in colourless silence: almost palpable, as though some dreadful confinement was about to be brought to term. I finished my

cigarette and lit another. I shouldn't really smoke at all, but I'd
been made to pretend to give up for most of High 5, and I decided
I was going to smoke freely for four years after to compensate.
You need to have goals.

The sound of the UPVC door gliding open and shut behind
me made me start, but I didn't look round. I knew it was Brett
even before she sat down beside me, hugging her knees through
a fleece, over a long white linen nightie that she'd unbuttoned at
her throat.

'Hey,' I murmured. I meant it to come out cool and confident,
indicating the calm psychological weather within, but it barely
came out at all.

'Hey,' she said. She peered at my nose. 'You should get that
treated.'

'Give me a hundred bucks and I'll take it to dinner.'

She laughed. Now the swelling was down I was beginning to
get used to it. Besides, I figured it would help me blend in in
prison.

'We need to talk?'

I didn't know what to tell her, because I wasn't so sure myself.
All of a sudden I felt a damn stupid tear rolling down the side of
my nose. I wanted to ask it what the hell it thought it was doing.
It was totally typical that it was on her side, and of course she saw
it.

So suddenly I had my face pressed into her chest and her hand
stroking my hair, and sort of rocking me, going shush-shush-shush.
I totally lost it then, naturally. I mean, this was like physical contact.

'C'mon, Jake,' she was saying. 'C'mon. You're feeling left out.
It's okay. Don't feel bad that we're taking this over. God knows,
we'd rather be doing our own thing on our own terms as well.
C'mon. Deep breaths. And blow.'

I sniffed, trying to suppress a snicker I couldn't help. She saw
it and smiled.

'There you go. Don't feel bad. We can work together, and we'll get where we want to go some day if only we can only bring this off. Okay? And I know how badly I've got to make that happen, because I'm never going to be able to let River alone if it doesn't.'

I kept it shut. I didn't want to make any response that might derail this.

'He knows it too, which is why he's so demanding on me. You know? He's my brother. He has a rich reserve of unfair pressures to bring in to play, deep-seated affinities to draw on. You do understand that I can't leave him, don't you? Not until I'm sure he can be left. And I know he will, one day. First we need to do what we need to do.'

I sat up, and fumbled out my cigarettes. We both lit one, and she exhaled heavily.

'You deserve to hear this. It's not fair of me to keep avoiding the issue.' She took a deep one. 'I can't begin to explain what it's like with him. We've been on the planet together twenty years, never out of each other's pockets for long enough to let ourselves become anything but, I don't know, analogues of each other. But we are different.' She held my eyes a moment, then looked down, then back out over the rooftops. 'I've often got to wondering, if we'd been born a couple of years apart instead of within an hour of each other, how we might have turned out. You know? Just a regular sister and brother. What different leverages we might exert on each other, whether we'd have any kind of relationship at all – or whether we could just be, I don't know, incidental to each other. He'd be someone who was around sometimes, if I went back to my uncle's; he'd be someone I'd hear about in letters, in phone calls; I could have the luxury of asking how he was, hearing what he was doing, you know? Being happy for him as a totally separate person. Which must be the most easy and satisfying emotional fix there is. And then I could tell all about what I was doing, and maybe someone could be happy for me too.'

She was murmuring now, like an incantation. I guessed this scenario represented real life to her. Escape.

'And we'd have, I don't know, jobs, friends, lovers; living our lives on totally different vectors, never meeting except by accident or obligation. People say – and I imagine this must be like having fatuous jerks coming up to *you* and being, like, it must have been so great to be in that band, when they don't know a damn thing about it – we get, oh yeah, it must be wonderful to be that close to someone, you know? Never being stuck for someone to confide in, never having to square up to a night on your own. And yes, I'd have to concede that we do have that. But I've never known how it might feel to be alone. Really alone, and having to face up to yourself, and thinking about who you are, what you're doing, where you're going and what you're going to do when you get there. It's so easy to deflect that, when there're two of you. You can make yourself so busy just trying to keep things straight, that you can defer all the regular kinds of decisions that people get forced to make while they're living. And yes –' she sighed '– I know that most of those choices involve losing sight of the kind of person you wanted to be; but at least you're going somewhere, even if it's not where you thought you'd wind up. I get to feeling like I'd be happy to take anything, sometimes, instead of this awful responsibility.' She threw her cigarette away. 'God, you don't know how much I'd like to be the one to weird out once in a while – to do the leaning instead of getting leant on the whole time. But this is the way we've become. This is the deal we have, and until there's a way out for both of us, I don't have any option but to go along with it.'

We were so not talking about it. She turned back to me, and put her hand over mine.

'He knows that too, which is why he's so demanding. But I

think you know what it would mean for you and me – for us, Jake – if I knew he wouldn't go straight off the rails the moment I left him to his own devices. But I can't do it now.'

'Did you want to? When you slept with him?' I didn't look at her. She was quiet a moment.

'It just happened. Like I said. We could have been anyone. We were just two bodies, and that's all. We've never talked about it, and I don't think we ever will. It's not true, this share-your-feelings-with-the-group crap. Some things are best left alone.'

I drew away from her and sat up, took a cigarette out of the pack then decided I didn't want it. I lit it anyway and let it burn in my fingers.

'Is he going to be around forever?'

'Don't do this to me, Jake.'

'Is he?'

She sighed. 'I couldn't bear to lose either of you, okay? And if we can make this work out I can have both of you forever. But if I put a foot wrong now then I'll lose you both. I need you to be here for me now. I can't do this on my own.'

We smoked fags for a while then went back to bed. There was an unspoken agreement that we should make an effort. This was free time, probably the last we'd have for several years if everything went off like we wanted. And if it didn't, we would have the rest of our lives to couch in. I proposed all going clubbing together, though I was kind of prompted into it by Brett. It was a bit rich – the two of us creating elaborate fictions for River's benefit, like he was the wounded one instead of the neanderthal ape who spread my nose all over my face – but it made me feel like I was in collusion with her against him. I got to be the adult, while he was the weird one. It was putting one over on him and he knew it. It was pretty childish, and I did feel bad about it, but you know.

We all made a big deal of being cool about going out, and Brett kept giving me encouraging glances as we drank through the afternoon. They got more and more up for it, and when the time came, I trailed into my room and changed, making an effort to shift up to their plane of excitement. I kind of gave myself a pep talk in the mirror. *Don't pussy out on me now; you're a fuckin' Beretta.* It was stupid to get gimpy now; this had been my idea. There really was nowhere else to go, and I had better get used to it. Knowing that never really helps, but I was a Beretta, however.

As we dressed, three different stereos competed for air time. We were making a concerted effort to be still at that early stage of sharing a flat when you think hard about what you put on before you jack the volume up to eleven. I turned mine (Tricky) down for a moment and wandered out of my room to hear what the others were spinning – Brett had middle-to-late-period Velvets, and River Frank and Nancy. It was after midnight, but our evening was just beginning. This was a reason to feel good, so I tried to make the most of it.

I'd been putting off meeting up with any of the rest of High 5 until I'd done something with my life. Ollie had done something with his way before me, and I was surprised at him – not that he'd done it, but that he'd done it so quickly. I saw the first notices of his club within weeks of High 5's official dissolution, though we hadn't seen each other for months before that. I suppose he'd been planning it for ages, and I was too busy mooning over my PowerBook to notice.

He would have been the easiest one to see because of his club. I kind of hadn't gone because I didn't want to have to queue up with a bunch of civilians just to be able to see my friend, yet the same time I didn't want to have to explain to some camp git of a rope-raiser that I was who I was while the whole line looked on. But mostly I hadn't gone because I hate the whole stupid scene now, and especially the people who run it. In every club I'd ever been in, the DJ was supposed to be some kind of star; way up on a podium, spotlit and radio-miked, twiddling more knobs than Neil Armstrong, fiendishly sliding fake EQs, cross-arm mixing. I mean, jesus, you're only playing records. But everyone's supposed to get all kind of reverent in an off-your-chump sort of way when some old casualty with an agent climbs up and informs you that they're in the house. I couldn't stand to see Ollie doing that, and everyone taking it like it was incredibly cool in some hyper-ironic kind of way, and waving their dumb hands in the air. I couldn't stand going to clubs after a while because I spent the whole night waiting for someone to do something phoney. Even at ones that didn't have their titles in the possessive case.

I couldn't have been further off the fairway. The club – the Gargoyle – was like nothing I'd seen before. The guy on the door was wearing a plum velvet tux coupled with a rayon shirt and aviators. He seemed to recognize me, and waved us through to a rickety old lift that took us up to a weird, note-perfect simulation of a mirror-lined Fifties supper club, tables and all. Peggy Lee's Latino version of 'I Enjoy Being A Girl' was drifting, barely audible, out of subdued speakers.

We were waved to a table, and ordered tequila and Luckies from a passing cigarette boy. This was a pretty cool place, I had to admit it. Up to the Eighties clubs used to have VIP rooms, with studded plush banquettes where fading celebs could network with gangsters, free from interruption. The Gargoyle seemed like one huge VIP room, where everyone was inside the charmed circle just by virtue of wanting to be different. Best thing of all was there was no sign of a DJ. I knew Ollie was here though, and I knew he knew I was. Two tracks after we came in, 'Louie Louie' came on. It was an old joke. Ollie used to call me Louie, after the song, because I could never be arsed to learn the words very well, and used to slur over the bits I forgot. Listening to live tapes, I did sound exactly like the guy from the Kingsmen in places. Fahn lil gur/Zwayn for me/Catch ur shi/Uh guzzerzeay. River and Brett had got up to get more drinks, and on the pretext of looking for the men's room, I went to find Ollie.

A bartender took me through a door at one side, and showed me into what looked like an editing suite, with Ollie at the controls.

'Hey,' I said.

'Big Jake,' he said, 'hold on.' He slid the faders down on one side and up on the other, and I heard 'Somethin' Stupid' come through the wall. He slipped off his cans, and got up and gave me a hug. It was good to see him.

'So what's with this tuneage?' I said. This was more my stuff than his. He was always dragging us off, in Kangol-and-Oakley disguise, to the Ministry when we were in London; and to Boy's Own, DiY, Up Yer Ronson and Cream when we weren't. There was an element of necessity rather than choice though; we were, as you can imagine, fairly universally reviled, and parties were one of the few places we could go without getting our faces pushed in. For a start, everyone there looked like us – we'd shaved our heads by this point, Shelley having decided that we were entering our spiritual, CKOne phase – and besides, it's easy to blend in when you're with twenty thousand people off their chumps somewhere in an old aircraft hangar. And when the bass shanghais your pulse, and the world stops turning . . .

'You can't get a decent DJ to play London any more,' Ollie said, to my question. 'The people are so sniffy. They'll walk out if they don't get exactly what they expect on the playlist. You can't experiment, can't try out new stuff. It's like being in some dope record store, where everyone, like, smiles and nods their heads when the track changes to show how cool they are, and if you don't know the guy behind the counter you can't buy the records. It's no fun. And I knew I couldn't compete with some corporate theme-park. So I thought, something different? Turn it down? And they love it. Look at them.'

It dawned on me that the glass above the mixing desk was a

two-way mirror into the club. Though it wasn't four-to-the-floor, hands-in-the-air out there exactly, it looked like there was a nice buzz. People were actually sitting round talking, getting up, wandering from table to table, smiling. Moreover, there wasn't a single person with their sunglasses on their head.

'They're not behaving like they're in a club at all,' Ollie said, smiling out at his little empire. 'Do you see anyone being cool?'

I didn't.

'They're acting like they never have to go home,' he said. 'You know? Cool exists because, all the time people know they're going to get hoofed out pretty soon, then all anyone has time to go on is surface. But if you don't have to go home in a couple of hours, you can talk without it just being a line. I never close. There aren't any locks on the doors, because they're never shut.'

'Don't people have to go to work?'

'I guess. But I think they don't all go to work at like, nine-to-five. You know? It's not necessary. We have electric light now.'

'Why aren't you out front?' I said.

'Same reason.' He took a woof on his Snapple. 'You're only playing records, y'know? Want some bud?'

I grinned, and he rolled a fatty, dropping some Julie London into the mix. We blazed up and sat back in the big, barber-shop chairs.

'Old times,' he said, with a sardonic smile. It was kind of like being in the studio. Not that we ever spent much time there. 'Seen any of the others?'

I shook my head, and chuffed out smoke. 'You?'

'I went down to see Max, couple of months ago. Not doing anything much. Total downer. How's your screenplay?'

'Oh, you know,' I said. 'I'm just kind of tinkering with it now. It's pretty much done.' I looked out the window at Brett and River, and decided something. 'Hey, do you have to stay in here all night? Want to come and meet my friends?'

He called someone up on the phone, and a Japanese guy came in and took over. Ollie handed him what was left of the smoke, and we went out.

It took a while to locate them, and Ollie dragged me round the tables to say hi to some people. He seemed to know everyone – boys in hipsters and Cenci tops, girls in Holmes and Kool Action. Then I picked them out on the floor, and waved. They waved back, and I watched them a while while Ollie talked with some friends. They were horsing around, doing real dances with real steps – the Pony, Walking the Dog – dances that Parlophone and Decca and Capitol had put a marketing spend behind a decade before we were born. Before even our parents had been old enough to dance them. I liked this stuff because it meant nothing to me; it belonged not to my past, but to someone else's, long ago. I loved these songs because they weren't part of my life – they didn't remind me of anything, couldn't reproach me for wasted chances. The Japanese guy put on the *Bewitched* theme, and the whole place went quiet.

Eventually Brett and River came over, and I introduced them.

'Ollie *Silverton*? Like Jack Silverton? The composer?' said Brett.

'Uh-huh,' said Ollie. 'My dad writes film scores, my mum restores Moogs, my sister plays bass in some guitar band. Our family put the funk in dysfunctional.'

General laughter. The talk evolved into a long discussion about the music he was playing. Ollie said this generation was only able to be into it because the last fifty years were suddenly available on CD. The old, insatiable desire for the new only existed because the old wasn't available; you couldn't have got hold of this stuff in the Seventies. Brett said that was all very well, but this stuff was only available now because the people who'd bought it first time round were affluent again; they'd bought it on 78s and 33s when they first had disposable income; then they'd had houses and kids and things to spend their money on; now, the kids had left home and the mortgages had been paid off, and they could afford to buy the same old stuff again. So a new format was invented, to persuade them to upgrade.

'We could have had CD technology in the Seventies, but there wouldn't have been any point. Like we could have had unleaded petrol and catalytic convertors in the Seventies. They did in America, but not here. Things have to wait until the market's ready.'

Things became fragmented for a few hours from here. Ollie and I did some E, but mine turned out a bit speedy. I freaked for a while, and failed totally to chill. Finally I dragged Ollie aside and hit him up for a valium ('Sure. But, jesus, who's that girl? Some kind of agent? Does she ever lighten up?'). I went home on my own.

I felt ill for days, but it had been a moderately successful experiment. I didn't want to push it though. There were still weeks before Ellmann would have anything for us to do, and though I didn't want to leave Brett alone with her brother I didn't want to hang around either. Besides, it was Christmas, so I went home.

I couldn't deal with that either. It didn't seem to have much to do with my life. Quite apart from anything else I found my old Filofax in my room, with the diary from the year before last. Reading it was torture. I envied this person who had so much to do. I hated him. My life had not turned out how I thought. I needed to get out of here, but I didn't want to go crawling back to the apartment too soon. I decided to go and see Max. I remembered what Nancy had said, about getting back together. I mean, over my stiffening corpse, but, you know. Maybe I shouldn't have been so quick to assume everything was over. We were all in the same boat, after all. I'd been meaning to call him – all of them – for ages, but I wanted to have done something with my life first. Which probably meant never. I couldn't get him that night, but his mum was quite nice on the phone when she realized who I was. She said to try again next day, and I got him the next morning. He was really surprised, and said to come down if I wanted – there wasn't much to do, but we could hang out, whatever. It was only half an hour on the train besides. I left after lunch, feeling pleased that I was doing it. Going to see him was like the anticipation of seeing a favourite film. You know what they're going to say, how they're going to behave. I got a cab from the station out to the terrifying suburb he lived in, located the house and rang the bell.

An unfamiliar shape loomed up behind the frosted glass and the door opened a crack. A balding guy in a slacks 'n' slippers combo revealed himself.

'Yeah?' His eyes were dead. Dead eyes. I thought for a moment I'd got the wrong house, but the squirly numbers by the letterbox were a pair of threes, same as on the gate.

'Uh, is Max in, please?'

'Who're you?'

'I'm Jake . . . Mr Williams? We haven't met but I was in High 5 with Max.'

'You'd better come in,' he said, grudgingly, and shuffled back to admit me to a daytime-soap hall that smelled of carpet shampoo and fabric conditioner. We stood uncomfortably facing each other for a second, him eyeing me as though I were catching.

'Is he . . . at home?' I inquired.

'He's asleep,' said Max's dad. 'Do you want me to wake him?'

No, hey, why don't you and me crack open a couple of cool ones, shoot the breeze a while? I'm sure we have so much in common.

'He's, uh, expecting me?'

'Is he? Is he?' He looked away for a moment, running a last check on what I'd said in case there was anything there that might reasonably justify his slamming me up against a wall. I let my face go slack, and stared into the middle distance, trying not to give him a reason.

'You,' he said flatly, gesturing at the kitchen, 'go in there. I'll go up and talk to him.' He climbed the stairs.

I walked stiffly into the kitchen, convinced I'd got the wrong house. Norman Bates here was clearly just slipping the wig off its mannequin and running a trembling Watney's thumb down the length of the blade. How long would it be before my body was found? I'd kind of suspected the only TV I'd ever get on again would be the news. The back door was Chubbed and Yaled, and the windows were security-locked also. Back out the way I came meant going blind past the foot of the stairwell. But standing on lino was asking for it. The hall carpet was a pale blue – maybe the thought of getting stains out of that might stay his hand for the vital seconds I needed. I ventured gingerly back out, and then Max was grinning down over the banister, thinner, in his bathrobe, than I remembered him, and with his hair all scrunched up on one side.

'Hey, snakehips,' I said. A teen magazine called him it once.

'A'right, sunshine? Come up.'

I followed him into a box bedroom and he closed the door behind us, punched me on the arm; then looked suddenly grave, put a finger to his lips, and flipped the stereo from standby with a remote. Some nice chunky Bach came on, and he nudged the volume down to a level that made talking possible but would scramble what we said to anyone outside.

'My dad,' said Max. 'I'm sorry. I meant to get up earlier.'

'Jesus,' I said, 'what happened now?'

'Oh, just more of the same,' said Max, looking kind of haggard. All the time in High 5, Max had been bombarded with permanently depressing news from home. His father got made redundant around the time we started, had a breakdown, spent eighteen months getting it together, started his own business that went to the wall after six months, then got another job, got ill, didn't have sick pay in the new job, used up his insurance with the breakdown, got let go again, and so on. 'It's worse now,' he said. 'I mean, he's better and everything, and remission's really unlikely, but they remortgaged this place for his business, then had to borrow more for his treatment, and they still owed for this home office thing he set up to try and make it seem like he had a life. And then the bank foreclosed. You know? Like it was a softball game and they could call time out, the bastards. It was because they knew about me. I paid them off the first time with most of what I had, but they still think I've got way more stashed away somewhere.'

'Oh look, hey Max, if you're short now . . .'

'Nah, don't be silly,' he said. 'You'll need it, and it doesn't go far, trust me.'

'No really, come on, man,' I said. 'I've got more now.'

'That's okay,' he said. 'I wish I'd never done it. He's so weird with me now.' He looked down and sighed, and a thick comma of hair fell down over one eye, the way it had on a million posters. He pushed it back irritably. 'Oh screw it. I try not to think about it. I'm working on something anyway. Check this out.'

He pulled across the sliding doors of a fitted wardrobe closet thing. It was stuffed with equipment, stacked high on punched steel shelves. I gaped. It was like Burt Bacharach's bedroom in there. Four Tascam 4-tracks feeding an ancient 8-track desk, a $1000 sampler, a Mac Classic, a Roland 808, a bunch of phasers and delays and flangers seemingly welded together. I don't know what else.

'Jesus, Max, where'd you get all this?'

'*Loot*, liquidations, wherever,' he said. He slapped the desk. 'You should see inside this thing. *Valves*. You wouldn't believe what you can do. It's like reverb, cubed.'

'What are you doing with it all?'

'Grab yourself some cans, boy.'

We both slipped on a pair, and he booted the Mac, then flipped a dozen power switches. If it had been eight hours later we would have seen the streetlights dim. He handed me a battered old Telecaster, plugged it into one of the channels, clicked a few times on the Mac screen, sparked up the 808 and instructed me to play a fairly standard progression, while he plunked away at a Casio kids' keyboard. I hadn't picked up a guitar since the last tour − I only learned, as we all did, so as to while away time while we were on the bus, or sitting out soundchecks − and the integrity of my changes left a little to be desired, but he seemed unconcerned. When we'd run it through a couple of times he signalled to stop, then sat down at the computer, clicked a couple more times, then slid some stuff around on the desk. Then he hit return.

A perfect, six-piece band playing the same progression as we just had flooded back through my cans. I could count at least three guitars, one a twelve-string, all playing perfect counterpart variations to my own sloppy chordwork, which I could just make out on one faint channel, way over on the right. There was a seamless bass, a Philly Hammond, and a drummer slapping seven shades of shit out of a ten-grand kit in there too. I gaped over at Max. He grinned back and clicked again with the mouse; a six-piece string section kicked in. And again, and they took it into a middle eight we hadn't played, and out the other side into a mirror variation, with a brass section too. It was kind of cheesy, but cool. He let it run awhile, then moved some stuff around on the desk, clicked up a few menus, and I nearly fell over. It had turned into thumping, full-on techno, but the same basic progression. He clicked again and we got handbag. Again; trip-hop. Four-to-the-floor. Hi-NRG. Old school acid house. Acid jazz. I was reeling. Still the same progression, still my crappy phrasing in there some-where, on a distant channel. Yardbirds-y R'n'B. Bluebeat. Prog-rock. White-knuckle hardcore. I couldn't take any more and pulled off my cans. The Bach was still on his little stereo. He slipped his off and beamed.

'Jesus, Max, what've you done?'

He laughed.

'I learned C++ on the laptop they gave me.'

'I thought you were playing Doom.'

He snorted. He was always hunched over his, as I was over mine for the last couple of years. The others used to rip it out of us.

'Then I wrote this application, and started collecting hardware. I'm trying to refine it, so you don't need so much stuff. You don't if you just use samples. But it helps to play it yourself – gives it a margin of deviation to jam from.'

'Jesus. It's so *good*. It's seamless. You really wouldn't know that wasn't a dozen different recordings. How did you think of it?'

'It came to me on stage, actually. You know how you'd drift off?'

I did. We were so well rehearsed, down to the last wink and swagger, that after the first couple of dozen shows you really could just tune out and think about something else, for the rest of that promotional cycle anyway.

'I was just thinking about the way they put us together, and it came to me.' He sat down cross-legged on his bed. 'You know? The one thing wrong with High 5 as a concept is the market fragments as it grows up. They get into genres. So what if you could make the same product – a song built around the same basic riff or progression or sequence – for a dozen different markets, and sell it to everyone? So I started playing around. Hey, you want a smoke? It's okay if I open the windows.' He started to roll one. I did too, for the sake of companionship.

'But, come on, Max, that sucks. That's just, like, such a UriZen thing.'

'Don't I know it,' he said. 'Can you imagine what they'd pay for this? Licensed, naturally.'

'But Max, come on. The one good thing about High 5 was that people naturally don't put up with it forever. They get into real bands. Something that means something, something that's different from the usual stuff you get force-fed.'

'Yeah right,' said Max. 'Alternative. Alternative to what? Like in *The Wild One*, someone asks Marlon Brando *What are you rebelling against?* And he says *What have you got?* Well what have you got? The CEOs of the biggest corporations in the world grew up listening to the Grateful Dead with their hair down to their ass. Policemen have piercings and *Tatler* models have tattoos. Lawyers smoke dope and city boys get on one every weekend.'

'So? That's got nothing to do with music. You can still do something different.'

'It doesn't matter if you do, because it won't be different anymore the moment you start to sell it. Alternative used to mean something that was too different to be mass-marketed in the usual way. Those structures exist now. If MTV had been around in the Sixties the Velvet Underground would have been on ten-year-old kids' bedroom walls. All the music UriZen used to do sucked, right? But there used to be independent labels, who were cool. Now they're just divisions of the majors. Miramax is part of Disney. All the kick-ass new films we think are so cool use a funding, marketing and distribution network controlled by the same corporation that owns ABC and builds ultra-secure family compounds in Florida.'

'Yeah, okay,' I said. I didn't need to be hearing this; I'd thought I was coming down here on some kind of mercy mission. I'd assumed it would make me feel better. 'But what's wrong with that? I don't see a problem. They're good movies. They deserve a wide audience.'

'Do they? When it means everything that's cool or different gets snapped up straightaway and turned into something it never wanted to be? Look at Nirvana. SubPop and the whole Seattle thing existed for ages before the mainstream picked up on it. Nirvana were just the first SubPop band who weren't fat, didn't dress in black the whole time, and had a singer with blond hair and blue eyes. Kurt Cobain never wanted it. Think about it. He was playing in a band that defied all marketing sense. They looked like shit. They wore clothes from K-Mart. They played in a genre that was notoriously uncommercial. Things were pretty cool in Seattle; the Melvins, Tad, Mudhoney; little gigs, people hanging out, no one getting fucked up. But then MTV picks up on it, the rest of the media follow, and everything gets stupid. The only thing they knew what to do with him was turn him into some kind of John Lennon/Jesus hybrid. He knew he wasn't, but no one would listen. So he blows his face off, and two days later you can buy his suicide note on a fucking T-shirt.' He pushed a hand through his hair.

'That's just Nirvana,' I said.

'It happens with everything. Jungle. Used to be pretty cool. Now you have to go to some corporate cattle market. When you go to the video store you know you ought to rent one of like, three films every time, just to show their market research dorks how totally disinterested you are in everything else they carry. But you know if you do there'll just be a shelf full of crappy imitations of *Mallrats* next year. Cool is over. Things that are good aren't allowed to stay that way anymore.'

'There'll always be good new bands. Proper ones.'

'Real bands blow,' Max said disgustedly. 'Come on, there's no difference between that and what we did anymore. Either you're, y'know, the next big thing, front covers of every magazine on the stand before you've even recorded anything, then six months later they're wondering why your first record sucked so bad. Or you slog away for years and years, you play anywhere you can, you put out a record you pay for, and no one notices. Then maybe you get lucky, you hit a wave, you make it big. Then you're playing some stadium tour after your third or fourth LP, and you drop in a couple of old songs that you know ninety-five per cent of the people there can't possibly have heard. If you don't announce them, they go along with it like it's new stuff. But if you say, this is off our first LP, most people don't own it, you'll get the biggest cheer of the night. They'll all be trying to prove to the person next to them that they've been into you forever. Not like it really is, like they thought your first top five was your first record. I hate that.'

He had a point. I do the same thing, even if it is kind of to myself.

'Are you really going to license that program?' I said.

'Do you see any other way out of this room?' he said. 'Oh jesus, I just don't know anymore. Look, forget it. I'm sorry I brought it up. I spend too much time in here. I haven't even asked you about what you're doing.'

'I'm not doing anything,' I said. 'Don't be sorry. I'm not sorry I came. Max, it is so good to see you,' I said, and gave him a hug.

We'd never really done that sort of thing before, except as part of a routine on stage or wherever. There was an awkward silence, but Max broke it after awhile.

'Look, d'you want to jam? That's one thing this stuff's good for,' he said, waving a hand at the computer. I said sure. He gave me back the guitar, picked up an old Squier precision, programmed the 808 and we lost the afternoon. We played 'Sixteen', 'Seventeen', 'Teenage Kicks', 'Teenage Riot'; 'Teenage Rampage', 'I Was A Teenage Werewolf', 'Teenage Lust', 'Teenage Lobotomy'. Anything I wasn't sure on he did on the Mac and we jammed and sang along, so it was mixed straight back into our cans. Kick out the jams! It was cool; we couldn't miss the irony, and that made it even funnier. Our faces were indelibly engraved on the memory of a whole generation of adolescents, and here we were, jerking around with crappy guitars in a suburban bedroom, playing ten-minute versions of three-chord garage songs because we didn't want them to end.

But by then it had been dark six hours, and Max said he had to take a shower and go to work. I carried on fooling around with the guitar, but my fingers were sore and it wasn't the same on my own. I thought it was probably best if I kept quiet about what I was doing with Brett and River. He'd just think I was as bad as whoever had a metaphorical finger on the trigger of Kurt Cobain's shotgun. I didn't know what he was telling me all that stuff for anyway. I had a plan. Things were going to be okay. Maybe I could even get him a job working on the soundtrack or something. Everything was going to be fine. He'd see. I doodled away on the guitar.

He came back in jeans and a V-neck over a white button-down, and we went downstairs. His mum was back from work and we ate some pasta with them. It was kind of how you'd expect. Then we were out in the cold and the dark, and walking away from there.

'You ought to live on your own. Why don't you move out?' I asked him, when we were out of earshot of the house.

'Because I'd never see anybody. I don't want to have the kind of life where the only thing I say out loud all day is thank you when I go to buy a paper. The same reason I do this job. The irony doesn't escape me, believe me; but it gets me out of the house.'

I didn't want to press him on it, even though I could scarcely believe it, so I kept quiet, and we walked on in silence. Two streets away we passed a municipal building with a TO LET sign outside. Someone had magic-markered an 'i' in between.

'Check this out,' Max said, and cut over the grass in front of it. 'This was the library. When I first came back I thought I could go here during the day, but it was already shut. Come and see.' I followed him past doors shackled across with chains, and around the side to a grilled window. We peered in to a padlocked cube of security-lit air.

'What d'you think they did?' said Max.

'Huh?'

'To get banged up like this.'

'Who?'

'The books. Must've been pretty bad.'

'The books are still in there?' I squinted harder through the glass. 'How long's it been shut for?'

'Six months. I used to think it was like a prison. Dead barcodes on flyleaves instead of numbers on arms. But now it's more like a mausoleum. They're dying,' he said. There was a kind of funereal air in there, now he mentioned it, that was quite distinct from the gloom, but I saw that Ollie meant about Max losing it a little. There were more important things to get upset about than this.

'Come on, buddy,' I said patiently, getting down from the window. I didn't want to set him off. 'Nothing's dying here. Books don't die.'

'Yes, they do.' He came over and sat next to me on the wall, started rolling a Drum. 'If books stay shut – if the paper doesn't get aired once in a while, the paper starts to turn. It deteriorates. Books give off a nastier, grimier dust than any class of object invented – except maybe money. I used to get covered in it. First month I was back, I used to spend most days at a second-hand bookshop in town, for the same reason I'm doing this stupid job now. It was the only place I could find where you can malinger without getting slung out.' He licked the paper. 'You want one?' I shook my head. 'Well, let's go. I'll be late.'

It was a fair schlep to where he worked. I said I'd walk out with him then call a cab and get the last train back. When we finally got to the place, on a road leading out of town, it was just after ten. Max made me wait round the corner while the evening shift clocked off, then let me in the back.

We made some popcorn in the microwave, then sat in the little perspex capsule waiting for my cab. There weren't any punters at all. Presently, though, a gang of kids, about fourteen or fifteen maybe, appeared at the far end of the forecourt, and just sort of hung out.

'Do you see them?' said Max. 'They come most nights. They're our old audience.'

'Jesus. Don't they recognize you?'

'Oh, come on,' he said. 'They're never going to believe I work in a petrol station.' He snorted. 'When I first started, one of them'd look at me, and do, like, a double take. Then I'd see him turn to the others, and they'd all look. They couldn't quite believe it was really me; I think they genuinely believe we're lounging around in Nassau or wherever now. So they'd assume I was someone who looked like me, and take the piss on that premise. God, I hope one of them comes over now, while you're here. That'd really freak them out.'

'Do they mess you around?'

'No. They're the least trouble of anyone. They always buy the same things; Snapples, juice, cereal bars, Bombay mix. It's people in cars that arse you about. They come over and point at something, Diet Pepsi or whatever, and you go and get it, then they say they wanted the decaf one, so you go and get that. Then they wait till you get back and say, oh yeah, and a cheeseburger. So you have to both stare at the microwave for two whole minutes. And then they're like, I told you I wanted extra cheese, and no bacon. And I'm like, it comes frozen, in a packet, okay? You want à la carte, don't come to a fucking gas station.'

He didn't need to add, but the gas station is all there is. We were both thinking about High 5. About UriZen. I wanted to go home now, but I didn't want to walk past that gang there.

'I meant to ask you,' he said. 'Do you know anything about some journalist? Nancy Stuyvesant?'

'What do you want to know?' I tried to sound nonchalant, but hearing her name again was like the ground opening up beneath me. I couldn't deal with things as they were, without having someone hanging around making notes on everything you did. But at least if she'd been bothering him then it meant she was in England for good, and wouldn't know about LA and the last time we were there.

'Just if she's okay. I mean, she seems okay. But I only spoke to her on the phone. She wants to come down and talk.'

'She's probably okay. I don't really know her that well.'

'Oh. Right. I just didn't want to see her if she was like, you know. I don't want that all again.' He was quiet for a moment. We both were. 'You know what bothers me most about that library thing? I used to go there when I was their age – thirteen, fourteen. When you most need evidence that other worlds exist outside this town, or you'll never leave. Now it's shut, and what have they got? High fucking 5. Or whoever else it is now.'

Beam me up. Max gazed off into the middle distance, tilted his chair back and put his One Stars on the desk. We sat silent for a while, trying not to look at the kids across the concrete. I wanted to say, hey, c'mon. It's okay, I'm doing stuff, we'll make up for it; some day we'll do something good. I wasn't so sure anymore.

My cab arrived and I said I'd call him when things were a bit straighter. He didn't look so convinced. I asked him if he wanted to come up to Ollie's club some night, and he said yeah, sure, whenever. I couldn't stand it any longer and just left.

I said to Brett I'd be gone a few days. I suppose I didn't want her to imagine I moved outside circles where putting someone up for a week wasn't any problem at all. Ten minutes with Max's parents had been too much, as I'd known it would be; I'd meant to go to a Travelodge for a few days after, just to be somewhere totally anonymous. Now I couldn't face it. I couldn't face the trouser-press, the stupid little kettle, the depressing half-assed club sandwiches from room service. I got the last train back to London and went back to the flat.

Weirdest thing. They were in bed when I got back and next morning I heard them getting up unnaturally early. I tried to ignore it a while and just sleep but after a while I got tired of it and got up. I staggered through just in time to hear the door slam, so I went over to the window and looked down at the street. After a moment, they came out the front, and walked down the street in business suits and overcoats and dark glasses. Which I found scary enough to send me back to bed for the rest of the morning, and most of the afternoon. I stayed in my room all evening, heard them come in, unpack a takeout, watch a rented tape – I could tell by the trailers at the start. I was feeling odd anyway so I took a couple of Temazepam and went back to bed. The same thing happened next morning. This time, watching from the window, my curiosity got the better of me. I thought about it all morning, and on the off chance went along to the little office space we rented. I hadn't really paid much attention to details at the time, but it was possible it was still ours to use. The blinds were up, and I could see from the street a desktop fan on a slow swivel from side to side. I buzzed up and was let in without inquiry. Inside were a girl and a boy, about twenty-one. They knew who I was and were so deferential I kind of did that Travis Bickle thing – *You talking to me?* No sign of Brett and River, but it turned out this was still our office, they were off having some power lunch, and the two kids were desperate graduates who wanted to get any media kind of media experience to put on their CVs. I suspected they were working for nothing. The business of the place was as an agency. The clients were people from *There*, the properties were under discussion. She was doing that thing from when we raided DIS, that first night in LA, after all. They told me like they didn't care. The only embarrassment was on my part, at clearly knowing so little about what was being done in my name. And it was; I was listed on the letterhead as a non-executive director. The kids didn't seem to have any kind of problem with the clearly fly-by-night nature of the operation. Should I have asked them, they would probably have informed me that the bulkiest corporations in the universe (there may be aliens and they may be very strange, but I don't think they can possibly be weird enough to have gone for corporate capitalism) were founded securely on a fairy's wing.

I parked myself in Brett's office and went to the HotWired chat room till they came back. River did kind of a doubletake when he saw me, but Brett came right in and closed the door behind her. I started the kind of argument you might expect. She exploded.

'You can't go on treating this world like it's some kind of *joke*.' She was leaning over the desk at me, her face a few inches from mine. I liked it, I'm afraid. 'Do you know what it does to people? Do you know what it costs most people to get here? And what it costs to stay? Jesus, you had it handed to you on a plate, and you fucked it up. Well, some of us have got to get to seventy. You can do as you please.'

'I'm . . .'

'What are you? You haven't the faintest idea what you are, because you've never had to look too closely. You know what you aren't? You're not a fucking kid anymore, with Shelley Volante there to cluck over you.'

She turned away in disgust. I'd never seen her angry before. She'd gone quite pink. I tried not to sound too whiny.

'I just thought we were going to do different things, is all, Brett. I don't *know* what. But there must be other ways than this. This is just so . . . so ordinary.'

She caught the sadness in my voice, I suppose. She calmed down anyway. I really was sad. It wasn't possible for us to do ordinary things, and we really shouldn't try. I mean, I don't despise people who do regular jobs, have ordinary lives. I'm jealous of them. I think anyone who's found themselves on the other side of the line is, in an odd kind of way. But it's just not *for* us. Not anymore.

'Look,' she said. 'We've escaped. Can you understand how much that means? From a world where the biggest decision you're going to make all day is whether to change the delay time on your screensaver. And we're never going back. It's time to stop pretending to ourselves that following someone else's rules justifies the ends. That's not the way. You have to have a game plan and stick to it. You can't just go around letting events force you into things. What's the point of being part of a scene if you don't control it? Why trust the industry when it doesn't trust us with power now? It only gives you power at the end of your career, when you don't know what to do with it. That's the wrong end, as far as I'm concerned, and so should you be.'

'Yeah, but . . .'

'We're changing. This isn't like some stupid small business thing. We don't sit in here every day, in suits, grubbing away. The way things usually go is, you have some talent, you go to work for someone, they exploit the hell out of you, hardly use a tenth of your abilities. Why do it anymore? We don't need to. We have everything we need and everything they haven't got. There used to be some kind of responsibility on their part; they chose to abdicate it, not us. These are the people who turned feminism into a moderately lucrative self-help sub-genre. Who turned politics into the Pepsi Challenge; the one thing that's meant to stop people from having all the power and none of the responsibility. So why pretend we owe them anything? We know their jobs better than they do.'

'But you're just playing along with them. All you're doing is what they do, and frankly, Brett, I think it blows.' This wasn't the sort of argument you can have sitting in chairs until you've done it a thousand times. I was pacing the hell around, let me tell you.

'No we're not. We're inventing a new kind of life, where there's no difference between work and play. That's what our real work is going to be now. Dissolving distinctions that were disappearing anyway.'

'The hell you are. All you're doing is offloading more crap into a market that's – jesus, Brett – full of it anyway. Do you really think the business needs more product? Or that we need more competition, for christ's sake?'

'Actually I do. One, having lots of product is good for cashflow – distributors have to settle their accounts to get the next product, on the offchance that it's going to do well, regardless of how the last one did. Two, this makes everyone's relationship better because it eliminates late payments. Three, it increases the provider's market share which is cool, because although consumers aren't generally brand-conscious in the entertainment sector, executive bonuses are linked to their slice of the market pie. Four, this makes everyone like us, five, it earns us money and six, that means we get to do what we want how we want.' She took a breath, put a hand on a tailored hip, and gazed out the window. 'So. You want to be pushed around forever, or you want to do some real work?'

'Your screenplay?'

'Yours. Ours is quite finished; all we need is finance. But yours needs work. You didn't know half of what you do now when you were writing it. You didn't have me around to help you. Nobody works like that. It's time to get back to it.'

'A polish?'

'A rewrite. You're doing a screenplay from an original novel now. But it's still your story. You have a better understanding than anyone of what the fundamental elements were, and where you were trying to take them. So I think you should do another draft, with both of us around for consultation, and we'll go from there.'

In spite of myself, I felt a warm flush, like I'd just got promotion.

'I'll start tomorrow.'

'There's no hurry. We can't afford to mess this up. In any case, I think we ought to get right away from all this before we get down to work. What do you say we take a few weeks out in the country, to hammer out the beta version? Closet ourselves away. No distractions.'

It sounded pretty good to me. 'Where?' I said.

'We've got the perfect place. A couple of days ago I called that accountant guy who executes our mother's estate, to let him know we were in England. He was horrified that we were renting this flat; he said if we're not tied to London, there's a cottage in Yorkshire, on the moors, that's still technically our mother's. Part of some probate thing that's still going on. It's extremely unlikely anyone's going to object to our using it, and even if they do, there's nothing they can do about it. So he's sending me the key. We have to go to Glasgow anyway, for the festival. Juliana's set some stuff up for us to do. We could go to this cottage for a couple of weeks before and brainstorm the first draft, leave you alone to work on it, then come back and all work together before we go off on the promo tour. What do you think?'

'What about River?'

'He's straight. We're both sorted out. We had some talks. It's not going to be a problem, trust me.'

Nonchalant as hell, I gave a half-shrug and a gesture of acquiescence.

'Okay. Let's do it.'

'Cool,' she said. 'It means you won't be totally alone for months on end, but you'll have a window of space to really get down to it, and we can come back from the festival and go over what you've done. And then we'll be off on the promotional tour for a couple of months. We can e-mail drafts back and forth, and by the time we're finished doing promotion for Ellmann we should have a ready-to-shoot screenplay to capitalize on straightaway. Okay?'

'Cool. When do we leave?' I was all set to go. The possibility of a chance to do some real work made me feel all kinds of better.

We bought an old Volvo saloon from the Seventies for four hundred pounds. Brett said it was the first car they'd had, when they were sixteen in Australia, though they'd chainsawed the top off theirs to make a totally cool convertible. They suggested we keep it till the summer and do the same.

It was a six-hour drive but totally worth it. The cottage was a real old place, pre-Aga oven, the lot. We just went to bed the first night, but the next morning I drove into the nearest village with Brett to buy groceries. It was quaint cubed. We laid in a few boxes of provisions at a genuine old village store, and Brett pointed out a weird old pyramid in the churchyard that was the tomb of some mad squire from the eighteenth century. He once asked Dr Johnson's cousin to marry him and when she turned him down for the third time, had her followed everywhere she went for a year by three prostitutes from Harrogate. Now he was supposed to be sat in an iron chair in the pyramid, with a bottle of port on a table beside him and broken glass set into the floor, for if the devil ever came for him. She knew all about the place; they'd had a famous holiday with her mother there before she married.

Days disappeared, then weeks. By the time they went to the festival and left me to it, I was beginning to get with the program. It'd taken a while; it had been strange coming back to it, after all this time. May in Los Angeles seemed light years away.

Casting was a problem, and one I needed to address now, Brett said. Specific parts needed to be written with specific people in mind, but I was sick of stars. I didn't have the energy to hate the whole thing anymore, or even to be especially jealous, but that's part of the reason I've become allergic to print media. I'm tired of them. There's never anyone worthy of your desire; anyone who sounds as good as they look; anyone who can be famous without presenting it as some kind of personal growth trip; anyone who can make a fortune from something tacky without pretending it's a table-turning triumph.

Brett had different ideas.

'We need stars,' she said. 'At least, someone with a track record. They're another hook for investors. This ought to interest you of all people. Stars are a recent invention. The silents didn't have them; there wasn't even a credit sequence at the end of a picture. The players weren't named. Studios assumed, quite correctly, that if you started making actors into personalities they'd want more money, but then they realized they could offset that against the box office they'd get from brand loyalty – going to see a picture because someone you liked was in it, regardless of whether it sucked or not. Using unknowns is going deliberately against the grain. It generally works with this kind of dirty realism, but we can't afford to be so iconoclastic. We're not interested in being that kind of new. We need names.'

We came up with a dozen suggestions and narrowed those down to two or three whose stars were waning and might be persuaded to do it as a kind of loss-leader.

Brett's screenwriting class had begun soon after we arrived. I wasn't a very good pupil, it has to be said. First off was a load of unfathomable stuff about the forty-eight cheques of film-making. At first I thought she said checks, but it turned out there were forty-eight people you had to pay at one time or another, and each cheque represented a different stage in the process of putting a film together. I didn't see that this had much to do with the task

255

in hand, but she said it was important that I understood the economic context this would be happening in.

'That's what's going to be upmost in investors' minds. Yes, they'll be interested in the story itself, and whatever evidence of a market we can present them with. But that's all pretty much taken as read; they wouldn't be considering the proposal without it. What they'll really care about at this stage is that it can be made with as efficient a budget as possible. So there mustn't be anything in there that isn't necessary.'

'Isn't necessary to what?'

'The story. The look of the picture. The production values. Everything that's going to make your target audience feel good about going to see it. At the same time you have to make it work visually. If you're reading the story, you supply the deficiency of what's on the page with your imagination. But on the screen everything has to be there so you can see it.'

Which was why I was worried about the setting; there wasn't going to be much to show, by virtue of it's being what it was. I began to wonder if she'd read the stupid thing. More worrying was how much she knew about film-making. I knew she'd said her interest was on the production side, but she didn't seem interested in the story at all.

The first evening I got the next lesson. We'd brought up the VCR and TV from London, and a bunch of tapes. *Less Than Zero*, *The Big Chill*, *Pump Up The Volume*, compilations of *My So-Called Life*. I set up the video, while she and River swilled Diet Pepsi.

'Why are you doing that?'

'So we can see it better.'

'We can see it perfectly well as it is. You don't turn the lights out to watch TV. So why do it now? Think about it.'

'I don't know. Does it matter?'

'Yes.'

'Jesus, I don't know. To make it more like the cinema?'

'Quite,' she said, looking smug. 'Why is it so dark at the movie theatre? The same reason bars have frosted glass windows; so we won't be seen by people who aren't engaged in the same thing. So it's slightly shameful; but more so in a cinema. In a bar you're allowed to see each other; in a cinema you're not. You don't want to be aware that there are other people there, because you know you're being given a kind of access to other people's lives that's basically prurient. The heroine never looks at the camera; especially not when she's undressing.'

'Tilda Swinton did in *Orlando*,' said River.

'The exception that proves the rule. So why do you turn the lights down? It's why going to an open-air play while it's still light out, or I don't know, going to Glastonbury, feels so unlike any usual kind of audience-thing. You want it dark because you don't want anything else to exist for the duration, like closing your eyes when you kiss somebody; but, staring at the screen, you want to suspend your own existence too. You don't want to feel any responsibility for what you're watching, because you know you're doing something you oughtn't. That's all. Go off and write now, and make sure you don't forget it.'

'What, can't I watch the movie?'

'You have work to do. So do it.'

Which was a terrific help. They refused to do anything at this stage because they said they had the hardest job; they'd have to pitch to direct it. They didn't want to get involved now because it risked them burning out in the next phase, when they'd write in the types of shot, the camera angles and stuff. They'd need to show that they already directed it, in their heads; otherwise, it was highly probable the investors would hire a director with a track record, as risk management; we'd get a flat fee for the script, which would probably be Writers' Guild minimum, and it would be taken away from us altogether.

By the time they went away to the festival I was torn in two. I'd only chosen to do what I did because there was nothing else I could imagine doing; it was the only thing that had the kind of opportunity for anonymity about it that I needed. I still had it on my hard drive, though I really ought to have deleted it because it was cluttering things up and slowing it down. What did I need it for? We had paperback copies now. It occurred to me, for the first time, that it wasn't very good. Actually it was terrible. Ellmann were only doing it because Brett and River looked so good. Which had been fine, apart from what you know about, but going back to it now and trying to rework it for another medium was like the difference between playing bass lines and bass chords.

I felt like the last person who ought to be doing this, but it was difficult to stay despondent for long. Every day pulled incredible still blue skies out of its autumnal misty morning silk hat. It was more of a pleasure than it ought to have been to charge up the PowerBook, take it down into the cellar, propping my chin in my fists as I frowned over what had seemed like a good idea a few months ago. And at night, with the windows shut against the cruel satire of winter, the lamplight warm on old wood and old stone, it felt almost real to drudge away at the kitchen table. The place should have been hell in winter, but it was perfect; the country thickness of the walls kept it warm even when it was howling outside, and I slept nine hours a night. To my amazed dismay, I worked sensibly, steadily, without bingeing or goofing off at all. By the end of the fortnight all I had left to do was a few chunks of dialogue; I was pretty much done.

I'd seen the instruction to write about what you know in a dozen dumb unleash-your-creativity-type textbooks that I had joined the ranks of the credulous by buying during especially low ebbs over the last few years; but I don't think it was meant the way I ultimately came to apply it. Most of my problems were to do with investing the characters with enough inner life to make them attractive enough to an audience for them to be interested in what happened to them. This kind of missed the point, I felt. This is not the way with reality – we all come from the same place (here), so we all have the same history; we all do or don't do the same things and we all like or don't understand the same things, because there's nothing else available. Making my characters *rounded* would be like using caps in e-mail; it would be like shouting. Besides, it didn't fit the story. There wouldn't be any reason for them to do any of the things that they did if they had lives. There would be no reason for them to be on some endlessly unsatisfying peripatetic quest for some kind of real, authentic, no unpleasant aftertaste or your money back experience.

My original story wouldn't do, I saw that now. A movie needed big emotions, big explosions, big tears. So I wrote about what I knew. There were originally six characters; I doubled it, and made each one appeal to a different demographic and/or style fad that the audience could pick up on. I'd refused to do this before because I was sick of lifestyles, sick of style magazines, sick of clothes that only looked good on the racks. Now I saw the point. I made three of them into crackheads, and wrote in a drug-dealing sub-plot that wound up with kneecappings behind steel doors in Rusholme Gardens or Atlantic Road or Compton or wherever we wound up setting it; some of the characters fell in with rich kids and disappeared; one got pregnant, one bought a house; two died in a car crash; pointless, senseless. And my male and female leads, who started off at opposite ends of the gang, get brought together by the waste, the tragedy, the cheap metaphors splashed all over the screen. But that still only brought it in at just over an hour. So. The female lead goes off to college, leaves him behind. She gets drawn into a new life, he watches from a distance. When she goes to the end-of-term ball with some fatneck in a kilt, he follows them. While they dance the last reel he fixes the brakes on the guy's MG. The quarterback dies, she lives, but in a wheelchair –

he's there for her. In traction, in physio, in the gym. Sweat and tears. Finally she learns to walk. But. She learns to walk away. *And* credits. Hour and forty. It's a wrap.

I could barely contain myself the day they were due back. I thought that finally we could get out of this damn country and have something worthy of our attention to focus on again. Things had blown, since we came here: it wasn't anyone's fault in particular; the place is just too small. You want to hit the road here, it'll run out on you by tomorrow night. The only place there is to go is around. Just around here. Small wonder there seemed to be so few people with so few ideas; why *There* was the best anyone ever expected; why anything with any potential will get turned round and dumped on before it has a chance to be good here. I didn't know what possessed us to come in the first place; there had to be better reasons to be somewhere than just that its currency was forever the first to get gang-raped on the foreign exchanges when the good ol' boys got that gleam in their eye.

I'd already begun checking out flight prices by the time they came back. They were due to do America after they'd hawked themselves round the circuit here, which wasn't going to take long. I thought I might as well go with them. The worst of the summer heat would be over now. I could hole up in Chapel Hill or Austen or somewhere; wherever they were, they'd be stuck on their own in a Best Western or a HoJo's or whatever, somewhere with a phone port anyway; we could e-mail drafts back and forth, and by the time it was over maybe we'd have a shooting script.

But this was when everything started to really blow. They both turned up wan and wide-eyed with lack of sleep, came straight in and started throwing things into suitcases. They practically ignored me. I had two bottles of Veuve Clicquot on ice – I'd had to drive all the way to Harrogate to get them – but Brett told me we had to be back in London by six and they'd tell me about it in the car. I thought it was best not to argue and complied, binning the red pepper pilaf I'd made for lunch like a fishwife doormat, emptying ashtrays and coiling up cables. It was pretty obvious something wasn't as it ought to be, but I wasn't prepared for this.

Everything had gone perfectly. Most of the kind of media people we were relying on for an initial push were in town for the festival anyway, so Brett and River could do the circuit in one fell swoop, with the added advantage of a holiday humour to take the edge off the grind of it all. Interviews were conducted in cafés, over glasses of Long Island iced tea. Most of the *There* crowd were around, so for Brett and River, a crowded afternoon of back-to-backs with magazines, trade people, arts programming editors or whoever had simply meant detaching themselves in a good-humouredly world-weary way from the gang, sauntering over to a quiet corner, trying not to drink anything and sticking to the script. Evenings were given over to parties: first-nights, launches, receptions, that sort of thing. They were steered round by Juliana, meeting all the right people and talking things up. It had become almost boring, Brett said. Juliana would drag them over to someone and go, here are the two writers I was telling you about, and Brett would tell them whatever she thought they wanted to hear while River hung around looking spectacularly bored by the whole process, which was generally taken as artistic detachment. Which was fine; everything was fine. They met just about every style journalist on the planet, which was kind of the point. Then things fell apart.

'Charlie and the rest all went off; they go to Goa for most of the winter. We all went out one last time the night before their flight. That was the first time it happened. There'd been one American guy who was with them who looked kind of familiar. He came over to me – we were at some party – and muttered something. He was really drunk and I didn't think anything of it. We all were. You know.'

She'd been staring out the window as she talked, in a low monotone; now she leant her forehead against the glass, while raindrops traced trails inexorably backward around her. 'But he stayed on at the hotel after the rest were gone. I think he was supposed to be covering the whole thing for *There*. But then he started turning up everywhere we were. When we were doing interviews he'd be sitting at the bar, watching us. I kind of, you know, made eye contact a couple of times – rude not to, since we all know each other – but he cut me dead. That kept happening, and then it snowballed. Suddenly he was everywhere. It wasn't like, when we went out of the hotel at night he'd be on a Vespa across the street, waiting to tail our cab. He didn't need to. There's only one like really *key* party a night and all the same people show up. I suppose he'd been around the whole time, but now he was like Banquo's fucking ghost. Every time I turned round he'd be there, staring at me, with this look of like, cheerful malevolence. Last night he even toasted me with his drink across the room and sort of sneered, and I couldn't take it any longer.

'I was cool. I excused myself, went over and said like, hey, how ya doing, heard from Charlie and the others lately, blah blah whatever. He just looked at me like I was from another planet. So I'm like what's the problem here? You know? And he says, he's trying to get a book deal too. And I'm so, what, you're sizing up the competition? Why don't you get out there and hustle, like everybody else? Hate to break it to you, kid, but people haven't come here for a holiday. Or d'you think you're above that kind of thing? You know.

'I realized this was kind of taking the wrong tack because he clearly did have some kind of problem, and we don't need any bad influence on Charlie and the rest. So I said, look, you want some help getting a deal? You want us to recommend you to our editor or something? Why don't you drop some of it off at our hotel and we'll read it, send it on if it's any good, maybe suggest some changes if it doesn't look quite like the kind of thing they might be interested in. I'm afraid I did kind of lay it on with a trowel but I just wanted him to stop bugging us. I mean, he really was. It was enough of a drag anyway without him always away in a corner like Nemesis with a toothache, you know?

'So I'm like yada yada, know how lonely it is before you get your first deal, feels like no one else in the world can possibly know how you feel, stuck out on the end of an event like that and you expect like a tickertape parade but no one else gives a crap, yada yada yada. And he's just staring at me like I was some kind of exhibit. And I lose patience and go, fine; I can help you, but you don't want it, so do it by yourself. And he sort of goes, you really would give it a read-through for me? And I say, yeah, you know, I'm serious, like I said. And he sort of half-laughs, and I thought it was like relief and all this time he'd been giving us the green-eye, despairing of ever being where we were. I mean, like he must've got a thousand rejection slips already. But then he goes, really loud, you'll read my typescript when you haven't even read your own? It was like, suddenly the rest of the room fades away. I must have said, what, or something, and he just goes, real nasty, you heard. You fuckin' heard. And walked out.'

Her voice had got more and more catchy and now she was almost in tears. She caught her breath a moment before going on.

'I ran over and grabbed River as calmly as I could, and we set off after him. But he was nowhere. Vanished. We got a cab and just went all over town looking for him. About two hours just cruising around. We tried every hotel the driver could remember, asking the night porter if a journalist his description had just come in because he'd left his notebook at our flat or something and we had an idea he was flying back to London first thing. But it was no use. I don't know why I left it to the last night to go over to him, because there was obviously some kind of problem there. I guess I just wasn't so interested in finding out. But that's it.'

She sat back and put her face in her hands a moment, rubbed some colour into her cheeks and looked up at me. I was kind of dumbstruck. This hadn't been in the brochure at all.

'How does he know?' I said eventually. 'How much does he know?'

'It doesn't really matter; and I assume everything,' she said. 'This could ruin everything. We're going to get the most absurd amount of coverage when it comes out. We met everyone there was to meet, and charmed the pants off them. We were the buzz. It's going to start this weekend; people's festival diaries, that sort of thing. Which is perfect. The first reviews will be in the glossies when they hit the stands next week and everything will snowball over the next few weeks to when the thing's in the shops, and we'll be everywhere. Just like you said. I think it's the age thing that's really clinching it.' She stopped a moment, then went on. 'I have no idea what he plans to do. It doesn't matter. We just need to find out what he wants to keep it to himself, and give him it.'

'How are we going to find him? Wait till Charlie comes back and find out who he is? Have you tried calling Charlie?'

'I've no idea where he is. I sent him a really non-specific e-mail, just there's a Fed-Ex for you back at the ranch, looks kind of urgent, let me know if you want me to open it for you. That ought to make him get in touch; why would anyone send him something care of us unless it was someone wanting to commission some work? But I don't know if he's even taken a modem out there. It's kind of remote, they said.'

'Can't we like, set up a ping with, I don't know, a disabled timeout, to see if he ever connects?' I didn't even know if you could do this.

'What's the point? There isn't time anyway. This guy could go to an editor right now with this.' She fumbled in her bag for cigarettes, and lit one. 'We're meeting him tonight. I e-mailed the generic *There* address, saying just at least let's talk, name your time and place. He came back first thing this morning saying Tattershall Castle at ten. I called the directory and there wasn't anyplace there, so I tried London and it's like some kind of anchored paddle steamer on the Thames. By the Embankment?'

'I know it.'

'There anyway. God help us.'

Brett needed some sleep – they'd been up most of the night – so we were quiet the rest of the way.

Seven hours later River and I were standing on the concourse at Charing Cross with a new mobile. I dialled the number of Brett's phone and she answered.

'I've got a table toward the back. I'm sitting on the river side, so he should have his back to you. You'll be able to see it from the pavement, but don't come down until you hear him come. I'm putting the phone in my bag now. Try it.'

There was a kind of scuffing noise then not much. I could hear her, but not enough to make out what she was saying. It scuffed again, and then there was Brett's voice saying, *How was that?*

'Nothing.' I said. 'Try the bag on the table.'

She did, and it was fine. We'd be able to hear whatever he said.

'Okay, I'd better put it back now,' she said. 'Don't come down till you hear him arrive.'

We waited. I could hear a faint hum of talk, but nothing else. At quarter past there was still nothing definite. I folded the phone up and told River we'd better go and check. We walked down through the tube and under Hungerford Bridge. We saw her almost immediately, with some blond guy hunched over with his back to us. I tried the phone again, but there was just hiss. There must have been a breeze catching it or something.

'Great,' I said to River, and explained the phone. He shrugged, leaned against the wall, and started rolling up a joint. This was really too much.

Up to now I'd always been prepared to cut him some slack on

this, if nothing else. Yes, he was a total goof-off, but maybe that was the way it went. He'd been knocking things out a lot longer than I had, and I dreaded to think what that might entail after ten years or however long it was. According to Brett he'd written four features and at least a dozen shorts. Perhaps there was this incredible burst for a few years when you start, then after a while you start to take it when you can get it, and understand that if it's not coming of its own accord it isn't likely that you're going to be able to force it. Like you can spend years going to parties or clubs and either just meeting morons or phonies or people who are physically allergic to you. Then one day when you're really not expecting it, when your hair could do with a cut and you could quite easily have stayed home and watched *Frasier* instead, some absurdly complex matrix-system of almost infinite variables clicks into sequence all at once and there they are, making eye-contact across the last room you expected to find them in. It had been like that meeting Brett and I suspected it was kind of like that with ideas. If you can genuinely, and without a sniff of conscious self-delusion, put aside the panic of not doing anything constructive, then someday you'll be poodling about when suddenly there are a whole regiment of ideas falling in for inspection; turning up for audition, all quietly confident that this is their lucky day, this is their break, this is the one. Trouble is, I never can. So I kind of admired him for being so laid-back he was practically flatlining, at the same time that it irritated the hell out of me. Because if Brett didn't have to take the strain the whole time she might have a little more of everything left for me.

'This is just so typical,' I said. 'For fuck's sake, man. How long are you going to let her do all the work while you just stand fucking by, blazing up?' I knocked the jay out of his hands.

I thought for a moment I'd gone too far and he was going to take a swing at me again. But he just sort of looked at me, coolly, and said, 'She's never going to sleep with you, you know.'

That. I'd almost forgotten about it. Jesus, you know? People who have time to worry about their love lives must be like people who have time to stand on the escalator. So 'Yeah,' I said. 'And what the fuck do you know about anything?'

He laughed. I glowered at him. But it made me feel bad that I didn't care.

'Have you finished?' he said, stopping abruptly to stare over my shoulder. 'Because he's coming back up.'

'Then walk,' I said, disgusted. I got in a kind of daggered look at him, before we sloped off back to the bridge.

Out of sight, we turned round and I got a good look at the loser who was trying to fuck up my life out of having too much free time on his hands. I couldn't believe it. It was the kid. From that first night in LA. It was the generic mid-Nineties oval glasses that did it. I actually staggered. What went around did actually appear to come around. Bugger.

That night in LA had seemed pretty stupid at the time, but now we were really going to pay for it. This seemed logical. I tried to concentrate instead on hating his guts. I don't know what he was whining about, when we stuck him up. Everything seemed to have turned out pretty well for him. Bastard. I don't know how he got us to swallow that line. He didn't have a problem at all. Everything about him screamed it. I could see his whole goddam lousy life just in the way he walked. Labradors, lacrosse games, parents who made family life seem like some kind of an elegant hobby. Clam-bakes on Cape Cod porches. Dartmouth, maybe, Pencey preppy definitely. Weekends sailing, in a fisherman's sweater, in the waters off beautiful Nauset. Where the sea pours bean green over blue. Or whichever. Ivy League bastard. How he got mixed up with the *There* crew I don't know, but they were all practically related anyhow. How had he got the internship to begin? He turned toward Westminster and commenced looking for a cab. I heard Brett's voice in my pocket shouting, *Follow him.*

I broke away from River and tried to find a cab myself, but the traffic sucked and I could have walked and kept up with the one he'd gotten into. I ducked between the bumpers to an empty cab eight cars behind his in the gridlock and got in. I told the driver Chelsea, then made a big show of spotting his cab, pointing it out and saying, *Hey, I believe there's an old friend of mine, can't believe he's in town, just follow his cab, will you?* I mean, what can you do? The driver looked back in the mirror at me like I was mad and said, *You want me to drive you, you tell me where first.* The traffic started to move and I just waved a twenty at him and said, *This really would be such a surprise for old . . . Josh, I'm sure he's headed the same way and this is for you if he isn't.* The driver sort of went *chuh* and shook his head, but he started to go on anyway. I pulled out the mobile and called Brett. She picked up straightaway.

'You still behind him?'

'Yeah,' I said. 'What happened? We couldn't hear.' It wasn't worth telling her he was the kid. She probably wouldn't have remembered, and things were complicated enough already.

'He's got a fucking tape of us at the houseparty. Slimy little fuck. Some stupid little electronic memo thing he had in his pocket. You know, he's the kind of jerk who carries one round the whole time so he can breathe earth-shattering insights into it whenever they strike him. He must've overheard us and switched it on. Probably thought it was good copy. I bet he makes a habit of it. Jesus. You still with him?'

I hadn't taken my eyes off him. 'Yeah,' I said. I couldn't believe I hadn't noticed him at the party. What can I say? He looked like everybody else. But so does everyone else.

'Follow him wherever he goes. If he goes in anywhere, wait outside till he comes out. We need to find out where he lives. I offered him money, but he turned it down. He must want something else.'

'How much? Did he turn down?'

'Five.'

'Shit.'

'Stay with him. Call me as soon as you can.'

She hung up. We were along the river now, approaching the Tate. His cab moved into the outside lane, and my driver followed before I had to ask him. Then into Vauxhall Bridge Road, and he turned left into Pimlico while we got stuck at the lights. My driver hunched over his wheel, just waiting for me to say something but I didn't want to give him the satisfaction. When we did turn though, and went a way up a street to the west, I saw the other cab stopped a hundred yards or so up a side road. I told the driver to pull over, thrust the twenty through the window and ran back. His cab was just pulling away and he was trotting up the stairs of a house. I hung back as he disapeared inside, then ran as lightly as I could along the pavement to where he'd been. The houses were so narrow and my perspective had been so tight that I couldn't be entirely sure which one he'd gone into. It was one of three, but they all had lights on and curtains drawn. I walked quickly on, then over to a square. I felt a little conspicuous hanging around so I got up over the rails into a communal gardens, up against a tree, and called Brett back.

'Where are you?' she said. 'Are you still with him?'

'Somewhere in Pimlico. Yeah. He's in a house down the street.'

'We'll go back to the flat and I'll send River round with the car. You can watch from inside, it'll be less conspicuous. What street are you in?'

'I don't know. Hold on. Hertford Square.'

'Is there anywhere to park?'

'Uh, hello? This is the late twentieth century?'

'Well, I'll send him anyway. You might get lucky. Have you got the number of his house?'

'No, could be one of two,' I whispered. 'Why do we need to know anyway? Can't we just e-mail him again with a better offer?'

'Are you insane? Then he's got documentary evidence.'

'We could phrase it like it was something else.'

'We can't afford to offer him much more anyway.'

This was true.

'Then what are we going to do?'

'I don't know. I'll have a think. You sit tight. If he goes out follow him and call me.'

'What if he gets a cab and I can't get one? I was lucky before.'

'You call this lucky? Just let's cross that bridge when we come to it. And try and stay out of sight. He knows who you are. We don't want to force his hand if we don't have to.'

She hung up. I hung around in the street again. A guy came past walking his dog, so I checked out my watch and kept looking ostentatiously up and down the street like I was waiting for a minicab. He was the only one though. I chained about fifty cigarettes and after half an hour River cruised up in the car, so I sort of waved him over. He was wearing glasses and a baseball cap. He cut the engine, drifted to a halt and raised an eyebrow at me. There was nowhere to park. I gestured, you may as well go back, and he nodded and went for the ignition. On second thoughts I grabbed his arm, and motioned to him to give me the baseball cap, and a rug that was in the back of the car. I could at least look as if I was homeless if I was here for the long haul. He gunned the engine and drove sedately off. I walked round the square and came in from the other side, then rolled myself up in the rug under a bush, so I could lie on my side and still keep my view down the street clear. It was incredibly boring and uncomfortable. After a couple of hours it started to get cold too. I was pretty miserable. I'd begun to get the feeling that, if my life was a town and I needed to draw a map of it, I'd need a piece of paper larger than the place itself just to fit it all on.

Brett drove up in a scarf and glasses around three. I waved her up the street, then caught her around the corner. She looked familiar in her disguise somehow, kind of like Grace Kelly or Jackie Kennedy, though I couldn't remember seeing her in a headscarf before. It was like a weird kind of *déjà vu*, sense-memory as well, to do with being cold and tired. But I was feeling pretty weird anyway. She cut the engine and handed out a sixteen-ounce coffee, grilled pepper and mushroom sandwiches on tomato bread from Cullens, and a largish wrap of whizz.

'Don't inhale it,' she said. 'Especially not in one go. You'll be manic for two hours then fast asleep. Rub a little on your gums at a time.' ·

'How much longer do I need to stay here?'

'Till morning at least. He might not live here. He might have just come round for a smoke or sex or whatever. If he doesn't leave before morning we know it's probably more than a casual thing and he's apt to come back. Follow him again, whatever happens. Call me around ten if you want.'

'Can't I call you before? We could, I don't know, talk? I'm bored stupid, Brett. I've hardly slept the last couple of days anyway.'

'I need to sleep,' she said. 'We have to go to New York tomorrow.'

I gaped at her, aghast.

'Didn't I tell you? Sorry. Juliana sprang it on us. They've got a few extra slots for us that're too good to turn down. The only place to put them was on the front.'

'What kind of slots?'

'Maybe Letterman.'

'Whoa.' I was kind of impressed, despite everything. It was my stuff after all.

'So. We'll need to talk before we go. Call me later.'

'Okay.' I watched her pull away, then walked down the street past the houses, in case anyone had been woken by the car and was watching. I waited a while at the end, then walked quickly back up to my blanket.

It was a hellish night. It wasn't that cold, but just sitting motionless under a bush with your life collapsing around your ears is kind of disagreeable in itself. I ate everything at once out of boredom, then did a little of the speed to keep me awake. When it got to six I snorted all the rest just to get through the next hour till it was light. I was still there at nine, and had been playing give-it-another-five-minutes-there-that-wasn't-so-bad-do-it-again   for two hours. Finally, I went to call Brett. But just as I got the phone out of my jacket a door opened across the street, and out he came. I huddled down behind the bush, then followed him up the street, round two corners to a newsagent, which he disappeared inside. I carried on past and ducked in a doorway. He came out with a sheaf of papers and some milk, and went back. So that was that. If that wasn't his actual flat, then he lived there near as dammit. I turned back to get a cab up by Victoria, so as to avoid going past his house again.

Back at the flat, Brett and River were furiously throwing things into suitcases. Brett received the information that I knew where he lived with a non-committal grunt, then carried on packing. I went into the kitchen and made some coffee, looked at the paper. There wasn't much in it, but Brett and River got a mention in some old love's festival diary. It didn't cheer me up much. I got another cup of coffee. That speed must have been cut with like, Alka Seltzer. Hopeless. Presently Brett must have heard the Krupp's mumbling furiously away to itself, and she came in and sat wearily down. I made her a latte and sat opposite her. She looked terrible.

'What now?' I said, more to break the silence than because I expected any kind of an answer.

She shrugged dejectedly. 'I don't know. I've thought about it all night and I – just – don't – know.' She put her head in her hands and spat words out at the table. 'In three hours we have a nine-hour flight, and someone from the *Voice* an hour and a half after we land. And that's it. For four weeks. New York, Boston, Washington, Chicago, Seattle, the Bay, LA. And as many college towns as we can fit in between. Not a morning off.'

We sat for a moment.

'Did you see you in the *Post*?' I said. She hadn't, so I spread it out in front of her. She looked at it miserably.

'This is just the first. It'll snowball from this weekend. The worst thing is, he could go to a diary editor any day after that and they'd probably take a chance on him. People love that kind of story, even if it's just a rumour. Entertainment industry gossip doesn't seem to count as libel. It's the way it's played. Build you up then dump all over you.'

'But what's in that for him? A diary column's not going to pay much.'

'Yeah, but they'd just run the diary as a prelude to a feature, that he'd write and get paid for. But still no more than we offered him. But this – this is like a feather in his cap at the *Post*. That's why he's doing it. To show how good he is at sniffing out a story. It'll guarantee him work in the future.'

'You know they're all getting laid off?'

'Uh-huh. Neat plan though.' She exhaled toward the floor and shook her head. 'The whole *There* thing. The union won't even get sniffy. On the contrary, they'll probably find it quite amusing. Bunch of vacuous rich kids getting the can.'

We sat in silence for a while. Then she folded up the paper, walked over to the swing bin and slung it in. She stood looking out the window a moment, hands in the pockets of her jeans, then turned round.

'You know we can't even afford a story in a gossip column, don't you?'

'Kind of.'

'Even a rumour would be enough to have Ellman get antsy about it and start winding down. We can't let that happen. We need this to be the absolute maximum success it can possibly be. Without a hint of a hitch. Or it'll strangle everything that was going to come after at birth. The slightest whiff of irregularity and investors aren't even going to return our calls.' She came back and sat on the edge of the table, tracing patterns with the ring of condensation under a diet Dr Pepper. 'The most irritating thing is this won't even be a scandal. Who cares? Like, this is news. A supermodel didn't write her S&F novel. Really? Some politician doesn't write his thrillers. Chuh, you don't say. The most we'll get will be just like some sniffy little facetious piece about the last gasps of postmodernism. Can see it already, can't you? But it'll finish us off. Every last gram of credibility we have will disappear in that one sniff. None of us will ever work again.'

'There must be something we can do.'

'There must be.' She sighed, rolled her eyes and got up. 'But you'll have to do it. I have to go.'

'I can't . . .' I didn't know what I couldn't. She came over and put her hand on my arm.

'Jake, you're the writer. You'll think of something. If you ever needed to, then it's now.' She walked back to the window. 'Tell him what he needs to hear. Do what needs to be done. He may take it better from you. I don't know though.' Her voice caught, and she seemed about to cry. 'You know he started coming on to me on the boat?' She turned away and her shoulders hitched, once, twice, then all at once. I got up and went over, tried to turn her round so she could cry on me. She wouldn't though, so I just kind of put my arms round her from behind.

'I buh-bet if I suh-slept with him,' she forced out, then a paroxysm took her. I put my face to the back of her neck. We couldn't let everything go. This wasn't just work anymore. Every part of my life would be over if I didn't get some resolution here. I had to do something, and do it quickly. There was no margin for any kind of procrastination. I couldn't take that kind of risk.

'It's going to be okay,' I said firmly. 'I'll take care of it.' It would mean the end of everything if it went wrong. I was too tired to care much. I had to at least give it a shot.

I held her for a while and she quietened down, then she saw the time, cursed, and went off to shower and change. I went into the living room and tried to doze off in an armchair. I'd think about it later. She shook me awake in what seemed like seconds, though it was almost one by the clock on the VCR.

'Cab's here,' she said. 'You going to be all right?'

I nodded, to give me time to think of something to say. Nothing came.

'I'll send you an itinerary when I get a complete one,' she said, stretching her lips to check her lipstick in the mirror by the door. 'Otherwise I'll look for e-mail before dinner every night.' She pivoted around, walked over, sat down on the arm of my chair. 'Remember the time difference is going to get wider after the first couple of weeks.'

'Okay.' It wasn't just the speed and the tiredness, but I really was kind of welling up. All of a sudden this felt like the last time I was going to see her; though in the kind of way that it feels like your lottery numbers can't fail to come up, the first couple of times you play. 'I finished the screenplay.'

She gave a half-sigh, half-laugh. 'Send it on in a few days, huh?' She kissed my cheek. 'So long.' She held my gaze for a moment, then was gone down the stairs. I watched her get into the cab down on the street, and drive off. It did turn out to be the last time I saw her, in a funny kind of way.

I took the car back to Pimlico about seven; I figured people would be going out for the night and there'd be no arguments about being in someone's space, and I was right. I found a spot just along his street and sat back, listened to the radio. I knew what had to be done. Exactly how was kind of a problem, but either he gave me a chance or he didn't. If he didn't I was going to kill myself. My only problem with that before had been my family; but if I could make it look like I just disappeared, it wouldn't be so bad. I'd worked it out that afternoon, even gone to the library and looked out a few possible sites. You found a railway bridge over a river somewhere remote. You bought some bodybuilding weights, a rope and a bottle of Mount Gay. You looked up the train times. You put the weights in your pockets, the rope around your neck and tied the other end round the outside rail. You sat on the edge. You drank as much as you could before you heard the train. When you saw it, you pushed yourself off. The fall breaks your neck, the train cuts the rope, and the weights take you to the bottom of the river forever. I was ready, if that was all the option he left me. I'd make sure everything was totally irretrievable first, but then I'd do it. No Brett meant no future; death-in-life. But I'd see the kid in hell first.

He came out about eight and strolled down toward the river. I followed. This set the pattern of the next three days. I stood at the intersection of his street in dark glasses and bandana, squeegee in hand, shivering, my gloves dripping wet after the first few windscreens. He wouldn't show all day, but after dinner he'd saunter out, nonchalant as hell, and lead me a dance all over the city. It was like he knew I was following him, as I'm sure he did, and spent all day devising new grindstones for my nose. Now we went north, now we went west, now over the river and along and back; now as fast over Chelsea Bridge as his stride would allow, so that I had almost to run to keep the fifty-yard gap constant; now lounging along Battersea Park Road in a manner that tested me in other ways. If I'd had any kind of plan I wouldn't have bothered, but I hadn't. There was nothing else for it.

Should you find yourself desperate, the struggle is not against committing crime but towards it. Motive, means and opportunity don't mean shit. The last one is all that counts. If he only gave me opportunity I would unconscionably have taken it. The third night he led me along into Chelsea, up and along the King's Road, then back through Cheyne Walk to the river. The tide was out, and there was no one about; if I only thought I had the leverage I might have rushed at him, pitched him over the wall, down on to the dark Thames mud. I saw myself forcing him down into it, while the lights of a late-night pleasure-cruiser threw monstrous shadows on to the concrete behind us. A dark thing done in darkness, in ooze-sucking slime that would have taken me down with him too. I no longer cared; I was ready. One of the tragedies of life is that the people most in need of a good duffing up tend to be huge, however, and he had forty pounds on me.

But he stopped before Battersea Bridge, cupped a hand round a lighter, then stood smoking, looking out over the river. I couldn't take it any longer. I was at a pitch of emotional and physical exhaustion. I had a short-handled Sabatier in my pocket. I started to close the gap, when he suddenly turned away, crossed the road and turned into Old Church Street. I followed. He went into a pub halfway up. The Front Page. I'd give them a fucking headline. I looked in through the window, watched him buy a drink and sit down at a table. The place was half-empty. I went in, walked up to the bar without looking at him and ordered a Scotch and soda. I studied him, in the mirror that ran the length of the bar behind the optics. He was reading a *Standard* that someone had left behind. I got my drink, paid the money, and didn't even bother to stand and vacillate. I was too near the end of the rope. Way too near. I went over and sat down opposite him. He looked up, then down, then up again with annoyance.

'Isn't it customary to ask if the seat is taken?' he said, in some Bryn Mawr accent he'd acquired since LA.

'Let's just leave it,' I said. 'What do you want?' I took a swallow of my Scotch. He blinked placidly back at me.

It was then that I lost it. I pitched him the Director's last speech.

It was all I had left. Brett had sold the interview she did with him for fifty (plus syndication) when he was dead. I'd cut it out and saved it because I loved her.

The kid claimed that his problem was that we were degrading the whole notion of authorship, presumably by Brett and River fronting my book. I thought I could swing it, since the principal author-guys at this juncture in history were movie dirctors. I knew the interview off by heart now, so I explained that directors weren't important until the studios broke up. I argued that the studios only broke up because of import levies imposed by European countries after the Second World War; because only a certain amount of foreign-made movies were allowed, pictures had to start being made on location. Once there was less reason to be in Hollywood, there was less reason to be tied to a studio. Directors hadn't meant shit before; they were just another kind of studio employee. Now they saw their chance. They formed production companies and promoted themselves as players, as authors. They weren't, of course – if their pictures had some consistency about them that could be taken for a common vision, it was just because they used the same technical crew every time. I claimed that it was all a marketing thing, to have a single point of focus for promotion. I cited the release of The Director's Cut-type video, once the sale of the regular tape was drying up. The Director hadn't said it, but it was the best example I could think of. The kid looked at me like I was mad. I felt mad. He didn't give a crap anyway.

'Look,' I said, cutting to the chase. 'She took it from me, okay? I gave it to her. I can prove it. It's mine. My agent will vouch for me.' There was an off-chance the jerk still had something about it on file, I guessed. It was unlikely he did his filing himself, so there was an outside chance the original treatment I sent him got put in the right folder, and might still be there. 'I want her to use my stuff for me. I can't promote it like she can. It was mine, okay? I gave it up of my own free will.'

'What are you talking about?'

I moaned. 'What are *you* talking about?'

'The story archive?' He blinked at me incredulously.

As I'd said to Nancy, when I was drunk and didn't think I meant it, the only time I'm ever going to surprise myself is when I think I've got no mistakes left to make. I had now given away the thing that could really hang us. He hadn't even known she hadn't written *Seventeen Forever*. There was no overhearing us at the house, no little tape machine. Not that he mentioned anyway.

The bar closed but there was no way we were finished. It turned out that altruistic shit didn't cut so much ice when there was shtum money on the table. He knew who I was, but only after I told him, and I guess he thought I must be pretty loaded. And clearly interested in keeping this between us. I'd begun to get an idea of his position, meanwhile. He wanted to write a piece of journalism about this, and get paid for it. That was money for fact, not fiction. My guess was Brett had offered him an idea to work on and he didn't have the ability to do it. He was in Fact not Fiction. So he was just sore at not getting a cut. It wasn't maybe so far off the mark. It isn't like I'm ever going to know. But when I offered him twice what Brett said she had to forget it he started getting interested. We'd left the bar and walked down to the river. I wrote him out, there on the parapet, a cheque that represented the last of my High 5 money and then some. He took it, and that was that. So much for the inviolable morality of authorship. Jesus.

It was only later that it occurred to me Brett hadn't even offered him money.

I spent the rest of the night back at the flat, oscillating between stoned calm and blind panic. I was in kind of a fix. Effective now, I had no money of my own. All the casino money had gone on living, setting up the agency, whatever. There was probably still a fairly sizable chunk of change tied up in the business but there was no way I could get at it without the other two knowing. The rent was paid up on the flat for another three months so I had somewhere to live, but after that I was lost. I couldn't afford to be mad at Brett, even if I'd been capable of it. She'd lied rather a lot, but I kind of expected to be treated pretty badly. Jesus. It didn't matter. I had other things to think about now.

Honesty is commended and starves, but if you're going to lie, you ought to have a damn good memory. I ran it through as best I could.

Events seemed to indicate the possibility that Brett knew I'd lied to her about the woman in Nice – and that I'd drawn upon High 5 reserves to provide the final stake at the casino. This was why she hadn't wanted to buy the kid off; hadn't wanted to because it seemed she hadn't tried. She knew she could rely on me. The kid wouldn't have come out with all that morality crap if she had. Unless this was a bargaining strategy? It was possible, but I have to say, it was pretty damn low of him if it was. But he was an industry type; so was I, and we invented that author stuff for not unselfish reasons, it has to be said. Whatever. If she did know I'd lied about killing the woman, she ought to despise me, after all she'd been through, but I didn't think she did. Rather, I wasn't prepared to accept that she did. I had no choice in the matter, trust me. It was unthinkable that she should despise me. I wasn't having it.

If she didn't know I'd lied in Nice, she didn't know I had any extra money of my own. So she couldn't have expected me to be able to buy him off.

If she didn't know I'd lied in Nice, then she thought I was a murderer; if only as much of one as she was.

If she thought I'd let us murder to get out of one fix, she might reasonably expect me to murder to get out of another. To murder for her, by proxy. As I had discovered, means and opportunity are far more difficult to come by than motive, and she'd been denied them by the publicity tour. I wished I could remember what she'd said when she left. Do what you have to do? Okay then.

First I needed to think of how. It is irritatingly difficult to despatch someone with whom you're not on friendly terms. She'd be justifiably angry with me if I notified her that I had executed the kid in the street. I had to come up with something slightly better. After an evening's thought I had it.

The *There* gang hung out at the Gargoyle. They were all still away in Goa but it wasn't unfeasible the kid would go there alone. If he did, I would, of course, follow him. I had backstage access at the Gargoyle. A vial of 2C-B – an eyedropper – a special birthday bottle of Bourbon for the kid's sole use and a fifty to the barman, along with the suggestion that 1) This is the best club the barman's ever worked in and 2) a club lives or dies on its ambience and 3) the ambience of a club depends on its guests' perception of the staffs' demeanour and attitude and 4) I know the fucking owner, pal, okay? The kid gets off his chump. I lead him quietly outside when he starts to admire the colours. A cab back to the flat. If the drugs don't kill him, then gaffer tape over his nose and mouth will. So, a body. The only place in the world the police weren't going to be anxious to go looking for a corpse was in the house of a person they made a royal horse's ass of themselves banging up for murder in the recent past. That Johnny Marlboro guy lived in England. It wouldn't take much to find out where. We could get out of here and the future could continue unchecked.

There was nothing to tie us here. It became clear over the next few weeks that the deals she'd been doing as insurance against the success of *Seventeen Forever* weren't necessary anymore. The thing was huge, or as huge as a book can get these days. Brett and River were everywhere. Every paper I bought for two weeks had features on them, with more space taken up by pictures than copy. This astonishing new talent. These remarkable new voices. Fingers firmly on the pulse. Truly a modern-day . . . what the inteviewer or reviewer actually meant, of course, was, sod the book, *look* at them. Don't you want to make one, or, better, *both* of them bite the pillow? And, more to the point: does creative union imply other kinds of congress? They may be brother and sister but, jesus, check them out. Imagine if that was around you every second of the day. The personal nature, the general drift, of most of the questions was appalling. They were practically saying to Brett, because she did most of the talking, go on. You can tell us. Or rather, don't tell us. We'd much rather imagine. Ah, me. *Ach, du*. Still. It was kind of what I expected. It was kind of what I'd hoped for, if you really want to know. I knew that would sell the damn thing even if nothing else would.

There was even a half-assed attempt to start a scene around them. BritPop had just been and gone, so get this: BritFic. Putting the sparkle back. Just the tonic. No kidding. But no one gave a crap already. It didn't work.

So. I e-mailed Brett an assurance that our business in London was concluded. I faked up a few local newspaper cuttings in Quark – *No leads in disappearance of American journalist: friends, neighbours baffled* – and Xeroxed them a few times to degrade their resolution, before I scanned and e-mailed them. I e-mailed the screenplay too. I got cursory e-mail back. Things were going mad over there as well. They weren't getting much time off. I also got e-mail from Nancy Stuyvesant. I read it, I didn't reply, and I don't want to talk about it. I stayed in the flat, weeks on end, and listened to the blues. The blues, how fucking quaint. Give me someone to *do* me wrong, pal. I mean, really.

Weeks passed; Spring punched its clock. I drifted along on a current of Mount Gay; spirit of the seas. The worst punishment this country can devise is solitary confinement, but that's how you live when you're young and you have no money. I slept a lot; sleep so close to waking that it barely deserved the appellation, with what passed for consciousness bubbling back as soon as the rum wore off. I woke with pulses pounding in my temples, mouth dry and foul-tasting, and flitted round the flat, a grey ghost in the half-light; looking for water, looking for a light. I lost it bad here. You don't want to know. So time out.

The call finally came in. E-mail from Brett, at the end of the line.

>We're in Heavenly, caught between UriZen and DIS. Get here *now*.

LA was done. America was done. Now they were in Heavenly, Ca.

Heavenly is a ski resort, on Lake Tahoe, on the state line between California and Nevada. When a bunch of nineteenth-century wagon-trainers came up over the ridge to escape the infernal heat of the Carson valley, they saw the Tahoe basin falling beneath them and named it Heavenly. And sat upon the shore, fishing, with the arid plain behind them. So I'm going back to Cali.

Going back to Cali. Any further West and I'd be East; a weird constructed mental flip, like the fighter planes with glitches in their software that make them flip over on their backs when they cross the equator. You better hope none are in the air when that illuminated ball in Times Square makes its descent in a couple of years. Will their software deal with the year 00?

I'm going back to Cali. If it were a separate state, it would be in the top ten industrialized powers. Way up in the charts, straight in with a bullet. California; a new Sumeria of fecundity and wealth; a cool place to be if you're an orange. I'm going back to Cali; the world centre of the simulated, unauthentic and unsatisfying. The world's first theme-park will be my last. I'm going to stop now.

Or soon anyway. The first rite-of-passage into giving up and giving in is when someone asks how you are and you don't tell them. They don't really want to know. So; *I'm fine*. It's taken me a while, but I'm going to be fine. Pretty soon now. But first, I had to go back.

I flew in to Oakland International, then an hour's hop to Tahoe. Brett met me at the airport. There wasn't much time to explain. She took me back to town in a rented Toyota, talking as fast as she drove.

And then we really were in Heavenly, caught between UriZen and DIS. When we first met, Brett had been seeing Shelley about a new biography of their mother. Shelley had been prepared to be decent about it. Brett and River's existence was one of the shock revelations that had occasioned (there were already a dozen) a new book; now they were over twenty-one their mother's estate could do nothing to prevent UriZen or anyone else with an interest publishing details of their existence. But it wasn't going to be a big deal. The sensational fact of their birth, the cover-up by the studio, was the story, and little space was going to be devoted to them beyond that. They'd agreed that it could be known they'd grown up in remote rural Australia, and were now living in California; nothing beyond that. There had been nothing much else to tell.

But now of course there was. The publicity in LA had been as mad as anywhere else, and Shelley had seen it. She'd bought a copy of *Seventeen Forever*, read it, and recognized it as mine. So now an extra chapter was being written to take recent developments into account, and when the biography came out it would blow us out of the water.

'We're going to be exploded,' Brett said. She really did look like shit, hunched over the wheel. She hadn't slept for almost a week, she said. 'We're going to be a fucking laughing stock. And so will you.' She rolled down the window and spat. 'This didn't even *occur* to me. I'd practically forgotten about it.'

She'd met Shelley at a party ten days ago. Shelley had explained the situation, Brett had begged her to retract. Shelley had laughed. Brett had spoken to every lawyer she could trust. It was hopeless. We couldn't get DIS to slap an injunction on UriZen without revealing we'd scammed them too. So here we were. A last, desperate call to Shelley two days ago had been stonewalled by her assistant, who'd let slip the information that she was here, skiing, for one week only. And so Brett and River came to Heavenly, and so I came here too.

'We've followed her. It's easy in skiing costume. Everyone looks like everyone else. She takes the same trail through the forest every day, on her own. It's steep. Her *partner* is too much of a pussy to tag along. She goes above a ravine, every day, same time. We stake out that section; one at each end, one in the middle. We get in her way – she'll be moving pretty fast, and it's narrow – and send her over the edge. Two of us she might just avoid, and keep her balance; three she can't possibly. We've got three hours, almost. If we miss her today, she might not come tomorrow. It's her last day.'

'What good will getting rid of her do?' I spoke quietly, with quiet resignation. 'The book will still go ahead. The story will still break.'

'No, it won't. She's obsessed with her own importance. I suppose her life's pretty boring, and she has to try and make it like a big fat thriller any way she can. She's kept this totally to herself. She's worried the story might have leaked otherwise. I mean, this is pretty hot shit. We are who we are; we're our mother's children, and suddenly we're all over the media anyway; but we've pulled off the intellectual property equivalent of a diamond heist. There are three huge stories there. She wants total impact; so total embargo till she's ready. No one else knows. Other people at

UriZen think she's delayed publication because the typescript needed a serious edit; I called pretending to be a journalist, and though they'd obviously been briefed to totally stonewall anyone about that, I kept calling back till I got an intern, who'd get carried away with having a chance to be so professional. And that was the impression I got; they didn't exactly say so, but they didn't have to. So. I'm pretty sure she took this holiday to write the extra chapter, and she'll spring it on them when she gets back, as a *fait accompli*.'

There was nothing I could say. Money wasn't going to buy me out of this one. There was none left anyhow. I couldn't object. If she had time to ask any more about the kid I would have to explain how I killed him. There was no way to get out.

So I told myself this would be like going for a series of shots. It was going to hurt, and there'd be a reaction period. But once that was over, the holiday could begin. All we were doing was protecting ourselves against the future. As the nurse would say, you might feel a bit of a prick – but hey, what else is new?

We got into Heavenly, and drove to her hotel. It was a weird place. When it snows in a normal town, the cloak of white over the prosaic, functional asphalt and concrete makes everything strange and ethereal. But this place was built for snow, like Disneyland was built for polyester pantsuits and obesity. It would have looked strange and unreal without it. It was also lousy with casinos. It was right on the state line; between California, where gambling was illegal, and Nevada, where there was no other reason to live. But there wasn't time even to look around. River was waiting in the lobby, and threw holdalls and skis into the rented Toyota while Brett idled the motor, chuffing huge clouds of exhaust at the kerbside. Then we were away, and driving on up to the slopes.

Finally I was really going to execute someone, or be party to a real death anyway. There was no time to feel bad, and I don't think I would have anyway. Necessity has no feelings, and this was the end of the line.

On the drive around the lake we talked about what we'd do after. They said we should just drive to LA – no flights that might connect us with Heavenly – rent a flat and get to work. Shelley's death would easily be attributed to accident. The automated snow system would put paid to any tracks we might leave, long before her body would be found. Our lift passes were in false names, but we were going to hike four miles across absurdly arduous country anyway, just in case. We got to the lift station and parked; put on the ski clothes, strapped on the Fat Boys, waited in line, and were carried up the mountain.

All the skiing in Heavenly is through trails cut into the forest. It was childishly easy to give the other skiers the slip and disappear into it. Brett and River had done the route the day before and the day before that too, and we plunged off the main trail into a tributary, then trekked through the forest. We hadn't enough breath for talking. They were better at cross-country than me too, and I had a hard time keeping up, but we couldn't slacken the pace. There was no guarantee she'd come through today, or tomorrow either. But Brett said that she had every day this week, at a little after three.

It was ten minutes to when we finally stopped. It was astonishingly quiet; so much so that the cold seemed almost a part of it. It tasted like you'd just brushed your teeth. Our breath hung in huge plumes in the static air.

'We're here,' said Brett, breathing heavily. She dug into the pocket of her salopettes and handed me a mobile. 'Take this. In case we get split up somehow.'

I took it, gasping, bent over for breath, and put it inside my breast, into the pocket of my shirt. My limbs were so tired I barely had any control over them. 'What now?' I forced out.

'River, get going,' said Brett, and he turned and poled off up the trail. She turned to me. 'He'll wait about a quarter of a mile away. You can see up the mountain for about a third of a mile there. We'll see her long before we hear her. She wears a yellow suit. When he sees it he'll call me. Then he'll ski back down here, ahead of her. I'll lie on the ground like I've fallen. You and River stand over me blocking the way right here.'

She led me to the narrowest part of the trail, and we took off our skis. It was maybe two metres wide, overhung by pines on one side and a two-foot snowbank on the other. I didn't want to look over, but Brett led me to it. The earth fell away beneath us, down to Tahoe, sapphire-blue in the sun.

'There's a two-hundred-foot drop. If we block her there and there –' she pointed '– then her momentum may carry her over. If she manages to stop, we shall have to round on her and push her. If she sees who we are she might try and get away. So put your goggles on and keep your hood up. No don't. Come here.'

I finally got the girl. Her mouth was shockingly warm, silky, after the sharp edges of the frigid air. I tore at my gloves and buried my hands in her hair. There was no time for tender caresses, or fainting or swooning at the wonder of it all. The world sang in my ears. Her hands were inside my jacket, then tearing up under my shirt, running over my stomach, my chest. Mine found her breasts, and she ducked away, shrugged her shoulders out of her jumpsuit, then pulled me back to her by the waist of my jeans, pushing down my padded overall. The world turned and the wheel span.

I replayed it a million times, but there wasn't much there. My jacket was half off, caught below my shoulders. I'd kind of shrugged at it, my hands still on her chest, involuntarily pushing my hips forward as she pulled me into her. Then, as she fell back, the world turned. A swish, a crouching yellow flash, the wind knocked out of my body in one giant *whoosh*. My legs flipped out from under me and I fell heavily on my back, spun round, half over the edge. Brett had collapsed back on the snow. Gravity wanted me more urgently than she did. As she crawled over toward me, as I slipped away; her shirt was torn open, and her flesh looked shockingly real, against the gaudy skiwear and achromatic glare of the snow, like a cash bet next to a pile of chips. That was the last thing I remember. I'd never seen her naked, and how *real* she looked.

I came round a while later. I don't know how long. I turned my head on its side. It screamed at me. I gave it a moment before I opened my eyes again. The sky looked like the sky, the lake looked like the lake. I was lying kind of upside down. From what I could see, I'd banged myself up pretty bad. It didn't hurt, but one of my ski boots was turned the wrong way. My head was aching fit to bust. I lay still a while, not thinking of anything. I seemed to be on some shelf or ledge, ice or rock or whatever. I wasn't cold at all. I was warm and drowsy. I wanted to sleep but my head hurt too bad. One arm was underneath me and felt strangely hot. I didn't see a pressing reason to get off it. The other one seemed to be functioning okay, and I felt around in my jacket for my Kents. I shook one out on the snow beside me, located my lighter, and put the cigarette in the corner of my mouth. It felt wet, like someone had bummed it. I took it out and held it up to my eyes, saw blood diffusing up the filter, spreading little tendrils, shockingly red against the white. I tossed it away and shook another from the pack, and put it in the other side of my mouth. This seemed okay, so I lit it.

It tasted good, like a cigarette should. The air was still enough to blow smoke rings, and they hung in space above my face. I even got one to go through another. I supposed the plan was blown. Shelley must have stopped, after she ran us down, and come back. Maybe Brett had got away, into the trees before she could recognize her. Why hadn't River alerted us? Where the fuck was he? No matter. We'd have to think of something else. Not really my problem, anyway. It seemed I had a Blighty one. I wondered idly if Brett was going to take me to bed now, when all this was mended. At least I knew she wanted me for real now. I remember hoping she didn't meet anyone else while I was in the hospital.

Presently I heard a helicopter. I supposed there was no other way to get to me. I was thinking that my leg would probably hurt a lot when they got the winch round me. But Brett would be there, leaning out. Concerned, relieved, tearful maybe. Whatever. The chopping got louder, and louder, then started to recede. After a while I remembered I'd heard one earlier, when we were queuing for the lift. It must be for heliskiing. I'd done it in Italy once. It was excellent; totally eco-nasty, but you could get up into the kind of silent, virgin powder you used to get before everyone got into it and all the best slopes got fucked up. I wondered how long it took to mobilize the mountain rescue team. Brett must have got to a phone by now.

The blood in the corner of my mouth froze. I picked at it, out of boredom. The brightness of the sky was making my eyes ache, and I was starting to feel kind of cold now. Deep cold, down in my bones. I smoked three more cigarettes, in quick panic, when I realized I was probably going to be in hospital at least a week, and they don't let you smoke much there. I don't see why; I should have thought it was good for business. I thought that they were taking a self-defeatingly short-term view there.

I wasn't worried at all. I was actually kind of bored. It was like *Starsky and Hutch*. You know the show ends at nine, and with ten minutes left they're both tied up in a warehouse, no one knows they're there – you don't even know precisely why they're there – and the ugly, low-rent-looking guys with the guns want to kill them very badly. But there's ten minutes left to go and besides, this is only the third episode and the run has to be at least six weeks. But I wasn't so sure I was a Starsky, or even a Mulder. Characters in serials do sometimes die in hideous accidents or of terrible diseases, and though you know they're just being written out because they're going to a better job or Betty Ford, they die anyway. I didn't want to die so much. Not anymore.

I was half-asleep, but there was this really irritating noise. Shrill. I lifted my head, and frowned about me, more annoyed than surprised not to find myself in my room. Presently, by a process of elimination (my arms don't make that noise, my leg doesn't make that noise) I remembered the mobile Brett had given me – it seemed like days ago – up on the trail there. I hunted round with my free arm till I found it, still inside my jacket.

'Hello?'

'Jake! Oh, Jake, thank god.'

'Hello, Brett.' I tried to sound cheerfully surprised, in a drawly, drunken sort of way.

'Oh god I only just remembered your phone, how are you?'

'Oh, I'm fine,' I said, breezily. 'Pretty good.'

'No,' she said, shocked. So I told her about the growing-up thing, and not telling people how you really are. I got a laugh. It made me feel good. Everything was going to be all right. I wanted her children. She had nice feet. I could have stopped the world for the way her ankles had descended into her pretty pink Vans last summer, and attempted to communicate this to her. But she cut me off. She wanted to know where I was, how badly I was hurt, where the blood was, how much of it there was, whether I was cold, whether I was tired, whole bunch of boring stuff. I filled her in as briefly as I could because I needed to know what sort of conditioner she used. I must have seen it a thousand times in the bathroom at the flat, but I couldn't remember, and there were a thousand things I needed to know about her now. It struck me for the first time how wonderful it was that we'd already been sharing a bathroom, showering in the same shower. I told her this.

'They told me I had to keep you talking, but I'm clearly not going to have a problem.' She giggled, and I giggled back. I felt kind of drunk.

'Who's "they"? Hey, where are you anyway?'

'I'm at the hospital in Heavenly. They're coming to get you, Jake.'

'In a helicopter?'

'Uh-huh.'

'Coo-el.'

She giggled again. I heard her take a swig of something.

'Hey, what you got?'

'Coffee,' she said. 'Instant. From the machine. Awful.' She took a theatrically loud slurp. 'Bleurrgh.'

I sniggered, and she giggled back. 'How's your charge? On the phone?'

I held it up in front of my face and checked the LED. 'Fine.' The green didn't look so bright though.

'Good. So talk to me. You have to keep talking. And if you start feeling sleepy, tell me. You mustn't fall asleep. The paramedic guy specified. No sleeping. You have to talk.'

So I talked. I told her all the things you tell someone when you know this is it. My lousy childhood — all that. Holidays, first time I slept with Cara. Yada yada yada. I'd been quiet for a long time before I noticed I was quiet.

'Brett?'

'Still here.' She took a drink of something. I wanted a drink. My mouth was sore. 'How's your charge?' she said, swallowing.

'Okay.' It was too much effort to look. 'When are they coming for me?'

'Real soon.'

'I want to see you again.'

'You will. Real soon now.' Her voice was so soothing. I could listen to it every day now. Murmuring in her sleep. Half-awake. Soft and dreamy. Half-full or half-empty. Half-awake and half-asleep. Sleepy. No.

'I'm feeling kind of cold, Brett.'

'It's okay.'

'My leg hurts.'

'It's okay. You're a tough guy. Who's a tough guy?'

'I am. I guess. Is River with you?'

'He's gone with them. They'll be there real soon now. Real, real soon.'

'You don't think . . . he's taken them to the wrong place?'

'He hasn't done that.' Slow and low.

'I'm cold.'

'Soon you'll feel warm. Warm and tired. So warm, Jake.'

'Warm.'

She sighed. 'You're in your bed now. I'm here with you. It's cold outside but we're in here. Where nobody can hurt us. We're warm; we're making each other warm. Come down into me, Jake. Don't push against it anymore. Let me make you warm. Close your eyes now. Warm, now. You're so tired, you poor thing. So warm and so tired. Close your eyes and let it wash over you. Like a tide, Jake. Go *with* it, Jake. Close your eyes now. Go with it. Close your eyes, and let the waters close above you, buddy.'

I closed my eyes.

This is the next century.

I'm fine. Okay?

This is the next century. It's not so different, except some things got worse, and will get worse still. You will think (till you're tired of it and then some), no, it can't possibly go beyond this. This has to be the living end. But it will get worse, if it's ever going to get better.

    Last New Year's blew; the worst, ever. It's usually pretty bad. You expect significance where there is none. But this was like the worst one you ever had, cubed. No one kissed me, or anyone else. It wasn't a time for kissing. You'll see.

If you want something badly enough, you'll get it: but you'll get it by degrees, and so slowly you won't even realize that you finally have it.

    I was so wrong about everything. I knew the industry sucked, but I had too little imagination to think of doing it any other way. I thought you could play along up to a certain point, but still have things your own way. I thought that in every theme-park there is something that looks like a rollercoaster, and something that resembles a carousel. The carousel is cheaper. People want to ride the carousel because though they know the only place they're ever going to go is round and round, they can watch from there; and when the rollercoaster disgorges its riders – once shiny-eyed and brash, now green-faced and broke – they chuckle to themselves. The people who chose the rollercoaster have to go now, but the people on the carousel have a long time left to ride. How they chuckle. How they murmur snide asides to their fellow passengers, there on the carousel. How they jeer, in whispers, behind their hands. How they laugh, quietly, among themselves.

I thought there was no carousel. I thought the fucked-up rollercoaster was all there ever was. The carousel was just a turnstile, to get you into the shittiest cars on the train; the ones that were going to hit the ground first. And you thought we were the reckless ones. But I was so wrong. The only reason I wasn't on the carousel myself was that it wouldn't have me. That's the only reason anyone chooses the rollercoaster, whatever they tell you. But maybe I'm just saying that.

We needn't have worried about the kid. They knew all along I wouldn't kill him; it was a test, a double-triple-bluff, to get me halfway up a mountain in Heavenly. Waiting for my next victim.

The kid wrote his story anyway, and it got spiked. No one wanted to know. The story may have had legs, but it didn't have enough of a kick. Too complicated. And all that's wanted is kick and fizz, with no lingering aftertaste. The truth doesn't matter and is not wanted. Brett and River were good copy exactly as they were; would remain so for a year or two, till the backlash started. So his story was spiked.

As for Shelley's new chapter; Shelley knew who Brett and River were all right. Shelley works for UriZen, so rarely takes holidays. She hasn't been to Heavenly in her life.

Back on the mountain there. I woke up again and it was dark. The sky was busy with stars, going about their stellar business. It occurred to me that Brett had told me to go to sleep. She said the paramedic guy told her not to do that. I located the mobile; there was still an ounce of charge. I tried to call 911, but I couldn't call anywhere. The line was still open: Brett had never hung up. I lay the phone against my ear and listened to the sounds of sex, in Brett and River's hotel room.

When I first met her, Brett congratulated me on my forthcoming marriage. If she'd picked up the receiver that night, and found I was still alive, she might have asked me to congratulate her on hers.

They were married in secret, of course, as befits couples who are famous for being brother and sister. No People magazine shindig. No reception at the Oak Bar, or the Ivy. It's more than three years now, I believe. If they get to five, I think I'll send them a card. I'm not bitter. I was wrong about everything else, and I wish I hadn't been, but I'm not sorry I was wrong about that. That was the only thing I couldn't have done differently.

I still don't understand River. I do Brett. I was sent, anonymously, a copy of The Sun Also Rises while I was in hospital. I don't see who else it could have been from.

I'd never read it. I knew if I wanted to be a writer I should know about Hemingway, but I thought a biography would do. I thought knowing about the life would tell me all I needed to know about the work. Deep background. It was a lot easier to deal with the one and not the other.

The Sun Also Rises was pretty good. It was better than the biography. Jake and Brett. Jesus.

Brett's real name is Susan Kahane, and she's from Manchester. But why River? I had him tailed, two years ago. He signs his real name Kurt; a hip version of Curtis. Was it Curtis Cobain, I wonder? No matter. River is nothing so star-shaped. Curtis Michael, if you please. River my ass. Still, he's stuck with it.

They didn't have any famous mom. They hadn't been to film school. The only time they were in Australia was when they met, travelling after they graduated. They went from there to LA, where they landed work-for-nothing internships at UriZen. Being British like Shelley helped. They were desperate to get media experience, and were happy to work for free. Brett was Shelley's assistant. She used to take my calls. I remember her on the way to Ellmann: don't suck up to the juniors – they'll hate you for it.

They'd been there eighteen months, the day I met them. Eighteen months working for free, and working two other jobs at night to pay the rent. I think this intern thing may be wrong, if that's what it can push people to. If that's how it makes you feel.

They had eighteen months that taught them Shelley was going nowhere, and could get another intern any time she wanted. Brett maybe started to wonder what her work experience was really worth; whether the access it gave her couldn't be used somehow, in a way that might actually pay someday. There was nothing Shelley could do that she couldn't, because she did all Shelley's work for her. She knew about my screenplay; she knew why Shelley turned it down. Why anyone would. Brett suspected this was something that could open the kind of doors that generally stay shut to penurious interns. And she knew I'd offer it to her, if I was led round to it. That film-snobbiness was just to get me hot for it. If you really want something, and someone offers it you, the first thing you should do is tell them to fuck off. The rest followed. If I wrote a saleable screenplay, that was just gravy. They had no intention of making the movie themselves. That film, or any other. I might have asked them to show me some of their work sometime. It wouldn't have been unreasonable. But I was more interested in the biography.

Brett and River ditched DIS after Seventeen Forever and got a five-book deal with UriZen. With Shelley. The first came out two years ago. I think Brett wrote it, with maybe some help from Shelley. It was about me; about us. It was okay, if you like that sort of thing. Brett tells a good story, but then she always did.

What hurts the most is the way they thought of me. When they were just slaves at UriZen. They saw me in the same light as they saw Shelley. All the power, and none of the reason for having it. What was I thinking of? I'd been given power to do as I pleased with, as long as I kept on doing the thing I started with. We should have reformed, like Nancy said. But I hated it too much. The people who loved us were still there, and would have taken us back. But I hated it. It never occurred to me people like Shelley hated it too, but did it anyway. Because sometimes you have to play the worst game, the one you know is a mug's punt. You spin the wheel. You play the lottery.

Old Brett. I have to kind of hand it to her. I missed her, for a long while. Still do. I can't think of her as Susan. She's Brett.

I wonder, if Shelley had really been in Heavenly (it was River, flashing past in the yellow, who knocked me off my feet); if she'd really been there, and I'd seen her and Brett together, could I have told the difference? Like at the end of Animal Farm. *He looked from one to the other, and back again . . . no, that's not fair. On Brett anyway. She was desperate, and right to be desperate. It would have killed her, to stay an assistant forever. I think it does actually kill you, if slowly, what they pay them. In whatever currency. Because there are a thousand, keen and fresh, behind you. Too few people doing way too much; the many wasting away for the few. We are behaving like insects. Striving for air, when we could be diving for pearls. Real drowners. And no one is going anywhere — just around here.*

But Shelley? Or maybe she didn't know what Brett had done. Maybe she didn't read it the first time I took it to her. Maybe she forgot it. Maybe she hasn't read it now. Maybe she's known all along and doesn't care. Maybe she's too busy to care.

Whatever. I shall follow their progress with interest, anyway. I can kind of see how it'll go. Their literary career is founded on nothing except how they look. Right now, the two of them are like a daytime soap star picked up by Hollywood — tolerated, good for TV movies and straight-to-rental, just so long as they keep smiling, show a lot of cleavage and avoid bumping into the furniture. Pretty soon they're going to be too tired by it all, not to mention too old, to do anything but roll with it; bumbling along in some has-been literary scene, knocking out a few hundred pages of half-baked assumptions regarding their conviction that everyone's lives are at the same stage as their own (being loved, time's blurring of love, children, love's dying gasps, infidelity, revenge, the change, maudlin self-pity, psychotic bitterness, etc.). I shall watch them writing for ever-diminishing markets, seeing their page number in the publisher's new catalogues rise from their shoe size to their age and beyond, travelling inexorably from the lobby-like hallowed ground behind the contents page, past the staples in the middle, till they finally hit the goods entrance just before the index. Unless, of course, they do break into the movies.

I'll be sorry, for Brett, because I'm pretty sure she'll end up going solo. They'll need a new angle, and her looks will be . . . not gone, but different. Not mass marketable; though I'd still kill for her, in twenty years, in forty. Even though she tried to kill me, and damn near succeeded, I still find her consummately attractive. Probably because of that. It kind of shows some taste, I have to admit it.

I survived, anyway. But we're all survivors. Ex-potential DOAs. We made it, then we made it as far as the car-crash age, and then we made it some more. Winners in some kind of economic/genetic lottery. We made it through. Group hug. C'mon now.

I was saved in all the wrong ways, then as now. Some wonderful little geek saved me, then as now. Misappropriated and misapplied technology saved me, then as now.

Someone once invented a machine that was meant for something else; but someone else saw that it could be used to listen in on phone calls. It's called a scanner, and they're very popular with geek kids. Tyler Moore, 13, of Portland, Oregon, wanted to go windsurfing on Tahoe for Easter like he wanted to wear the matching bowtie-and-waistcoat his mother was going to give him for his birthday next month. He knew about the bowtie because he found it. He found me also. History doesn't record whether he was a High 5 fan. The newspaper does, but that's something else entirely.

I spent five weeks in the hospital. My parents had to pay, because I didn't have any money left. I've paid them back now. I have steel pins in my left ankle and shoulder. I can't dance too well anymore, but I don't have to.

Nancy and Max and Polly came to see me when I got home. Nancy knew Max because she was doing a story on High 5: where do you go when there's nowhere left to go? She never wrote it. Max showed her his music machine, and she quit journalism.

I was glad to see them. I'd been back home a while, doing things I ought to have done before now but couldn't. Like going to see my grandfather. I made it into the building this time. I sat and held his hand for two hours. He didn't know who I was. The TV in his room was on, but I turned it off every time I came. He had a choice of forty channels on it, but he couldn't see or hear any of them. They were all shit anyway. I went as often as I could; twice a day usually. I cut his nails when they grew; this was the only visible sign he was alive. He's dead now. He died of a cold I gave him, a cold I nurtured, breathing carefully into his slack mouth. So I got my victim, in the end.

When Nancy and Polly and Max came to see me they told me a plan. That was four years ago. We are now – well, no, not bigger than UriZen, but that isn't the way you keep score anymore. We scare people who thought they could never be scared. I, who was ruined by a multinational conglomerate, am now a founding partner in something that seriously pisses them off. But we have no flashy LA HQ, no quoted stocks, no executives. No interns. We live in a hundred crappy shared flats and houses, and work from there too. We make frightening amounts of money; we pay ourselves what we need to live.

The plan Nancy told me was shockingly vague. It was founded on the idea that we should decide what it was in the world that blew; isolate it, and evolve away from it. It was pretty easy to see.

UriZen and DIS traded on the idea that, if they came up with something good, lots of people might want to pay to experience or own a copy. A CD, a cinema ticket, a video, a book. This worked perfectly well for most of the twentieth century. But what happened when they didn't have anything good anymore? What happened when all they had was hooey? Nothing happened, was what. They still owned the only distribution network there was, so all that was available was hooey.

Freedom of the press used to apply only to people who owned one. You own a newspaper? Go ahead and be free with it. This was the case until very recently. Until someone thought of using something for something else entirely.

Misappropriated and misapplied technology. PCs and phone networks were meant to be used for work, but suddenly it was like playtime for ever. Anyone at all could be their own radio station, publisher, TV network, whatever; and reach everybody, instantly, and very very cheaply.

Nancy's idea was this. UriZen and DIS only had hooey to offer, and everything they touched turned to hooey; they owned the distribution network; and they charged people for copies of the hooey. But we had access to a new and more efficient distribution network; we could make hooey as easily as they could; and, because our distribution system had practically zero overheads, we could give it away. Hooey for free.

So we reformed High 5. We used Max's music machine to write and record material; Polly and Zeke and a bunch of other kids set up a web site, and we gave it away for nothing. Anyone could click on our site and download a CD's worth of new songs for free. Our old fan-base had, by now, better access to, and better understanding of, computers than anyone else on the planet. Within weeks our site was getting hundreds of thousands of hits a day. The people who were coming there are, traditionally, the hardest demographic to market to. So we sold ad space on the sites, and client profiling and focus grouping that we made up ourselves. We made a terrifying amount of money. Money you can't imagine. We did it for a year precisely, then stopped. We didn't need to do hooey anymore. We came up with new things we could give away, now we had money to make them; things that weren't hooey; and people kept coming. More and more people.

I hate to tell all this because it stinks of kick, and it reeks of fizz, and I don't do that shit anymore. It's like, when the Net first came into the viewfinder, back in the mid-Nineties, the media went stupid. They said, this is going to change everyone's lives. They said that because they wanted to stop it. They said that, because they knew that it really could change things forever. They said that to sensationalize it, so regular people thought it was just another crock of shit from the media. They said that to build *it up, so when it hadn't changed everyone's lives six months later, they could knock it down again and they would be safe. They said that, because they were scared it was going to put them out of business. They were absolutely right, and their strategy worked, pretty much. Except for us. They made us, do you see? They brought us up, they jerked us around, and then we left home.*

I am now here. I'm dealing with it. I always hated here and having to be here, but I'm taking it a little at a time. I do quite a lot of drugs now, which other people are occasionally a bore about — however, I like them. They are entirely themselves and there is no marketing involved whatsoever. Nancy says you shouldn't; as long as the government can posit some kind of lawless drug-crazed underclass they can make people scared, and push through whatever laws they like. So all the poor kids who died drowning in Evian were supposed to have died of Ecstasy poisoning. That was another of the many final straws that propelled Nancy out of journalism. If anyone genuinely wanted to stop poor hick kids dying, they might have pointed out that if you get on a bad one, lots of water isn't like an antidote. It doesn't look it, but it can kill you. But where's the story, buddy? Far better to interview the stricken parents over and over, and leave it at that. This is what we call tact; this is what we call discretion.

When I was still getting better I told Nancy about turning the lights down to watch a video, to make it like the movies, and she agreed with Brett. She said that it was because you knew you were spying, you knew you were doing something bad, and you feel better about doing bad things in the dark. She said: turning the lights down is something we've learned so well, that we've come to treat all of our exposure to information in the same way. So we have a model for the way we feel when we read about Bosnia, Rwanda, Bahrain—wherever the hell it is now. The only possible argument for a media is that it should inform, that it shouldn't allow injustice or atrocity to be perpetrated in a dark place. But we've come to put it in a dark place ourselves, she said. It's the only kind of spectating we know.

*

303

Nancy agreed with Brett about a lot of things, which surprised me at first. Brett was right about most things, it turns out, except the way to go about them. She saw that things blew, but thought there was no way we were going to change them, so we might as well go along with them. So did I.

There have been a dozen High 5s since us. They were based on us, and we were awful. We were based on a thousand other formula bands, who were based on the Monkees who were based on the Beatles, who ripped off black R'n'B. Chain of crap, getting stinkier and stinkier till you get to the crock of shit at the end of the rainbow. Which was us. How many more do we need? And the worst thing is, there isn't anything else now. Welcome to the next century. I've seen the future, and it blows, believe me. Trash culture used to be good: it taught you alternative literacies. A horse will sneeze when it smells bad hay. If all the hay is bad the sneeze reflex gets confused. Now the alternative is the mainstream. When everything is the same, there is nothing to define alternative against. The reflex got confused: there was no way to see what was going down.

This was the key to what we started off doing, and it's kind of key to what we do now. Everything the conglomerates had was hopeless, because they had all the style and none of the substance. They took all the old successes and just kept copying them, without understanding why they worked in the first place. Like the story archive Brett plundered. Like Max's music machine. Like all the movies now: car chases, femmes fatales, the idealistic rookie and the cynical old-timer; all used to have a reason to be there. Now they're there because they've been there before, and for no other reason. A kiss is still a kiss; a sigh is still a sigh. It's still the same old story. You must remember this.

But skip it if you don't want to know the future. Skip this if you want to watch the game before you get the result. You're not going to like the game, and you'll wish you'd known where it was going to end up; but skip this if you want.

Stories used to pick you up, carry you off, and put you back down where you started. You were slightly different afterward. They don't take you anywhere anymore — just around here. You don't expect them to, *and your guard is down. Things get snuck past you. Movies or stories, or whatever you want to call them, have power, and power wants to go bad like DNA wants to replicate. When I was growing up, the only cars my friends and I knew were GT1s, MR2s, XL5s. Even though there was nowhere to drive them — just around here — and thought you wouldn't think it to look at them, sometimes there was nothing to hold them to the road. People died. You wouldn't have though it to look at the cars. So shiny, so cool looking. You wouldn't have thought it to look at the movies, the magazines, whatever. But this is the next century, and bad things have happened. Because meaningless crap is all anyone knew, it's all anyone expected. It was meaningless; couldn't hurt you. Guards were down. Things got snuck past. A new house edge accumulated. It worked terribly slowly, and a little at a time. But this is the next century. Bad things have happened, and they're going to get worse.*

We're not changing the world, but we see what we can do. No one is stopping us because we're way too successful. We're making far too much money with the superficial things, and that's as far as anyone looks. They wouldn't understand a lot of the rest of what we're doing. We're too spread out. There is nowhere and no one that anyone can put their finger on and say, there. Stop that.

It's not really me. I'm still some kind of loser-dork-patsy already. I don't care because I haven't earned anything better. I haven't even earned this. I still don't deserve it, but I didn't deserve to be in High 5. It just happened. But like Brett said, the cards have no memory. Things aren't going to even out, and if you think they are, you're going to start worrying there's something wrong with you. I'm a liar and a thief, but I try not to think about it too much.

It isn't me, and it's not even Nancy. It's mostly Polly and Zeke and the rest of them. Nancy thinks of things that blow and comes up with the opposite; they get to work; the rest of us do what we can. I, for example, spent all of the last month printing delivery notes. It was okay; it was cool. I got paid enough to live on. I got some evenings off.

One of the first things we did was news. Nancy was sick of journalism because the existing media gives away its lunch. Scandals go unreported because everyone is blitzed out of them. Abuses go unchecked if they don't fit five hundred words of copy and a punchy headline every day until they're sorted out. People die or people get hurt or people are made miserable and if there's no new angle then no one cares.

But Nancy said journalists — for the most part — have a call. They have to, because most of the time they're not getting paid. There is no structure, no graded career-path, and few salaries. They have a call, and it is this: they feel that truth is a virus. It wants to replicate and it wants to make itself known. They hunt out the stories, they write the stories; but the people who have to decide what's going to sell spike them.

Intelligence is determined not by how many cells a brain has, but by how good the connections are between them. The old media ran millions of stories, but the laws of kick and the laws of fizz precluded much effort to connect them. If things seem random, it's because you're standing too close to a very large pattern. Nancy said it was time to step back a little.

We run the stories that get spiked because they have too much legs and not enough kick; stories that might pass some kind of sell-by date. We don't have to worry that there aren't enough to make a headline every day, because we don't have to come out every day. We don't have to have a cover price. Anyone can read them for free. We're not selling anything, and it doesn't cost us anything much, so we can do it. And millions of people get to read them, for free. Millions of people get angry, and stop buying; bad things, which tend to be done by a very few, who tend to have something to sell, tend to decline.

The joke is, the media that lived on hysterical 84-point said the Net was going to erode communities even further; people would never go out of their rooms. It turns out it brings good people together; it makes them act like a community for the first time in their lives. People who blow don't get a look in. People whose interests we threaten can't stop us because they don't know where we are, and they can't stop us because they wouldn't know how. They don't understand us.

This is the real difference. This is what the ruckus was about. This is the cool thing. All of this stuff is difficult to understand: you can do it but it takes a long time. There is no quick payoff here. So it tends to be only intelligent and committed people who know how. Intelligent and committed people are always pretty cool, by definition. So cool things tend to happen.

Things that blow don't get a look in, or get palmed off with something superficial. The cool stuff goes on elsewhere. The build-it-up-and-knock-it-down hype job that was done to the Net in the mid-Nineties looked like it worked, but it didn't. The superficial stuff – the stuff they could understand, and fit into five hundred words of copy – was meant to be superficial. The cool stuff went on elsewhere.

A lot of the world – it tends to be the parts where the worst things are happening – can't afford computers. This blows. Nancy said it's because computers are too expensive; they're too expensive because they have too many features, too many selling points. I'm typing this into my old PowerBook, and I'm not using five per cent of it. People buy mountain bikes to cycle round the park on. People buy 4×4s to go to the superstore in. They buy them because someone wanted to sell them, and pretty soon that was all there was. A computer that can do everything you need shouldn't cost more than a cheap, 3-gear bicycle. No gears, if you live in a flat country. This thing on my desk is history; it cost ten bikes. It's a 4×4 that I use to go to the store in. So we make the future, lots of little building-blocks of the future, and we sell them at cost – the price of the cheapest bicycle – in places where they're needed. The places where the worst things are happening.

Actually, we pay lots of other people to assemble them for us, in lots of far-off places. No one knows it's us because we encrypt everything we do, in a code that's so cool it would take the biggest government supercomputers three weeks working flat-out to decode this paragraph. It has existed, and been free on the Net since the early Nineties. Some effort has been made to make it illegal; this effort would have been more productively spent pissing against the wind. It's called PGP – Pretty Good Privacy. I, who was undone by fame and the getting of it, have been saved by privacy. Which sounds pretty good to me.

Where information is needed – which tends to be where it's suppressed on point of death – we use PGP and High 5. Even the scummiest old governments love High 5. The generals with the big moustaches, the jumped-up duces with the jouncing quiffs; they love High 5. We're good for the kids. We keep them quiet. No one objects to a High 5 tape coming into the country. Even if they listen to it, it's High 5.

The tapes we send in are DATs; good for making copies from, good for the local economy. DATs break music up and store it as data; binary code, a bunch of ones and zeroes, a list of instructions to tell circuits whether they should be on or off; just the same as the way magnetic tape stored music as positive or negative charge. On DATs the quality is better because the data is kept in 16 different sections – call them one to sixteen. The low parts – the bass and the drums – are in the low numbers; the high parts – the keyboards, the vocals – are in the high numbers. Anything above fourteen, human ears can't hear. So we can put whatever we like in the sixteenth section and no one will know it's there. Stuff like news and information. Stuff like how to build your own computers and send or access information. Stuff like how PGP can stop the secret police or whoever from knowing what you'd rather they didn't. Stuff like how to put your own information on to the tape, above the music, and send it back. There used to be a news blackout when things got bad somewhere; when the army took control, when martial law was imposed, when genocide was going down. There isn't any blackout anymore.

We do one little thing, that isn't half so sensational. No kick, no fizz. On all of our sites we run little ads, politely asking people to vote, and explaining how to get on the register; how you can vote even if you owe the government money. You can't do anything on our sites without seeing one. It's not like we don't know that if voting changed anything it'd be illegal. It's just that, the last time, if anyone had bothered, things wouldn't be so bad now.

*

So that's some of what we do. I say we, though I do very little. I'm kind of a foil, more than anything. A front, a face. I was so wrong about that. But neither was anyone else right. I'm old now, but some things never change.

But time out here. This is still a story, and stories shouldn't tell you too much. Stories should have a hook, and the payoff you expected; the one you knew was coming all along. Stories shouldn't take you anywhere much; just around here. The cars in my old story didn't go anywhere much, and that was kind of the point; just around here. Having nowhere to go isn't the same as having any reason to stay. They crashed all the same.

Stories want to be like life, but they're not. Love works in the movies because you have movie stars having sex with movie stars. You don't get tired of having sex with movie stars; not in ninety minutes, anyway. Even Walter Matthau gets some. You know? Stories say I should get back with Cara here, but I shan't. I don't want to; she'd still spend the whole time in the bath anyway.

Besides, I don't think she'd have me. I'm old now, and I don't look as good as I used to. Gravity, which wanted all of me in Heavenly and was cheated, has settled for taking me a little at a time. It started with my face; the thing I'd been taught to trade on.

Now it doesn't matter what I look like. I'm glad, because I look like shit. I, who was shit, now look like it. But I don't do that shit anymore.

I still write though. Little stories. I'm not any good, but it doesn't matter. No one needs to review them, and dump all over them. No one needs to build me up to knock me down. This way I get to practise. Little stories. They're given away, with the rest of it. It doesn't matter who wrote them, who's the face to promote them, because no one has to buy them. They're free.

It doesn't pay to think too much of all the things you leave behind. We have it in our power to begin the world over. Kind of.

*

309

We are now here. We've been here all along. We haven't been anywhere much — just around here. The here is what matters. The here *is what's important.*

We put things to bed here. We think about the wake-up call here.

So the story begins.

THE END

READ MORE IN PENGUIN

In every corner of the world, on every subject under the sun, Penguin represents quality and variety – the very best in publishing today.

For complete information about books available from Penguin – including Puffins, Penguin Classics and Arkana – and how to order them, write to us at the appropriate address below. Please note that for copyright reasons the selection of books varies from country to country.

In the United Kingdom: Please write to *Dept. EP, Penguin Books Ltd, Bath Road, Harmondsworth, West Drayton, Middlesex UB7 ODA*

In the United States: Please write to *Consumer Sales, Penguin Putnam Inc., P.O. Box 999, Dept. 17109, Bergenfield, New Jersey 07621-0120.* VISA and MasterCard holders call 1-800-253-6476 to order Penguin titles

In Canada: Please write to *Penguin Books Canada Ltd, 10 Alcorn Avenue, Suite 300, Toronto, Ontario M4V 3B2*

In Australia: Please write to *Penguin Books Australia Ltd, P.O. Box 257, Ringwood, Victoria 3134*

In New Zealand: Please write to *Penguin Books (NZ) Ltd, Private Bag 102902, North Shore Mail Centre, Auckland 10*

In India: Please write to *Penguin Books India Pvt Ltd, 210 Chiranjiv Tower, 43 Nehru Place, New Delhi 110 019*

In the Netherlands: Please write to *Penguin Books Netherlands bv, Postbus 3507, NL-1001 AH Amsterdam*

In Germany: Please write to *Penguin Books Deutschland GmbH, Metzlerstrasse 26, 60594 Frankfurt am Main*

In Spain: Please write to *Penguin Books S. A., Bravo Murillo 19, 1° B, 28015 Madrid*

In Italy: Please write to *Penguin Italia s.r.l., Via Benedetto Croce 2, 20094 Corsico, Milano*

In France: Please write to *Penguin France, Le Carré Wilson, 62 rue Benjamin Baillaud, 31500 Toulouse*

In Japan: Please write to *Penguin Books Japan Ltd, Kaneko Building, 2-3-25 Koraku, Bunkyo-Ku, Tokyo 112*

In South Africa: Please write to *Penguin Books South Africa (Pty) Ltd, Private Bag X14, Parkview, 2122 Johannesburg*